THE
BECKONING

B.K. PETERSON

This work of fiction contains parallels to events and persons from antiquity. Other names, characters, and details are products of the author's imagination. Any resemblance to persons or events not from antiquity is purely coincidental.

For Charity Ann

CHAPTER 1

"Well, the cards appear to be in her favor," rumbled a powerfully deep voice. His large frame eclipsed the door as he emerged from the emergency operating room.

Allison had been preparing herself for the worst, and her crystal blue eyes yearned for the life of her only child. "So does that mean she is going to make it?"

"By the looks of things, I would say that she is going to pull through. At the same time, I'd love to see her in better condition." Dr. Khai Oughten smiled sympathetically. "In addition to fusing the rods to her spine, she has five broken ribs, a fractured wrist, ruptured spleen, and a severe concussion. She's going to be out of commission for a long time."

Allison shook her head in disbelief. "I swear, that girl is going to be the death of me. Maybe this will have finally knocked some sense into her. Seriously, I have no idea what she was thinking."

"You've certainly got your hands full with this one, don't you? Avery is extremely fortunate though. Honestly, I've seen much worse from rock climbing accidents. Falling thirty feet typically doesn't end well. But as far as we can predict, it appears she and the baby are going to be just fine."

Allison was caught completely off guard and glared blankly at the doctor in disbelief, not certain she understood him.

"I'm sorry," Dr. Oughten said, stroking his graying beard. "Is everything okay?"

Allison stumbled into an adjacent chair. "You didn't just say – baby – did you?"

"Forgive me. I thought you knew." Inhaling deeply, he rolled his eyes sheepishly and took a seat next to Allison. "She's about twelve weeks along, give or take."

"I beg your pardon, but that's impossible. Certainly there must be some mistake."

"This is tough news," Dr. Oughten continued. "I know. My daughter became pregnant at age seventeen as well. Let's face it - it's a little younger than any of us would hope for, but people successfully work through these challenges all the time. Things will work out. You'll see."

"Thank you, Doctor," Allison began to clarify, firmly looking him in the eyes, "but it just doesn't make any sense." She took a deep breath, pushing strands of her platinum blonde hair out of her face. "Avery hasn't had any ovaries since she was twelve years old. She's a cancer survivor."

"*Really?*" Dr. Oughten mused on the concept for a moment. His thick eyebrows accentuated a forehead wrinkled in contemplation. "That's always been the thing about Mother Nature. It seems she always has a few tricks up her sleeve."

∞

Trying not to make any noise, Allison stepped into her daughter's hospital room and carefully closed the door behind her. A worn reclining chair was waiting adjacent to the bed where Avery slept, and as welcoming as it was, it had been where she spent the night for the past three weeks, and she longed for the comfort of home. Allison ached for things to go back to the way they used to be – before Avery's accident, before they found out she was pregnant. Nestling herself into the chair, Allison took the remote off the bedside table and turned off the TV.

"Hey, I was watching that," Avery grumbled.

"Good grief! You startled me," Allison piped. Pushing the long black hair behind her daughter's ear, Allison kissed Avery's forehead. "Why aren't you asleep?"

"Nightmares."

"Same one?"

"Yes. I just hope it doesn't come true."

"Well, your track record certainly doesn't help at all. Cancer, the staph infection, and then you go rolling off the edge of a cliff!"

"Dad would've been proud of that one."

"Maybe. But even *he* wouldn't have gone rock climbing without any gear. Seriously. That was just asking for trouble."

"I know, I know. I promise I won't do it again."

"I *know* I've heard *that* before."

Avery looked up toward the window at her right and watched the moon with envy. It wasn't fair. The moon always got to stay the same. But not her. Whenever she began to feel like she knew who she was, she was forced to reconsider. Normally it was something being taken away. First her father, then her ovaries. But this was going to be different. So much different. Specialists from all corners of the globe were being brought in to try to figure out just how in the world a girl with no ovaries was able to conceive. It soon became apparent to Avery and her mother, however, that rather than help her, they were all more interested in simply being among the elect who got to see the girl whose body had broken the laws of nature. It seemed there was a new 'subspecies' named Avery, and medical spectators were lining up in droves just to get a peek.

"Mom?" Avery's deep brown eyes began to moisten.

"Yes?"

"I'm scared. I'm not supposed to be pregnant." Tears began rolling down her angelic cheeks. "I don't know what to do. What am I going to say to Taylor? He's going to hate me, isn't he? Mom, he's going to hate me. I just know he is."

"Now, now. He's not going to hate you. Calm yourself, child." Allison reached for her daughter's quivering hand. "I'm going to help you through this. And you have all your friends and – "

"I didn't do anything wrong though, Mom – I mean – I never meant for this to happen. I just – I don't see how it could have. Like I told you before, we never let things get out of hand. This wasn't supposed to happen."

"Avery look at me. We've already been through all of this. Of course things got out of hand. You wouldn't be pregnant unless they had."

"I don't have any *memory* of it though, Mom!"

Allison sighed in frustration. It had come as no surprise that Avery couldn't remember almost the entire week prior to the accident. So it wasn't altogether unreasonable that other parts of her memory had also been affected.

"It's okay for people to make mistakes, Avery. None of us could ever hope to be perfect. It's just not realistic. You've got a lot of hormones running wild at your age, and sometimes people lose control."

"I know what I know, Mom!" Avery insisted. "Taylor respects me, and I promise you nothing ever happened!"

"Sweetheart, a woman doesn't just conceive out of thin air. If it wasn't Taylor, then – then it was somebody else." Allison's stomach churned at the thought. "Avery, I know it's hard, but you've just got to be able to talk openly about these things. If something happened to you, you need to tell me." She paused for a moment, scared to death of asking the question. "Were you raped?"

"No!" Avery looked away. *I don't think I was.*

"Avery, please be honest with me. That's the only way we can hope to work through all of this. It's toxic to keep it bottled up inside of you. It will end up driving you insane."

"I *am* being honest with you! Something's not right here! You don't know what it's like. I've felt like enough of a freak as it is, knowing all this time that I could never have kids. Now I'm told I have one growing inside me, and I have no idea where it came from! Why is this happening to me?!" Avery was breathing much harder now and the heart rate monitor began to flash.

"Avery, honey." Allison quickly leaned over the bed to embrace and console her terrified daughter. "Honey, please relax. It's okay, love. Just relax for a moment. Things are going to be okay."

The smell of her mother's perfume was incredibly pacifying. Inhaling one deep breath after another, Avery surrendered to the pervading essence of her mother's unhindered love. As her tense muscles began to relent, she closed her eyes, concealing the emotional hurricane that raged within.

CHAPTER 2

"What's this?" Taylor Beckman asked through a mouthful of roasted veal. His father Nathan had just reached across the fancy dinner table to hand him a manila envelope. Taylor wiped his mouth and then examined the return address. It was from Garvis University. The excitement and anticipation surged through him like wild fire. "I'm so nervous right now, I can't even stand it."

"Just open it," his mother urged with confidence as she sipped a two-hundred-dollar glass of wine.

Taylor set the envelope down and closed his eyes. "I just need to breathe for a second."

"Look at your son, Jane," Nathan chuckled. "He acts as if he doesn't already know he's been accepted."

"Do you guys really think Uncle Kevin could have pulled some strings for me?"

"You're such a tease, Taylor," Jane said. "Even if he wasn't the Dean of Admissions, I assure you that you haven't a thing to worry about. So open the confounded envelope before I call Kevin and say you're not interested."

"Alright, here goes nothing." Taylor tore eagerly through the paper and pulled out the packet. "Mr. Taylor Beckman," he read aloud, "we're pleased to inform you of your acceptance into Garvis University and the School of Biomedical Engineering." Filled with relief, Taylor sat back in his chair and gazed up at the intricate woodwork in the restaurant's vaulted ceiling. "YES!!" he shouted, drawing the attention of the surrounding guests.

"Congratulations, my boy!" Nathan smiled approvingly.

"See that, Sweetheart?" Jane looked at her husband with satisfaction. "I told you we didn't pay off my brother's boat for nothing."

Glaring at his mother, Taylor sat up in his chair. "You paid off his boat?!"

"Never mind about that, Taylor," Nathan insisted as he handed the waiter his credit card. "The important thing is that you're in. Isn't that right, Jane?"

"Precisely." Retrieving a mirror from her snake-skin purse, Jane began admiring her new nose. "Well that's healed up perfectly, now hasn't it? Remind me to thank Sydney for referring me to Dr. Shaw. His work is absolutely flawless."

"Sweetheart, I'm fairly certain you're lucky to still *have* a nose after all you've had done to it."

"Speaking of surgery," Taylor interrupted, "what do you say we head over to the hospital? Avery is expecting us."

"You know, Taylor," Jane said while applying more lipstick, "I don't know if that's such a good idea."

Disappointment flooded over Taylor's face. "What? Why not?"

"Don't you think she'd rather recover in peace? I mean, the poor girl could hardly carry on a conversation *before* she threw herself off the side of a cliff. I can't imagine trying to speak with her *now*."

"Mom, you've never really *tried* to talk to her. Whenever I've had her over at the house, the only thing you've found to say was how you thought she should do her hair and nails differently."

"I was just trying to be nice, dear. But that's not the point. Your future is beginning now, and you need to stop wasting your time with low-class girls who are only going to get you into trouble."

"Avery isn't low class! She's different from all the other girls I know. She actually likes to talk about things besides fake-baking and contraceptives. Dad likes her, don't you Dad?"

10

"She seems like a nice enough girl, son. There's no doubt about that. But I think what your mother is trying to say is that there will be plenty of well-bred women at Garvis to entertain you. Personally, I think you've been spending a bit too much time with her."

"C'mon! I really like Avery, you guys. I feel like she understands me."

"Think about it rationally." Nathan tried not to look irritated. "While Avery finishes up her last year of high school, you're already on your way to a distinguished career. You have nothing in common. She'll probably still be cleaning houses with her mom five years from now. Does that sound like a good match to you?"

Remaining silent, Taylor pulled out his phone and looked at the picture of Avery on the screen's background. Perfect strands of silken long black hair, accented with one blue streak in the front caressed her flawless dark complexion. This particular picture had been taken right after she got a nose jewel, an addition Taylor was rather fond of. Her potent dark brown eyes were hypnotizing. In fact, it took his mother's imposing shrill voice to remind him where he was.

"Taylor, trust me," Jane urged. "You're too young to be able to see this situation clearly. Stay away from her. She's only going to get you into trouble. Girls from her walk of life only hang around people like us for *one* reason. The last thing we need is some illegitimate grandchild leeching off of us for the rest of our lives."

"Avery's not like that. You guys are wrong about her."

"Son, be realistic," Nathan persisted. "Now is not the time for you to lose focus on your goals. You've worked hard to get where you are. So stick with it. All this will pay off in the end. You'll see."

"Sure, Dad."

Nathan perceived how crestfallen Taylor had become. "You know, I think we steered a little off course with that conversation. You're going to Garvis! And I think that calls for a special treat. Don't you agree, Jane?"

"Nathan, I'm not really in the mood for dessert tonight," Jane whined. "Let's just go."

"I'm not talking about dessert." Nathan stood and began for the door. "Follow me."

As they exited the restaurant, Nathan spoke quietly to a valet attendant who then promptly disappeared into the adjacent parking terrace. "Alright, son, close your eyes until I tell you to open them."

Surprises were good. Taylor's imagination was running wild. "Can I open them now?!"

"Stop it. Of course not." Nathan placed his hands over Taylor's face. "And no peeking."

"Good grief, Nathan. You are such a little devil!" Jane squawked as she saw the bright yellow Porsche Carrera emerge from the shadows.

Taylor couldn't take it any longer. Pushing his father's hands away, he couldn't believe his eyes. "Dad, I'm in love." Practically drooling, he nestled into the driver's seat and inhaled the exotic aroma that accompanies a brand new sports car.

"It's a bit overboard, Nathan, don't you think? What on earth was wrong with the Benz he's been driving all year?" Jane complained.

"You've spent over a hundred thousand dollars on your face in the past two years alone. I think I'm allowed to buy our son something nice every now and then. Now don't stay out too late, Taylor," Nathan called out. "Go make a few of your friends jealous and then meet us back at the house, alright?"

Taylor acknowledged his father's advice with a thumbs-up and sped off.

"He's not going to listen to us about that girlfriend of his, is he Nathan."

"I wouldn't say that. He's a smart kid. He'll come to his senses."

∞

"What's taking those Beckmans so long?"

Taylor could hear Avery's mother as he approached the hospital door. *Oops. Late again.* He usually was.

"Mom, chill out," Avery replied. "He sent me a text like ten minutes ago saying he'd be right over."

"Still, it's a little inconsiderate, don't you think? They were supposed to be here thirty minutes ago."

"Sorry I'm late you guys," Taylor announced as he entered the room. "There was an unusually long line at the flower shop."

"You didn't!" Avery exclaimed as she struggled to sit up in the hospital bed.

"I should have brought more." Taylor revealed a dozen long-stem red roses he had been hiding behind his back. Kissing Avery's warm cheek, he placed them on her lap.

"You are so sweet." Avery glowed with contentment and noticed he still had three more roses in the other hand. "And who are those for?"

"Why, for your gorgeous mother, of course!" Taylor winked at Allison, who responded with a manufactured smile.

"You seem a little more perky than usual, Taylor," Allison pointed out.

"He's just excited to see me, Mom."

"Always." Taylor's expression was genuine as he pulled up a chair next to Avery's bedside. "You look terrific, casts and all."

"You're too nice."

"I still can't believe your timing with this! What was it – like a half hour after I left for The Keys with my folks that this all happened?"

"I'm pretty sure it was less time than that. Honestly, I just couldn't bear the thought of being separated from you for that long, Taylor," Avery said playfully.

"I doubt that." He grinned. "Something tells me you'd be just fine without me around."

Even though Avery knew he was joking, she didn't like the way it sounded. "No I wouldn't."

Taylor noticed the shift in her tone. He watched for a few moments as Avery traced some of the rose petals with her finger. Something was clearly on her mind.

On the other side of the room, Allison began to grow uncomfortable with the extended silence. "So Taylor, where are your parents? I thought they were coming too."

Avery looked sharply at Allison, trying to dissuade her; she knew full well where her mother was trying to steer the conversation.

"I'm sorry you guys, uh," Taylor began, looking troubled, "they weren't able to make it. Jet lag seems to be taking a bigger toll on them than usual."

"I see." Allison didn't believe him, but tried to seem as understanding as possible. "So uh, Taylor, how's school going for you these days?"

"It's going really well, actually. Thanks for asking."

"Have you started looking at any colleges yet?"

"Yes. I've had my sights on one in particular."

"That's great. Hopefully it's not too far from home."

"I'm hoping for Garvis."

"Oh, wow. That's quite a ways from here."

"My folks have a house within about thirty miles of the campus, so it's not too bad."

"I really hope you make it in. A friend of mine has a boy who tried to get into Garvis. The kid had straight A's too. Pretty competitive, I guess."

"It is. It's a lot of stress." Taylor looked back at Avery who was being unusually quiet. "You know, I guess now's as good a time to tell you as any."

Avery was curious. "About what?"

"I got an acceptance letter from Garvis today."

Avery had never doubted he'd get in. Not only was he an exceptional student, but his family was well-connected. She always knew he'd eventually go away to college, but didn't expect it was going to be so soon. Avery's mind ached. *I don't even know if it's his baby. He's never going to want to see me again.*

"Well, that's terrific, Taylor." Allison stood to shake hands, and Taylor accepted the gesture with enthusiasm.

"Thank you! It's a really exciting time for my family right now."

"That's great, Taylor." Avery faked a smile. "But I thought you weren't going to apply for another year."

He was embarrassed for not having told Avery sooner. "I wasn't going to, but you know how my parents are. They're pretty driven when it comes to stuff like this. They pushed pretty hard to get things rolling."

Avery was visibly upset now. "I just don't understand why you never told me."

Taylor felt confused and irritated. *Why am I getting in trouble over this?* He didn't appreciate being made out to be the bad guy.

15

"Are you really upset about this? I thought you'd be happy for me, Avery."

"Well, I guess I am." Avery was trying to refrain from crying. "It's just that – " *No. I can't tell him.*

"I'm sorry, Taylor," Allison began, "but Avery's still in a lot of pain. It's been really hard for her these past few weeks."

Avery felt as though her heart would explode.

"Classes don't start until this fall, Avery," Taylor assured. "That's still six months away. It's not like I'll be leaving tomorrow."

The emotions could be held back no longer and Avery began weeping uncontrollably. Allison desperately wanted to take her pain away, but knew there was nothing she could say. All she could do was watch helplessly as tears flowed down her daughter's face.

"We'll still see each other all the time," Taylor continued. "I'll fly out to visit you, or I'll bring you out to be with me. It's really not going to be as bad as you think." Sitting next to her on the bed now, he put his arm around Avery's waist.

Avery leaned her head on his chest while the heavy tears that prevented her from speaking began to soak into his white polo shirt. As his heartbeat resonated in her ear, she somehow felt safe, like he'd love her no matter what happened. "Taylor?"

"Yes."

"Taylor, I'm pregnant."

"What?" Taylor choked, feeling as though the wind had been knocked out of him.

Raising her head to face him, Avery's intoxicating eyes pleaded for forgiveness. "I'm so sorry, Taylor."

Struggling to look at her as he spoke, Taylor repositioned himself closer to the foot of the bed. "How long have you known about this?"

"For a couple of weeks now." Avery reached for a tissue and blew her nose. "I wanted to tell you sooner, but you've been away. I just wanted to tell you in person."

Taylor stared blankly out the window for a moment. His whole world seemed to be spinning out of control. "How far along are you?"

"Fifteen weeks."

Taylor wasn't even certain he wanted to know, but felt compelled to ask anyway. "So – who's the father?"

"I don't know, Taylor." Avery put her face into her hands and wept. "I have no idea whose baby this is."

Taylor was dumbfounded. None of it made sense. How could she have made him believe she adored him all this time? Was it all just an act? But why? He said nothing.

Avery was crushed by Taylor's countenance. Something about the way he looked at her in this moment reminded her of when he had first asked for her phone number six months ago. She had a boyfriend at the time, but he appeared so devastated at her response – as though he'd been informed he had two weeks to live – that she changed her mind. But things were different this time.

Allison could remain quiet no longer. "Are you saying you're *not* the father?"

Standing slowly, Taylor took two steps back toward the door. "You think *I'm* the father?" He then looked at Avery, hoping she would vouch for him, but she said nothing.

"You've been dating for six months now. You need to take responsibility for your actions. Wouldn't you agree?"

"Well, yes, but Avery and I have never – "

"We realize this throws somewhat of a wrench in your college plans, but you *have* been spending an awful lot of time together, Taylor."

Taylor felt like he was being assaulted from all sides. Walking back to Avery, he took her by the hand. "Avery, please! Tell your mother the truth!"

"There are a lot of things I don't remember right now, Taylor. I don't know what the truth is anymore." The greater part of her actually hoped Taylor would confess to what she had no memory of. That would have been far more comforting than the alternatives. But seeing he would offer no such consolation only increased Avery's despair. Picking up the roses, she pushed them into his arms. "Here. I don't deserve them. You deserve to be with someone who isn't going to try and screw your life up. Not a *freak* like me!"

"I truly care about you, Avery – more than you could possibly know. But I'm not responsible for this. I just can't have any part of it."

Allison stood and approached him as he turned to leave. "You both should realize the only way to know for sure is through a paternity test."

"Alright. Have it your way. But I assure you this is a *huge* misunderstanding."

Looking back into Avery's stormy eyes for the last time, Taylor imagined everything that might have been. His greatest desire in this moment was that she *was* carrying his child. But it wasn't true. And that changed everything.

As Taylor exited the hospital parking lot, he made a phone call. "Mom?"

"What's wrong? What's taking you so long? You didn't wreck the car did you?"

"No, Mom, the car's fine. It's about Avery. You and Dad were right about her. It's over."

"You did the right thing. It's for the best."

18

As the traffic light turned green, the yellow Porsche peeled out, leaving a trail of smoke and a dozen red roses in its path.

CHAPTER 3

Avery regretted not having worn a jacket. With her long black hair dancing in the breeze as she walked, she donned a pair of pink tennis shoes, blue jeans, and a yellow cardigan. Despite the slight chill, the sun felt wonderful on her chocolate-toned face as she made the final stretch of her ten-block trek to school.

She'd almost forgotten how good it felt to be outside. Four weeks in the hospital had felt like six months, and Avery was ready to get back to some normalcy. But then again, normal had recently begun to take on a whole new meaning.

New Hope East was one block away now. As she approached, the calm and freedom she felt during her first walk outside since her accident was beginning to dissipate. Just what awaited her behind those white brick walls? If nothing else, there was ceramics. How she'd missed it!

Taking one of the less-busy entrances, Avery pulled open the heavy door and passed a few hundred turquoise lockers before reaching number 1136. Setting her backpack on the floor, she wondered if she'd even be able to remember her combination after all this time. Attempting to turn the dial, Avery was perplexed to discover it wouldn't budge. She gave it another exerted effort, using both hands this time, but it was in vain. "Great," she blurted.

Rolling her dark brown eyes in frustration, she retrieved her white canvas backpack and began for the main office. Commencing her descent down the main stairwell, Avery observed a group of girls on the landing a few meters in front of her. Talking quietly amongst themselves, they were glancing in her direction. When she was a few steps past them, she heard the unmistakable word 'slut'. She was taken back for a second as she continued down the remaining stairs, but tried to convince herself they were referring to someone else.

She would soon be passing through the commons area, which was buzzing with activity. Groups of guys and girls stood around chatting, many holding their morning coffee, waiting for the first bell to ring. Navigating her way through the crowds, Avery discerned a notable reduction in the volume of conversation as she passed by. Many were looking at her with smirks on their faces, while others appeared embarrassed and looked away.

Okay, this is weird, Avery thought to herself. Now at the main office, she timidly opened the door and entered.

"Good morning," squeaked the elderly female office secretary, keeping her eyes on the computer as she typed. "How can I help you?"

Avery briefly looked behind her to make certain the woman was actually speaking to her.

"Yes," Avery began. "My locker dial is stuck. I was wondering if a custodian could come by and help me get it open."

"Why is it stuck?" the gray-haired woman insisted. She peered at Avery over the top of her reading glasses, apparently anticipating a well-detailed explanation.

"I don't know," Avery said, trying not to look annoyed. "I've been gone for a month. Today's my first day back, and my locker dial won't turn. Can someone please help me?"

"A month?" the woman leered. "Sounds like it probably *rusted* shut. I'll see if I can get Dave on the radio."

After verifying for the secretary it was actually *her* locker she was trying to access, Avery was accompanied by a burly, round gentleman in his fifties back upstairs to number 1136.

"I really appreciate you taking the time to help me," Avery said as they walked up the stairs.

"No problem," he growled. "I needed a break from cleaning that nasty boys' bathroom anyway."

Pulling out a flashlight that seemed like a toothpick in his large hairy hands, the custodian bent down clumsily and scrutinized the dial. Using a pocket knife, he cut and dug at the stubborn adhesive, but without success. Some students in the proximity took notice of what he was doing and began to watch.

"Looks like super-glue," he huffed, blowing his nose on a hanky that he retrieved from his front pants pocket. "Blasted pranksters. We're probably going to have to replace it. I'll take care of it within the next hour. At least I can get you unlocked for now though."

Now thumbing through an enormous key ring, Dave found what he was looking for and inserted the small key into the lock while giving the latch a firm pull. As he swung the door open, immediately a large collection of thin square packets poured from the bottom of Avery's locker and onto the beige laminate floor. Before he or Avery could discern what they were, Dave struggled down to start putting them back where they came from. Then it hit her. Her chocolate-toned skin flushed into a deep red. She opened her mouth to speak, but nothing came out. Some students passing by recognized the little packages instantly and began to laugh.

"These are *not* mine," Avery asserted as she began grabbing fistfuls of condoms and walking them across the hall to the nearest garbage can. Some fell to the ground during the process, which were promptly picked up by eager hands of students walking by.

"You just want me to throw these away then?" the large custodian questioned loudly. His enormous hands were cupped and overflowing with the little square packages.

"Yes," Avery replied. "And thanks for opening my locker. I can handle it from here."

"What are you all looking at?!" Avery barked at the gathering crowd as she plopped the rest of the mess into the garbage.

"What a *whore*!" boomed a deep voice from the crowd. It was echoed by laughs and giggles.

Seeing one more of the disturbing packages on the floor, Avery picked it up and noticed there was hand writing on it. In bold black capital letters it read: BETTER LUCK NEXT TIME.

The crowd was now dispersing, as approximately one minute remained before the first class would begin. Placing her math and history books onto the top shelf of her locker, Avery saw his picture out of the corner of her eye.

"Thanks a lot, Taylor," Avery said under her breath. Removing the photo from the inside of her locker door, she tore it into little pieces and tossed them into the garbage can.

∞

"Now I want you to approach this assignment in a very specific way," Mr. Murray explained as he paced around the room.

He was certainly one of the more engaging English teachers at New Hope East. Always clean shaven, with reddish brown curly hair, he stood about two meters tall, even with his slouch. Due to his pale skin and well-proportioned face, he looked much younger than he was. And that silly bowtie and suspenders look he insisted on; Avery couldn't help but smile every time she saw him. Indeed, for Avery, watching him lecture this morning was a welcome diversion to the nightmare she'd experienced thus far.

"This anthology," Mr. Murray continued, "is about focusing on the journey of your lives, rather than the destination." Now sitting on the edge of his desk, with chin-in-palm, he looked at Avery for a moment. "Ms. Renshaw, it's good to have you back."

"Thank you," Avery smiled.

"The due date is in two months," he went on. "It will consist of twenty one poems, each with a minimum of fifty words, and with a max of two hundred. There are some key aspects I want you to incorporate in your writing. Each poem will have three versions, so to speak. First will be the way you interpret subject matter now, right here, in this moment. Second, from the point of view of someone at the outside, looking in. Third, of how you think you may interpret the subject matter twenty years from now."

Groans of disapproval were heard throughout the class. Avery, on the other hand, pulled out a spiral notebook and immediately got to work.

Mr. Murray was now pacing about the room again as he concluded his instructions. "Now, to assure you are given ample time to finish this, we will be dedicating the last ten minutes of every class session to developing our poems." Taking a seat in the black swivel chair behind his desk, he started some new-age instrumental music on his stereo. "Now, begin."

There was so much to say. So much she felt. So much she didn't *want* to feel. How could her life have taken such a turn? Why did the universe seem to single *her* out? Was she being punished for something? Was there something inherently wrong with her? The previous month's events were replaying constantly in her mind, her logic desperately trying to make sense of it all. But it was no use. All that remained was confusion, pain, and resentment. *I don't deserve this. I don't deserve to be pregnant!*

"How's it going over here?" Mr. Murray asked, taking a seat in the desk to Avery's left.

"I'm sorry, what?" Avery mumbled as she looked up, her hand throbbing from writing so much so quickly. To her surprise, the room was empty.

24

"That's what I love about writing," Mr. Murray commented as he looked at the clock on the wall. "Everything around you just sort of, disappears."

"Sorry about that," Avery began as she packed away her things. "I didn't realize the bell rang."

"No need to apologize. Is there anything I can help you with?"

"Honestly, Mr. Murray," Avery said as she stood up, "I wish there was."

"Alright," he smiled as he accompanied her to the door. He could sense she was on the verge of tears. "Try to hang in there, okay?"

"I will. See you tomorrow."

∞

History class was particularly difficult to endure that day. It was a boring discussion on the current reckoning of time, which was measured as years transpired since the Fall of Rome, 1,536 years ago. Not only was the aged instructor's monotone voice savagely annoying to follow, but the conversation between the two girls a couple rows up made it nearly impossible.

"I heard the look on that girl's face was priceless," said a curly-haired brunette in a loud whisper. Avery was pretty sure her name was Carla.

"I wish I could have seen it," responded the short-haired blonde sitting next to her.

"Misty said she about died laughing."

"Whose locker was it?"

"I'm not sure. It was up on the second floor, somewhere by language arts, I think."

"Who did it?"

"It was a couple of guys on the basketball team. Do you know Jackson and Stue? Devin told me it was them. I guess it was the girlfriend – well, ex-girlfriend of someone who graduated last year."

"That *was* pretty messed up though, don't you think?"

"Not really though. Apparently this chick was totally sleeping around on him."

"How do you know?"

"Stue and Jackson are friends with the guy. Devin said she had no clue who the baby's dad was!"

"Seriously?"

"I know, right? The girl's a complete slut."

"Wow. Maybe it's her boyfriend's baby."

"Nope. Devin said the paternity test was negative."

Avery's stomach was practically in her mouth. Quietly excusing herself, she slipped into the hallway and darted for the bathroom. Ducking into one of the yellow stalls, she crouched down and began projecting her breakfast into the toilet. Taylor's face flashed through her mind with every heave. *What am I going to do? The entire school knows about me!* What she needed was to bawl her eyes out.

Exiting the stall, Avery looked in the mirror for a moment and tried to compose herself. Taking a step back, she placed a hand on her stomach and stood sideways. Scrutinizing her reflection, she determined she *had* begun to show a little, but it wasn't yet *obvious*. Was it? Maybe it was. Or maybe, just maybe, she would wake up – wake up and realize it had all just been a bad dream.

East High's lunchroom began to hum with activity as the first wave of noisy students began pouring in. Sitting at her and Marnee's usual table along the far wall, Avery reluctantly opened her lunch bag, removing a banana and a bag of potato chips. Food did *not* sound good right now. Pulling out her pink cell phone, she noticed her mom had sent quite a few text messages. 'How are things going? Are you feeling the morning sickness today? Love you.' While thumbing in a response to her mother, Avery noticed Marnee taking a seat with her lunch tray on the opposite side of the room. Of course, she couldn't really read into it. After all, she hadn't been to school in over a month.

Taking her food with her, Avery carefully traversed the bustling cafeteria and took a seat directly across from Marnee.

"Hey, stranger," Marnee said as she pulled her curly blond hair into a pony tail.

"I love your shirt," Avery commented.

"Isn't it cute? Burke got it for me for my birthday." Marnee pushed her black-framed glasses to the top of her pointy nose and began smearing butter on a roll.

"Oh crap, Marnee," Avery sighed in dismay. "I totally forgot. I'm so sorry."

"Seriously," Marnee began as she took a bite of her whole-wheat roll, "don't even worry about it. You've had enough on your plate these days."

"Thanks for visiting me in the hospital." Avery opened her bag of chips and popped one in her mouth. "It got a little lonely in there."

"I can imagine." Marnee picked up her turkey sandwich and took a massive bite.

"I see you're done with the whole vegan thing."

"Yup," Marnee affirmed as she set down her sandwich. "I knew it wouldn't be a good match with track and everything. Coach Hansen said I was crazy. But Burke wanted me to try it out. His snobby vegan club gives him crap for dating a carnivore, but they can just kiss it."

"You're funny." Avery grabbed a couple more chips and began to peel her banana.

"So when were you planning on telling me?" Marnee took another bite of her sandwich and dabbed a napkin to the corners of her mouth.

Avery's eyes widened at Marnee's question, who glared expectantly in return.

"Is it true?" Marnee insisted, her dark green eyes fixed on Avery's.

"I guess I'm still in a bit of denial."

"The whole school is talking about it."

"Oh really? Why don't you tell me about it?" Avery's tone had shifted from calm to cynical.

"I don't get you, Avery," Marnee said as she flicked a piece of lettuce off her white shirt sleeve. "We've been friends for like two years. And you can't even tell me what's going on? That's a little messed up, don't you think?"

Avery looked away for a moment in silence. The incessant babble in the room was now beginning to make her feel claustrophobic.

"Don't judge me," Avery said as she resumed eye contact with Marnee.

"I'm not judging you."

"Do you have any idea what this is like?"

"Not really. No." Marnee opened her can of cola and took a few swallows. "I guess I'm just a little surprised. That's all."

"What's that supposed to mean?"

"Nothing."

"What are you so surprised about? Do tell. I would love to know."

"I guess I was just under the impression that one of my good friends would clue me in on the fact she was getting so much action. You've always acted like such a prude."

"What?"

"Well you have. According to you, you didn't even kiss Taylor until like the tenth date, I swear. And then just out of the blue, you get yourself knocked up, and you don't even know whose kid it is?"

"You know, you're one to talk."

"You *know* who I've been with. It's not some big secret. The least you could do is talk to me. But apparently that's too hard for you."

"What do you expect me to say to that?"

"Nothing, Avery. I guess I shouldn't expect you to let me know anything that's going on in your life. Enjoy your banana."

Leaving her tray, Marnee grabbed her sandwich and walked toward the exit. As she watched her friend go, Avery pushed her food aside and dropped her face into her hands.

CHAPTER 4

The walk home from her first day back at school had been a blur. Emotionally bankrupt and physically spent, Avery's hand quivered as she turned the key to their old downtown apartment. Dropping her backpack by the front door, she slogged over to the kitchen to see if there was anything to snack on. On the fridge was a note from her mother: 'Doing some cleaning bids. Be back around seven. Love you.' Avery mused on the fact that Allison still used notes so much. *You could have just texted me, Mom.*

Finding nothing worth eating, Avery downed a glass of water and headed for bed. The cruelty she'd endured that day gnawed at her incessantly as she lay. Trying to get comfortable, she turned from her left side to the right, staring into space. As she replayed the events of the day over and over in her mind, something in the closet caught her eye. She'd forgotten it even existed. The elegant yellow dress was long and slender, made of a sleek satin. It reminded Avery of better days.

∞

"What are we doing here?" Avery had questioned, feeling surprised and flattered.

Taylor clenched her hand and smiled. "I just thought it might be fun to take a look around."

A wave of excitement surged through Avery as the pair walked inside the upscale clothing retailer. She'd never been in a store *this* fancy before.

"Welcome to Ashton's," greeted a well-dressed woman in her late thirties. "Can I help you find anything?"

Avery shot a nervous look at Taylor. They'd only been dating a couple of weeks and she had no idea what he had in mind.

"Actually, yes," Taylor replied with confidence. "Do you carry Etienne?"

The woman's eye's widened as she smiled. "Absolutely. Please follow me."

Guiding them to a section on the far right of the store, their host turned and smiled. "I believe these are about the size you're looking for. Dressing room is to your left. Please let me know if you have any questions."

"Thank you," Taylor beamed.

Avery didn't know what to think. "Taylor? Seriously. Why did you take me here?"

"I'd like you to try some of these on."

"But why?" Avery blushed.

"Come on, Avery. Just humor me a little. It'll be fun."

"I don't know, Taylor. I'm not really a dress girl."

"I'm going to try something on too."

"A dress?!"

"No, silly!" Taylor laughed. "One of those tuxedos over there."

"Oh."

"Hey, what about this yellow one, right here?"

As Taylor pulled it from the rack, Avery had to agree. It was the most beautiful dress she'd ever seen. Holding the long gown directly in front of her, a smile of pure satisfaction emanated from his well-proportioned face. "Wow. Yes. This is definitely the one. Well, that settles it. I'll take a minute and change into my tux, and we'll meet right here in a few minutes."

"If you say so," Avery grinned.

The female employee unlocked the door for Avery and smiled. "You'll need help zipping that up. Just let me know when you're ready."

"I guess I will, won't I?" Avery replied. "Thank you."

After a few minutes and some help from the attendant, Avery admired her reflection in disbelief. Having always considered herself somewhat of a Tom-boy, this was a side of herself she'd never really explored. The radiant young woman staring at her through the mirror looked like a princess from the fairy tales she'd read as a kid.

"Avery," Taylor called. "Are you going to let me see you?"

"Sorry," Avery replied. "Be right out."

With mouth agape, Taylor looked on as Avery appeared from behind the dressing room door.

"I can't even tell you!" he exclaimed. "You make that gown look *so* much better."

"You don't look bad yourself, Handsome," Avery smiled.

"Ma'am," Taylor called to the attendant, "could you please take a picture of us?"

Scurrying over from the cash register, the woman took his phone and snapped a photo. "You two look absolutely dazzling."

Returning Taylor's phone, the woman returned to the register and printed off a receipt. "Alright, guys. When you're done changing, I'll go ahead and get that dress ready to go for you."

Avery was flabbergasted. "Oh. I'm not actually buying this. There's no way I could ever afford a dress like this."

"Well, that's what boyfriends are for, right?" the woman laughed.

"Taylor, I can't let you buy this dress for me! It's almost six hundred dollars!"

Being well over a head taller than Avery, Taylor leaned down to kiss her on the cheek and whispered in her ear. "How much trouble would I be in if I already did?"

Avery was speechless.

"So not that much then, I take it?"

"But why? When would I possibly wear it?"

"Don't you have a Senior Prom coming up?"

"You want to take me to the Prom?"

"You're not surprised are you? Why wouldn't I?"

"Well, I don't know."

"I've got to try and hold on to you, Avery. If I don't, some other guy will come and scoop you up."

"Well, Mr. Beckman," Avery grinned, "you certainly know how to sell."

"So does that mean you'll let me take you to the Prom?"

"Of course I will."

Gently pushing wisps of blue and black hair behind her ear, Taylor leaned down and kissed the angel in the yellow gown standing next to him. And Avery, who tip-toed up to reach him, enjoyed every moment of it.

But it was a Prom she'd never attend. A memory she'd never have.

Instead, there was pain. Confusion. Guilt. Regret. And the yellow dress – the most beautiful gown in the history of the world. Hanging in the closet, it seemed to be taunting her. Mocking her. *He's better off without you. And you know it.*

Tears welled up in her eyes. *Why did this happen to me? Did I do something wrong? Why am I such a freak?*

Then their conversation in the hospital came back with full force. 'Who's the father?' Taylor had said. And she didn't know. She still didn't know. It was doubtful she ever would. Not like it mattered though. *Why are people so cruel?*

I'll never get to wear that dress for him.

Hanging in its splendor, the satin yellow gown continued to taunt her. Continued to remind her that she would never wear it because she was a whore. A slut. That's why Taylor would no longer have anything to do with her. She was a pregnant seventeen year-old. And not by him. A pregnant *teenager*. A whore. Avery closed her eyes in anguish.

But that's not *who I am. No. That is* not *who I am.*

Rising to her feet, Avery strode into the kitchen and returned with a pair of scissors. With a deep resolve radiating from her bloodshot eyes, she tore the gown from its hanger and threw it in the middle of the floor. Then kneeling beside the heap of yellow fabric, she began at the neck and frantically severed it all the way to the bottom. Now making a dozen or so cuts around the perimeter, Avery used both hands to fiercely rip the yellow satin to shreds.

The task was exhausting.

The elaborate dress, like Avery's soul, had now been reduced to rags. Crouching into the fetal position atop the pile of torn yellow fabric, Avery closed her swollen brown eyes. She needed sleep. But she knew it would bring no solace. Because eventually – she would have to wake up.

CHAPTER 5

"You are an absolute genius," sounded a familiar raspy voice.

"How's it going, Mr. Kunz?" Turning to smile at her mentor, Avery kept her hands in contact with the cool smooth clay. "I thought you weren't going to be here today."

"Jury duty can't keep me out of this place *all* day," he chuckled as he approached from the door.

"Did you go dressed like that?" Avery commented as she continued smoothing the edges on the face of her newest creation.

"So my super-hero t-shirt and board shorts aren't quite doing it for you, are they?"

"Oh, they are. And the flip-flops."

"Well, they *did* make me wear a tie."

"Then it seems you performed your civic duty in style," Avery laughed.

"You know it. So, how are things going?"

Avery hesitated. "They're going."

"Good. That's good. Feeling okay?"

"Yeah."

"Glad to hear it. I have to say, it's been pretty weird not having you around for the last month. Everyone's been asking about you."

"Well, it's been interesting. I will say that."

"I can imagine."

I greatly doubt that.

"Hey, uh, you didn't happen to see Landon here today by chance, did you?"

"I did. He stayed after with me for a little while, but said he had to drop his dad off at the airport."

"Crap." Mr. Kunz stroked his bristled chin. "I was hoping to catch him so I could hand off his scholarship packet."

Walking to the opposite side of the table as Avery, Mr. Kunz placed a weathered hand on the dusty surface and brought the pointer finger of his other hand to his forehead. "And wait a second. I think I'm getting a signal here. Something about – yes, something about another student of mine. Yes. A student named Avery. That's right. A student named Avery who is nearly finished with her scholarship packet."

Avery made brief eye contact with him while she worked and forced a slight grin.

Mr. Kunz had both hands on the table now and leaned forward as he spoke. "Well? Hmmm? Help me out here, Avery."

"I'm sorry, Mr. Kunz. It's just that – "

"Now, I know you've had a bad time lately with the accident and the hospital stay and everything. I totally get that. You're obviously feeling well enough to be at school though. So that's good, right?"

"Yes. The pain is pretty minimal now. So I'm happy about that. Yes."

"Awesome. You look like you're doing okay. Your hands still seem to be doing what you need them to. How long ago did I give that paperwork to you though?"

"I know, I know."

"The deadline's in four weeks. That's nothing. That'll fly by like that."

"I guess I'm just a procrastinator."

"C'mon now. Don't label yourself like that, Avery. You're not. You've got what it takes. You're the most gifted student that's ever stepped foot in this room. It would be a shameful waste of talent for you not to go to art school. You're light years ahead of the game, Avery."

"You're *supposed* to tell your students those kinds of things," Avery blushed.

"I'm not just blowing smoke at you. I really thought we were on the same page about this." He could sense there was something bothering her. Her expression was reserved and somewhat somber. "I can't imagine your mom giving you flack about wanting to go."

"Well, even with a scholarship, room and board *are* pretty expensive."

"That's true, but you've got an excellent shot for a full-ride, Avery. You really do. I mean, just look at this piece you're working on right now! This is the kind of stuff you see in an art museum or some billionaire's mansion! You're more skilled than I'll ever be. We need to get moving on this. We're running out of time."

Slowly lowering her hands to her side, Avery looked at her mentor in silence. He reminded her so much of her own father. The square jawline. The scruffy beard. The incessant enthusiasm. The way he cared.

The low-hanging sun had now found a direct route through the classroom windows, illuminating tears as they trickled down her bronze cheeks. "Thank you for believing in me."

"Good grief, Avery. How could I not?"

With a blank expression on her face, Avery looked at the table and traced her finger aimlessly through the dust. "I'm not going to apply for that scholarship, Mr. Kunz."

He was dumbfounded. "Why?"

Directing her gaze toward the sinking sun, Avery bit her lip for a moment and spoke barely above a whisper. "I'm pregnant."

∞

"I see it's the usual for you today," commented a middle-aged male cashier with a pierced eyebrow.

"Yes, thank you," Avery responded as she handed him a single red rose and a candy bar.

"Total comes to three fifty seven."

"Here ya go."

"Out of five. And here's your change."

"Thanks, Dale."

"No problem. See you next week."

"Bye."

Heading toward the grocery store exit with the rose under her right arm and the candy bar in her pocket, Avery texted her mother. 'Visiting Dad and Kendra. Love you.'

Stepping into the cool evening air, the seventeen year old began the twenty minute uphill walk from the store to the cemetery. It had been her weekly Monday ritual for nearly the last five years. Large maple trees lining the street swayed to and fro in the wind as she made the climb. The low hum of lawnmowers in the proximity could be heard, while the beginnings of tulips, orchids, and roses were manifesting in the residents' yards. Avery was running out of breath sooner than usual, and she made note of just how much a month in the hospital had taken out of her. No matter though. Her destination wasn't too far away now.

The sun hung low on the horizon as she arrived, enveloping Avery and her surroundings in a deep orange glow. Spotting a cement bench under a towering weeping willow, she took a seat to catch her breath, and the crisp moist air was refreshing to her exhausted lungs.

She was grateful to be outside, but the pending sunset, although beautiful, was a dismal reminder that tomorrow would be another humiliating day of school. Another day of ridicule. Maybe she just wouldn't go back.

Now continuing up the narrow crudely paved road, she spotted the familiar secluded nook. This place was one of the few places she could go to think. And although the view it afforded wasn't overly appealing, it was a view nevertheless. Avery felt she could discern more clearly the true nature of things from here. She had even developed a sort of kinship with the decaying cityscape in the distance. In her silent oasis she had watched it deteriorate by degrees over the years. It seemed to follow the same course as a human life, its youthful pillars inevitably crumbling with the unforgiving passage of time. The myriad of buildings in the distance cast long shadows over the outskirts of town, much like those created by the sea of lifeless tombstones that Avery currently took solace in. This was Avery's favorite time of day, for the imposing shadows seemed to empathize with her. These dark sprawling shapes, somehow more than the grave markers themselves, represented a void – a void that truly understood her.

Pulling the chocolate bar from her pocket, she placed it at the base of a shiny red marble gravestone.

"I love you, Dad," Avery whispered. She gazed longingly at the letters engraved in stone.

Richard Steward
Husband, Father, Friend
Nov 4, 1495 – July 2, 1532

From a distance, the grounds keeper noticed Avery had arrived and was very much accustomed to the candy bars being left. Generally, the hunched-over old man would leave it there for a couple of days and then throw it out with the countless other items routinely left in cemeteries. As he leaned on his shovel and watched her, he reflected on her consistent visits. Although some graves were visited with some frequency, once a week was definitely outside the norm. And such a young person by herself, week after week. It was rather remarkable. How he would have loved to have a conversation with her. But naturally, she didn't know sign language, so all he could ever do was wave hello and goodbye. How he appreciated this thoughtful young woman's visits! They were a constant reminder to him that people could be knit together in love, even when death insisted on getting in the way.

As the sun bid farewell over the horizon Avery walked a few meters to the east and traced her finger along the words on a simple granite gravestone, which words, according to Allison, had been Kendra's last.

Avery, I love you, even now.

How Avery longed to have memories of this remarkable woman. But all she had to go on were stories she'd heard from her parents. A refugee from India's war-torn Southern Reach, Kendra had managed to travel half way around the globe for a new beginning. Life had not been kind, and Kendra arrived in the Western Republic with one possession: an unborn child. Starving, sick, and homeless, she was taken in by Allison, who discovered her nearly unconscious at an inner-city bus stop.

Over the following months it was heart-wrenching for Allison and Richard to learn of all that Kendra had experienced throughout the years. They both grew to appreciate and love this mysterious dark-skinned beauty from the Southern Reach. She was so gracious and kind, always doing anything she could to help the Stewards with housework, yardwork, and errands. To their deep dismay, however, Kendra departed almost as abruptly as she had arrived. Suffering a serious stroke two weeks before her due date, she died during an emergency C-section, leaving little Avery to carry on the new beginning her young courageous mother had only just begun.

Avery affectionately looked at Kendra's name emblazoned in cursive on her right forearm and smiled. *I wish I could have met you. You sacrificed everything for me. I don't deserve it. But thank you so much.*

Pressing the delicate flower petals to her lips, Avery laid down the rose and departed. As she walked across the soft velvet grass, her calves glistened in the sun, the left bearing a small tattoo of Richard's name, and the right displaying Allison's. She could see the old grounds keeper trimming a row of lilac bushes in the distance. She waved goodbye, which he noticed with a warm smile, and promptly returned the gesture. That simple friendly human interaction was remarkably comforting for her on this particular evening. She had been feeling so completely alone. And yet, an elderly man who couldn't speak had somehow made her feel like – like she mattered.

CHAPTER 6

"C'mon, Sweetie," Allison said as she gently wobbled Avery's shoulder. "We need to get going."

"Ugh," Avery groaned. "It's too early."

"It's nearly noon, Avery."

Turning over in her blankets, Avery looked at her mother through droopy brown eyes. "I don't want to go, Mom."

"What do you mean, you don't want to go?"

"Uh, let me rephrase. Mom, I don't want to go. How's that?"

Raising her eyebrows at her daughter's sarcasm, Allison reached across the bed and opened the dusty aluminum blinds. "Alright, Miss Attitude. Thank you for sharing your opinion. Now it's time to get up. This is important."

Expressionless and staring at the floor, Avery felt as though she were a prisoner in her own skin. "Fine. How long do I have?"

"Twenty minutes. Then we have to leave. What do you want for breakfast? Oatmeal? I could throw some pancakes together real quick if you want."

"I'm not hungry."

Allison shook her head as she turned to leave the room. "Teenagers."

Realizing she didn't have time for a shower, Avery threw on a white hoody and some jeans she hadn't worn in a while. She was disappointed, however, to discover she couldn't get the pants to fasten without a struggle. *Great.* It was yet another reminder of her new life. The one she hadn't chosen. The life she would change if there were any possible way.

Without saying a word to her mother, Avery walked past the kitchen where Allison was unloading the dishwasher and closed the front door behind her. Allison caught up with her a few minutes later.

"Well, aren't we just a bundle of joy this morning," Allison chimed as she opened the driver's side door of their gray clunker.

Without looking up, Avery finished sending a text and slid the phone in her front hoody pocket.

"Better buckle up," Allison insisted as she fastened her own seat belt. "Gotta keep that baby safe."

Avery followed suit with a moan and then pulled her phone back out, pretending to be busy.

Doing her best to ignore her daughter's discontent, Allison turned the key. The old engine wheezed and moaned for a moment before consenting to fire up.

"Well," Allison began as she backed down the cracked apartment driveway, "I'm excited to find out if it's a boy or a girl."

"That makes one of us then," Avery mumbled. "Wow, this car sounds like it's going to die any second."

"Can we shoot for just a little less negativity, please?"

Without responding, Avery looked out the window and reflected on what a nightmare her life had become. Despite the loss of her father and her own bout with cancer at age twelve, things had calmed down and were starting to look pretty hopeful. She had discovered her talent and love of sculpting and was headed for art school. Things were going to work out. Life was going to be good after all. Or so she had thought.

∞

"Yes," Allison smiled as she stepped toward the receptionist's desk. "You should have an appointment for Avery Renshaw."

"Let's take a look here," came the reply. "Ah, yes. Dr. Blaire will be with you shortly. Please have a seat for a few minutes and we'll call you back."

"Thank you."

Finding a chair next to some magazines, Allison watched the door for Avery, who entered a few minutes later with her eyes glued to her phone.

"Who are you talking to?" Allison asked casually.

Avery spent a moment finishing another text message before responding. "Marnee."

"I thought you two weren't talking. What's she up to?"

"We weren't, but we've talked it out. Things are fine. She wants to go see a movie tonight."

"You can go, but remember I need some help cleaning for a while today."

"You're going to make your pregnant daughter clean houses with you," Avery smirked. "I don't know how I feel about that."

"Nice try, Sweetheart. It's quick money. It will only take a couple of hours."

"Whatever. Sure. The movie's at seven. We'll be done by then, right?"

"Should be, yeah."

While Allison flipped through a home-decorating magazine, Avery sat quietly with her white hoody drooping over her forehead. She couldn't help but notice she was easily the youngest person in the room. Most of the other women appeared to be in their later twenties to early thirties. As she looked about the room, Avery reflected on how she had never in a million years thought she would be sitting in an OB's waiting room! How she detested being here. A curly blonde haired woman in a bright pink shirt had been eyeing Avery from across the room. Her expression seemed one of sympathy and concern. It was difficult for Avery

44

not to feel judged, sitting in a room like this. She was piecing stories together in her own head about the others waiting to be seen. So why wouldn't they be doing the exact same thing about her? Of course they were. A pregnant teenager? Those girls were easy to figure out. She knew what they thought of her. If they had any idea.

"Avery?" announced a female medical assistant in her mid-forties.

A nervous wave swept over her as Avery stood. All eyes in the room now had permission to look directly at her since she was the one called back. She could almost feel them sizing her up as she and her mother followed the woman toward a narrow hallway.

"Alright," the woman said, directing Avery's attention to a scale. "Go ahead and step up there for a second."

Great, Avery thought. "I'd really rather not, if that's alright."

"Avery?" Allison said in surprise. "Please cooperate."

Rolling her eyes, Avery stepped onto the digital scale. She'd gained five pounds since her accident. *Whatever*.

Taking note of the numbers displayed on the screen, the attendant directed them into an adjacent room.

"So, I'm sure this is a clerical mistake," the attendant began, "but I'm showing this is your first appointment."

"That's correct," Allison said. "It's a little complicated. But yes. It's the first one."

"That works. Just making sure. So do you know about how far along you are?"

"I think something around twenty weeks or so," Avery guessed.

"Well, when was your last period?"

Avery paused for a moment. "I've never actually had a period before."

The attendant looked confused. "But – "

"I don't have any ovaries."

Allison could tell the attendant was trying to make sense of what she was hearing, but without success. "She had a rare form of ovarian cancer when she was in elementary school and they had to be surgically removed."

The woman opened her mouth to speak, but couldn't seem to formulate all the questions she wanted to ask. "Um, gotcha. Well, moving on then. I'm going to take your blood pressure and ask you a few quick questions, and then Dr. Blaire will be with you a few minutes after that."

Avery's blood pressure had been normal, and she confirmed that she didn't smoke, drink alcohol, or indulge in hard drugs.

"Alright," the attendant continued as she made notes on her clipboard, "are you in a monogamous relationship with the child's father?"

"A monoga-what?" Avery queried, looking at her mother for assistance.

"She's asking you if you're sexually involved with just the baby's father."

Avery looked frustrated. "I'm not sexually active with anyone."

"Okay. That works," the attendant responded. "Do you have any health concerns regarding the father's side of the family?"

The three endured a moment of awkward silence while Avery tried to formulate her response. "Well, I do have one concern about the child's father."

"And what is that?"

So she does *know who he is?* Allison was eager to hear what her daughter had to say.

"I'm concerned because I don't know *who* the child's father is. I don't know how on earth I'm going to raise a baby. I don't even know *how* I got pregnant. So there. Those are my concerns. I could list a few others, but I'm sure your clipboard doesn't have much more room."

Allison smiled nervously and slowly shifted her gaze from her daughter to the attendant, who listened intently with raised eyebrows.

The medical assistant silently reflected on how these types of situations always made working for an OB rather interesting. "I see. This is clearly an extremely delicate situation. If the both of you can wait here, the doctor will be in momentarily."

As the attendant closed the door, Avery looked at her mother in dismay. "I don't want to be here, Mom."

"Oh, Avery," Allison sighed as she placed her arm around her daughter. "I don't know what to say."

Closing her eyes, Avery leaned her head back against the wall. "I just want all of this to go away. I can't deal with this anymore."

"All we can do is just take it a day at a time." Allison tried to be consoling, but sensed she was falling short. "I wish your father were here."

Avery had just been thinking the same thing. "Me too."

"He was always so much better with words than I am."

Avery's mind drifted to when she was ten years old and about to jump off the high dive for the first time. "Now I know you can do this," her father, Richard, had said. She would always remember those caring, enthusiastic blue eyes beaming at her. He pushed back his wet wavy brown hair and continued, "There's nothing to be afraid of, Aves. Just keep your arms to your side, take a deep breath, and step off the edge."

Avery wanted to do it, but still wasn't convinced. "Dad, I don't know. I don't think I can do it. It's so far. What if it hurts?"

"Do you want to know the secret? I'll tell you if you really want to know."

"What is it?"

"It's all in how you look at the water."

"What do you mean?"

"Let me put it this way. When you were standing up there, did you view the water as your friend, or your enemy?"

Avery hadn't been certain she knew what her dad was getting at, but she tried to go with it. "My enemy, I guess."

"The water is going to catch you, Avery. It will always catch you. It's waiting *just* for you. It's excited for you to jump in and be its friend. Do you see what I mean?"

The concerned expression on her face had begun to give way to a smile. "I think I get it. Yeah."

Richard then placed his large hands on her little shoulders. "We don't run from our challenges in this family, Avery. We run towards them. Okay?"

"Okay."

Climbing the ladder to the diving board felt so much different after her dad had explained it like that. She took each step with confidence and then walked calmly across the board with certainty and a sense of eager anticipation. And just like her father had promised, the free fall was brief, and the water caught her, enveloping her in a blanket of safety. Emerging from the pool with a huge smile on her face, her ears were met with booming cheers and hoots from her father as he clapped.

"Nicely done, Aves! Nicely done!"

Helping her to her feet as she climbed out of the pool, Richard embraced his daughter tightly.

"See! What did I tell you?!"

"I know dad! It really worked! Can I go again?!"

"Absolutely."

Avery's body jerked with a start, her attention being brought back to her current surroundings. Dr. Blaire had just entered the room and unintentionally slammed the door behind her.

"I'm so sorry to startle you like that!" chuckled a casually dressed woman in her mid-fifties. "We haven't been in this particular office for very long and I'm still getting used to these doors." Extending a strong, albeit slender, hand to Avery and then Allison, she introduced herself. "Hi. I'm Holly Blaire."

"Are you the doctor?" Avery asked.

"That's what they keep telling me." Dr. Blaire smiled, revealing a striking smile with dazzling white teeth. "And you must be Miss Avery Renshaw, is that right?"

"Yes. Pleased to meet you."

"Likewise."

Avery was instantly put at ease by Dr. Blaire's cheerful demeanor. And donning a snug black T-shirt and green scrubs, she came off very unimposing.

"And this must be Mom."

"Allison Steward. Thank you for taking the time to see us today."

"Oh stop it. The pleasure's all mine." Taking a seat in a black swivel chair by a small wall-mounted computer, Dr. Blaire pulled her shoulder-length silver hair into a pony tail. "I apologize if I seem a little sleepy this afternoon. I ran a half-marathon this morning and I don't think I was quite prepared enough for it."

"You are certainly more ambitious than most," Allison laughed. "I probably couldn't run around the block if I wanted to."

"Oh you could too!" Dr. Blaire insisted as she briefly looked over the notes on her clipboard. "So how was the drive in for you two? Hopefully not too hectic."

"I slept through it," Avery admitted. "So it was pretty nice."

"It wasn't bad," Allison explained. "Took the Central Corridor from downtown. It's never too congested this time of day."

"Well, good. Very good. I suppose it's time to get to work then, right? So I'd like to clarify something before we proceed, just to err on the side of caution. By the sound of things, Avery, you're not certain who the child's father is. And you have no ovaries. Is that correct?"

Avery looked at the floor and sighed. "Correct. I have no ovaries. And no. I – I don't know who the father is. No."

With deep concern in her large hazel eyes, Dr. Blaire looked at Allison for a moment and then back at Avery. "So, I just have to inquire about the obvious here. Now, you're seventeen, so I can't imagine why you would have been, but – I still have to ask. Did you have any procedures performed that would artificially induce pregnancy?"

Avery laughed out loud. "I apologize for laughing, but why on earth would I do that?"

"Absolutely not," Allison insisted. "We can't even afford to pay the rent. No."

"I apologize," Doctor Blaire began. "I just had to ask. It just seemed like the only viable possibility. But I agree. I mean, there isn't a reputable organization in existence that would perform that procedure on a teenager. No question about it."

"Believe us," Allison said with wet eyes, "we're more confused than you are."

"Of course," Dr. Blaire conceded as she handed Allison a tissue box. "I certainly don't want to make things any more uncomfortable than they no-doubt already are."

"We appreciate that," Allison said, dabbing a tissue at her eyes.

"Now there's a comment here," Dr. Blaire continued, "that you've never had sex with anyone."

Avery knew it sounded crazy. "At least not that I have any memory of, anyway."

"She had quite the accident a couple of months ago," Allison explained, "and it seems like some of her memory was impacted."

"And the reason I bring this up," Dr. Blaire went on, "is because depending on the nature of the event itself, it could have been traumatic enough to cause some severe psychological damage. Can I be completely open and frank with you, Avery?"

Despite the very personal nature of the conversation, Avery felt safe talking with this kind woman. "Yes. Please do."

"I have a couple of concerns. Now, it's clearly been some time since you learned you were pregnant, so I'm sure you've possibly explored this. But I'm worried you were forced into a sexual encounter. And I really hope we're not dealing with an ongoing abuse situation here."

Tilting her gaze toward the floor for a moment, Allison put a hand on her forehead and took a deep breath. She had spent many a sleepless night worrying about the same thing. But Avery had given no information about it. Nothing whatsoever. Leaning forward in her chair, Allison looked with raised eyebrows at Avery, who sat still and expressionless.

"I know it must seem that way," Avery offered, "but I really couldn't say. I mean - "

"*Why* can't you say, Avery?" Dr. Blaire pressed.

"I can tell you right now, if I had something to say, I would say it."

"Were you *threatened* at all?"

Avery could discern that Dr. Blaire truly cared about her and wanted to help. But she simply had no memory of the event that led to her child's conception. "I really don't have any information for you. I don't remember anything about it. I wish I did. I'm sorry."

"I apologize for being so avid," Dr. Blaire continued, "but it's my responsibility to act when something just doesn't look right to me. And this entire situation is a huge red flag. Will you promise me something, Avery?"

"Yes. What?"

"When you start to remember what happened, promise me you'll say something. You have people who care about you. Please don't keep any of the details a secret, okay?"

Shrugging her shoulders, Avery smiled and nodded her head. "Okay."

"Alright. Thank you. And then one other thing before we move on, have you been screened for Sexually Transmitted Diseases?"

"Yes," Allison confirmed. "We had all that done as soon as we learned she was pregnant."

"And?"

"She's free and clear in that department."

"What a relief. At least you don't have *that* to worry about. That said, if you two fine women will follow me, we're going to head down the hall to have a much closer look at this baby."

Following Dr. Blaire to the end of the hall, Allison and Avery entered the last room on the right.

Warmly ushering the two women inside, Dr. Blaire closed the door behind her. "Allow me to introduce you to Brinn. She's our ultrasound technician."

A curly-haired brunette in her mid-thirties stepped forward and shook both of their hands. "Good afternoon. I'm Brinn."

"Nice to meet you," Avery smiled.

"Brinn, would you explain to our guests what you're going to be doing and how this all works?"

"Certainly. In a moment, Avery, we're going to have you lay down right here." Brinn motioned to a comfortable-looking reclining chair which was adjacent to a cart carrying sophisticated equipment. "Then I'll be applying some of this blue gel to your abdomen, which allows this instrument to see the fetus."

Avery felt as though she were on a rollercoaster and was slowly nearing the top of that first ascent.

"You look a bit nervous, Avery," Dr. Blaire commented.

"I might be," Avery agreed. She noticed how sweaty her palms had become in the last thirty seconds. "I just don't know if I'm ready to see the baby yet. That's all."

"Avery, why not?" Allison queried. She constantly found herself striving to see things from her daughter's point of view, but sometimes she just wasn't sure where she was coming from.

"I guess I'm just in a little bit of denial. That's all."

"You certainly don't have to watch if you don't want to," Dr. Blaire offered. "This procedure simply allows us to take some accurate measurements, as well as detect crucial developmental abnormalities. It shouldn't take long."

"So Avery, if you would lie down right here," Brinn began, "I'll grab this gel and we'll go ahead and get started, okay?"

"Okay," Avery consented as she nestled onto the cushioned surface.

"This is going to feel a little cold at first," Brinn advised right before squeezing some of the blue gel onto Avery's distended belly.

"Whoah!" Avery exclaimed. "You're right about that!"

"So just relax," Brinn continued. "I'm going to take this sensor and move it around to access different angles."

Grabbing a nearby chair, Allison took a seat right next to her daughter. As Brinn worked the sensor and took measurements, Avery reached for her mother's hand and held it tight.

With eyes glued to the monitor, Dr. Blaire stood hip-to-hip with the technician, speaking softly while intermittently pointing at the screen. With eyes closed and gripping her mother's hand, Avery lay still while Allison failed to make any sense of the shapes coming in and out of focus on the computer display.

As ten minutes turned to fifteen, and fifteen became twenty, Allison began to be concerned. While it was true she'd never been through this experience herself, she could sense something was off. Trying to help Avery stay at ease, she switched to holding her daughter's hand with her left, and used her right hand to softly stroke Avery's long black hair. As she gazed at the young woman who lay beside her, she could hardly believe this was her daughter. Although she hadn't carried Avery in her own womb, she couldn't imagine loving her any more if she had.

Turning from the computer monitor to discuss the findings, Dr. Blaire took a seat a meter away from the pair. Brinn then took a moment to wipe the gel from Avery's belly and helped her sit up.

"So Avery, Allison," Dr. Blaire began with concerned eyes, "I have some crucial news for you."

Allison's stomach was now in her throat as her premonitions began to materialize.

"This is going to be quite a challenge to cope with, but Avery, the fetus you're carrying has substantial developmental abnormalities."

"What abnormalities?" Avery asked in surprise. "Is the baby going to be okay?"

Clearing her throat, Dr. Blaire scooted her chair closer to the two women. "The liver is far behind where it should be for this stage of development. There is only one kidney, while there should, of course, be two. And while those items alone are very significant, the lungs are riddled with holes."

"Holes?" Allison said in bewilderment.

Avery sat speechless, gripping her mother's hand.

"Regrettably, Avery," the doctor continued, "I'm afraid if you were to go through with the remainder of the pregnancy, the baby wouldn't survive more than a few minutes after birth."

"How can you be certain, though?" Allison probed. "I mean, shouldn't we get a second opinion?"

"Absolutely," Dr. Blaire agreed. "I would insist, actually."

Avery's mind spun. "Is there no surgery that could be done to fix the lungs?"

"I'm afraid not," Dr. Blaire affirmed. "They literally look like nothing I've ever seen before. I truly hate to say it, but this baby cannot survive without you, Avery." Compassion flooded the doctor's face as she looked at the two women squarely in the eyes. "My professional medical advice – is for this pregnancy to be aborted. I'm so *terribly* sorry."

Both Allison and Avery remained silent for a few moments, trying to process what they were hearing. For Allison, the news came as more of a blow than when she discovered Avery was pregnant. She had grown thoroughly excited to be a grandmother, regardless of the peculiar circumstances surrounding her daughter's pregnancy. She had been looking forward with eager anticipation to be able to hold that precious grandchild in her arms. But now – those noble aspirations were dissolving like a sand castle to the waves.

A kaleidoscope of emotions surged through Avery, ranging from sorrow and regret, to relief and rejuvenation. But what remained was the guilt. Guilt for feeling at all relieved that her own life might finally go back to normal. Yet the prospect existed only because another life wouldn't actually come to fruition. Life could never go back to normal. Not after this. Either the phenomenon she carried in her womb would die for lacking the ability to survive after birth, or expire at the hands of medical intervention. Hopelessness seeped painfully through her veins as Avery came to the realization that no matter what happened, she would *never* be the same again.

CHAPTER 7

What is this place? Avery wondered as she stepped cautiously along the steel-paneled flooring. The din of high-pressured steam and pistons, along with the opening and closing of valves reverberated around the expansive tiered enclosure. *What am I doing here?*

Perplexed as to how she arrived in such a place, Avery continued along the rusty walkway, struggling to see in the dim light. Then without warning, she felt the impact of her left shoulder making forceful contact with the wall. It was as if the floor had started to move, causing her to lose her balance. It wasn't an earthquake. She'd experienced one of those before. Then another shift in the floor's orientation took place. *Am I on a boat or something?* Instinctively reaching for the railing to her right, she noticed something peculiar on the tier just below her. An open brown duffle bag sat next to an orange calico blanket that had been loosely spread out on the floor. She also noticed what looked like a pair of green exercise pants that had been folded to serve as a pillow. *Is someone sleeping in here?*

"Hello?" Avery called out, keeping her hands fixed tightly to the railing, but her voice was immediately swallowed by the symphony of the mechanical activity in the room. Carefully making her way down a short set of nearby stairs, she inched toward the duffle bag and blanket, pausing again to keep her balance as the entire room teetered. Now crouching over the bag, she quickly determined the items belonged to a young woman. *What in the world is she doing here?*

Taking another look around, Avery noticed a faint strand of natural light across the room and up some stairs. An exit. Becoming slightly more adept at keeping her footing in her awkward environment, she maneuvered along the narrow path and climbed the stairs. Taking a moment to examine the bulky door latch, she got it to open by thrusting upward and then across. Avery's long black hair was immediately blown back by a gust of icy wind, which caught her off guard and ripped the breath from her lungs.

Gasping and shoving the door closed to protect herself from the bitter cold, Avery scurried back down the stairs to retrieve the calico blanket. Imbued with a subliminal sense of purpose and with the blanket wrapped about her, Avery returned to the steel exit door and stepped into the arctic night.

Avery's jaw dropped as she surveyed her surroundings. She was indeed on a boat. An enormous cargo ship. There were hundreds of steel containers the size of rail cars stacked all over the place. *But how did I get here?* Numbing winds swirled around her from every direction. Without having to think, she knew she was here for a reason. *Go left,* came the internal prompting. *Now right.* As if being steered by someone else, Avery obeyed every command. *Head up those stairs.* The stinging she'd felt in her unprotected feet had now begun to subside as she continued to race along the deck of the freight liner. *Stop!*

To Avery's left was another door, similar to the one she'd encountered before. She immediately opened it and stepped into the darkness. Grateful to find a light switch on the wall to the right of the entrance, Avery flipped it on and looked around. She seemed to be in some crude type of office. There was a lengthy hallway directly ahead of her which she instinctively started down. Then she heard it. Pausing in her tracks, Avery strained to discern the noise past the howling of the wind and the creaking of the massive vessel. *There it is again!* Someone was crying. Following the noise a little further down the hall, Avery happened upon the source of the crying. A door on the left was slightly ajar,

58

and she slipped cautiously inside, discovering she was now in a bathroom.

"Ma'am?" Avery said as she walked slowly toward the prostrate figure. "Ma'am, are you hurt?"

Sobbing was the only reply.

"Ma'am, I'm sorry to intrude, it's just that I heard you crying, and thought I might be able to help."

Still no verbal response. However, the twenty-something turned and pushed herself up from the floor and slowly rose to her feet. Pulling her long jet-black hair behind her shoulders, she approached a nearby mirror and hesitantly took a kitchen knife that had been laying across the rim of the steel sink.

"Ma'am," Avery's voice quivered as she spoke, "what are you going to do with that knife?"

Continuing to cry, the woman acted as if she had no idea Avery was even in the room. Moving in closer, the mysterious woman closely examined the ghostly figure staring back at her through the mirror. She then placed a hand on her belly and turned ninety degrees to her right, briefly observing herself from the side.

Oh my goodness, Avery thought. *She's pregnant. And she's afraid.*

As Avery took in the desperate expression on the terrified woman's face, she could feel her pain, her fear of the unknown, her yearning for a respite from her deep personal hell. *I know how you feel*, Avery thought. *I know too well.*

With closed eyes and clenched teeth, the quivering woman then raised the knife and delicately placed the tip just under her sternum.

Don't do it, Avery yearned. *Please don't do this.*

"It's okay," Avery spoke now through tears of her own. "Everything is going to be alright."

Although she'd not yet acknowledged Avery's presence in the room, the woman now opened her bloodshot eyes and dropped the serrated knife to the ground. Her sobs subsided and the expression on her face shifted from terror to one of surprise and curiosity.

Can she see me? Avery wondered. Continuing to stare right through Avery, the woman began to step lightly in her direction. The beginnings of a smile now began to emerge on her lips and she extended her right hand.

Avery reciprocated the gesture, and at the moment when their hands would have touched, Avery was shocked to see that their fingers actually seemed to disappear into each other. Both women paused, each closing their eyes, with warm smiles emanating from their faces. Avery had no idea why, but she felt a remarkable connection with this enigmatic stranger.

With great tears of joy now rolling down their faces, the two women retracted their hands at the same time. Returning now to the mirror, the woman pressed her finger to the glass and began to write something in the condensation.

Avery gasped as she watched the letters materialize on the mirror. A – V – E – R – Y.

Avery's head spun as she tried to process everything she had just witnessed. With a chill jolting down her spine, she began to understand. Glancing down at the name tattooed on her right forearm, Avery knew. But it wasn't possible, was it? *No.* How could this possibly be real? And yet, she was here. There was no denying it. *You're Kendra.*

"Mom?" Avery called.

Kendra then instantly turned and looked Avery directly in the eye, her smile one of indescribable joy. Avery rushed toward her, wanting desperately to embrace her courageous biological mother. But as she did so, the scene began to recede before her eyes. It was as if two intersecting dimensions were being rapidly torn apart.

Maintaining eye contact with Kendra as long as she could, Avery screamed out to her as she was pulled upward and away from the ship. "Mom! No! Please come back! Mom, *please*!"

Within a brief moment, Kendra and the freight liner were swallowed up in the dark distance of the night. Out of sight. Out of reach. But Avery knew. Yes. *Everything* had changed.

Jarred out of sleep at the sound of her daughter's hysterical screaming, Allison grabbed the wooden baseball bat that lay at her bedside and dashed across the hall.

"What's wrong, Aves?!" Allison shrieked as she barged through the door. "Who's here?! What's happening?!" Not seeing the threat in Avery's room, Allison took a quick step back into the hall, scanning the area for the intruder she was intent on bashing in the face. Panicked and breathing heavily, Allison scoured the rest of their small apartment, but found nothing.

"Mom!" Avery called, her face wet with tears.

With bat still in hand, Allison rushed back to her daughter's room and flipped on the light. "What is it, Avery?! Why are you screaming?"

"Mom?"

"Yes, Baby?" Allison panted. "Were you having a nightmare or something?"

"Mom, we're not going to that doctor's appointment tomorrow. We're not getting a second opinion."

Relaxing from her poised attack position, Allison took a seat on the bed and laid the bat on the floor. "Oh, Sweetheart. I thought someone was trying to hurt you."

"We're not going to listen to them, Mom," Avery said, tears rolling down her cheeks. "I *have* to protect this baby."

61

Taking a deep breath, Allison wiped a tear from Avery's cheek and smiled. "I know, Sweetheart."

"You do?"

"I've stayed up all night thinking about it."

"You have?"

"Yes. And for some reason, I've been thinking of Kendra too."

"Really?" Avery sobbed.

"She talked about you all the time, Avery. She really did."

"I've been thinking of her too."

"This probably sounds strange, but it was as if she had already met you. She had such a connection with you. She said you were her inspiration – that you'd saved her life."

"Really?"

"Oh, yes. She said it all the time."

"She was so brave."

"I've only ever known one person as brave as Kendra."

"Dad."

"Oh, he was pretty brave alright. But I was actually referring to someone else."

"Who?"

"*You*, Avery."

"Oh, Mom. You don't have to say that. I'm afraid. I don't know what's going to happen."

"Neither do I. But you know what?"

"What?"

"That's okay."

"Yeah."

"I'd better let you get back to sleep," Allison said, gently kissing her daughter's forehead. Retrieving the wooden bat from the floor, Allison headed for the door. Then just before exiting, she turned back. "By the way, I've never seen that orange calico blanket before. Where did you get it?"

CHAPTER 8

Avery attempted to motivate herself as she made the trek to school. *I only have four more months of this.*

It had been two months since the accident, and three weeks since her harrowing visit to the OB.

School is over in four months. I can do this. Just ignore them. They don't even know you.

She could always just take the GED and move on. She'd heard of a few other people doing that. But she didn't want to look weak. Because she wasn't.

If I drop out, then they win.

While it was true the taunting from the other students had subsided for the most part, the dirty looks and raised eyebrows in the halls were ongoing. If there was one thing Avery had learned over the past eight weeks, it was how easy it is to judge. She knew all about arriving at rapid conclusions about other people. She'd done it herself many times.

Now shuffling through the sea of students heading to first period, Avery made the turn down the hall for her locker. *Hmm. That's odd. What's* he *doing here?*

"Hi, Mr. Kunz," Avery said as she approached. "Are you lost or something?"

"No," he grinned. "I couldn't wait to tell you. Something fortuitous has come up, and there's something I need to give you before you leave today."

Avery was incredulous. "What do you mean? What is it?"

"All I'm going to tell you right now, is it's something you're probably going to like."

Avery was used to her ceramic teacher's quirky sense of humor, and chuckled at how giddy he seemed. "Okay, Mr. Kunz. Whatever you say."

Practically trotting down the hall, Mr. Kunz turned and gave her two thumbs up. "Don't forget!"

The remainder of the day seemed to fly by. Avery knew Mr. Kunz had something silly up his sleeve, and she was ready for a dose of cheer. Having finished up her work in the ceramics studio, she washed her hands and walked across the dusty floor to the adjacent office.

"Alright," Avery chuckled as she entered Mr. Kunz' sculpture-laden office. "What crazy thing do you have planned?"

"Ah, yes!" Mr. Kunz chimed, looking up from his computer. "The surprise."

Avery couldn't help but laugh. "I don't know about you sometimes."

"First of all," he began, standing up, "do you happen to notice anything missing?"

Avery glanced curiously around the room at the jumble of prior students' ceramic pieces, super hero posters, and heaps of old papers. He even had two mini-refrigerators. She shook her head and smiled. "Well, aside from a toilet, I'd say you've got everything you could possibly need, right here in this room!"

Mr. Kunz appreciated the comment. "You know, you're probably right! But do you remember what used to be right *here*?" He was pointing to the only vacant spot on his large desk.

"My Dolphin Warrior piece."

"Precisely!"

"I knew you had some kind of joke planned, but – "

"And don't worry. I didn't break it."

"I would sure hope not! It took me two weeks to make that!"

"A beautiful piece, to be sure. It's always been my favorite."

"So, what? You took it home or something?"

"Nope."

"Well, where is it?"

"So here's the skinny. I have an eccentric well-to-do cousin that pays me a visit a couple times a year. She's a big shot land developer and happened to be here this week on business."

"Okay."

"Well, she's never actually been to the studio here at school and wanted to see it. And get this – not surprisingly, she loved your Dolphin Warrior piece. I mean, she just really, really loved it!"

"So you just gave it to her?" Avery was feeling a bit perturbed.

"No, I didn't *give* it to her, Avery." Reaching into his desk drawer, Mr. Kunz pulled out a white envelope and handed it to his perplexed student.

Avery stared quietly at the envelope and then back at Mr. Kunz.

"Go ahead. Open it!"

Slowly pulling back the flap, Avery's dark brown eyes widened significantly as she cautiously removed the contents. Holding the slip of paper in both hands, Avery's jaw dropped as she examined the document. "This *has* to be a joke."

"I *told* you I didn't just give it to her. She insisted on buying it from you. It's possible I jumped to conclusions a little too quickly on this deal, but I figured you wouldn't have any objections. It *is* four thousand dollars, after all."

Avery was speechless. Indeed, the document she held was a certified check made out to Avery Renshaw – for *four thousand* dollars.

"Surpriiiiise!" Mr. Kunz looked like he'd just hit the lottery himself.

66

"This can't be real, right. You're messing with me. I know you're messing around. You have to be. That's what you do. Only this is just a little on the twisted side, if I'm being completely honest."

"C'mon, do I look like a guy who can't be taken seriously?"

"Actually, you kind of do."

"Okay. Fair enough. Don't go anywhere. I'm going to make a quick phone call." Pulling out his cellphone, Mr. Kunz looked up a number and placed the phone to his ear. "Yeah, Liz. Do you have a minute? Fantastic. So you know that piece you loved so much? Well, I have the student in my office right now, and she's reluctant to believe what I'm telling her. Yeah. Okay. Sure. Here she is."

In quite a daze, Avery took the phone. "Hello? Yes, this is Avery. Why, thank you. That's very kind of you to say. I suppose so. Yes. Yeah. I could definitely do that. Oh, I'd say I'll have it done in a day or two. I'm not uncomfortable with it, no. It's just I've never had anyone ask to buy my work before. Wow. Okay. Thank you so much. Okay. Bye."

"What did I tell you?!"

"This is crazy, Mr. Kunz."

"So what else did Liz tell you?"

"She wants to buy the piece I'm working on right now too."

"I told you she's eccentric! Talk about striking gold, right?"

"I don't know what to say. I really did *not* see this coming."

"Who needs art school when you're already this good? Hey, you deserve it, Kiddo. Go take your mom out for a nice dinner. I'll see you tomorrow."

With the four thousand dollar check in hand, Avery exited the studio and pulled out her phone to place a call. "Mom?"

"Yeah, Sweetie?"

"This is going to sound strange, but I don't think we need to worry about another eviction notice this month."

CHAPTER 9

"Well," Allison sighed, opening the car door for Avery, "that money sure went fast."

"You're telling me," Avery conceded, stooping down into the passenger seat.

"Wait a second. You should be the one driving."

"I don't know, Mom."

"Hey, you bought it."

"I'm actually feeling pretty nauseous right now. But thanks though."

"No problem."

Settling down into the driver seat, Allison placed her hands on the steering wheel and inhaled. "It certainly *smells* better than Oscar."

"That's for sure!" Avery laughed. "Those stray cats really did a number on that back seat, didn't they?"

"Yeah. Nasty. Let's not make that mistake again, shall we?"

"If I remember correctly, it was *you* that left the window rolled down that night. Not me."

"You'd think the smell of Oscar alone would have been enough deterrent for those punks."

"Seriously, right? Oscar was the ugliest car on our street. If I was going to go out for a joyride, I'd have broken into the Smith's convertible. That thing is *nice*."

"If it wasn't for you, Avery, we'd be royally screwed right now."

"It wasn't anything *I* did. Getting that money was totally random. We got lucky. Plain and simple."

"Well, we were due for some luck. Don't you think?"

With a hand on her distended belly, Avery watched a mother and her toddler child walking down the sidewalk. "Let's just hope there's more luck on the horizon."

"How much did that lady say she'd pay for your other piece?"

"Six."

"Thousand?"

"Yeah. Six thousand."

"That is amazing, Avery! Do you know how long it takes me to make that much money?"

"Probably a while."

"It would take me four months to do that. You pulled it off in two *weeks*."

"Like I said mom, it was just luck. Mr. Kunz' cousin isn't going to just keep buying my sculptures. And after I graduate, I doubt I'll have access to the kiln anymore."

"You know what though? It's always been a day at a time for this family. It might as well stay that way, right?"

"I'm sure it will." Avery took a deep breath. "And not to change the subject or anything, but I could really go for some steak and pickles right about now."

Allison looked at her daughter in disbelief. "Steak and pickles?"

"Pregnancy cravings, *Mom*," Avery said, pointing to her abdomen. "I've been thinking about eating steak and pickles all morning."

"You have?"

"I can literally taste them in my mouth, right now."

"Well, we still have a little money left over, don't we?"

"Forty three dollars."

"Alright then." Allison fired the ignition. "Steak and pickles it is."

"So we've got a turkey club with fries," grumbled a short male server in his mid-fifties. "And then the twelve ounce prime rib – with sliced pickles on top, correct?"

"Yes," Avery confirmed. "And make sure the pickles are on top of the steak while it's cooking."

"Right," the server tried not to roll his eyes as he turned. "Will do."

"Hey," Avery said, looking in the direction of the entrance, "I know that guy."

"Who? The server?"

"No. The guy in the wheel chair that just came in with his dad. I'm assuming that's his dad. He's in my creative writing class."

"His dad sure is handsome."

"*Mom?*"

"What?"

"I don't usually hear you make comments like that."

"Well he is. I'm just making an observation."

"I think his name is Erik."

"The dad?"

"No, Mom. The son."

"I'm pretty sure Erik was born blind."

"That's unfortunate."

"Look at that. I think they're going to end up sitting right next to us. I'm going to say hi to them."

"Please do."

"He's probably married."

"He might not be."

"Hey, Erik," Avery said, taking an adjacent seat. "It's Avery, from school."

The young man turned to his left to face her. His eyes were a glossy green, with no defined pupil. "Avery? Wow. I certainly didn't expect to see you here. Well, I never expect to see anyone. But you get what I mean."

Avery laughed. She admired his sense of humor, as well as his handsome jawline, which she hadn't really noticed until just now.

"This is my much older brother, Gavin."

"Hey, I'm only nineteen years older," Gavin chuckled. "Nice to meet you, Avery."

"My mom, Allison, is sitting over there."

Gavin waved, admiring Allison's deep blue eyes.

"Avery, Erik's mentioned your name a few times in the past."

"Is that right?" Avery grinned.

"Yes he has. You guys have the creative writing class together, right?"

"Gavin, please try not to embarrass me too much," Erik recommended.

"Why would you be embarrassed?" Avery questioned.

In the process of trying to take a sip of water, Erik was startled by Avery's direct inquiry and spilled some down his shirt. "Here goes nothing, I guess." Nervously setting his glass on the table, the young man turned again in the direction of Avery's voice. "I'm kind of a shy person, and so this is rather awkward for me."

"It's okay," Avery reassured him.

"This is so nuts. So, I've been wanting to ask you to the prom, but I was certain you probably already had a date. I mean, you must have a date, right? How could someone with a voice that beautiful not have a date? I don't even know why I'm telling you this because even if, for some odd reason, you didn't have a date, you'd most definitely be busy with something else. And that's okay. I would totally understand, and it wouldn't hurt my feelings if – "

"Erik?" Avery stopped him, placing her hand on his shoulder. "I would absolutely love to go with you to the prom."

"And I totally get that. I thought you probably already had plans, so that's totally – "

"Erik, stop talking!" Gavin laughed.

"What?" Erik blushed.

"Weren't you listening to her?"

"Of course I was."

"She said she'd love to go with you."

"She did? You did?"

"Yes, Erik," Avery giggled. "I'd be honored to go to the prom with you."

"Oh, wow. This is big. This is really, really big. Sorry, I'm just a little astonished right now."

"So are you ready for my phone number?"

"I've never been as ready for a phone number as I am right now."

"Four one nine. Three two two. One two, nine two."

"I won't forget it as long as I live."

"How about you call me tonight at around eight, and we'll talk some more."

"Sounds fabulous!"

Gavin mouthed a silent thank you to Avery as she stood. Returning to sit with her mother, Avery's smile was beaming.

Allison grinned. "It's a shame you didn't hold on to that dress."

CHAPTER 10

"You'd better hurry up in there, Aves!" Allison shouted through the bathroom door. "Didn't you say he was coming at six?"

"My hair is making me mad!" Avery yelled back, fastening the final curl to her head.

"At least he won't know the difference!" Allison mused on the concept. "You could have just woken up, and it would be all the same to him."

The bathroom door then swung open, and Avery shot her mother a long disappointed glare. "That's *not* funny, Mom."

"You're right. Sorry. And wow. You've never done your hair like *that* before! It's absolutely gorgeous!"

Avery smiled. "You really think so?"

"All those tight curls pulled up and under like that. Hot stuff, Aves. I'm surprised you were able to do all that by yourself."

"Marnee and I were practicing the other day. Her hair cooperated better for her."

"I highly doubt that. My hair will not curl like that. You're lucky."

Looking at the clock on the bathroom wall, Allison rushed into Avery's room. "Crap! We've got like ten minutes to get this amazing dress on!"

Using some of the money from her second sculpture sale, Avery had purchased the exact same dress from Ashton's.

"Alright, Aves," Allison beamed, pulling the satin gown from the closet. "I'm glad you went with the baby blue. I think it contrasts better with your skin tone. Well, let's give this a go, shall we?"

Helping her daughter to slip on the six hundred dollar dress, Allison imagined what it might be like to some day help Avery prepare for her wedding. Tears were gathering in the corners of Allison's bright blue eyes as she zipped the back of Avery's gown. The waning sun crashed through the window, splashing beams across the shimmering satin, which held snugly to Avery's back, then flowed gracefully from her hips to the floor.

In the mirror's reflection Avery witnessed a tear fall from Allison's cheek and tried not to cry herself. "Mom! You're not allowed to cry. I've already put on my makeup. So stop it, right now."

"I know. I'm sorry. I just can't believe you've grown up so fast. I wish Dad could have been here to see how wonderful you look tonight, Aves."

"I wish he was here too." Unable to keep back the tears, Avery turned and hugged her mother.

As the two embraced, Allison thought of all the two of them had been through over the years, particularly within the last few months. How it was possible they were even still standing was beyond Allison's comprehension. And yet, through the hardship, chaos, and uncertainty, they had arrived at a peaceful moment. This moment. Somehow, she knew – if they could have bursts of joy like this along the way, they could face anything life threw at them.

"I love you, Mom," Avery sighed.

"I love you too." Wiping a tear from Avery's cheek, Allison returned to the closet and removed the shoebox Avery had returned with earlier that day.

"I'm almost as excited about the shoes as I am the dress!" Avery exclaimed as she eagerly revealed the box's contents.

"Nice, Aves!" Allison agreed. "Glossy white criss-cross straps, with the silver base. Isn't this fun?! I can't believe I'm helping my daughter get ready for the prom!"

"There," Avery said, having fastened the second shoe in place. "What do you think?"

"You really do look like an absolute dream. I still think it's a shame your date won't even be able to see you."

"He likes me for my personality, Mom."

"I thought it was your voice."

"Whatever."

"Besides, he hasn't spent time with you just after you woke up."

"Rude."

"Hey, where's the camera?"

"Just use your phone, Mom."

"No," Allison refuted, shuffling into the hall. "This event calls for an actual *camera* to be used."

"Well, you better hurry." Attempting to keep the hem of her gown off the ground, Avery wobbled after her mother into the front room. "Erik's supposed to be here any minute!"

While Allison was hunting for the camera, a long, shiny black object was coming into view on the street outside. *Is that him?* Avery hoped, watching intently out the window.

Within the stretch Escalade, Erik wiped more perspiration from his furrowed brow.

"We've arrived, Sir," announced the chauffeur over the vehicle's intercom. "I'll be over in a moment to help you."

Opening the rear passenger door, the driver assisted his passenger onto a hydraulic lift, an amenity Erik had searched high and low for.

Avery's heart fluttered as the doorbell rang. "Mom, forget about the camera! He's here!"

"Found it!" Allison chimed as she scurried into the entry way. "Okay. Let's see, um. Avery you stand right here, and then I'll let him in."

"Open it already! He's waiting."

"Don't *you* look handsome," Allison smiled, swinging the door wide.

"I don't know about that," Erik blushed. "I'm sure it's more the tux than me."

"Please, come in," Allison insisted.

"Thank you."

Traversing the threshold, Erik turned slightly to his left and paused. "I guess Avery is probably still getting ready, huh?"

"Nice try, mister," Avery smirked. "I've been ready for over an hour, just waiting by this window."

Erik's face went from cherry red to ashen in an instant. "Didn't we agree on six? I am so sorry, Avery. I really thought – "

"Avery!" Allison interrupted. "Don't scare the poor kid! Don't worry, Erik, you're not late. Avery's just a big tease."

Thoroughly amused by his reaction, Avery was attempting to stifle her laughter. "I wish you could have seen the expression on your face!"

"Oh dear," Erik grinned. "I didn't know you were a prankster!"

"Get used to it," Allison chuckled.

Pulling out a handkerchief from behind his lapel, Erik wiped his glistening forehead. "I'm sorry if I seem a little nervous. I've never actually been on a date before."

"I'm your very first date?" Avery asked, stepping closer.

"I suppose it's not the sort of thing you're supposed to admit."

"What, that *I'm* your date?" Avery grinned mischievously while Allison shook her head in disbelief.

"Oh no. That's not what I meant." The color began again to drain from his face. "I'm way excited you said you would go with me. I was simply trying to say that – " The sound of Avery's laughter was exhilarating to Erik's ears, like the New Hope Symphony. "That was another joke, wasn't it?"

"She's terrible," Allison commented, giving her daughter a light whack on the arm.

"Sorry, Erik," Avery giggled. "I'll stop razzing you. For a couple of minutes, anyway."

"Oh, I'll find a way to get you back," Erik chuckled. "Wow. So what's that smell?"

"My perfume, of course," Avery insisted. "I bought it just for tonight."

"If I had to describe it, I would say it's Vincent Conrad's Fourth Concerto, but sprayed from a bottle."

"I don't know what that is," Avery laughed, "but it sounds good to me!"

"Oh," Erik remembered, "before I forget, I brought something for the two of you."

"Presents?" Allison smiled.

"Actually, Ms. Steward, would you mind opening the front door again? I need to have the driver bring a couple of things in."

"Certainly," Allison consented.

Giving the stalky Asian driver a thumbs up, Erik took another quick dab at his forehead. With a nod, the chauffeur opened the Escalade door and arrived bearing a fancy chocolate bar and a corsage.

"Thanks, Spencer," Erik said. "The candy is for Avery's mom."

Receiving the candy bar, Allison sighed with anticipation. "Kaufman's? This is my absolute favorite! How did you know?"

"I have an informant."

Erik's hands gyrated like a jackhammer as he retrieved the delicate corsage package from the driver. "Sorry. I'm just a bit nervous right now."

Watching him remove the delicate contents of the clear plastic container sent a thrill through Avery's extremities. Two white roses flanked a larger red rose, with Baby's Breath proffering bursts of light blue. Extending her left wrist, Avery beamed with satisfaction as her date clumsily slid on the elegant ensemble.

"It's so beautiful, Erik!" Avery sighed. "Thank you."

"Not nearly as beautiful as the person wearing it," Erik replied, sweat trickling down his face.

"Alright," Allison said playfully, "you two are getting just a little mushy. Let's not keep the driver waiting too long."

"It's fine by me, Ma'am," the gentleman conceded, adjusting his sunglasses. "These two have me booked through one o' clock."

"One o' clock?!" Allison placed her hands authoritatively on her hips. "The party's over at twelve! You got that!"

"Oh, don't worry, Ms. Steward," Erik insisted, panic flooding his face. "I can have her home sooner than midnight if you need me to."

"Leave him alone, Mom," Avery chuckled. "This is his first date. He didn't know any better."

"Okay then." Allison put a hand on Erik's shoulder. "I'm her mom. It's my job to give you a hard time. Before you two go, I need to get a picture."

As Avery stood directly to his left, chills shot through Erik's spine as he felt her drape an arm across his back. He'd never smiled so big in his life.

With the assistance of their driver's muscular arm, Avery hoisted into their mode of transportation for the evening. It was like stepping into another dimension. Her nostrils were instantly met with the rich aroma of leather, a smell she hadn't often encountered. Once Erik's wheelchair had been anchored, the door closed with a thud, enclosing the two in a world of luxury.

"Wow," Avery exclaimed, taken aback by the ambience. "We get all this to ourselves?"

"Yeah. It's just us. I tried to see if I could get one of my friends to bring a date, but he wasn't up for it."

"I like it like this. I'm glad it's just you and me."

"Me too." Breathing deeply, Erik was mesmerized by Avery's perfume. "Avery?"

"Yes?"

"What's it like in here. I mean – what does it look like?"

"What's really neat in here are the lights. I'm trying to figure out a good way to explain this. So, you know what the sun feels like, obviously, right?"

"Amazing. I know it's bad for you, but I can actually detect a faint glow from the sun if I look directly at it. It's the closest I've ever come to seeing."

"Alright. Okay. So there's a faint ribbon of blue light that goes around the entire perimeter of the limousine. It's coming from behind the tops of all the seats. And then there's a similar pattern on the ceiling too."

"Sounds cool."

"It really is. And I wanna say the inside of this thing is like twelve feet long."

"Really?"

"I swear we could fit like twenty more people in here! You're really spoiling me, Erik."

All Erik could do was smile. *I'm spoiling you?*

"Seriously," Avery insisted. "You've got to reach out and touch these seats."

Shuddering as her skin came in contact with his, she took his moist left hand and gently guided it to the smooth leather upholstery.

"Doesn't that feel amazing?" Avery said enthusiastically.

"It really does." Moving his hand across the surface, he briefly brushed into a warm silky surface and then instantly pulled back. *Her leg! Dude, you're not supposed to touch her leg!* Pulse racing, Erik hastily retrieved the hanky from his inside jacket pocket.

"What's wrong?"

"Sorry," Erik mumbled. "I didn't mean to touch your leg like that. I was just – "

"Hey," Avery spoke softly, scooting closer to her panicked date. "It's okay. Just relax. You probably just wanted to see what my dress was made of right?"

"Oh, no. I mean – my hand just slipped."

"Here," Avery said, snatching the white cloth from him. "Let me do that for you. We're on a date. We're supposed to take care of each other."

As she dabbed at his wet brow, Erik could barely breathe. Closing his eyes, he inhaled another wave of her symphonic scent.

"This really is your first date, isn't it?" Avery giggled, inserting the cloth into his front jacket pocket.

"Is it that obvious?"

"You sort of told me that back at the apartment."

"Right." Looking straight ahead, Erik cleared his throat.

"But yeah," Avery conceded. "It *is* that obvious. It's cute."

Turning to face her, he forced another deep breath. "Well, maybe we'll have to hang out more often. You know, just to help me get used to – being with an angel."

"Erik Harper!" Avery exclaimed, resting her head on his shoulder. "Are you hitting on me?"

"I was trying to be honest."

∞

"I still can't believe you ate all of that food!" Avery commented, stepping from the Escalade onto the street.

"Like I told you," Erik called over his shoulder, "I never know when I'm going to eat again."

"There you are, Sir," said their driver, unbuckling the straps that secured Erik's wheelchair to the hydraulic lift.

"Thanks, Spencer," Erik said. "Are you still wearing your sunglasses?"

"Always."

"Even in the dark like this?" Avery questioned.

"Streetlights hurt my eyes."

"So I guess we'll just call you when we're about ready to leave then?" Erik inquired, attempting to straighten out his tux.

"I'll be right over there, right in that cul-de-sac. But yeah. Call me."

The duo then began their descent down a dimly lit ornate stone path, flanked with drooping ribbons of red and white. Leaves from the adjacent ground cover and hundreds of scrub oaks danced playfully in the cool evening breeze, while the sound of running water could be heard from a waterfall in the distance.

"So, looks like this part might be kind of tricky for us," Avery pointed out, looking at all the twists and turns that led to the Prom venue.

"Tell you what," Erik smiled. "How about you steer us?"

"Just like I did at the restaurant?"

"No. I've had enough crashes for one evening."

"Ha ha." Avery gave him a light slug on the shoulder. "Nice try, mister. I told you to stop, but you weren't listening."

"I'm pretty sure you told me to stop *after* I bumped into that poor server with all the cups."

"Hey!" Avery laughed. "I was doing my best."

"That *was* kind of funny though."

"The part where all the drinks spilled on that old man, or how she ended up in your lap?"

"You know what though, we'll always remember it, right?"

"Yes. And I'm sure they will too. Okay, so we're going to take a left in about ten feet."

"No. No. You're not going to steer us like that."

"How else am I supposed to do it?"

"You're going to drive."

"Drive that thing while I'm walking next to you? I'll end up rolling it over my toes or something."

"This chair can be just pushed from behind too. Either way, it won't be that hard. Just try it."

"I've got a better idea."

"Wow," Erik exhaled nervously, with Avery's hips now directly atop his thighs. "That is a *much* better idea."

"Not too heavy for you, am I?"

"Not at all."

"Alright then," Avery chuckled. "Let's do this."

"Just try not to get us high-centered."

"But that would take all the fun out of it."

Taking it slowly at first, Avery soon felt comfortable with her abilities. "I think I'm pretty good at this!" Avery yelled as she finished the second turn. "How about we speed this up a bit?"

"I don't know, Avery," Erik gritted his teeth. "We're going to end up hitting somebody."

"Watch out, everyone!" Avery screamed as they passed a group of startled Prom-goers. "The brakes on this thing are broken!"

Holding on for dear life with white knuckles, Erik held his breath as they veered a hard left. "You're crazy! I swear we're gonna die!"

"I seriously need to get me one of these!" Avery hollered. "Wahooooo!"

Now taking a hard right, Erik detected they were up on two wheels. "Holy crap! I swear we're going to crash, Avery!"

"Brace yourself, Erik! I think I see a short cut!"

Erik's heart felt like an engine roaring within his chest. "Shortcut?! I don't think that's a very – "

Heavy vibrations reverberated through the seat and into Erik's legs as Avery led them off the smooth path. Whipped by leafy branches as they barreled through the vegetation, Erik's fear merged with pure exhilaration as he screamed. "Yeeeehaaaaawwwwwww!"

Avery's primped black hair frolicked in the wind, tickling Erik's face as they blazed along her alleged shortcut. Inertia was in complete control, however, as one of the wheels met with an elevated tree root. No longer in contact with his cushioned seat, and Avery's angelic scent leading the way, Erik's muscles contracted, preparing him for impact. Both screamed during their brief flight above the brush, then tumbled on top and over each other down a slope that led to a shallow pond.

Gasps from dozens of confused onlookers could be heard as the pair rolled with a splash into the cold water. Soaked and shaken, Avery struggled to help Erik into the sitting position. "Erik, are you okay?! I'm so sorry!"

Panting and hunched over, Erik tried to spit out mud and debris from his mouth.

"Erik, please say something!" Avery pleaded, her hands on his shoulders. "Are you okay? Say something!"

Like an ignited trail of gasoline, panic surged through Avery's limbs as she felt Erik's back suddenly stiffen. Choking for air, he flung his right hand to his throat, thrusting himself backwards into the water. Head cocked and mouth agape, he gurgled while his pulsating body created ripples through the pond.

"Erik, no!" Avery shrieked, frantically casting her gaze about for assistance. "Somebody please help us!"

Now abandoning his feigned brush with death, Erik rolled towards Avery and began laughing uncontrollably.

The sudden shift in Erik's behavior was deeply vexing to Avery. *What is he doing? He's not – laughing, is he?*

Completely peeled over, Erik's hands were at his abdomen while he carried on, his laughter chasing the panic from Avery's overloaded nervous system. With her burst of adrenaline gone, she felt like a deflated raft, washed upon the shore.

"You think you're pretty hilarious, don't you?" Avery chided, creating trails of ebony down her cheeks as she wiped water from her eyes.

Struggling to speak through bursts of laughter, Erik echoed Avery's own words, spoken back at her apartment. "I wish you could have seen the expression on your face!"

∞

"Hey, thanks for the help guys," Erik sighed as he settled back into his seat. "My wheelchair has to weigh a ton."

"For a couple of drama class geeks," Jeremy began, running a comb through his bronze hair, "yeah, it was pretty heavy."

"Maybe, for you," Jeff scoffed. Brushing dirt from his shirt and slipping on his jacket, he shook his head and chuckled. "I have to say, you two, that was the funniest thing I have ever seen, bar none."

"Every moment spent with Erik is an adventure," Avery said, slugging her date lightly on the shoulder.

"Whoa, watch it," Erik playfully winced. "Haven't you beaten me up enough for one night?"

"Not even close," Avery grinned, bending the dark streaks of mascara that accented her face.

"Well," Jeremy said, "we're going to head back to our dates. You two try to stay out of trouble."

"Sounds great," Erik said. "See you guys on Monday."

Guiding Erik to one of the salmon-colored granite benches that surrounded the outdoor atrium, Avery took a seat and breathed deeply. "I am so sorry about crashing the wheelchair."

Erik leaned his head her way. "Don't be."

"If it's broken or anything, I promise I'll pay to have it fixed."

"Trust me. This thing is built to last. Besides, that's what insurance is for."

"You're probably not going to let me drive it anymore, are you?"

"It's obviously dangerous." He beamed, pausing for a moment. "But well worth the risk. Tell you what. Why don't you drive us to that picture station over there?"

Sliding some soggy blue and black hair behind her ear, Avery looked curiously in the direction he was pointing. "How did you know there was one over there?"

"I can hear it."

"Over all this music? That's amazing."

"You can just tell by the way the people are talking with each other. It's a little bit different than the people who are out dancing."

"That's a great idea. But before we do, can we dance to this song first? It's one of my favorites."

86

"I would love to, but how are we – "

Before Erik could finish his sentence, Avery was back in his lap, sideways this time, with her left hand on the back of his neck and her right across his chest. Melting like butter in the hot sun, Erik rested his face atop her wet hair, which smelled like heaven, and closed his eyes.

Raising her head for a moment, Avery spoke softly into his ear. "Dance with me. Take us out in the middle of all those people and dance with me, Erik."

"Alright. But you steer."

Placing her hand on his, the two rolled out into the crowd. Making a wet trail through a rainbow sea of dresses and tuxedos, Erik took the lead and began maneuvering his wheelchair in a steady circle. Like a slow-spinning top, the drenched pair began devouring the attention of all who witnessed them.

Warmth from Avery's body seeped through Erik's soaking tuxedo, lulling him into a trance. He heard nothing, smelled nothing. All that mattered was the gentle heaving of this angel's chest against his. There were no names anymore. No limits. No pain. No sorrow. Just her. Just him. Alive. Together. This moment had no flaws. They lacked nothing. They had conquered the world.

∞

From the upper terrace which flanked the venue, the sight was truly magical. Within the densely populated atrium was an empty circle, about seven meters in diameter, with a motorized wheelchair in the center. Bursts of light bounced off a satin baby blue gown and a matching tie, the spectacle being photographed from all angles by onlookers.

"Taylor!" Jackson shouted, his blonde mop bouncing as he shuffled away. "The girls wanna do pictures. Let's go!"

Ignoring his younger friend, Taylor continued to focus on the scene below. Straining his narrow hazel eyes, he placed both hands on the stone railing and leaned slightly forward.

"Are you coming, Taylor?" questioned a scantily clad redhead to his right.

"Oh uh, sorry, Kate. I'll meet you guys over there in a couple of minutes, okay?"

"Whatever," she mumbled, rolling her eyes. "I guess I'll see you down there then."

Thirty seconds later, Taylor's attention was interrupted with a slap to his back. "Dude, Jackson! What?!"

"Are you just gonna stand up here all night? Stick with the group, man."

"I can't believe I let you convince me to come here tonight. I needed to leave this high school prom crap in the past."

"Why? What's wrong with Kate?"

"Nothing's wrong with your cousin, per se. It's just that...well, never mind."

"Well, then let's *go!*"

Returning his gaze to the pair in the wheelchair, Taylor removed his jacket and laid it across the railing.

"Freak, man! What are you looking at down there anyway?" Striding up to Taylor's side, Jackson scrutinized the crowd below. "What? I don't see anything! What is wrong with you tonight, man? You're not gonna score with Kate if you don't start paying attention to her."

"What makes you think I want to do that?"

"Have you lost your mind? That's why we're *here*, bro!"

"You and your one-track mind."

"So sue me. You coming or not?"

"Do you see who's in that wheelchair down there?"

"Some gimp and his lady. What do you care?"

"Look closer, numb-nuts!"

"Whatever." Slightly tilting his head, Jackson leaned against the railing and watched the oddly-matched couple below. "You've *got* to be kidding me. That's not Avery, is it?"

"Yes." Retrieving his jacket, Taylor brushed past Jackson, marching toward the wide stairs that spilled onto the atrium floor.

∞

Still cradled in Erik's lap, Avery was assisting with their slow progress through the picture line. Music continued to animate the air, along with voices and laughter from the others waiting to be professionally photographed.

"I haven't had this much fun in a loooong time, Erik," Avery said, her head nestled on his shoulder.

"Me too," Erik agreed. "I'm so glad we found each other. I mean, you know, at the – "

Placing her pointer finger on Erik's lips, Avery whispered into his ear. "I'm glad we found each other too."

As they inched their way with the line, the crescendo of a waterfall began to drown the blaring music in the background.

"I wonder what the rental place will have to say about all the dirt on your tux," Avery said, wiping at his left sleeve.

"Forget about the tux," Erik said. "I feel bad about your dress. It must be ruined."

"It's just a silly dress. Besides, you only wear a prom dress once, anyway."

"I think our little fall down the hill will make for some funny pictures though."

"You know what?" Avery asked, lightly squeezing Erik's hand.

"What?"

"I wouldn't change anything about tonight."

"No?"

"Not one thing."

Avery's heart then screeched to a halt as a familiar sound invaded her ears. It was the last voice on earth she expected to hear tonight. "Avery?"

Pretending she had no idea he was standing there, Avery closed her eyes and shifted slightly in Erik's lap.

Squeezing Avery's hand, Erik straightened his posture somewhat. "Avery, I think someone's trying to talk to you."

With pulse pounding, Avery remained silent, taking only short spurts of breath.

The unsought male voice was closer now, directly to Erik and Avery's left. "Avery, can we talk for just a second?"

Remaining in her huddled position, Avery offered no response. Now clutching Erik's pant leg, Avery's terse breaths and thundering heart rate persisted.

Erik leaned his head to the left and spoke cordially but authoritatively. "You're really bothering her. Why do you need to talk to Avery?"

"Avery, I know this is a little awkward, but I saw you here and just wanted to apologize." He took a deep breath and paused. "You know, for everything."

Gradually raising her face from Erik's chest, Avery glared intently into the narrow hazel eyes she once adored.

"I never should have walked out on you that night at the hospital. It was stupid of me. I was being a coward."

"Don't you think it's a little *late* for apologies?" Avery demanded.

"Avery," Erik muttered, "who are you talking to?"

"Someone I used to know," Avery answered. Bringing her eyes back in line with her unwelcome guest's, she didn't speak, but her message was heard loud and clear.

"I guess I'll see you around then," the young man sighed, receding back into the crowd.

"Yikes," Erik managed. "What was that all about?"

"Please don't make me talk about this now," Avery lamented. "I promise, I'll tell you later."

With head hung low, Taylor rejoined his party. Noticing his friend's sunken demeanor, Jackson ducked out of the line and slithered a few meters back to the motorized wheelchair. "So this must be the baby's daddy. Is that right?"

Avery cringed at the stinging appearance of yet another one of her tormentors. "Can't you see I'm on a date, you low-life? Just leave us alone."

"I can see you're on a date," Jackson chided, throwing her a sinister grin. "You're always on a date though, aren't you? That's how you got knocked up." Lightly nudging Erik on his right shoulder, Jackson produced a demeaning chuckle. "Dude, regardless of the load of crap she's fed you, it's probably not your kid. So don't worry about that. She gets around so much, she'd never be able to find the sucker who got her pregnant!"

"Erik, don't listen to him," Avery insisted, her voice quivering. "He doesn't know what he's talking about."

"Oh, I do. She's got a locker full of condoms, man," Jackson went on. "Loads of 'em. She's probably got ten rubbers in her purse right now. But that's good news for you though, right? Oh yeah, Casanova. You will get a piece of pie tonight. Sad part for you is, it'll be leftovers."

Having noticed Jackson's absence, Taylor spotted him doing what Jackson did best. Shoving past a few human obstacles, he arrived to hear the final portion of Jackson's deriding remarks.

"Dude!" Taylor bellowed, shoving Jackson in the back. "What do you think you're doing?"

"Chill out, man," Jackson rebutted, wheeling back around. "I'm just trying to do this crippled guy a solid. Let him know what kind of a skank he's got sitting in his lap."

"What did you call her?" Taylor barked.

"Dude, you of all people know how much of a freaking hooch that girl is!"

Within a split second, Jackson's head flew back, flipping blood and saliva as he endured the splintering impact of Taylor's unforgiving left hook. Exclamations of astonishment were made as Jackson went sprawling backwards, plowing into a group of bystanders. Staggering like a flimsy piece of sheet metal, Jackson recovered his balance and charged his assailant like a psychotic bull. Stepping to the side, Taylor used his water-polo-toned upper body strength to send Jackson crashing into the adjacent brush. Planting a shiny black shoe firmly into Jackson's gut, Taylor then crouched down and grasped his prey by his blonde mop. "You can tell that hooch cousin of yours she can ride home with you tonight."

Delivering one final blow to the left rear of Jackson's skull, Taylor trekked through the undergrowth toward the stone-paved path which led to the exit.

Dazed and head throbbing, Jackson elevated his bloodied face from the leafy groundcover. Snarling and growling like a wounded badger, he watched his attacker retreat. "You're *finished*, Taylor! You hear me?! You're *done*!"

∞

"Aves?" Allison called, glancing at the clock. Nine thirty. "Aves, what are you doing home so early?" Placing her mystery novel face-down on the nightstand, Allison plodded toward her bedroom door and peered down the dim hallway at the dark female silhouette in the entry way. "Avery?"

Flipping on the light switch, Allison halted in her tracks, gasping and cupping both hands over her mouth. A ragged remnant of what she had looked like four hours earlier, Avery stood emotionless, her face marred by dull streaks of inky eye liner and mascara. Her once perfect black curls now resembled a mangled birds' nest that merged into her soiled damp dress. "Avery, what happened to you?"

Clenching her eyes shut, the muscles in Avery's face contracted and twisted as she collapsed to her knees. Her low whimper then rapidly escalated into an agonized and elongated shriek as she clutched fistfuls of hair on either side of her head.

Rushing to Avery's side, Allison stooped and embraced her wailing daughter. "Oh, Avery. Erik couldn't have done this to you, could he?"

"I wanna be dead, Mom," Avery managed to get intermittent words out between heavy sobs into her mother's neck. "I can't do this anymore."

"Honey, don't talk like that," Allison insisted, stroking Avery's tangled hair.

"It's too hard. Please don't make me go back there, Mom. I can't ever go back."

"Honey, look at me," Allison said calmly, her hands now on Avery's slender shoulders. "Where? Can't go back where?"

"To school. It's torture. It's about to get even worse too. I can feel it. Something happened tonight at the Prom."

"Avery," Allison implored, wiping more tears from her daughter's face, "tell me who's giving you all the trouble. I *need* to know."

"It's not that easy, Mom." Avery bowed her head, plopping into a sitting position. "Freak, these shoes are killing me." Hastily unfastening the tiny buckles, she then threw them over her head. "It's complicated."

"Give me a name, Avery." Allison's blue eyes were ablaze with indignation. "*Now*."

CHAPTER 11

"So that's it, right over there," Jackson said, pointing to the far corner of East High's parking lot as two brunette cheerleaders accompanied him across the black top.

"Wow," the girl to his left commented, pulling her wavy hair into a pony tail. "I can't believe your dad actually let you take his new GT to school."

"Well, he didn't actually *tell* me I could," Jackson admitted, casually dribbling a basketball as they walked. "But what he doesn't know can't hurt him, right?"

"Those are some nice rims," the taller brunette to his right commented, applying another coat of shiny pink lipgloss. "So you gonna take us for a little ride?"

"You bet."

Upon reaching his father's navy blue GT, Jackson popped the trunk and began showing off the dual subwoofers inside. "Here. I'll let you hear what they sound like real fast." While unlocking the driver's door, an approaching black tank top with a platinum head of medium length hair caught his attention. *The more hotties, the better*, he thought.

"Hey, Jackson," the blonde smiled, strutting toward him from the opposite side of the car.

"What's up?" he acknowledged, trying to figure out if he'd met this girl before. She definitely looked a bit older than high school age.

"Is this pretty thing your car?" she said, setting down her oversized turquoise handbag.

"Yeah," he said, slightly hesitant. "Do I know – "

"Good."

The sound of shattering glass then pierced the air, inciting sharp screams from the two pining brunettes. With his jaw practically on the ground, East High's power forward watched in horror as the passenger side window exploded into pieces all over his father's black leather seats.

"Do you know who I am?" the freckled blonde grinned as she cocked a wooden baseball bat for another blow. "What, no answer?" With another swift burst of strength, the crazed woman sent the blunt piece of wood plowing through the rear passenger window, creating the same devastating effects.

Paralyzed with shock, Jackson stood in a limp stupor, his forgotten basketball rolling down the slope of the parking lot.

"Excuse me, ladies," she said, closing the trunk. The two wide-eyed girls immediately stepped back, watching in disbelief at the spectacle unfolding before them.

"Let me ask you again, you pathetic douche bag. Who am I?"

Taking two steps toward the rear of the battered sports car, Jackson's open mouth failed to articulate anything.

"What a shame," came the reply. Giving way under the forceful impact of the bat, the GT's rear windshield had now imploded, scattering shards of reflected light throughout the vehicle's pristine interior. "You were at the Prom two nights ago, weren't you?"

"Uh, um," Jackson uttered.

"I'll take that as a yes." Taking a moment to demolish both taillights, she then turned and walked along the passenger side to the car's front. "You spoke with a girl named Avery Renshaw that night, didn't you?"

"I, uh – "

"What pretty headlights you have, Jackson." A moment later, what remained of them lay scattered on the ground below. "You must think you're a real man, don't you? Calling a helpless pregnant girl a slut right in front of her prom date? You're such a man, Jackson."

The two witnessing brunettes slowly turned in unison to look at each other, then resumed watching the school's star basketball player get verbally ripped to shreds.

"Let me ask you again, hot shot. Who am I?"

A blank stare was all Jackson could muster.

"You're even dumber than you look, you know that? It's a pity too, you worthless waste of space, because it's such a beautiful windshield." Two vicious swings and five seconds later, the only glass that remained intact was on the driver's side. "Alright, pee-brain, you listen to me and you listen well. I had better not hear about you saying one more word to my daughter as long as you live. You or any of your loser friends. You hear me?!"

"Yes, ma'am," Jackson muttered, his hands quivering at his side.

"Seriously! You don't know anything about my daughter! How dare you have the gall to prance up to a pregnant teenager and accuse her of anything! She could have been raped for all you know, you ignorant pathetic excuse for a man! Oh, and let me guess. Are you going to go home to your mommy and daddy and cry about how a mean lady came and destroyed your pretty little car? Is that what you're going to do? Run home like a little girl and cry to your parents?"

"No," Jackson conceded, his eyes fixed on the raging blue ones before him. "I deserved it."

"You're going to make sure my daughter is left alone, you understand me?"

"Yes. I understand you."

Slipping the bat into her bag, Allison threw Jackson a smile as she turned and strutted off.

Plate glass crunched beneath him as Jackson calmly took a seat in his father's destroyed vehicle. Closing the door and placing his hands on the leather steering wheel, he turned to his left at the two cheerleaders gawking at him. "You can keep this quiet, right? Nobody needs to know."

"I think it's probably too late for that," the taller of the two remarked, pointing across the vehicle.

Shifting his gaze to the right, Jackson was met with half a dozen phones and awe-struck faces pointed in his direction.

∞

Having stayed home from school that day, Avery lounged comfortably on the couch in some black sweats and a pink tee shirt. Flipping through the local channels, she brought another spoonful of Rocky Road to her lips and savored the smooth chocolate ice cream and crunch of the almonds.

"Hey, Sweetheart!" Allison hollered as she burst through the front door.

"Geez, Mom!" Avery yelped, dropping her spoon. "You don't have to yell. I'm right here."

"Oh, sorry," Allison said, continuing down the hall. "I just figured you'd be in bed."

"What's with the bat, Mom?" A nervous wave surged through her as Avery's imagination began calculating what on earth her mother had been up to.

"Oh, nothing serious, really," Allison called out, returning the bat to its designated spot beneath her bed.

Avery stared blankly at the infomercial host as her mind continued conjuring the possibilities. "What does that mean? Nothing serious, Mom? That sounds kind of serious, if you ask me."

"Stop worrying," Allison insisted, walking now into the kitchen. "What should we do for dinner? Frozen pizza? Burritos? We have some leftover chicken and rice."

"Mom, you're freaking me out. Tell me what you did."

With a frozen pizza in hand, Allison stepped briefly into view to make eye contact with her daughter. "Let me put it this way for you. You're not going to need to worry about being made fun of at school anymore, okay?"

"How can you be *sure*?" Avery moaned incredulously. "I wish you would just tell me."

"Mothers' secrets," Allison asserted, preheating the oven to 425.

Two hours later Avery received a video link within a text message from Marnee. The shocking footage, dubbed 'Blonde Rage', had accumulated nearly twenty thousand views within three hours of being posted.

"Mom?" Avery stammered as she trudged into her mother's room.

"Yes, Honey," Allison said looking over the top of her mystery novel.

Handing her phone to Allison, Avery took a seat on the bed beside her mother. "What have you *done*?"

CHAPTER 12

Avery awoke to a rhythmic buzzing, as some loose change rattled atop her particle board nightstand. Knocking over an empty green plastic cup in the process, she clumsily retrieved her vibrating phone. "Erik?"

"Um, hi, Avery," came the hesitant reply. "Have I caught you at a bad time?"

"No. No, you didn't," Avery yawned, taking a moment to stand and stretch. "I just woke up, actually."

"I'm sorry to wake you up. Maybe I should call later."

"No. I'm good. It's fine." Slumping back over in bed, Avery laid on her side, facing the closet. "Wow. What time is it?"

"Lunch time."

"It's probably about time for me to get up then. It's good you called."

"I'm just glad you're okay. I've been trying to call and text you, but you haven't been responding. I was really worried about you. And you haven't been in class the past couple of days."

"Yeah," Avery sighed. "I'm sorry if it felt like I was ignoring you. I've been pretty much ignoring everyone. The other night was really rough on me."

"Avery, about that. I've been wanting to apologize for not doing a better job of standing up for you. I just sat there and didn't say anything while that jerk spoke about you like that. My mind went completely blank."

"It's fine. You don't have to apologize for that."

"Yes I do," Erik asserted. "You were my date and I shouldn't have let him speak to you like that. I'm so sorry."

"You had no idea what you were getting yourself into that day at the restaurant, did you?" Straining back into a sitting position, Avery stood and walked to her closet, running her fingers across the soiled prom dress.

"No." Erik paused, taking a deep breath. "It was much better than I had even imagined."

"Ha! That was the right thing to say, but I know you're lying."

"I mean it. I haven't stopped thinking about you."

After the unpleasant end to their date, Avery had expected never to hear from Erik again. But when the calls and messages had started to come in, she'd been too embarrassed to engage him. Smiling from ear to ear at his sincere tone, Avery left the gown and sauntered down the hall, heading for something cold to drink. "I've been thinking about you too."

"Really?" Erik gulped.

"Yep." Opening the fridge, Avery crouched down and grasped a pitcher of water and poured herself a glass. "You sound surprised."

"Well, uh, it's just that – "

"It was the best night of my life." Taking a refreshing sip from a ceramic mug of her making, she plopped onto the couch. "Up until the end, that is."

"It did have quite the ending. There's no doubt about that."

"I'm not gonna lie, though. It was pretty awesome when Jackson got punched in the face. I've always hated him."

"I can't imagine why," Erik said sarcastically.

"I shouldn't say that though. It's not good to be a hater."

"I'd say he earned your hatred."

"Yes. He certainly did."

"So, speaking of Jackson, I think he's changed his tune a little."

Closing her eyes in anguish, Avery sighed and felt the all-too-frequent surge of anxiety again pulsing through her back and limbs. "I was worried about that. My mom is so nuts! I don't think I'm ever going to be able to step foot in school again. It would be suicide."

"No, it's not like that at all. That's part of the reason I called you during lunch. I just had a conversation with him."

Avery's eyes widened. "He talked to *you*? That can't be good. What did he say?"

"He said he was sorry for causing us trouble that night, and that he didn't know what his problem was. He said he wanted to apologize to you directly, but that he'd promised your mom he'd never speak to you again. He wanted me to tell you how sorry he is for disrespecting you."

Running her free hand through her matted morning hair, Avery arose and commenced pacing up and down the hall. "That doesn't sound like Jackson at all. I don't think he's ever apologized to anyone in his life!"

"I guess your mom really made an impression on him."

"Wow." Avery halted pacing momentarily, trying to let things sink in. "And you're sure you were talking to Jackson?"

"Who else would I have been talking to?"

"It's just so weird."

"I'm guessing you saw the video."

"Yes."

"One of my buddies had me listen to it with him. He said Jackson looked like he'd seen a ghost."

"I still can't believe my mom did that. But just watch. His parents will probably press charges."

"I'm sure your mom could probably persuade them not to."

"What, with her bat?" From her vantage point in the hallway, Avery could see the infamous Louisville Slugger lying under her mother's bed.

"Just saying. So did you get my message about the symphony?"

"I don't know if you want to be seen in public with me anymore."

"I told you my brother plays the cello for them, right?"

"You mentioned that during dinner. Yes."

"He can get us some really good seats."

"When is it again?"

"This Friday. I hope you'll come."

"You wouldn't be embarrassed to be seen with a pregnant teenager?"

"I would prefer it."

"If you say so."

"So that's a yes then?"

"I would like that a lot, actually. Thanks, Erik."

"Awesome. I'll let Gavin know so he can reserve the tickets. Are you going to be in class tomorrow?"

Avery hesitated, still wary of any unwanted effects from her mother's incident in the parking lot. "Sure. Yeah. I'll be there."

CHAPTER 13

"Thanks, Mom," Avery said, kissing Allison's cheek.

"So are they giving you a ride home afterward then?" Allison asked, grabbing Avery's white leather purse from the console. "Here, don't forget this."

"Oh, thanks. Yes, they are." Pulling down the visor, Avery took a final assessment of her makeup, applying a touch more silver to each eyelid.

"I still can't believe that's the same dress," Allison commented.

"I know, right?" Avery agreed. "It's not perfect, but I think that dry cleaner did a pretty good job. They couldn't get all of it out of the back though."

"That's what your mom's cute white jacket is for, right?" Allison grinned.

"Thanks, by the way. I promise I won't roll around in the dirt with it."

"You'd better not."

"Well, he's waiting inside. I better get going."

"Have fun, Sweetie. You look gorgeous."

"Love you."

∞

The scent of Vincent Conrad's Fourth Concerto gracefully fluttered an unseen path through the expansive foyer of New Hope's renowned Monument Theater. Above the polished white marble floor it glided, weaving its way around human forms, climbing through vines of decadent crystal, and eventually washing across the pale freckled face of Erik Harper.

Taking a seat on an oak-legged bench with cushy maroon velvet upholstery, Avery quietly took a seat directly in front of him, admiring his full reddish-brown hair. Shoulders erect and legs at nearly perfect ninety degree angles, he resembled a Marine awaiting his assignment. His large chest heaved with each slow breath, accentuating his muscular upper body.

Removing his cell from his tan sport coat, Erik quickly typed something, then returned the phone to his inside jacket pocket. A brief moment later, Avery's phone jingled in her purse. Grinning suspiciously, she unsnapped the clip and reached inside to read the incoming message. 'You're wearing that amazing perfume again.'

Inputting her response, she crossed her legs and waited. Within a few seconds Erik retrieved his phone and pressed the speaker button. A female computer voice then orated, "Oh, so that's how you knew I was here."

"Actually, no," Erik confessed, placing the phone in his lap. "I heard you walk in."

"No," Avery chuckled. "With all these other people walking around?"

"Oh yes." He leaned forward. "You have a signature step."

"Is that a bad thing?" Avery squinted, tilting her head.

"Not at all. Everyone walks differently. I just happen to have memorized yours a long time ago."

"Mr. Harper," Avery giggled. "Have you been spying on me?"

"If you want to call it that. Sure. Ever since algebra in tenth grade."

"Mr. Stott's class?"

"Yep."

"I don't remember having that class with you."

"Trust me. I was there."

"I feel like I would have remembered someone in a wheelchair. Now I just feel like an idiot."

"Remember the guy with the dreadlocks?"

"You're kidding me! *That* was *you*? But what about the wheelchair? I was thinking you'd always had to use it."

"The wheelchair is kind of a newer thing, actually."

"What happened?"

Erik faced the polished floor for a moment, then returned his gaze in Avery's direction. "It's been kind of a gradual thing. I started losing my balance a lot about fifteen months ago. Fell down the stairs a few times. Stuff like that."

"Geez. That's weird. What caused it?"

"The doctors haven't really pinned it yet, but it's kind of like multiple sclerosis, similar to muscular dystrophy, and a bit like amyotrophic lateral sclerosis."

Avery's eyes were wide with concern. "That's quite the mouthful."

"Basically, it's a motor neuron disease."

"Can it be treated?"

"So far, no."

Avery was silent for a moment, searching his eyes, which behaved like two little children wanting to tell an exciting story, but unable to find the words. With her delicate touch, she placed his left hand in hers, gently caressing his rough skin with her thumb. "It's not fair, Erik."

"What do you mean?"

"I don't know. Just, everything that's happened to you. I've thought a lot about what you told me the night of prom. At the restaurant."

"Oh?"

"Have you ever been angry with her?"

Erik's gaze was reflective, but he said nothing.

"With your biological mother, I mean."

"I wouldn't call it anger, no. I've been sad for her. I think she has a lot of regrets. Gavin had it worse than I did. All those boyfriends of hers were really hard on him growing up I guess. Beat him up a lot. Stuff like that."

"That's horrible."

"Yes it is."

"Isn't she the reason you were born blind?"

"Gavin thinks so. He thinks it was the drugs. He said when he was born, she wasn't into crack yet. She was actually fourteen when she had him."

"Wow. That is so crazy. Makes me feel like I don't have much to complain about."

"It was really hard on Gavin. Having the upbringing that he did. Sure made him responsible though. Man, that guy is by the book about everything!"

"How old was he when he ran away?"

"And it wasn't like he totally ran away. But by the time he was twelve, he had found a way to spend most of his time out of the house."

"I don't know," Avery sighed. "If it were me, I would have ended up dead in a gutter somewhere or something."

"He did what he had to do to survive. That's when things started getting really bad with the drugs. He said they were bad before that. But I guess she really started going downhill. And it wasn't like he was living on the street. There was an older foreign lady named Cornelia who lived on the same block that sort of took him in. He spent most of his time over there."

"I'm surprised he didn't end up in foster care."

"I think Cornelia may have guessed he may have been better off with her than being pulled into the system. You know? He could easily have ended up in foster care though. I don't know why he didn't. Just didn't work out that way. Maybe it was for the best."

"Well, it seems like you two are a good team." Releasing Erik's hand, Avery took a moment to straighten the front of his jacket. "Have I mentioned how handsome you look tonight?"

"You're a lot like my brother, you know that?" Erik's voice quivered with emotion. "You're just so caring and encouraging all the time."

"That's nice of you to say, but – oh my goodness, Erik. You're crying."

"You're like a ray of hope."

"I see what you're trying to do, Mister," Avery smiled, her wet brown eyes glistening like the chandelier crystals dangling above them. "You want my mascara to smear again." Gently pressing her lips to Erik's moist cheek, Avery then whispered into his ear. "You're too good to me. So what about those seats your brother was able to score for us?"

∞

Avery's return home was announced by the screeching of the hinges on their front door. Exiting the bathroom wrapped in a robe and a towel about her head, Allison padded toward her beaming daughter, embracing her firmly. "And I half expected you to be covered in dirt. So, how was it?"

Grinning bashfully at her mother, Avery remained silent for a moment.

"What, Aves?" Allison questioned, ushering her daughter to the couch. "Did you two kiss or something?"

With her grin stretching like a taut rubber band, Avery had to look away to break from Allison's expectant glare.

"Oh, wow." Allison's back stiffened. "Well *that* was fast."

"Ah?" Avery chirped, slapping Allison's knee.

"I would have never kissed a guy on a blind date."

"What do you mean, blind date, Mom. He wasn't a blind date." Avery's eyes then widened in response to her mother's wry grin. "Mom?!"

"Sorry," Allison laughed, pulling the towel off her head. "I had to. It was just too easy!"

"You are the worst sometimes, you know that? Seriously." Avery swiftly wiggled free of Allison's button-up sweater, and playfully tossed it into Allison's face. "There's your sweater back, you jerk."

"Watch it now, little lady." Allison issued a firm look.

"You shouldn't make fun of people," Avery chortled, kicking off her black heels. "It's not nice. You'd better watch out or somebody will end up bashing in your windows to teach you a lesson."

Allison gleefully welcomed the comment. "So," she continued, dragging a large round brush through her moist yellow hair, "besides your little romantic moment, how else did things go tonight? Does the symphony compare at all to those obnoxious rock concerts you and Marnee love so much?"

"I can't really compare the two. They're completely different. The symphony has a much more soothing feeling about it, but there's still some exciting moments. Going to see a band is more about the rush, and you get all sweaty jumping around. You know, that sort of thing. But tonight had a different sort of thrill about it. It was really neat. It was – inspiring."

Finishing with the round brush, Allison set it aside and clasped her pale hands on her lap. "Well, good. I'm glad you had such a nice time."

"I wish you could have seen Erik's face while he listened to the music tonight." Avery looked away for a moment and sighed.

"It was like he became part of the music. He would close his eyes, and kind of sway back and forth."

"I'm pretty sure that's what your dad used to do when he was falling asleep."

"Ha, ha. Very funny."

"Sorry. You were saying?"

"I don't know." Avery paused for a moment, looking intently into Allison's large blue eyes. "Because he's blind, I think he's able to enjoy the music more. It's like he can hear more of the sounds, or something. Does that make sense?"

"I think so. Yeah. That's really neat. Sounds like the second date was much better than the first."

"And that *kiss*," Avery sighed.

"Oh, no," Allison smiled, rolling her eyes. "Here it comes."

"Not too short," Avery went on. "Not too long. Yeah. Just perfect."

"What? Right in the middle of the performance?"

"Absolutely! Why not?"

"Oh, to be young again."

"Don't be jealous, Mom. Forty is still young."

"Who are you calling forty? I'm thirty nine and twelve eighths."

"Well, Mom," Avery said, standing up, "I'm beat."

"Hey, wait," Allison called out as Avery strode down the hall. "Aren't you going to stay up and watch Kidswap reruns with me?"

"Sorry, Mom," Avery hollered back. "That show is for old people!"

CHAPTER 14

"Aves!" Allison called from their apartment entryway, frantically brushing lint from her black knee-length skirt. "Aves, it's time to *go*!"

"I said hold on a second!" Avery yelped from the bathroom. "I'm looking for my mascara! Did you do something with it?!"

"No. I have my own makeup, thank you very much." Stomping across their worn out gray carpet in a pair of black flats, Allison thumped her fist on the bathroom door. "Just use *mine*. You can put it on in the car. We're running late as it is."

Flashing a squinty-eyed glare at her mother as she opened the door, Avery forced her way past Allison and headed for the front door.

"Nice skirt," Allison commented, "but aren't you *forgetting* something?"

Feeling a gust of air from their open front door across her exposed rounded belly and shoulders, Avery marched into her room and moments later walked out donning a light pink three-quarter sleeve cotton blouse. "There," Avery couldn't help but laugh at herself. "You happy now?"

"I don't know," Allison laughed. "Maybe you *wanted* to show off your pregnant self while the principal hands you your diploma! I think it would make the experience more memorable for everyone."

"Thanks, Mom, but no thanks."

As Allison backed the gray sedan out of their parking stall, Avery pulled down the passenger visor and began dragging the mascara brush through her already jet-black lashes.

"Aves," Allison began, making a right onto Thirteenth East, "this'll probably sound corny, because I'm your old mother and all, but I just want to let you know how proud I am of you."

"Well," Avery said jokingly, "I guess it is a *little* corny, but go on."

"Seriously though. A lot of kids don't ever graduate. And this last year has been especially hard on you. It's been – it's been hard on both of us."

Avery closed the mascara bottle and placed it in Allison's purse. "It could have been worse."

"Dad would have been proud."

"Yeah."

Ten more minutes passed as Allison navigated through the inner-city traffic. "Well you sure have gone quiet."

"Yeah," Avery responded, keeping her eyes on the passing buildings, pedestrians and cars. "Sorry. I've just been thinking. I mean, this is supposed to be such a big day and everything, you know?"

"What do you mean?" Allison inquired, slowing down for a red light. "Does it not feel that way?"

"Sort of. But all I can think about is…"

"The baby?"

"Today I graduate. But what about tomorrow? And the next day? And the day after that?"

"Just a day at a time, Avery. That's all we can do."

Remaining silent, Avery closed her eyes and leaned back in her seat.

"Hey, no sleeping," Allison insisted. "We're almost there."

"Mom, chill. I'm not sleeping." Raising her hands to her eyebrows, Avery sighed forcefully, keeping her eyes closed. "I'm thinking."

Finishing a left hand turn, Allison placed her right hand on her daughter's shoulder. "We can do hard things, Avery. We already have."

Within five minutes, Allison was slowly driving through the ocean of parked cars, looking for a spot with minimal required walking. "Well, looks like this is the best we can do." Bringing their sedan to a halt, Allison pushed the transmission into park and the two exited the vehicle.

Warmth from the blacktop crawled up Avery's legs as the pair made their way to the rendezvous point they had arranged with the Harpers.

"There it is," Avery said, pointing off to their right. Beyond some aspen trees that adorned the campus walkways, there stood an imposing massive replica of the Western Republic's national flag. Fashioned entirely of clear glass, the eight-ton weaving spectacle was suspended in the air, hoisted by stainless steel rods, twenty centimeters in diameter, protruding from the ground at varying angles. There were ten rods in all, one for every province in the republic.

"How late are we?" Allison questioned, fumbling through her purse for her phone.

"Like ten minutes," Avery responded, double checking to see if Erik had responded to her last text.

"I guess ten minutes isn't too bad," Allison admitted. "Yikes, it's a hot one today."

"Well," Avery said as they arrived and stood under the enormous glass monument, "they should be here pretty soon."

The York University campus was a bustle of activity, with East High graduates and their families zipping this way and that, white and red tassels coupled with the platinum numbers 130 dangling from the awkward black caps. Photographs were in progress in every direction. Graduates posing in their white cap and gown with their parents, siblings, and grandparents.

Taking a shady seat on one of the many concrete benches, Avery looked longingly at the students with two parents standing beside them. Images of her father flashed in and out of her mind. A few times she thought she saw his curly brown hair and cheery smile coming through the crowd. Was that him in the blue suit, carrying a dozen roses?

"Why don't you try calling him?"

"Huh?" Avery was startled by the voice to her left.

"I think you should call Erik," Allison repeated.

"Oh. Right." Pulling up the number, Avery placed the phone to her ear and listened to it ring through to voicemail. "Hey, it's me. We're here. Please call me and let me know if you're running late, or if you're already here. We're just sitting by the glass monument. Love you."

"I didn't know you guys were using the 'L word'," Allison commented, raising her barely existent eyebrows.

"Yeah. So?" Avery looked at the ground, rolling her phone around in her hands.

"How long has that been going on?" Allison sat up for a moment, straightening out her skirt.

"I don't know. A couple of weeks."

"You think you really love him?"

"Mom," Avery glared, "I really don't want to talk about this right now."

"Okay."

"Yes," Avery conceded. "I think I do love him. And stop tapping your foot like that. It's driving me nuts."

"Sorry."

"It's just, you know, noises right now. Little noises like that are making me crazy lately."

"Is that them?" Allison asked. "In the blue SUV?"

"No," Avery said. "They're in a white SUV."

"How long do they expect us to wait out here in the heat like this?" Removing a wad of old receipts from her purse, Allison began flapping it across her face.

"I don't know," Avery sighed, standing up. "They should be here by now."

"Well, let's at least get your picture taken out here while we're waiting." Reaching into the bag that contained Avery's white cap and gown, Allison looked up to see Avery had waddled half-way to the parking lot. "Aves?!" Jumping to her feet, Allison began chasing after her fleeing daughter.

Turning to verify her mother had caught on, Avery frantically gestured for Allison to keep coming, then hurried toward their car.

"Avery, what are you doing?!" Allison hollered, desperately trying to keep up. "Wait up!"

Once in step with Avery, Allison tried to get a few steps in front and head her off. "Aves, what on earth are you doing? You have a graduation to go to!"

Quickening her pace, Avery pressed on. "He's not coming, Mom!"

"What do you mean, he's not coming?" Allison panted, shifting her purse and bag to her other arm. "Did he text you or something?"

"No. That's part of the reason I know something's wrong. Plus, they're not like us, Mom. Erik and Gavin are never late for anything. *Ever.*"

"Maybe they got stuck in traffic or something."

"Throw me the keys," Avery insisted, now standing at their driver's side door.

Allison reluctantly dug around inside her purse, then tossed them over. Catching the clanking key ring, Avery nearly had the sedan in reverse before Allison could even get her door closed.

"Avery, slow down!" Allison growled, firmly planting her hand atop the gear shift. "Let's just try calling again."

"I've been trying, Mom!" Avery rebutted. "The last time I heard from him was at like seven this morning. He hasn't responded to any of my messages or calls since!"

"That could mean anything. We have no idea what he's up to. Driving us over to their house isn't going to accomplish anything. I'm sure they won't even be home when we get there."

"We're not driving to their house," Avery said, throwing the car into reverse. "We're going to the hospital."

∞

"And you're certain he'd be here?" Allison said as they approached the front entrance of New Hope Regional.

"It's the closest one to their house," Avery insisted, halting her gate as the automatic glass doors slid open. Stepping promptly up to the information desk, she placed her quivering hands on the desk.

"How may I assist you, Miss?" a young bulky security guard asked.

"We're here to see a patient," Avery panted. "Erik Harper. He's eighteen, and would have arrived within the last two and a half hours."

"Hmm, let me see," said the security guard. Taking a moment to input the information, he looked up from his computer screen. "Do you happen to be in the company of Avery Renshaw?"

"I am Avery Renshaw."

"He's in room 213A. It's down the second hallway left of the elevators."

"Thank you."

Gently placing her hand on Avery's arm, Allison smiled empathetically at her daughter as they turned, their feet tapping along the gray tile floor.

∞

Rapping quietly on the door of room 213A, Avery and Allison were breathing deeply from their urgent walk from the foyer of the hospital. As the door slowly came ajar, they were met with Gavin's brilliant green eyes. "Please come in. I'm so sorry I wasn't able to phone you. I recently lost all my phone's contacts and during the madness this morning we didn't end up bringing Erik's."

"Don't worry, Gavin," Avery said, stepping into the room. Cupping her hands over her mouth, she cautiously approached the bed on which Erik lay.

"He always said he didn't want to be intubated," Gavin said quietly, ushering Allison into the room. "Maybe he'll pull out of it though, you know?"

"Of course," Allison whispered, gently squeezing Gavin's arm. "Absolutely."

Tears began making trails down Avery's cheeks as she ran her fingers delicately through Erik's thick reddish-brown hair. His face was even more pale than normal, which contrasted vividly against Avery's darkly toned skin. "Erik," she whispered into his ear. "You're in trouble, Mister. You know that? You stood me up this morning." Setting her purse on the bed next to him, she leaned over and kissed his clammy forehead.

Looking on from the opposite side of the room, Allison clutched Gavin's tan shirt sleeve, fighting back tears of her own.

A rush of hope swelled in Avery's chest as Erik began to stir. Coughing and gurgling into the ventilator tube that protruded from his throat, Erik arched his back and opened his eyes.

Rushing to his brother's side, Gavin crouched to one knee and took him by the hand. "Hey, buddy, it's me. You're in the hospital. Remember, you stopped being able to breathe very well this morning, so we had the ambulance come and haul you down here."

Turning to face his brother, Erik strained his neck to be able to nod in acknowledgment of what he'd just been told.

"And Avery's here, buddy. She's right next to you."

Leaning further to his left, Erik gazed longingly in Avery's direction. Feeling her soft warm hand against his cheek, he closed his eyes and tried to inhale a deep breath of her perfume. He was frustrated, however, to find the ventilator was doing all the work for him. Reaching for the apparatus jutting from his throat, Erik grasped the tube and began to yank on it.

"Erik!" Gavin interceded, prying his brother's fingers free. "You have to leave that alone. It's helping you breathe.

Swinging his right arm across his chest, Erik swatted at Gavin's hand and pointed his forefinger accusingly in his face.

Rising slowly to his feet, Gavin wiped a tear from his clean-shaven face. "I know you never wanted to be on life support. But buddy, this is just a ventilator to help you out until you stabilize."

Slicing both his hands back and forth through the air, Erik had signaled for silence. Now grasping the plastic annoyance that filled his mouth, he used both hands to loosen and finally remove it entirely. "If I'm – going to live," he gasped between words, "it's going to be – without – a tube – down – my throat." Struggling to breath, he managed a few good breaths, he turned again to face Avery. "You're wearing that – amazing perfume – again."

"Yes," Avery said, taking his hand. "Just for you."

"You're – beautiful. You know – that?"

Unable to speak through her tears, Avery knelt, closing her eyes, and held his weakened hand to her cheek.

"You need – to do something – for me – Avery," Erik coughed.

"What?" Avery sobbed.

"I need you to – say hello – to little – Ahmyn – for me."

"Who?" Avery squinted through her tears.

"Well, don't you – think it's a – good name – for – the baby?" Erik forced a smile through spurts of coughing, his chest fighting for air.

"Ahmyn?" Avery said, raising her eyebrows. "Yes. It's a beautiful name."

"Avery?" Erik continued.

"Yes, Erik."

"This – isn't – the end – for us. You – understand?"

"Erik, don't talk like that," Avery sobbed, squeezing his hand even tighter.

"The best – the best is – yet – to come."

"Erik, no," Avery pleaded. "Gavin? Can't you make him wear the ventilator?"

"This is what he wants," Gavin sobbed, trying to choke back tears. "I need to respect his wishes."

"Gavin!" Erik coughed. "Gavin, get over – here."

Avery attempted to step away and make way for Gavin, but Erik held her hand tighter, keeping her close. Walking to the opposite side of the bed, Gavin placed his muscular hand on Erik's shoulder. "Yes, brother."

"Thank – you," Erik managed. "For – everything. For being the – man – I'll never have – the chance – to be."

Then looking straight ahead, his grip on Avery's hand relaxed as he exhaled. "I love – you."

And then silence. Timeless and sacred, it saturated the room. It hushed all tears, and even drowned out the enduring tone that blared from the heart monitor machine. Leaning slowly over Erik's chest, which no longer fought for breath, Avery placed her lips upon his forehead – for the last time.

CHAPTER 15

"I just don't think it's a good idea, Avery," Allison blurted as she hastily restocked her cleaning tote.

"Why?" Avery whined from her bedroom.

"Do I really need to explain this to you? Because if I do, you're going to need to wait until *after* I'm done working."

Dropping a few more scour pads and a bottle of extra-strength Grease King into her tote, Allison headed for the door.

"Mom, please let me visit Marnee." Now waddling down the hall in some white sweats and one of Richard's old gray T-shirts, Avery was headed for the refrigerator. "I have to get out of here. I need a change of scenery for a couple of weeks. It's so stuffy in this apartment, and we might as well not even have a cooler. I swear that thing's older than *you.*"

"Thanks."

"And I don't know what the neighbors are always cooking over there, but it smells like dirty socks and vinegar. Seriously, living here anymore is a nightmare. The shower hardly has any pressure, and the people upstairs are always playing that obnoxious music and – "

"Avery, I really don't know what to tell you. I'm a little busy right now." Sliding some white-rimmed sunglasses onto her nose, Allison picked up her tote and opened the door. "I have a new client, and I'm late. This discussion is going to have to wait."

"Tell me you'll let me get my sanity back," Avery persisted, drinking a glass of chocolate milk. "Mom, *pleeeeease.* Marnee said her parents would fly me out there and everything. They have a nice big air-conditioned house away from the city, and a pool and -"

"Avery," Allison insisted, standing half way out the door. "I'm sorry your friend moved. Okay? I really am. But you're seven months along. I'm not going to let you go prancing across the country at this stage in your pregnancy. It just isn't responsible."

"According to who?"

"A doctor would tell you that. Oh, but you wouldn't know that, would you? Seeing as you refuse to go."

Avery looked away from her mother's piercing gaze and focused on a picture of her and her father that hung crooked on the wall. "You *know* how I feel about that, Mom. They told us to *kill* my baby. Did you forget? I'm *never* going back there again. *Never*. Besides, we couldn't afford to go to the doctor if we wanted to."

"Avery, I tried to find another doctor's office and you refused that too. Yeah, it's a little pricey without insurance. Well, a lot pricey – but what's a few doctor's visits compared to paying for cancer treatments?"

Slumping down onto the couch, Avery placed her glass of chocolate milk on the coffee table. "Well I'm sorry I've been such a financial burden on you."

"Avery, all I'm saying is there is no reason why you shouldn't be doing all you can for that baby. That child will become your *life*."

With tears welling up in her eyes, Avery turned to face her mother again. "You might have forgotten, but I didn't choose this for myself. Remember? I never wanted this to become my life. Whatever happened to someone choosing their own life, huh?"

Removing her sunglasses, Allison spoke firmly. "Regardless of the unusual circumstances, Avery, bearing a child is no curse. It's an honor."

"How would you know, Mom? You've never been pregnant!"

Allison was deeply hurt by Avery's cutting remark. "I would have done *anything* to have a child, Avery."

"Is that so?" Avery glared. With tears now streaming down her face, Avery struggled to her feet and padded down the hall to her room. "Well I'm sorry you had to settle for *me*."

As Avery slammed the door behind her, Allison locked their front door and placed the cleaning tote into the passenger seat of their sedan. Walking briskly around the back of the vehicle she opened the driver's side door and stepped in. Placing her hands on the warm steering wheel, she gazed intently through the windshield at the decaying fence in front of her. Life was hard. It had always been hard. But the future – the future seemed unbearable. "What are we going to do when she loses that baby?"

∞

Avery had been trying to get to sleep for over an hour. It seemed like every time she was ready for bed, the child in her womb was ready to play.

"You sure are a feisty little thing, aren't you?" Avery smiled as she placed her hand on her belly. "Are you dancing in there?" She couldn't help but laugh. "Well, at least one of us likes the neighbor's music." Avery reached for the remote. "I have an idea. Since you aren't going to let Mommy sleep, what do you say we see what's on television tonight?" She began flipping through the channels. "Ah, this looks good. Maybe I can get you to fall asleep watching Tom Barry."

"'So our first guest tonight hardly needs an intro. Would everyone please welcome international icon Darius Viyergo. First of all, we want to truly thank you for coming onto the show tonight.”

“Stop it. The pleasure’s all mine. Thank *you* for having me.”

“Now to be clear, this is your first television interview. Is that right?”

“Precisely. I’m finally beginning to overcome my stage fright. And just look – I’m making my debut on the Tom Barry show, no less! How’s that for striking oil?!”

“We wanted to give you the warmest welcome showbiz has to offer. What can I say?”

“Seriously though, how long have you been on the air now? You’re hitting the big ‘two – zero’ this year, right? I’d say that deserves a round of applause. Let’s give it up, everybody, for Mr. Tom Barry and twenty strong years on the best late show in the Republic!”

“C’mon now, you’re making me blush. Tell you what. I’ll let you buy me a steak after the show. That way I not only get to have the pleasure of interviewing the most intriguing man in the world, but I get to dine with him too!”

“I don’t know about the *most* intriguing.”

“People say you have a gift. How do you respond to that?”

“I don’t know if I would classify it as a *gift*, per se. Do you have any idea how many emails I get, how many letters through the post I receive? Not only that, but consider this – as a celebrity, when you encounter the public, what do they typically want?”

“That’s *easy*. An autograph and a picture.”

“Exactly. For me, it’s much more complicated than that. I should think that a gift would make my life easier. A person only has to take one look at me to know that my life has been anything but easy.”

“Indeed.”

"But don't get me wrong. I accept my experiences for what they are, and it's pointless to wish the past away, no matter how unpleasant it may be. In some ways, our pending future's most valuable asset is the unfortunate past. We should never be afraid to make mistakes. How else are we supposed to learn?"

"But that's the fascinating thing about you. You don't *make* mistakes. Everything you have ever said *would* happen *has* happened."

"I wish that were true, Tom. As a matter of fact, before flying out here yesterday I told my wife that you would have dyed your hair bright blue right before the show."

"Don't make me nervous! Now I really wish I had a mirror on me, just to double check!! Hey everybody, what color is my hair? Terrific. Now we've got the whole audience playing along."

"Just send me your stylist bill. I've got you covered."

"Now help me understand something here. Over the last fifty years you've been able to predict the annihilation of two major cities, the most catastrophic monsoon in recorded history, multiple earthquakes, a massive volcanic eruption in one of our polar ice caps, and yet you're able to sit and crack jokes with me on national television!! How do you maintain a sense of humor amidst all the chaos?"

"In general, people have a strong tendency to take themselves very seriously. I did too for a while, but I'd like to think that, deep down, it's been a well-developed sense of humor that's kept the human race going all these years. Just imagine where you'd be without yours!"

"Indeed. How old were you when you began to discover your uncanny ability to predict future events?"

"About six years old."

"I understand that there have been a slew of neurological tests performed to discover a potential reason for your unique capacities. Are you wired, so to speak, differently than the rest of us?"

"Absolutely not. There is absolutely nothing different about the way my brain works than anyone else."

"You've no doubt wondered why this has happened to you. Have you been able to make any sense of it all?"

"Nothing is completely clear to me. The conscious experience is altogether very ambiguous, in my opinion. But there are some notions that I simply can't ignore. I feel that existence, or that is to say, what we know of it, is an extremely small portion of reality. With all the collective knowledge humanity has accumulated, with all of our technology, our medical advancements, satellites, microchips, etc., we're really still in the same predicament that we've always been in."

"And what's that?"

"We still suffer. We still have to die. No prescription can cure that. No computer program can override it."

"Indeed. Well said. And what of this unprecedented supernova that is alleged to appear within the coming days? And what day did you say it would be again?"

"Well, depending on where you are relative to the International Dateline, it would be on the summer solstice, or the day after."

"Now this event seems, at least to me, somewhat different than others you have predicted. I mean, the rest were taking place on our planet. They were things that would directly impact people's lives. But a supernova?"

"That's an interesting point, Tom. But I think the supernova will prove to be very much a symbol of sorts."

"Of what?"

"I believe it will mark the beginning of a new era for humanity."

"What do you feel the next big challenge for the human race will be?"

"To believe."

"In what?"

"Something other than ourselves.'"

Pressing the power button on the remote control, Avery gazed at her swollen abdomen. "Something other than myself, huh? Is that what you're trying to teach me?" She felt another powerful kick. "Ah. I see. Well, you know what? I think you're alright." The obnoxious music from upstairs had finally stopped and the young mother-to-be could almost feel their two hearts beating in harmony. "You're going to have to be patient with me though." She tried to hold back the tears. "Because I have no idea what I'm doing." Another series of kicks came. "You're a boy, aren't you, Ahmyn?" There was a prolonged long stillness, then a light nudge. Avery wiped a tear from the corner of her mouth and smiled. "I've always known. I don't know how. But I've always known. Somehow I feel like you've told me."

Through her window Avery could see a young mother in the neighboring apartment building holding her toddler child. She'd witnessed many times before the mother's frustration as she yelled and sometimes spanked the boy. Now cradling him in her arms, the mother wept. Already feeling quite emotional herself, Avery cried as well and looked on as the mother and her child now laughed and wrestled around on the bed. There was good in the world. It was always there, beckoning, yearning to break through. Surrender was the only requirement.

"Avery?" Allison spoke softly as she cautiously entered the room. "Avery, I need to apologize."

Avery continued to gaze through her window, silently grateful her mother had come to talk. "No, Mom. I'm sorry for being so emotional lately."

Allison walked over and embraced her daughter, stroking her long black hair. "I've been doing a lot of thinking tonight, and I've decided I've been too hard on you." Picking up a black picture frame from Avery's nightstand, Allison placed it on the bed within Avery's view. "Why did you have this face down?"

Delicately running her finger across the glass, Avery flipped it over again. "It's all still too fresh, Mom. I just can't believe he's gone."

"You had so many good memories with Erik though. Don't you think you should focus on those? I've always loved this picture of you two in the entry way on prom night."

"I do focus on them, Mom. But that's the problem. That's what hurts. I wish they were more than memories."

"I think you'll find that in time, those memories will comfort, rather than torture you."

"I hope so. It was different with Dad, for some reason. I missed him so much, and I still do, but it was a different kind of pain."

"Well," Allison sighed, "it was a different kind of affection." Placing her hands on Avery's shoulders, she smiled and just gazed into her daughter's eyes for a moment. "I don't know if I've ever told you this, but Kendra was the most beautiful woman I've ever seen. And you look just like her."

Embracing her mother, Avery began to cry. "Oh Mom. You shouldn't tell a girl things like that. Because then she'll start to believe it."

"But it's true."

"If you say so."

"And I have some news for you."

"You're pregnant?"

"Funny."

"Sorry. Couldn't help it."

"I know. But I'll have you know I just got off the phone with Marnee's father and - "

"Mom!" Avery sat up and gasped.

"And you leave in two days."

"Are you sure, Mom?"

"Don't talk me out of it."

"Right."

"They wanted you for longer, but I would only let you out of my sight for a week. I must be crazy."

"Thanks so much, Mom! Wow. Doesn't the world just seem so beautiful right now?"

"I think this pregnancy is making us both a little loopy, Sweetheart."

"Let's have some ice cream."

"Deal."

CHAPTER 16

"I still can't believe they gave you a ticket for such a late departure," Allison complained as she carried Avery's suitcase out to the waiting taxi. "Don't they know pregnant teenagers become cranky when they don't get their sleep?"

"Very funny, Mom." Avery painfully made her way down the few remaining steps.

"Oh, Sweetheart," Allison exclaimed, looking in disbelief at her daughter's ankles. "I swear those poor things doubled in size since lunch time. And by the way, Princess, who gave you permission to wear my favorite skirt? Hmmm?"

"Well, your closet didn't tell me not to."

"Fine. Just don't ruin it. But seriously, how are you going to get through security? You can barely walk."

"I'll roll through."

"I'd like to see that."

"Well that's just too bad isn't it? Because you're not invited."

"Honestly, Avery. I don't know that you should be doing this."

"Mom, stop it." Pausing briefly, Avery closed her eyes and took a deep breath.

Allison noticed Avery cringing behind her and set the beastly suitcase down with a thud. "What? What is it, Aves? You really don't look good."

"Mom, I'm fine. I just needed to rest for a second." Wincing as she continued down the sidewalk, Avery smiled at the middle-aged taxi driver who was now taking the suitcase from Allison.

"Thanks," Allison said as the driver effortlessly lifted the suitcase without a word and brought it to the open trunk. She then turned back to Avery with her hands on her hips. "I'm just worried about you."

"You're the one who made the arrangements," Avery rebutted. "So just chill out."

"I'd feel much better about you going if I were able to drive you to the airport myself."

"Well, you'll be busy working. So don't sweat it. I'll be fine."

"I can't believe that client called me back. Aves, if I didn't have to be cleaning that office building in a half hour…"

"Please stop worrying so much," Avery glared, kissing her mom's cheek. "You said they're going to pay you well, and we need the money. I'm glad they called you back." Easing herself into the backseat, Avery closed the door, then leaned out the open window. Smiling, she blew her mother a kiss. "Thank you, Mom. I love you."

"Where to, Miss?" asked the driver.

Avery fumbled through her purse to find her ticket. "Haven International."

Allison rushed to the driver window to get his attention. "Now, you're a good driver, right?"

With a slight scowl, he stroked his whiskered cheeks with thumb and forefinger while peering over a pair of thick lenses. "So I've been told."

"Right. Of course you are. I say that because, well, as you can see, my daughter is seven months pregnant, and if there is even a *hint* that she is going into labor, you head straight to the nearest hospital. You got that?"

"Duly noted, m'am," he grumbled, glancing at his watch. "Anything else I should know?"

"Actually, yes. To be perfectly honest, I'd rather she didn't go at all."

"Wait a second. Didn't you call me?"

"Mom!" Avery interupted, "leave the poor man alone and let him do his job!" Leaning up to the front seat, she placed her hand on his shoulder. "I'm so sorry about her. She has issues with separation. Let's please get going."

Tipping his soiled tan hat, he placed the vehicle in gear and started slowly down the street.

"Love you!" Allison called out, watching in angst as the red and white taxi disappeared around the corner. Retrieving the phone from her back pocket, she checked the time. Nine thirty. She had ten minutes to get to work.

∞

Avery awoke to blaring horns from nearby motorists. Her driver, too, was contributing to the racquet. "You've got to be kidding!" he shouted, pounding the steering wheel.

Avery pulled her cell phone from her purse to check the time. Ten fifteen. They'd been driving for approximately forty five minutes now. "Why do you suppose there's so much traffic at this time of night?"

"Beats me, Miss, but we're gonna need to take side roads to get there. I've driven this route plenty of times and it's never been this bad before."

"Do you think I'll be able to make my 12:30 departure?"

"I think so. It'll be cuttin' it close, but I think I can getcha there."

"Thank you, Sir."

"Name's Trevor, Miss."

"Thanks, Trevor."

"Wow, Mom," Avery spoke softly to herself. "Seventeen text messages? Quit freaking out."

Dialing her mother, Avery could see a lightning storm developing on the horizon.

"Please tell me you're okay," Allison blurted into Avery's ear.

"I'm fine, Mom."

"Why didn't you answer any of my texts or calls? I'm freaking out over here."

"Because I'm tired and I fell asleep."

"Has that driver been weird at all?"

"What are you talking about?"

"He kind of gave me the creeps."

"No, Mom. Chill out. Everything's fine. Look, my battery is almost dead. I forgot to charge it before I left."

"You're just trying to torture me, aren't you?"

"Yes. That's my whole purpose in life. So I'm going to turn my phone off to save battery and then call you when I'm seated. Okay?"

"Just please be careful."

"You know me."

"That's what I'm worried about."

"Love you. Bye."

"Love you too."

Having exited the highway at the earliest opportunity, Trevor had now taken them into the heart of an old industrial zone. Avery had never been this far north before. Thunder grumbled and roared with more frequent intervals while rain flung itself into the streets and buildings.

"Where are we?" Avery jumped in her seat as a clap of thunder sounded from particularly close proximity.

"This here is East Bend. A lot of these were munitions factories back during the war. Long before your time, of course. Not a whole lot goin' on 'round here now. What the – ?"

To Avery's confusion and dismay, Trevor pulled to the side of the road and brought the taxi to a halt. Having now exited the vehicle, he was soaked completely through by the time he opened the trunk.

What is he doing? Avery opened her door slightly, trying to let in the least amount of water. The rain was almost deafening. "Trevor! Is something wrong?! What's going on?!"

Holding a car jack and wrench, Trevor walked back around to respond. "Got a flat!" He crouched down and immediately began to work.

"What?! Seriously?! Do I need to get out?!"

"No, no, no! Stay inside! Should be fine!"

Avery slammed the door and sighed as she sat back in her seat. Pulling out her phone to check the time, she was disappointed to discover it wouldn't turn on. What seemed like twenty minutes went by before a completely drenched Trevor closed the trunk and reentered the driver seat.

"Sorry 'bout the delay, Miss," Trevor grumbled as he plopped into the driver seat like an enormous load of wet laundry. "Never a convenient time to get a flat. Let's just hope the stars align for us the rest of the way." He chuckled as he began checking his pockets. "Now where did I put those blasted - "

"GET UP! GET OUT!" boomed a voice from outside the vehicle.

Completely bewildered at what was happening, Avery had witnessed the figure of a man approach and fling open the driver door of the taxi. Trevor was now staring down the barrel of a pistol.

"I said GET OUT! C'mon. Let's go!"

Neither Avery nor Trevor could yet see the man's face. With an iron grip now on his shirt, Trevor was thrown from the car and into the street.

"Stay back!" the man shouted. Now noticing there to be a passenger, he glanced inside and saw a pregnant terrified young woman. "Now, you're a pretty little thing, aren't you?"

Avery's heart was now in her throat. Trevor lunged for the gun and the two struggled fiercely, spinning this way and that, then slamming into the car. The shorter of the two figures was Trevor, whose back was now up against the driver side rear door. Avery's instinct was to flee, but her ankles were on fire, she had no idea where she was, and the man had a gun! She tried her phone again. Still nothing.

CRACK! CRACK, CRACK! Trevor's silhouette collapsed and their aggressor entered the driver's seat, slamming the door behind him. Avery could immediately smell the alcohol. The foul odor pushed her to the verge of vomiting. Breathing heavily, he rummaged for the keys, locating them on the passenger seat.

"So where to, gorgeous?!" he growled, laughing as he turned the key.

Avery's stomach did another somersault.

"Speechless, eh? I guess I've always had that effect on women, now haven't I?" He now had one hand on her thigh, tugging her skirt. "So whatta you say we go somewhere a little more private?"

Struggling to speak, Avery tried to move her leg out of his grip. "I'm just trying to get to the airport."

"I'm awfully sorry, beautiful, but something tells me you're gonna miss this flight." His poisonous crooked smile reaffirmed his intentions.

"Please – don't – hurt – me," she whimpered through rapid short breaths.

"Oh, I think you'll be fine." He smirked, looking directly at her stomach. "Besides, this won't be your first rodeo, now will it?"

She had to make a move. And fast.

He began driving now, pulling slowly down an even darker, narrower street. "This oughtta do just fine, don't you – hey!" He turned around to discover an open door and his prize missing.

Avery hadn't exited the moving vehicle unscathed. She held a hand to her throbbing forehead as she limped for cover. Every stride felt like searing hot coals and her lower back began to tighten under a menacing ache. The darkness and unrelenting rain made it difficult to navigate. Avery made a push toward what appeared to be a medium sized dumpster about twenty meters away. Turning briefly to assess the proximity of her attacker, a pair of headlights emerged in the distance, and the taxi veered clumsily in her direction. Then screaming as she fell, Avery's face was now in the gutter, the impact being absorbed by Trevor's motionless body. Light from the approaching taxi revealed torn flesh across the left side of Trevor's face. Death, Avery feared, was on her own doorstep now. But as the vehicle drew ever closer, she quickly pulled Trevor's arm and torso atop her own body, nestling herself between his lifeless frame and the gutter. Clenching her teeth, Avery endured another wave of agony through her lower back and abdomen.

Badly wounded and panting uncontrollably, Avery was on the brink of complete exhaustion. She felt as though her lungs would burst. Images of her unborn child flashed through her mind. If she couldn't escape, what would become of him? *Are we going to make it? What should I do?* She felt a kick. *You want me to hold still?* Then another. *I'll try.*

The taxi crept slowly by, surpassing Avery by fifteen meters. Then parking, her assailant stepped immediately from the vehicle. Storming down the opposite side of the street, he scrutinized every possible hiding place.

Another paralyzing ache surged down her body. Trying desperately not to cry, Avery groaned through another wave of agony. Then another, and another, each episode slightly surpassing the prior in magnitude. The pain was more excruciating than anything Avery had ever imagined possible. She now threw her head back, screaming in agony. Her unrestrained cries didn't go unnoticed, however, and within moments she was brutally pulled from the gutter by her hair and arm and thrown to the sidewalk.

"And to think you had me convinced I needed to be gentle!"

The blow Avery took from the concrete put her in a delirium as her rhythmic episodes of anguish persisted.

The predator inched methodically toward his helpless prey, slowly drawing a knife. "Rain always makes everything more romantic, don't you think?"

Then with the ferocity of a speeding train and the brilliance of a thousand suns, her assailant was planted permanently on his back. Blood seeped through his crushed skull while smoke rose from charred clothes and scorched flesh.

The explosion left a dull ringing in Avery's ears and her legs were completely numb. Amidst her cries of pain were mingled tears of cautious relief, as it appeared her would-be killer was now dead himself. With the immediate threat to her life gone, she could be more cognizant of the source of the relentless rhythmic contractions in her back and abdomen.

"Ahmyn, you're not supposed to come now!" She moaned under the pain, placing her hands on her belly. "Please not now!" Avery writhed in anguish. "We'll never make it through the night! Somebody please help me!"

The lightning strike had been more than enough stimulation to arouse Trevor from unconsciousness. Upon coming to, he was extremely disoriented, not clearly remembering how he ended up in the street. His chest felt as though a thousand pound weight was crushing him and both sides of his face throbbed incessantly.

The screams from a terrified woman immediately pierced his ears and he labored to raise himself to a crawling position.

"Miss," Trevor groaned, trying to get her attention. The onslaught of rain muffled his weakened voice and every drop felt like a dagger to his maimed face. The situation started to coalesce for Trevor as he pulled himself nearer the girl who now lay four meters away. It was his passenger. He could now see the man he had fought with, dead and disfigured. Certainly she hadn't killed him. Had she?

"Nooooooo! Please no!" Avery wailed.

"Holy crap," Trevor panted. "She's having the baby!" Stumbling to his feet, Trevor rushed to retrieve anything useful from the taxi's trunk and cab. He returned to Avery's side, placing over her a calico blanket he'd found under Avery's purse, as well as forcing a blanket from his trunk under her. "Miss, it's me, Trevor!"

Gritting her teeth, Avery responded with a groan.

Trevor's heart raced as he struggled to hold Avery's feet in place. "Don't worry! I saw this in a movie once!"

Heaving from her hips, Avery felt as though her insides were tearing apart at the seams. As the stinging rain continued to pelt her in the face, one agonizing push after another left her more and more depleted of strength. "Mom! I can't do this anymore! I just – " As Avery pierced the air with one final scream, the rain relented, and a new sound emerged from the chaos.

Gently wrapping the delicate infant in the calico blanket, Trevor tenderly placed the wailing child in his mother's arms.

"Thank you, Trevor," Avery replied weakly as she wept. "He's so beautiful. More beautiful than I could have ever imagined." Now noticing the calico blanket that encircled Ahmyn, Kendra's face flashed in Avery's mind. "You're here," Avery whimpered, closing her eyes. "How did you know where – to find us?"

Carefully lifting Ahmyn from Avery's exhausted arms, Kendra wrapped the calico blanket about the infant more snugly. With the child cradled in one arm, she kissed his tiny forehead, and extended her other hand to Avery, lifting her to her feet.

Kendra's elegant white flowing dress was like nothing Avery had ever seen. It was as though it were made of the sun itself, as if rays of light had been woven into fabric. Now returning the babe into Avery's arms, Kendra kissed her daughter on the cheek and motioned her to follow. As she struggled to keep up with the angel before her, her surroundings began to morph and twist. As though she were looking through a kaleidoscope, images of her own childhood, mingled with visions of Ahmyn's future transformed and dissolved into each other for what seemed like hours.

In time, these scenes began to subside. Uncertain she was dead or alive, awake or asleep, Avery now seemed to be traveling above a speeding red and white taxi. Curious to see who was inside, she approached the window and peered in, only to see Allison pacing back and forth in an office building of sorts, frantically checking her phone. Reaching out to comfort her nerve-racked mother, the scene began to splinter before her eyes as shards of searing light now found her on her back.

Attempting to sit up, Avery was frustrated to find her limbs wouldn't respond. Masked faces were coming in and out of view as she squinted under the imposing light. *Ahmyn! Where's my baby? Where is my baby boy?* She tried desperately to cry out for help, but couldn't make a sound.

"How's her little one fairing?" a scruffy male voice sounded from her left.

"He's doing great," a woman responded. "We're just monitoring his breathing in the nursery."

Relieved at what she overheard, Avery surrendered to the weakness that permeated her muscles. Closing her eyes, all she could see was Ahmyn's face, the great love of her life. Indeed, the one who had saved her.

CHAPTER 17

Allison was staring nervously out the living room window when her phone began ringing. It was a number she didn't recognize. "Hello? Aves?!"

"This is Megan Wright with New Hope Medical Center. Am I speaking with Allison Steward?"

"Yes."

"And you are the mother of Avery Renshaw, correct?"

"Yes. What's happened to her? She was supposed to be on a plane two hours ago!"

"Your daughter was involved in a carjacking incident and is being treated for a concussion."

Allison could feel the blood draining from her face. "You have to be kidding me."

"No. Your daughter is actually extremely lucky to be alive. She's in room 417A."

"I'll be there as soon as I can. Thank you."

∞

"Ouch!" Avery winced as a female nurse repositioned her IV.

"Sorry about that."

"It's fine," Avery whispered. "I guess I'm just a wimp."

"Ha! You're the toughest girl I've ever met. Giving birth on the side of the road after fighting off a rapist? I can't imagine."

"Well, I did have a bit of help." Sitting up in the uncomfortable hospital bed, Avery took another bite of the nearly flavorless chocolate pudding she had recently been given. "When do you think I'll be able to see my baby again? I haven't seen him since – well, since the sidewalk earlier tonight."

"Certainly, I'll go check on that for you right away. He is only four pounds, nine ounces. So he's a bit on the small side. He also needs some assistance with keeping his oxygen levels up. How far along were you, anyway?"

"About seven months."

"Yeah, so he's got some catching up to do. It could potentially be a couple weeks or so before he can go home."

"Really?"

"Yes. But trust me. I've seen much worse. He's actually doing a lot better than a lot of babies I've seen come early. He's a fighter. He'll be fine. We'll have you come say hi to him in a little bit."

"Thank you. I'm glad you feel like he's doing okay. That makes me feel so much better."

"I'm not worried about him. He just needs time. Things got rushed for him, so he just has to catch up. That's all. Oh, and I'm Susan, by the way. If you need anything else, just let me know, okay?"

"Before you go, can you tell me how Trevor is doing?"

"Trevor?"

"Yes. He was the taxi driver who was with me when we were attacked. He must have brought me here."

"Ah. Certainly, yes. I saw the two of you arrive. But honestly, I don't know how *he's* doing. I believe the police took him aside for some questioning, but more than that, I couldn't say."

"That's weird. He was shot in the face. He has to be here somewhere."

"Hmmm." Susan's bright green eyes shifted to the side for a moment. "Well, I *did* get a good look at him, and he didn't appear to have any injuries."

"Are we talking about the right person here? He was shot right in front of me! I saw the whole thing! He saved my baby's life! He needs help!"

"I don't believe he is here, but I'd be happy to leave a general message for him to contact you, if you'd like. And provided he's here, he'll have the info he needs to get back to you."

"Whatever. Fine. Yes. I just wanted to make sure he's okay. That's all."

"Absolutely," Susan smiled as she stepped out the door. "Oh, looks like you have a visitor. Are you Mom?"

"That's me." Allison looked relieved as she entered the room. "Avery, can you get a handle on all these close encounters with death, please?!"

"Hi, Grandma," Avery whispered in her mother's ear as they embraced.

"No!" Allison gasped, gently placing her hands on Avery's belly. "It's way too soon! Is the baby okay?"

"He's okay, Mom. He's fine."

"A boy? Oh, wow. He really is okay? I mean, I just. They scared us both to death with that ultrasound. I've been so worried about it."

"Ahmyn's good. They're keeping an eye on him in the nursery right now."

"I'm so happy, Aves. What a relief!"

"But I do have a bit of bad news for you though."

"What? What now?"

"I ruined your skirt."

Allison rolled her eyes and allowed herself to laugh. "I guess I'm going to have to ground you then." Holding Avery's hands in hers, Allison stared into her daughter's face for a moment.

"Mom, you look like you're going to cry."

"That's because I *am* going to cry. Geez, Avery. Are you okay? What happened to you tonight?"

"I'm fine, Mom." Avery embraced her mother once again, squeezing her tightly.

"Talk to me, Avery. What happened?" Allison wept as she held her daughter. "I feel like such a failure of a mother right now."

"You shouldn't feel that way, Mom."

"I told Kendra I would protect you. I haven't kept you safe."

Placing her hands on Allison's shoulders, Avery spoke firmly. "You have, Mom."

"Ha!" Allison blurted. "Are you kidding me? Everything that shouldn't happen to a person has happened to you! Everything. I swear, the universe is really out to get you! How can a mother possibly keep up?"

"I guess I *am* sort of rambunctious."

"That's an understatement! Carjacking incident? Seriously? You know, something just didn't sit right with me about that taxi driver. The whole thing just didn't seem right."

Avery looked at the floor in silence for a moment and then back at her mother.

"Avery. Please talk to me."

Now on the verge of tears herself, Avery opened her mouth to speak, but there was nothing.

"Ahmyn wasn't born here, was he?"

"No."

"In the taxi?"

"The sidewalk."

"On the sidewalk? Aves, I am so sorry." Allison searched her daughter's face for more answers. "Good grief. You must have been in labor before you even left!"

"No. I don't think so."

"So the carjacker throws a pregnant woman out onto the street to fend for herself? And I'm guessing the upstanding taxi driver didn't help the situation much either."

"He was shot, Mom. He was shot in the face right in front of me."

Placing her face in her hands, Allison slowly shook her head in disbelief.

"He was going to kill me. I could see it in his face the moment he looked at me. But only after he - "

"Oh no. Did he – "

"No. I jumped out of the car to get away, but didn't make it far."

Tears trickled down Allison's face as she listened.

"But then – the most absolutely random thing happened."

"What? What happened?"

"He was actually struck by lightning."

"Lightning?"

"Crazy, right?"

Allison's expression shifted from horror to amazement. "What are the odds?"

"Seriously? I couldn't believe it."

"I don't get it though. Who helped you at that point? Did someone overhear all of this?"

"It was Trevor, Mom."

"Who's Trevor again?"

"The taxi driver. The gunshot didn't actually kill him. He helped me through the labor and drove us here."

"Oh, Avery, I'm so glad you're safe. I'm – I'm kind of in a state of disbelief right now, honestly. Wow. I don't know how you do it, Avery, but somehow you always pull through."

"Wanna know my secret?" Avery donned a playful smile while wiping her eyes.

"What's that?" Allison smiled while wiping her eyes with a tissue.

"It's all in eating a well-balanced breakfast."

Allison chuckled and shook her head.

"Now I'm afraid I can't allow you to eat *this* little guy for breakfast though," Susan announced, pushing a portable incubator. "Say, Big-Shot, do you want to see the women in your life?"

With wide eyes, the infant gazed in his mother's direction.

"Hey, Ahmyn," Avery cooed. "Can I hold him?"

"Of course you can!" Susan replied, opening the incubator. "Just for a couple of minutes though, because he's not going to be able to keep his temp up for long. But look at that head of hair! And what a trooper, too! He's got strong lungs and heart. Like I said before, he struggles a bit with the oxygen levels, but that's common when they come early. We'll probably end up holding onto him a couple weeks, would be my guess. Just to make sure he can maintain temp and keep his oxygen up. But I don't suspect he'll be here long. Oh, and I'm pretty sure he's hungry, Mom, so I brought a bottle."

"He seems a little bigger than I would have expected," commented Allison.

"A little bigger than some," Susan responded. "Just imagine if he'd gone full term."

"What an absolute angel," Allison whispered.

"Isn't he though?" Avery said as she cradled her son against her chest.

"Oh my, Avery. What's wrong with his arm?" Allison said, delicately pulling open the blanket for a closer look.

"There's nothing wrong with it, Mom. It's just a little different, that's all."

"It *is* rather uncommon," Susan interceded, "but he appears to have a moderate case of phocomelia. You'll notice the poor little thing's also missing his right ear."

"I think he's perfect just the way he is," Avery insisted as she tucked the blanket back across his chest.

"You know, I have to say," Susan began, "Ahmyn has had such a calming influence on the other babies. It's really been quite peculiar. He's a very peaceful little guy."

"Well good," Allison smiled. "We could use a calming influence around our place, couldn't we, Aves?"

"I'll go ahead and leave you three be for a few," Susan said, her brown curly hair bouncing with her as she headed for the door. "Be back in about five or so minutes to return him to his incubator and bring him to the nursery."

"Thanks, Susan," Avery called. "Can you believe he's actually here, Mom?" Avery smiled as she kissed her infant's forehead.

"Honestly," Allison said, "I really can't."

"Being here, you know, in this situation, has really made me think of Kendra. I really felt like she's been with me tonight."

"She was an amazing woman, Avery. She really was."

"I wish I could have met her, Mom."

"I wish you could have too."

"It just seems so unfair."

"But when was life ever fair?"

"True," Avery sighed. "Here, Mom. You need to hold him."

Smiling from ear to ear, Allison received Ahmyn with joy. "Hello, you wonderful thing. We're so excited to have you with us. Oh, Avery, look at those eyes."

"I know! They leave you almost speechless, don't they?"

"I don't think I ever told you the last thing Kendra ever said to me and Richard."

"Yeah you did." Avery looked surprised. "She told you to tell me she loved me. Right?"

"She certainly did ask us to do that. Yes. And I told her how scared I was. Your dad and I had no idea how to raise a baby."

"What *did* she say, Mom?"

"I'll never forget it. Right before they wheeled her off for the emergency C-section she said, 'What if I were to tell you that everything is going to be okay?'"

Avery looked stunned. "But I thought she knew she was going to die."

"She did. I think we all did at that point. She was pregnant with you when she arrived in the Republic, you know. Very sick too. So sick. When I saw her for the first time, it was at that bus stop in Center City. It must have been eleven at night. I worried she was dead."

"Honestly, Mom, I've never known anyone who did for anyone what you and Dad did for Kendra. Taking in a perfect stranger like that. I'm so glad it was you and not someone else."

"Looking back, it all seems so amazing, doesn't it?"

"What?"

"I don't know. I guess everything that's lead up to this moment right now. So unlikely, and yet – " Allison gently kissed Ahmyn's hand as he grasped her finger. "But I guess in a way, everything has turned out okay. I mean, how could things not be more okay than they are right now? Life has dealt some blows. There's no doubt about that. But look at this angel, Avery. Where did he come from? He's obviously *supposed* to be here."

"Things do feel okay, don't they? But Mom, didn't you used to say there was no purpose to our existence? How is anyone *supposed* to be here? How was any of this *supposed* to happen?"

"Don't peg that one on me! That was your father! And I believe he said it like this – 'Don't waste your time trying to discover your purpose. All that exists are opportunities.'"

Avery laughed. "That doesn't even make any sense!"

"It made sense to him."

CHAPTER 18

Two doctors stood at the nursery window, observing Ahmyn as he slept.

"It just doesn't make any sense."

"Let's hear it."

"I had Cytogenetics rerun the tests five times because I was convinced they were screwing things up down there. But the data kept coming back the same."

"Well?"

"So get this. He isn't XY or XXY."

"Well he's certainly not touting ovaries."

"No. He's X0!"

"That can't be right."

"I know! But it's true."

"Then where did his testicles and penis come from? The Y chromosome confers maleness."

"X0 males *do* exist."

"Nice try. Not in our species. X0 should be female."

"Well we know of at least one X0 male, now don't we?!"

"What about chromosome eight?"

"Neither parent was a carrier. Chromosome eight is normal."

"But just look at him! That is a textbook phocomelia phenotype!"

"Maybe it's due to the absence of a second sex chromosome."

"There's no way to know."

"It's a shame the ex-boyfriend wasn't the father."

"One can't help but wonder if a male donor even exists."

"Parthenogenesis? Very funny. Put your mind to rest on that subject, Doctor. There is clear heterozygosity throughout his genome."

"Oh, there's a father out there somewhere."

"What I wouldn't do for a drop of his blood."

"This kid is a complete genetic anomaly. It's absolutely mind-numbing."

"Nature's secrets have made fools of us once again."

"Indeed. They truly have."

CHAPTER 19

"Knock, knock," Susan announced while cautiously opening the hospital room door.

"Oh, hi!" Avery called across the room. "Come on in."

"Well I see our little angel has caught on to the nursing thing."

"Yeah," Avery laughed. "It didn't take long."

Taking a seat in a bedside chair, Susan placed a pile of envelopes on the nightstand.

"What's all that? Medical bills?"

"Not yet. Those will actually be sent to your house. It appears, however, you may have become quite the local celebrity, young lady."

"Oh?"

"These look like personal letters. There must be at least thirty of them here! Some of them are even from neighboring provinces."

"Are you kidding me?"

"I know, right? You've been here a grand total of three days and your fan mail is already piling up. Take a look. Here's one from Durham, a couple from Burgandy, a few from Elstadd, and it looks like the rest are from York."

Avery seemed distracted. Standing up, she laid her now sleeping infant in his portable incubator. Then walking back to her bed, she began gazing intently out the window. "Have you noticed that before?"

Susan moved the chair closer to Avery for a better look. "Oh yes! You've got a perfect view of the supernova from your window, don't you?!"

"I'm surprised how bright it is."

"Yes. Isn't it beautiful? I guess they've named it too."

"What did they name it?"

"Grace."

"It's so pretty. It's not like a planet, is it? I've never seen anything like it before."

"They were talking about this on the news. It's a star that basically died. I guess it collapsed on itself and exploded. It was actually first seen the night you got to the hospital – the night you gave birth. Only, it's been so cloudy around here lately, we couldn't see it until today."

"The summer solstice. Just like Darius Viyergo said."

"Yep. That whole thing creeps me out though."

"What creeps you out?"

"I don't know. How he predicts those things. And then they actually happen. It's just weird."

"It is pretty strange," Avery agreed. "How long do you think it will be there?"

"They say it could be twenty to thirty years, I guess."

"Wow."

"I know."

Avery sighed as she glanced over at the pile of letters. "Look at all that mail. I'm really not a huge fan of this sort of attention."

"I suppose you can thank Channel Eight for that. It really is a remarkable story though, Avery. The whole thing is so crazy. It obviously wasn't your time."

Avery stepped past Susan and gazed upon her slumbering child. "In that moment, I wasn't really worried about what was going to happen to me. All I could think about was Ahmyn."

"Absolutely."

"I used to have this nightmare that I was alone and went into premature labor. And in my dream I was so worried about myself, about what was going to happen to me. So weird that it actually happened. Only when it did, the only important thing was that Ahmyn would be okay. Only I had no idea how we were going to escape. I couldn't imagine any possible scenario that would make things alright. I was certain we were both going to die that night."

Tears began to trickle down Susan's face as she listened.

"When I was hiding underneath Trevor's body, even amidst the horrible labor contractions, all I could think about was how I was never going to get to meet Ahmyn. I was never going to get to look into his eyes. I would never hold him, or kiss his precious little face. I'd never hear him laugh or cry. Never have a conversation with him. I loved him so much in that moment that it was as if I had never loved anyone or anything before."

"Oh, Avery," Susan sobbed, "I am so sorry you had to experience this."

"And then when I was thrown onto the sidewalk and watched him pull out that knife, I felt this overpowering peace flood over me. It was so unexpected. So odd to be able to feel that way under those circumstances. I was no longer worried about what was going to happen. In my mind's eye, Ahmyn and I were embracing each other. He was a grown man. It's hard to explain, but in that moment, I was completely happy and at peace. That must sound so strange."

"No, no," Susan replied as she wiped her eyes.

"I'm just so grateful Ahmyn is here, and that he's safe. I just hope I can be the mother he needs and deserves."

"Don't beat yourself up if you never feel quite up to the task. I've been doing the motherhood thing for fifteen years now, and I still feel inadequate at times." Standing up, Susan took a tissue and blew her nose. "And speaking of motherhood, I probably better get going. I've got a hungry pack of teenagers at home to cook for."

"Of course. Seriously, Susan, thanks for everything. You've been so nice to me."

"You're going to be a great mom. Don't ever doubt it. And in case I don't see you before you two check out, good luck. A new normal awaits you."

"Oh, it's new alright! But it certainly doesn't feel normal!"

Susan was nearly to the door, but returned and placed her hands on Avery's shoulders. Looking Avery directly in the eyes, she spoke calmly and assertively. "That little boy of yours is extremely special. This might sound a little out there to you, but when he looks at me…"

"Susan, you're crying again."

"When he looks at me, I – I feel like he knows me. You know? Like – he really understands me. I'm sorry though. How could he? He's just a baby, right?"

"He does seem to have a way with people."

"He's a special boy. And I just know you're going to be a wonderful mother."

"Here," Avery smiled. "Give me a hug. Thanks again. For everything. We'll never forget you."

"I won't be offended if you do, but I'll certainly never forget the two of you."

As Susan departed, Avery looked at her stack of letters with curiosity. Taking an envelope from the top of the pile, she sat on the stiff bed and tore through the seal. As she read, a perplexed look flooded her expression.

'Dear Avery, I have no idea why I'm writing to a person I've never even met, but I just couldn't help it. My name is Laurel and I'm seventeen years old. For the past six months I'd been having this dream – now, this is going to sound crazy to you, so I'm sorry – and the stuff that happened to you the other night, well, it was in

155

my dream. I must have had the same dream twenty times. There was a girl riding in a taxi, and she was wearing a white shirt and a skirt with flowers on it. I could feel how afraid she was, how she thought she was never going to see her mom again. I saw that evil man's heart, and it was the blackest, darkest place imaginable. So awful. But you were protected. Somehow you were spared. And the news didn't say it, but I know he was struck by lightning. That's how he died. He deserved to die.

'I don't know why I had that dream. I almost thought it was something that was going to happen to me. I'm so glad you're okay. I'm sorry, this must sound so off the wall to you. I just know you are supposed to be Ahmyn's mom. I wish you all the best.'

It didn't make any sense. Was this some kind of joke? And how did this random girl know Ahmyn's name? The news must have disclosed it. It was the only explanation. Avery cautiously took another:

'Dearest Avery, first of all, I want to congratulate you on the birth of your son. And in such incredible circumstances! Now, I apologize in advance, because what I'm about to tell you is going to sound unbelievable.

'About thirty years ago I had a dream so vivid and profound that it has never left me. I had shared it with a close friend and over the course of time, we lost touch with each other. She saw the news story a few nights ago and was able to find me online. She directed me where to find the story on the internet so I could see it for myself. I have to tell you, watching that was like dejavu for me. The dream I had thirty years ago was about you! I saw you thirty years ago in my dream. There is no way you should have conceived that child to begin with. But you did. And that taxi driver, Trevor. You saved his life.

'This must sound so odd to you, and I apologize for that. I'm an old woman now, with no children of my own. I hope you'll accept the enclosed amount. I know it isn't much, but hopefully you can acquire some of the necessities for that wonderful child of yours.'

Sincerely,

Enrah Lithgow

Avery picked up her phone and placed a call. "Mom, are you done working yet?"

"Almost, Honey."

"Because I'm kind of freaking out over here."

"Is Ahmyn okay?"

"Yes. It's just that – "

"What is it, Avery?"

"I think I'm losing my mind."

"Not you too."

"What do you mean?"

"You know how I was going to confront Dr. Blaire's office about the completely bogus information they gave us?"

"Yeah. How did it go?"

"Their office is gone."

"What, on a holiday or something?"

"No, Aves. As in the building doesn't even exist anymore. It's just an empty lot now, with a commercial for-sale sign."

CHAPTER 20

Under the windshield wiper of a red and white taxi laid a yellow piece of paper flapping in the wind. Smog filtered the light as the sun crept above the horizon, bathing Chester Street in a deep orange glow. As Trevor awoke, he clumsily raised the driver's seat into the upright position. Seeing the citation, he reached out the open window to retrieve it. *Wrong side of the street, eh? Whatever.*

Tilting the rear-view mirror towards him, Trevor examined his face again. No bullet holes. No wounds. No writhing chest pains. *Did last night even happen? The phone!* Upon removing it from his pants pocket, he immediately saw the shattered screen and bullet hole. *But I was shot in the face too! What is going on?! Did I use last night?* Examining the contents of the glove box, he concluded he hadn't. The heroin and paraphernalia were still there. And there was no urge to use either. The sight of it made him want to vomit.

Driving now to a nearby apartment complex, Trevor parked and popped the trunk. From it he removed a closed box containing a garden hose, duct tape, and a forty-ounce bottle of vodka. Then adding the contents of the glove box with the rest, he walked to a rusting dumpster and threw everything inside.

Everything was different now.

Retrieving his wallet from his back pocket, Trevor removed a worn picture of a woman with two beautiful little girls. *I must be crazy.* Taking a deep breath, he started towards the dilapidated apartment building and made his way up three flights of creaking stairs. There it was. Number three thirty seven. With his heart racing, Trevor reached out and knocked on the door. He was immediately startled by loud barking from inside. *I hope it's not too early. Who am I kidding? I shouldn't even be here in the first place!*

"Angus, shush!" came a girl's voice from inside.

Peering outside to see who it was, the girl immediately closed the blinds. More barking followed. Trevor's heart was now in his throat. *I've made a huge mistake.* Turning to leave, he walked hastily towards the stairs. He then heard a door open and his name called.

"Trevor? Is that you?"

Holding his breath, Trevor paused on the stairs.

"Who's down there?! Trevor, if that's you, you better come back up here and talk to me."

Slowly turning, Trevor prepared for what he might say. "Yes, Gretchin. It's me."

As their eyes met, he wished he could vanish into non-existence.

"Shouldn't I be calling the police right now? Did you forget what the words 'restraining order' mean?" Her stern glare pierced him to the core.

"I'm sorry, it's just that – "

"Oh, and by the way, aren't you supposed to be dead right now?" Taking an envelope from her robe pocket, she proceeded to tear it in half and threw it in his direction. "I got your messed up letter yesterday."

"I see that." Trevor took a few steps closer. "Look, Gretchin, that was all - "

"You're really screwed up, you know that? I'm not responsible for your failures. If you're gonna knock yourself off, leave me out of it."

Maintaining eye contact, Trevor returned no response and picked up the torn envelope from the ground.

"So why didn't you do it? It's not like anyone would've even noticed you're gone."

"It's true."

Lighting a cigarette, Gretchin blew a plume of smoke in Trevor's direction. "So why are you here, Trevor? Do you need money or something?"

"Look, I know I shouldn't be here. I know I've only caused problems for you and the girls."

"Oh, you actually remembered you have daughters? Because you sure didn't remember to show up for either of their births." Leaning against the railing, she took another long drag. "So tell me, Trevor. How old are they? Hmm? What grade are they in?"

Trevor said nothing.

"Do you even know their names? Which one of your girls has Downs? Hmmm? Can you tell me that?"

"I know I'm a poor excuse for a father."

"You're not a father, Trevor. Fathers are there for their kids. Fathers don't spend the grocery money on heroin. Fathers don't leave for weeks at a time without warning." Gretchin took a few strides in Trevor's direction and threw the cigarette in his face. "Father's don't *beat their wives senseless* in front of their kids!"

"Gretchin, I am so sorry."

"No, Trevor. I'm the one who's sorry. I'm sorry I was too weak to get away from you sooner. I'm sorry I ever laid eyes on you. That was the worst mistake I ever made." Gretchin was now twelve inches from Trevor's face. "I used to put up with your crap, Trevor. But not anymore. Don't ever show your face here again. I *mean* that. Leave now. I'm calling the police."

This really was a mistake. Trevor started down the first few stairs and then stopped.

"August eighteenth and February eighth," Trevor spoke softly.

Gretchin's hand was on the door knob, but she paused where she stood. "What?"

"That's what their birthdays are. August eighteenth and February eighth." Trevor's voice quivered as he turned to face her again.

As Gretchin cocked her head and glared back at him, she could see fresh tear streaks on Trevor's face.

"Bailey is eleven and Kenna is nine. Bailey's in sixth grade and Kenna's in third."

Releasing her grip from the door knob, Gretchin turned to fully face him.

"Bailey's favorite color is yellow and her favorite animals are whales. Kenna says she doesn't have a favorite color, is deathly afraid of cats, and bear-hugs everyone she meets for the first time."

Gretchin's expression of disgust began slowly to give way to genuine surprise.

"Bailey loves math, but hates reading. Despite Kenna's disability, she's a gifted artist. She mainly draws faces of people we've never seen. She calls them her helpers. I've had one of her sketches in my wallet for over two years, and I've looked at it every day."

"Alright, Trevor. I'll admit that was slightly impressive." Pushing some of her shoulder-length red hair behind her ear, Gretchin lit another cigarette. "But do you want to cut to the chase and explain why you came here in the first place?"

"Gretchin, something has happened to me. I don't know exactly how to explain it though."

"Let me guess. You woke up this morning and realized what a screw-up you've chosen to be? That's great and all, but that doesn't really change anything, does it?"

"Remember that dream you used to have all the time? Back around when we were first married?"

Gretchin looked at the ground as she took another drag. "Maybe, yeah. What about it?"

"There's only one face that Kenna has drawn more than once, right? And you've commented on how it looked exactly like the girl from your dream, right?"

"I guess so. Sure."

"It's one of those sketches that I've kept in my wallet all this time."

"Trevor, you're starting to ramble and I'm losing interest very quickly."

"Gretchin, that girl is a *real* person. I saw her last night."

"What are you talking about? Did you see her at a strip club or something?"

"I'm trying to be serious here. Gretchin, your dream came true last night."

"You're high-as-a-kite right now, aren't you?"

"Ironically, no. Last night was the night, Gretchin. I was gonna check out for good. Had everything I needed. But for some crazy reason, I decided to do one last run. Got a phone call for someone who needed a ride to the airport. And then it's *her*! Down to the very last detail!" Walking back up the stairs, Trevor hurriedly removed the tattered sketch from his wallet and pointed at it. "This girl got in my taxi last night. I seriously couldn't believe my eyes. Gretchin, she even had the blue streak in her hair, and the nose ring, and – "

"Trevor, do you have any idea how crazy you sound right now?"

"Do you see this?" Trevor pulled out his destroyed phone and held it out. "I was shot point blank in the face last night trying to protect that girl and her baby. If I'd never known about your dream, she would've just been another girl off the street. I would've watched the carjacker drive off with her inside. I stuck my neck out for her because of your dream."

Gretchin was intrigued, yet skeptical. "Carjacker? Shot in the face? You look fine to me."

"This is part of why it's so hard to explain. The bullet had torn through both cheeks and it had to have taken out teeth too. But somehow, through the intense pain in my face, I was able to help her give birth. Right there on the sidewalk, Gretchin! Right in the middle of the pouring rain! It was nuts! And then the moment I had that infant in my hands – " Trevor paused and began to sob. "The moment I held him – the pain – the pain was gone. Completely gone. I don't know why. I don't know how. But the pain was taken from me. By the time we got to the hospital, my face – my face was completely healed. It was as if it never happened. Like I'd never been shot."

Gretchin stared at Trevor in bewilderment.

"And the best part, Gretchin, is that my addiction – my addiction is – gone. I don't know what's happened to me. But it's like – it's as if – I've woken up."

"Daddy!" Kenna announced from the door. Holding a piece of paper, she ran up to Trevor, giving him a firm bear-hug. "My helpers!! Drew last night!"

Gretchin and Trevor looked in amazement at the life-like sketch. It was a young woman with a blue streak in her hair, a nose ring, and a baby in her arms.

CHAPTER 21

"And you're certain there aren't any other newscasts about this?" Allison said, her cellphone tucked between her shoulder and ear while she searched online.

"Yes, ma'am," came the reply. "Have you tried any of the other stations? I know we weren't the only ones who caught wind of it. Craig Burton was up there on York's most-wanted list, after all."

"I've called them. Didn't really come up with anything though. Sorry to bother you. Thanks for your time."

"Still nothing, huh?" Avery asked, bouncing her tiny infant on her shoulder for a post-feeding burp attempt.

"Nope," Allison sighed, setting down her phone and closing the silver laptop. "I honestly don't know what to tell you."

"Do you see how crazy this is, Mom?" Laying Ahmyn in his light blue bassinet, which was lined with the famed brown calico blanket, Avery plopped her exhausted body on the couch. "How could anyone who didn't know us possibly know his name? Folks living thousands of miles away?"

"I don't know, Aves."

Momentarily stepping outside, Allison reentered the apartment with her arms full. "Do you think it will ever stop?!" Allison chuckled in disbelief as she unloaded two jumbo-sized packages of diapers onto the growing pile of gifts in the corner. Heaps of formula, diapers, blankets, and clothes were stacked with myriad other baby toys, carriers, bouncers and the like, most of which had been anonymously left on their porch over the past two weeks in the middle of the night. "Thank social media, right?"

"I can't believe this," Avery said, watching her mother return to the porch for more.

Moments later, Allison dropped a stack of letters onto the table, then brought another baby-bouncer to add to the collection.

Plodding over to the table, Avery began sifting through the mess of over two hundred letters she hadn't had the time to read. "Do you think we can ask the hospital to stop forwarding them?"

"Well, what are they supposed to do with them?" Allison queried as she secured the deadbolt with a click.

Slumping into a rickety pine thrift-store chair, Avery pushed the pile of envelopes away and laid her head into her arms. "I don't know. Send them back, maybe. Or throw them away. I don't care."

"Well, we could ask them to do that," Allison conceded, taking an adjacent seat. "But some of them have had money in them. It would be kind of wasteful."

"I guess you're right. All of this is just a bit too much for me though, Mom. I don't know how to respond to all of this."

"People are just trying to help."

"It's not like I'm not grateful for the stuff. I am. I really am. It's just − I just. I don't even know these people!" Waving her hand across the table, Avery grabbed a handful of letters and began thumbing through the names. "These people have no idea who I am, and they're writing me letters! Most of them say they've had *dreams* about me. *Dreams*! It's creepy. They know things that only *I* should know. And that one lady − one of the letters I received while I was still in the hospital − she said she dreamed about me before I was even born! Mom, it's − bizarre!"

"I can't disagree with you." Placing her pale freckled face in her hands, Allison inhaled deeply and smiled at her daughter.

"Stuff like this isn't supposed to happen to people. It's just − weird!"

"Truth is stranger than fiction sometimes, Aves. It really is."

"It's like we've been sucked into the Twilight Zone, or something."

"I'm just glad our little one-armed wonder is okay."

"Don't call him that, Mom. You'll give him a complex."

"Oh, stop it." Allison said as she stood. Stepping to the bassinet, she scooped up her stirring grandson and landed a wet kiss on his silky bronze cheek. "He knows he's my favorite person in the whole world." Rocking him gently, she tilted her head downward and kissed him again. "And just look at that delicious head of hair. So handsome. He's definitely got your nose, Aves. Look at that little baby button nose!"

Now standing at her mother's side, Avery rested her head on Allison's white shirt sleeve. "He really is our little wonder, isn't he?"

"Don't you think he just looks so – I don't know – wise?"

"He really does," Avery smiled, delicately stroking his thick black hair. "The moment I laid eyes on him, I just had the sense that – that he knew why he was here. It's like he knows something we don't."

"You're going to make a difference in this world, Ahmyn. You know that?" Allison whispered.

Wiping a tear from her cheek, Avery ladled her child up from his grandmother's arms and kissed his forehead. "He already has."

CHAPTER 22

"So, I'm sure this machine looks familiar," said Kristin Cooper, a red-headed radiology tech at New Hope Medical Center.

"Yes," Avery agreed. A wave of angst swayed through her as she eyed the imposing x-ray machine. It was bringing back the initial shock of the news she'd received ten months prior. "I remember it well."

"We're glad you were able to make it in," Kristin smiled, her blue eyes sparkling in the fluorescent light. "It will just be good for the doctor to check on the rod he fused to your spine. You know, just make sure everything is looking the way it should."

"Alright, then," Avery said, pulling her blue-streaked ebony hair into a ponytail. "Shall we get this over with?"

"Absolutely." Ushering Avery onto the machine's hard bench, Kristin placed a thick heavy pad onto her lap. "Alright, so just straighten your posture just a bit and hold onto these grips. Perfect. Just like that. Hold that position and I'll go start the machine. This will be really quick and easy. I promise." Walking to the opposite side of the room, Kristin typed a few commands into the computer and placed her hand over the mouse. "Okay, on three, two, one."

Holding her breath, Avery closed her eyes as the white mechanical arm hummed around her torso.

"All done," Kristin announced. "I'll take that pad, and then you can just hang out on one of those cushy chairs over there while I grab Dr. Oughten."

"Sounds great." Stretching as she stood, Avery sauntered over to a brown leather loveseat and nestled into the overstuffed cushions. Pulling out her phone, she shot off a text to Allison. 'How's Ahmyn doing? Is he behaving for you?'

Moments later, a short ting emanated from her pink phone. 'He's doing pretty well. Not a big fan of the bottle though. Not quite the same as the real thing, I guess.'

'I'm not sure how long this is going to take, so I'm sorry if he starts throwing a fit.'

'No prob. Love you Aves.'

'Love you guys. Kiss my baby for me.'

'Will do.'

When the doctor arrived ten minutes later, Avery had dozed off with a copy of Hiker's Extreme open on her lap.

It was a face Dr. Oughten would never forget. The girl who had defied death. Such a fascinating case. The pregnancy, above all else, had perplexed him every day since. Had it really been ten months? Yes. Yes, it had. Recalling that memorable conversation he'd had with the girl's mother, he began pouring over the vexing images displayed on the computer monitor.

"Is there anything I can help you with before I take lunch?" Kristin chimed, leaning in from the hall.

"Yes, actually," Dr. Oughten responded incredulously, turning to face her. "These can't be the correct x-rays."

Joining him at the computer, Kristin looked at the time stamps on the images, and glanced at the time displayed on the bottom right corner of the computer monitor. "No. Those are them. Those are the ones. I just took them. See the times?"

"The software must be glitching or something," Dr. Oughten insisted. "If these are her x-rays, then I'm missing something."

With wide eyes, Kristin cocked her head to one side. "The rod."

"Exactly. I'm going to need you to redo these. Because this just doesn't make any sense."

"Absolutely." Padding across the room, Kristin placed a hand on Avery's shoulder. "Avery?"

"Oh," Avery gasped and pushed herself up in her seat, glancing rapidly around the room. "I fell asleep. Sorry."

"I'm so sorry, Avery, but I just need to have you x-rayed one more time. Something went wrong with capturing the image properly."

"Sure. No problem."

Standing by as Kristin repositioned Avery on the x-ray machine, Dr. Oughten watched closely as the x-rays were captured again. "Okay," he said, gazing intently at the screen. "This is just weird. We're going to need to try something. Avery, can I just have you sit tight for a few minutes?"

"Oh no!" Avery chuckled. "Did I break it?"

"I'm afraid so," he smiled, now turning to Kristin. "I need you to go retrieve a titanium rod from the supply room. I'm going to call Parker and let him know you're coming."

"Sounds good," Kristin agreed as she scurried into the hall.

"The machine is acting up, Avery. Which doesn't really make sense, but when Kristin gets back in a few minutes, we'll have a better idea of what's going on. If you'll excuse me, I just need to make a quick call."

Avery shrugged. "Okay."

"Oh, and go ahead and take a seat over there for a couple minutes. No need to hang out on that cold bench."

While Dr. Oughten informed the supply room Kristin was on her way, Avery tapped and slid her finger on the sleek surface of her phone, perusing her FlashBack page. There were quite a few comments about the most recent picture she'd posted of her blowing raspberries on Ahmyn's chubby belly, his face aglow with laughter.

"So, Avery," the doctor said, approaching from the doorway, "how are things going at home?"

Setting her phone aside, Avery looked up and smiled. "Oh, I guess they're going pretty well. Having a baby now sure changes things, that's for sure."

"I know what you mean. It definitely takes some time to get into the swing of things. So, boy or girl?"

"A boy. Ahmyn." With her right index finger she pointed to the inside of her left forearm where his name was emblazoned in cursive.

"Nice. I like the name. Very nice." Squinting his hazel eyes, he scrutinized her face for a moment.

"What?" Avery blushed, wiping her cheeks. "Do I have some breakfast on my face or something?"

"No, I was just admiring how well the stitches on your forehead have healed. I don't even see a scar. Are you wearing any makeup?"

"Some mascara and eyeliner."

"And nothing else, right?"

Feeling the blood continue to rush to her cheeks, Avery remained silent.

"Sorry," the doctor said, examining her forehead even closer, "I'm not trying to embarrass you or anything like that. I've just never seen anything heal up so well before."

"I've got it," Kristin announced, holding up a narrow shiny cylinder.

Wheeling around, Dr. Oughten stretched out his massive hand and retrieved it from her. "Very good. Thank you."

"What are we going to do with it?" Kristin said, adjusting the legs of her green scrubs to sit more evenly atop her white sneakers.

"Grab some tape, if you would, please. And then Avery, we're going to have you resume your place on the bench you're becoming so well-acquainted with today."

Following the doctor's directive, the two young women did as they were asked. Tearing off a few pieces of masking tape from the roll, Dr. Oughten began to adhere the titanium rod to Avery's right shoulder blade. After placing the protective pad once again upon his patient's lap, he walked as briskly to the computer as his wide frame would allow. "Okay. Three, two, one."

With a furrowed brow, Kristin peered around the doctor's left, trying to get a closer look at the screen. Stepping away from the monitor, Dr. Oughten closed the door. "Avery, if it's alright with you, we really need to take a look at your back for a moment."

"Sure," Avery consented.

"Just stay where you are, Avery. Kristin is just going to lift your shirt in the back. I just need to briefly examine the surgery site."

The air seeping in from the vent above felt cool on Avery's exposed skin. "Do you see anything wrong with my scar?"

"That's just it," Dr. Oughten sighed, removing the taped rod from her shirt.

"There is no scar," Kristin said in disbelief, gently pulling Avery's blue T-shirt back down.

"And no rod," Dr. Oughten added.

"What do you mean, no rod?" Avery questioned, standing up. "I don't understand."

"Come take a look for yourself." Leading the pair to the computer, he pointed to the screen. "These here are the x-rays taken two months after the initial surgery. You can see the rod we fused right here. It's very conspicuous."

"I see it," Avery said calmly.

"Well," the doctor continued in his deep voice, "these are the x-rays from today. These are the first images Kristin captured. As you can see, there's a significant difference. I obviously couldn't take them seriously. So we did it again. See here? Still, the rod in your back isn't showing up."

"Well that doesn't make any sense," Avery commented, staring at the screen.

"That's why I had Kristin get this titanium rod. I needed to see if the x-ray would pick it up. See these images here?"

"It shows up right where you taped it," Avery said, still trying to piece it all together.

"What I'm trying to say here, Avery, is that – "

"What?"

"The rod I fused to your spine – is gone."

Avery stared blankly up into his hazel eyes.

"It's like it was never there."

"How could it not be there anymore? It couldn't have dissolved, could it?"

"It wouldn't have dissolved. No. You have no scars from your accident. No rod in your back." Taking a step back, he took a long breath. "Honestly, I'm at a complete loss."

"I'm extremely confused right now," Avery said.

"It's like the accident – it's as if – well, like – like it never happened."

"How can that be?" Kristin asked.

"Seriously," Avery said, looking back at the screen. "I don't get it."

"To be frank," the doctor said, placing the titanium rod on the desk, "I have no explanation for it. In any case though, I guess we won't need to be checking up on your back anymore."

∞

Hinges squeaked as Avery closed the front door to the apartment. "Mom?"

Holding her finger over her lips, Allison tiptoed out of Avery's room and down the hall to greet her daughter.

"Thank you for watching him," Avery said softly, embracing her mother.

"He was an angel, as usual," Allison sighed. "I love that baby so much." Now heading for the kitchen, Allison pulled a plate from the fridge. "I made you a sandwich. Thought you'd be hungry."

"You're the best," Avery said, sitting down at the table. The turkey bacon and tomato sandwich was really hitting the spot. "So good, Mom. Thank you."

"You're welcome," Allison smiled, taking a seat on the opposite side of the small table. "So, how did it go?"

Setting down her sandwich, Avery seemed very reflective. "A little too well, actually."

"What? Did the doctor propose to you or something?" Allison chuckled.

"Funny," Avery smirked as she took another bite of her sandwich.

"Well, then what was so amazing about it?"

Closing her eyes, Avery took a deep breath and placed her sandwich on the yellow stoneware plate. "I don't know what's going on, Mom. All I have is questions. No answers."

"Aves," Allison sighed longingly, "what is it?"

"The scar on my back," Avery said softly. "Look at it."

"What? Is it infected or something?" Carefully lifting the blue cotton shirt, Allison traced her finger lightly across where the surgery site had been. "I don't understand. Where's the scar?"

"Better yet," Avery continued, "where's the titanium rod?"

"What do you mean?" Pulling Avery's shirt back down, Allison took a seat beside her bewildered daughter. "Did it detach or something? I don't get it, Aves. Just what is going on?"

173

"They took x-rays, Mom, and there's nothing there. The rod is gone. The scar is gone. It's like it never happened."

Looking intently into Avery's deep brown eyes, Allison slowly shook her head. "But that's not possible. It isn't possible, Avery. They obviously don't know how to operate their own equipment."

"No, Mom. They do. Doctor Oughten didn't think the machine was working properly either at first. But they taped a titanium rod to my back and took an x-ray and it showed up."

Placing her pasty white elbows on the worn down card table, Allison rested her face in her palms and stared blankly at the wall. "You are quite the intriguing young woman, aren't you, Sweetheart?"

"I don't know," Avery responded, placing a bacon crumb onto her tongue.

"You gave birth, for crying out loud. That never should have happened. But it did. And now you're spontaneously healing? People we've never met have had dreams about you? I think we need to start documenting this stuff."

"What do you mean? Like in a blog or something? I've thought about it. I don't know though. People will think I'm nuts. I feel like I've had enough of that scene. You know?"

"No. No. For some reason the internet doesn't seem like a good place for it. A journal. A diary. It would be good to look back on. We should both do one."

"Sure. Why not? Couldn't hurt, right? Do older folks really go back and read the journals they've kept?"

"I think so. But I think journals are more for others to read. To benefit from." Walking quietly down the hall with Avery closely behind, Allison placed a hand on the doorframe to Avery and Ahmyn's room and looked longingly at the sleeping child within. "The whole world will know his name, Avery."

174

Leaning her head on Allison's shoulder, Avery watched her son's chest rise and fall with each tiny breath. "Why do you think that? What if I don't want everyone to know who he is? How am I supposed to keep him safe if that happens?"

"If there's one thing I've learned through raising you," Allison continued, clasping her daughter's hand, "it's that a parent has very limited control over the future. I would have protected you from so much more, Avery. There is just so much that's out of our control."

"Even though I know you're right, I still don't like the way it sounds. I don't want Ahmyn to suffer. I just want to keep him by my side and protect him from the world. He's so tiny and precious."

"As much as a parent feels they can do for their child, we all know our children have done far more for us than we ever did for them. I think Ahmyn is going to teach us things, Avery. He's going to show us things we can't do without."

With her heart racing at her mother's words, Avery stepped toward the edge of the pine crib. Reaching for Ahmyn's cheek, she brushed her finger delicately across his silky skin and whispered. "Who are you, my love? And what have you come to teach us?"

CHAPTER 23

With legs crossed and a copy of Motherhood Magazine in hand, Avery sat in the waiting area of the pediatrician's office. She couldn't help but smile at her sleeping infant. Ahmyn had recently decided he was fond of his thumb, and was munching on it as he slumbered. Taking a mental note of the time, Avery would remember that two o'clock seemed to be the time to visit the doctor; besides herself, there was only one other mother and child waiting to be seen.

As she perused her magazine, Avery observed the kindergarten-aged girl across the room, about eight meters away, playing with some wooden blocks. Her hair was a glistening strawberry blonde and braided in pig-tails.

"Can I just comment on how gorgeous your daughter's hair is?" Avery smiled.

Looking cautiously upward, the twenty-something blonde with green eyes smiled, revealing some of her ill-cared-for teeth. "Thank you. She'll appreciate that." As the young woman spoke, she was signing in unison to her daughter, who watched intently with bright eyes. The two carried on a silent dialogue for a minute or so, the little girl's mother occasionally vocalizing remarks as she signed. "I don't know if that's such a good idea. I know, I know. Honey, I think you should just play with your blocks though. The baby's probably sleeping, sweetheart."

Avery smiled warmly at the little girl. "Does she want to come and say hello to my little guy?"

"I told her we really shouldn't be bothering you," the woman responded. "I'm sorry. Don't mind us."

"It's okay. He's been sleeping for a while. She can come say hi."

"I don't want to impose. We're just here for a couple of vaccinations though. She's not sick or anything."

"Not at all. What's your daughter's name?"

"Misty."

"Misty," Avery motioned, "Ahmyn would love to say hello to you!"

Signing to her daughter, the woman gave her consent.

With her buoyant pig-tails bouncing with her, the girl jumped to her feet and scurried over to the car seat where Ahmyn slept. Squealing in delight, Misty signed to her mother how cute Ahmyn was.

"I'm sure he *is* beautiful, just like his mother," the woman responded. "But remember that he's sleeping. Try not to wake him up!"

Ahmyn had been slightly startled by Misty's audible excitement and began to open his large, dark gray eyes. Stretching his little body, he let out a grunt and then made a connection with the lively green eyes staring at him from barely half a meter away. Excitedly signing something else to her mother, Misty then turned to Avery and started signing to her.

"Alright," the young mother responded. "I better come have a look at him. And Misty, I'm sure she doesn't want you to tickle her sleeping baby!"

"Actually, his feet *are* pretty ticklish," Avery smiled. "Go ahead and tease him a little. It's okay."

"If you say so," the woman chuckled. "Misty, she says it's okay. Gosh, I'm really sorry about her."

"Don't be. Ahmyn's a pretty social baby."

Kicking his chubby legs, Ahmyn let out a boisterous belly-laugh as Misty danced her fingers along the soles of his feet.

"See!" Avery exclaimed. "He likes the attention."

"Oh, sweetheart," the woman began as Misty signed, "that's very nice of you to say. She says she wishes he was her little brother."

Avery smiled. "And I'm sure he would love it if you were his sister."

"I really don't know what's gotten into her. She's normally not this outgoing. I'm so sorry. Misty!"

Pulling gently on Misty's arm, the embarrassed mother tried to prevent her daughter from planting a big wet kiss on Ahmyn's cheek. Her attempt was unsuccessful, however, and Ahmyn grinned from ear to ear at the display of affection. Avery couldn't help but laugh.

Taking a small step back, Misty stood still and watched him for a moment. Tilting her head to one side, she had a look of intent contemplation. Keeping her eyes fixed on Ahmyn's, she then tilted her head slightly in the opposite direction and furrowed her brow. It appeared almost as if she were trying to make sense of something the infant was saying. Then, to the bewilderment of her mother, the young girl approached Ahmyn slowly, bringing the left side of her head just within his reach. Pushing the pig-tail behind her left ear, Misty paused just inches away from Ahmyn's face. Extending his tiny arm, the boy placed his hand upon her ear and held it there for a moment. The two perplexed adult women watched on as the little girl turned herself about and presented her right ear to the boy, who repeated the same simple motions.

Raising a hand to each side of her head, Misty began to touch both ears simultaneously. With eyes wide with amazement, the girl pulled gently on each ear, rapidly looking around the room.

"What did he tell you?" Misty's mother inquired as she signed.

Misty shrieked in excitement while pointing at her mother's face. Then startled by a similar stimulus that seemed to emanate from her throat, she quickly cupped her hands over her mouth in surprise. Removing her hands slowly from her lips, she cautiously began to experiment.

"Aaaaaaaahhhhhh," came the noise from Misty's mouth. "Aaaahhhh oooooohhh aaaahhh oooohh eeeeeee oooohhh eeeeee."

In silent bewilderment, the girl's mother watched in complete awe, with mouth agape. What had just happened?

Suddenly whirling around, Misty fixed her attention on another young mother entering the office with her infant. A bell attached to the door made a glorious reverberation throughout the room as it opened and closed. Squealing in delight, Misty darted to the door. Laughing and gazing up at the bell as she did so, she began repeatedly opening and closing the door. Her astounded mother remained speechless and completely still as she tried to make some logical sense of what she was seeing.

Avery was nearly as stupefied at the scene as the girl's astonished mother. What on earth was going on? With her mind racing, Avery looked slowly down at Ahmyn, who was sucking his thumb and gently kicking his legs.

Rising clumsily to her feet, Misty's now extremely pale-faced mother walked slowly to the receptionist's desk.

"Kammie, are you alright?" asked the receptionist. "You look like you're not feeling too well."

"You guys have one of those instruments that tests how well a person can hear, right?"

"Yes. Yes we do."

"I know this sounds crazy," she mumbled as she turned to look at Misty, "but I think my deaf daughter can hear."

CHAPTER 24

"We're so glad you guys could make it," Allison said as she opened the door. "Come on in! It's hot outside!"

"It's not much better in here!" Avery called from the kitchen. "I'll be right out you guys, just washing my hands!"

"I sure hope we're not crashing the party," Gretchin said nervously as she ushered her daughters inside.

"Consider this a thank you party."

"Hey, ladies!" chimed Avery as she entered the balloon-filled living room. "Trevor's coming too, right?"

Gretchin was stunned as the girl she had dreamt of so many times rushed to greet her. "He's actually just grabbing a few things out of the car. He'll be right in."

"It's so good to finally meet you," Avery said as the two embraced.

"Oh my!" Allison exclaimed as she received the strongest hug of her life. "You must be Kenna!"

"Hello, Bailey," Avery said as she extended her hand.

"Hi." Bailey attempted not to smile, trying to conceal her new braces.

"What about my hug, Kenna?" Avery said with her arms out.

"Helper!" Kenna exclaimed as she nearly tackled Avery to the ground.

"What gorgeous girls, Gretchin!" Allison declared.

"I like to think they got their looks from me," Trevor announced as he struggled to carry a present and a child carrier up the door step. "Seeing as Gretchin still has *hers*."

"Good grief, Trevor!" Avery said with her hands on her hips. "Nobody said anything about being on number three!"

"That's actually our nephew, Evan," Gretchin clarified. "I watch him for my sister on Wednesdays and Fridays."

Allison looked puzzled. "He's a bit big for a child carrier, isn't he?"

"He's disabled," Gretchin began. "That's actually a special transport for quadraplegics."

"Oh my goodness," Allison said in embarrassment. "I'm so sorry. How old is he?"

"He's three."

"Yep," Trevor confirmed. "He's our little miracle man."

"Speaking of little miracles, where's the birthday boy?" Gretchin asked.

Avery smiled and pointed to a play-pen in the corner of the room. "Snoozing over there."

"Oh gads, and here we are making all this noise," Gretchin blushed.

"Ahmyn sleeps like a rock, so don't sweat it!" Avery insisted.

"Oh good. I'd hate to wake the little guy."

"We need to get him up anyway," Allison pointed out. "Here, guys, why doesn't everyone have a seat?"

"I'll grab a few more chairs," said Avery as she walked into the kitchen.

"Yes," Allison affirmed. "Please make yourselves comfortable. I'm going to tend to the food for a minute."

The Hansen family took a seat on a tattered brown leather couch, adjacent to the play-pen where Ahmyn slept.

"Are those two birds finches?" Bailey asked, pointing to the cage hanging in the opposite corner. "They're cute."

"Those *are* finches," Avery confirmed as she set up two folding chairs. "Do you like birds?"

"Yes," Bailey replied. "I actually did a science report on finches last year."

"That's awesome! What grade are you in?"

"Seventh."

"And what about you, Kenna?"

"She's in fourth," Bailey answered for her sister, who was crouched down and peering through the mesh of the play-pen.

"Ahmyn, wake up!" Kenna yelled.

"Kenna!" Gretchin snapped. "Let him sleep."

"It's fine," Avery smiled as she walked over to retrieve Ahmyn. "He's been sleeping long enough."

Reaching into the play-pen, Avery gently lifted her son and held him close. "C'mon my little goose-monkey. It's time to wake up. Some new friends want to meet you, buddy."

Ahmyn grunted softly and let out a peep as he yawned, his left hand extended as he stretched.

"What an absolute darling," Gretchin commented.

"I love his long curly hair," Bailey added.

"Yeah," Avery agreed. "We like to leave it long. You gonna wake up for us, Ahmyn?"

"What happened to his right arm?" Bailey questioned.

"Bailey!" Gretchin glared at her daughter, "that is *extremely* rude."

"Sorry."

"Don't feel bad about being curious," Avery said as she stroked Ahmyn's hair. "He was born like this. But he gets along just fine." Avery made momentary eye contact with Trevor and then continued, "Did you girls know your Dad was there the night Ahmyn was born?"

"Yes," Bailey answered. "That was when he got shot. But his phone stopped the bullet."

"If your dad hadn't been there, I don't know what Ahmyn and I would have done. We would have been all alone."

Ahmyn's stormy gray eyes were now open and alert. As Avery set him on the floor, he began shuffling on his rump in Evan's direction.

"Now that's a clever way to get around!" Trevor commented as everyone giggled.

Evan smiled as Ahmyn approached him. As the two looked at each other, it seemed they were having an in-depth discussion. Their silent conversation persisted for a few minutes as everyone quietly watched. Then using Evan's carrier to prop himself up, Ahmyn took the boy's hand in his. The room was completely silent. Gretchin then placed a hand over her mouth and watched in disbelief as Evan's hand clasped Ahmyn's thumb.

"Trevor, are you *watching* this?" Gretchin gasped. "Are you *seeing* this?"

Maintaining his grasp on Ahmyn's thumb, Evan's skinny, red-socked feet then began to move and stretch, along with his legs. Gretchin could barely breathe. Allison watched in astonishment from the hallway. Kenna knelt beside the carrier and then reached for Evan's other hand, which he took. Gently pulling, Kenna raised her cousin from his seat and embraced him. Ahmyn then plopped onto his bottom and scooted over to his speechless mother while Kenna helped Evan sit on the floor.

Then moving slowly, Evan stumbled into a clumsy crawling position. Placing one hand, then leg in front of the other, Evan began to advance across the floor in Ahmyn's direction, who watched and smiled.

"Thhhhhh," Evan muttered as he crawled. "Thhhhhh – aaaaaank – yyyyyooouu." They were the first words Evan had ever uttered.

Ahmyn took a few shuffles to meet him. Then placing his hand on the boy's right cheek, he too spoke for the first time.

"Evan. Walk."

As for the birthday party, it was no different than most. There was food, soda pop, ice cream, and laughter. Ahmyn covered himself from head to foot in his very first birthday cake. Pictures were taken.

Good-byes were said and the Hansen family began to depart. Kenna handed Avery a worn and folded piece of paper, then insisted on kissing everyone before she left. Outside, Bailey held Evan's hand, who clumsily walked beside her to the car.

Later that night, as Avery was preparing Ahmyn for bed, Allison methodically sipped a cup of black tea. She was mesmerized by a somewhat worn piece of paper hanging on the fridge – a very life-like colored pencil sketch, depicting Ahmyn and Evan on the floor together, with Ahmyn's hand on the boy's cheek.

CHAPTER 25

"Ahmyn, Sweetheart," Avery said calmly, gently nudging her slumbering child. "It's time to wake up."

In a cocoon of blankets, the five-year-old made no inclination of consciousness.

Arising from his bedside, Avery walked to the doorway and flicked on the light. Then running her fingers through Ahmyn's jet-black shoulder-length hair, she could hardly believe this day had actually arrived. "We have to get up, Sweetie," Avery continued, jostling him a bit more this time. "It's your first day of school."

Growling like a frustrated puppy, Ahmyn turned slowly toward his mother and shielded his eyes. "Hi, Mom," he managed.

Kissing his forehead, Avery resumed combing his long hair with her fingers. "Good morning, Sweetheart. It's your big day today."

Wide eyed and grinning, Ahmyn commenced wiggling free of his white sheet and cartoon-themed comforter. "Are we leaving right now?" he said excitedly.

"Almost," Avery assured. "We still need to get dressed and eat some breakfast first." Standing up, she pointed to the foot of the bed. "I've laid out some clothes for you to choose from. Grandma wants you to wear these pants, and then you can decide between these two shirts, okay?"

"Okay, Mom," Ahmyn agreed as he stood and rubbed his eyes.

"Do you want any help changing?"

"No, Mom," he yawned. "I can do it myself."

"Alright, Mister," Avery smiled as she headed for the door. "I guess I'll go get some pancakes going for you. Yell if you need any help, and come meet me in the kitchen, okay?"

"Yep."

As Avery poured the golden yellow batter on the electric griddle, Ahmyn emerged from the hallway in a pair of crisp dark blue jeans and an orange tee imprinted with a shark.

"Don't you look handsome?!" Avery exclaimed, rushing over to hug him.

Crouching down to look Ahmyn directly in the eye, Avery gently took her son by the shoulders. "I can't believe how fast you're growing up. You're not a little baby anymore, are you?"

"No, Mom," Ahmyn smiled, reaching for the tear trickling down his mother's cheek. "And don't cry. You always cry."

"Moms are supposed to cry." Embracing him tightly, Avery lifted him off the ground and twirled in a circle.

"Where's Grandma?" Ahmyn queried.

"She had to work early this morning, Sweetheart. She really wanted to see you leave for school this morning though. She's very sad she couldn't be here."

"We should save her some pancakes," Ahmyn suggested.

"Yes, we should." Setting her child on a creaky wooden chair by the table, Avery reentered their closet-sized kitchen and swiftly flipped the pancakes, making a flopping sound with every flick of her wrist.

As the pair sat down to eat, Avery gazed longingly at her boy. He was growing up way to quickly for comfort. "I think you're going to have a great first day of school, Ahmyn."

"Me too," Ahmyn replied with a bead of syrup gliding down his chin.

Finishing a bite herself, Avery set down her fork with a clank. Clasping her hands atop the table, she leaned forward and smiled. "Now remember what we talked about last night?"

Ahmyn took a swallow of milk from a green dinosaur cup and nodded. "Some kids are nice and some are mean."

"That's right." Avery sat back and inhaled deeply. "And if they say anything about your arm?"

"It's because they are curious," Ahmyn went on.

"School is good. It's usually pretty fun, and there's always something new to learn. I'm excited for you, Ahmyn."

As they finished up with breakfast, Avery couldn't help but laugh as she noticed Ahmyn's feet. "You took your shoes off already, silly boy?"

Nodding silently, Ahmyn grinned and wiggled his toes.

Crouching beside him, Avery pushed the gray slip-ons over his white-socked feet. "I know you have something against them, but you have to wear shoes at school. You can't go running around in bare feet at recess. It's not allowed." Embracing him once again, Avery kissed his warm cheek. "Shoes stay on, alright?"

Ahmyn reciprocated his mother's hug. "Okay." Hopping down from his chair, he skip-walked toward the bathroom.

"Are you brushing your teeth like a good boy?" Avery called while cleaning up the table.

"Yes!" Ahmyn chimed as he placed the toothpaste between the nub of his right arm and chest. Twisting off the cap with his left hand, he then placed the tube of paste on the sink counter and then positioned his toothbrush in the same fashion while applying a clumsy blob of blue-sparkled paste with his left.

"Need any help, Mister?" Avery asked as she leaned on the doorframe.

Shaking his head, he brushed vigorously for ten seconds and then spat.

"I just can't get over how grown up you are," Avery said. "I can't believe it's your first day of school already."

Ahmyn dried his face with the green hand towel that hung from the rack behind him. "I'm still a kid mom. I'm not a grown up like you."

"True," Avery smiled, "but you *did* use to be a lot smaller."

"You seem sad, Mom." Ahmyn's intense gray eyes were like two tiny oceans glistening up at her. "What's wrong?"

"Oh nothing." Placing her hand on the crown of his small head, she combed her fingers through his long dark hair. "It's just hard for moms when their kids go to school. We're so used to being with our kids, and then we have to let you go for a few hours. We have to share you with other people. Sometimes we wish we didn't have to do that."

Ahmyn just smiled. "I'll be okay, Mom. Don't be sad."

"I know, I know. Don't listen to me. I just worry too much. That's all. It's time to go now."

Shuffling into the front room, Ahmyn swiped his backpack off the couch and turned to his mother. "I'm excited for Miss Tindale to be my teacher."

"She's very nice." Avery smiled. "I'm excited too."

∞

It was a relatively short walk to Braxton Elementary, although it had seemed longer due to the imposing fog. Parents and students were ushered into the sandstone-colored brick building as they arrived, then directed to their respective classrooms.

Miss Deborah Tindale's curly brown hair bounced atop her sturdy shoulders as she zipped about the room, greeting her new students. Stopping at Avery and Ahmyn, she crouched down and quickly slid her yellow-framed glasses back up her skinny nose. Extending her pale-skinned hand, her cherry red lips parted into a bright smile. "Hello again, Ahmyn. I've been looking forward to having you in my class."

Nearly attached to his mother's leg, Ahmyn beamed back at the friendly face before him and gripped her fingers. She briefly shook his hand, then continued to make her way around the crowded room, her black skirt dancing above the floor as she walked.

A pleasant tone then chimed over the intercom, which prompted Miss Tindale to take her place at the front of the room. "Parents, thank you so much for helping your children make it safely to the classroom. I'm going to ask that you help your children find their way to their assigned seat, and while you're doing that, I'm going to take a quick roll count. As each student's name is called out, we invite the adults to take their leave, and we'll see you again in four hours."

As Ahmyn's name was called, Avery kissed his cheek and whispered, "Make sure you do everything Miss Tindale asks you to, alright?"

"Okay, Mom," Ahmyn smiled.

"Love you. I'll be back soon."

Avery made one final turn as she entered the hall. Locking eyes with her boy, she blew him a kiss and felt a deep sense of accomplishment. She had staved off the tears, albeit only until she was out of Ahmyn's sight.

∞

"What's your excuse this time, Will?" said a twenty something redhead in frustration as she locked the door behind her. Repositioning the phone on her shoulder, the young mother struggled to carry her son, purse, and diaper bag down the remaining steps of the eroding porch. "You're kidding, right?" Setting her two-year-old down, she took one last look in her compact and began making her way down the walkway.

"Ball!" the child shouted as he discovered a sparkly red treasure in the weed-ridden lawn.

"Stay close to Mommy, Nathan. It's foggy."

"Fug-eeeeee."

"That's right, Baby, good job! Did you hear that, Will? Your son just said 'foggy'."

"Fug-ee, fug-ee, fug-ee, fug-ee!"

Taking her son's hand, they commenced their morning routine walk down State Street. "Honestly? New seats for your truck? Did you forget about *my* car? I've been taking the bus for over a month now. And did you also forget that your son and I have to walk over a mile to get to daycare? You are such a jerk – you know that? You seriously only think of yourself."

"Daddy come home?" the little boy squealed. "Show Daddy ball?!"

"Not wanting to be married anymore is one thing, Will, but you still have responsibilities to your son. Look, I'm barely making rent as it is! Do you want us kicked out on the street?"

Now at the first crosswalk, the young woman reached out to press the pedestrian button, causing her purse to slip from the opposite shoulder in the process. As the grasp on her son's hand was broken, Nathan watched as his ball bounced off the edge of his shoe and into the street. Before his mother could think, her child had rushed into the busy intersection to reclaim his prize. Tires shrieked as the boy's delicate skull was crushed by the lethal force of an oncoming SUV. Having rolled over his arm and leg before coming to a complete stop, the toddler's body now lay lifeless behind the vehicle, which had traveled fifteen more feet before coming to a complete stop.

"My baby!!" The devastated woman rushed to her child's side, cradling his mangled body against her chest. "You killed my baby!!" she screamed as a teenage driver exited the vehicle. "You killed my baby!!"

Having already dialed 911, the young man began speaking with emergency responders. "I've just hit a pedestrian – a kid – uh, uh, a small child. Oh my – no – I think he's dead. No – I think he's dead – I've killed him. Please hurry – I think he's dead."

"Somebody help us! Please!" the mother cried, looking frantically in all directions. Her initial shock was now giving way to deep despair, as the horrible reality of her loss became more and more real. In this moment of utter chaos, she was startled by a gentle hand placed on her shoulder from behind.

"Sarah?"

A barefoot child, no more than five years old, now stood before her. He radiated kindness through large glistening gray eyes, and his expression was that of compassion and empathy. "Sarah, Nathan isn't dead. It's not his time."

Extending his left arm, the boy placed his hand on Nathan's head. As he did so, an unexplainable peace swept over Sarah, and she felt her son begin to squirm in her arms. Extending the child away from her crimson-stained white blouse, she now watched in amazement as Nathan smiled at her, his once-broken body now completely unharmed.

"Is this yours?" the boy asked as he handed Nathan something sparkling and red.

"Ball!" Nathan exclaimed.

The barefooted boy began to walk away and Sarah could see that he did so with a limp, one leg being slightly shorter than the other.

"Wait!" she called out. "How do you know our *names*?"

Without stopping, he looked over his shoulder and responded with more quiet confidence than Sarah had ever seen in anyone. "I know *everyone's* name."

CHAPTER 26

"Alright, friends!" Miss Tindale shouted over the din of outdoor recess, then blew her whistle three times. "Time to line up!"

Like tiny ducklings giving heed to their mother, the young students clumsily made their way from the playground equipment to the feet of their new mentor. Tapping their feeble shoulders with her pointer finger as she went, Miss Tindale counted her brood of ankle biters, falling one short of the needed count of thirty four. Gliding back to the front of the line, she repeated the procedure, arriving at thirty three yet again. The potentially alarming discovery kicked her pulse up a notch as she counted her antsy students a third time with the same results. Feverishly scouring the small playground, the panicking teacher made a discovery that sent her heart to the floor. At the mouth of the blue twisting slide, with white socks stuffed within, was a lone pair of gray slip-on shoes.

Ten minutes later, with the help of ten other staff members, the entire school had been combed for Ahmyn Renshaw. Local law enforcement was promptly notified, and while awaiting their arrival, Principal Menlo Grant and Miss Tindale examined the security feed for any leads.

"You say you found his shoes right here, correct?" Principal Grant said sternly, pointing to a flat-screen monitor.

"Yes." Miss Tindale responded, her heart knocking within her chest like a volcano about to erupt. "At least I think they're his shoes. All the other students have theirs."

"Okay," Principal Grant continued. "So here he is getting on the equipment. And then what happens? Let's see. Hey Bev, any sign of the police yet?"

"No, Sir," replied the office secretary from the doorway.

"So it looks like he must be sitting down right there. You can see the back of his head and his elbow," the principal observed, pushing his fingers over his thick brown mustache.

"And there he is coming off the slide," Miss Tindale pointed out, hoping desperately to see what direction he'd gone.

"And barefoot!" Principal Grant added emphatically. "So where does he go from there? C'mon, Ahmyn, where did you disappear to? So then he heads somewhat toward the camera, and then we lose him. If he kept in the same direction, then he's going toward Seventh East. So we'll check the Northeast feed and see what we get." With the flick of his wrist and a few mouse clicks, Principal Grant acquired the desired feed, then hastily loosened his red neck tie. "Wow, it's hot in here. There! There he is!"

"Headed north on Seventh," Miss Tindale affirmed.

"And then he disappears! Curse this fog today, geez!" Principal Grant shot out of his chair and headed for the door. "Bev, Debbie and I are leaving to start looking for him. Jenn is covering Debbie's class. Show the police his picture and let them know we've headed north on Seventh East."

∞

Removing the last of a load of darks from the dryer, Avery's phone began tinging in the back pocket of her jeans. "Hello?" she announced, not recognizing the number. "This is she." Cradling the phone between her ear and shoulder, she lugged the bulky laundry basket into the bedroom she and her mother now shared. "I'm sorry, what?" The orange plastic basket hit the ground with a thud as Avery tried to comprehend what she'd just heard. The words were simple, but their implications were too dire to be immediately understood.

"Well, where did he go? I mean, I just don't understand how a kindergartener just up and leaves the school playground without someone noticing! Was he with someone? Was he kidnapped? How come you people don't know what happened to my son?!"

Slipping into her white sneakers, she blasted through the front door like a race horse barging through the gate. "I don't even know what to do! My mom has our only car! Have you called the police? Should I call them too? I can't believe you lost my son!"

With phone in hand, Avery tore down the street, keeping pace with a blue-clad street cyclist for nearly a block before slowing her gate. Like a sailor bereft of anything to guide her, Avery felt the terrible storm of uncertainty swarming about her. *Where could he have gone? What if he was kidnapped? Maybe he's back now. Maybe they found him. Maybe he came back. Could he have thought school was out? Were there kids picking on him? I would have seen him by now if he were trying to come home. Does he even know how to get home? I don't think he does! Oh, Ahmyn where are you?!*

∞

"We have a pedestrian hit on the corner of Eighth East and Hansen," blared Officer Chuck Demsey's two-way. "Again, Eighth East and Hansen. Child hit."

"That's just great," the officer sighed through a mouthful of breakfast burrito. Flipping on his lights and siren, he maneuvered his cruiser through a U turn and assertively began the half mile trip to the destination. "People, pay attention! Geez!"

Applying the brakes briefly before banking hard right, extra caffeinated black coffee splashed against the lid of a white gas station cup. As he hurried on, he observed emergency lights in the distance through a brief clearing in the fog.

Arriving just before the fire truck and ambulance, Officer Demsey left the door to his black cruiser open and rushed to a young woman cradling a bloody-clothed child in her arms. "Ma'am! Is the child breathing okay?!"

Without acknowledging the tall dark haired officer to her right, the frazzled woman toggled her gaze from her child's face to peering down the misty street before her.

As the paramedics approached, Officer Demsey began consulting with the distraught male teenager at the wheel of the parked SUV. With his skinny elbows on the wheel and his face buried in his hands, the young man looked with bloodshot eyes at the officer before him.

"He came out of nowhere, I swear!" the desperate teenager sobbed. "Just ran right out in front of me! I didn't have any time to stop."

"Alright, buddy," Officer Demsey began, stepping right up to the open door of the vehicle. "Try to calm down a bit for me, okay?"

"I'm dead meat. I'm dead. Plain and simple. You're going to have to arrest me, aren't you?"

"I'm not going to arrest you, kid." Officer Demsey insisted, pointing straight ahead. "Look over there. The little boy is walking."

Wiping the heavy tears from his eyes, the teenager peered through the windshield in disbelief at the same child his SUV had just crushed only minutes prior. "He didn't die? He can walk? What a relief! I thought for sure I – . Oh, I'm so glad he's okay!"

Meanwhile, Nathan didn't want to hold still for the paramedics. "Tickles, Mom! Make 'em stop!"

"Hold still, Nathan," Sarah insisted, firmly grasping her child's wrist. "The men are trying to make sure you're okay."

"I'm okay, Mom. I'm okay. Doesn't hurt. Doesn't hurt."

"Jim, can you tell where all the blood's coming from?" asked one of the medics as he carefully inspected the child's skull.

"Not yet," came the response. "Ma'am, could you please hold him in your lap or something? We really need to figure out where he's bleeding from."

"Nathan, please hold still." Wrapping her arms around her rambunctious child, she watched as their mysterious barefooted rescuer was swallowed in the fog up ahead.

While Officer Demsey had his detainee filling out paperwork, he noted how wired the victim appeared to be and glanced at the fender of the red SUV. Deeply indented, and severed in half, one of its splintered edges bore a bloodied pale piece of what appeared to be human tissue. Stepping closer, he crouched for a better look. Mostly spherical in shape, the sight sent the officer sprawling backward when he discerned an iris and pupil. Whipping around to examine the victim again, it was immediately apparent the child still had both of his eyes. Which begged an obvious question.

"Excuse me," Officer Demsey said to young man who was still fumbling his way through the incident report. "But can you explain whose eyeball is dangling from your fender?"

CHAPTER 27

"Mom!" Avery panted into her phone as she sprinted. "Mom, you have to call me back! Ahmyn's gone missing. He disappeared during recess and I'm on my way to the school right now."

Saturated with paranoia, Avery watched every car that passed, trying to catch a glimpse of Ahmyn's hair or his orange shirt. Anything that moved was a potential lead. And everything that didn't. Trying her best not to entertain the worst possibilities, however, she kept speaking out loud to herself as she jogged. "He's going to turn up. He's happy and safe. He's going to turn up. He's happy and safe." Still, the tears emerged. "Ahmyn!" she screamed, her voice raspy and exhausted. "Ahmyn?! Ahmyn, where are you?! He's going to turn up. He's happy and safe. He's going to turn up. He's happy and safe."

∞

Principal Menlo Grant scanned the road ahead while his newest Kindergarten teacher was coming apart at the seams. Applying the brakes to his navy blue sedan, he took a deep breath and attempted to offer some words of encouragement. "We'll find him, Debbie. We will."

"I can't believe I lost him," she sobbed, pushing her hands into her now matted dark hair. "My first day teaching and I've already lost a student."

"Let's keep our eyes peeled. We're going to spot him. He probably just went for a walk or something." As the words came out of his mouth, Menlo Grant knew how unlikely they actually sounded. Reality was going to have to take a back seat to hope, however. For as long as possible.

"What if we can't find him, though?" Debbie whimpered. "I could never forgive myself. No, I couldn't. I've lost someone's child. I've lost him. I lost someone's baby! I should just turn myself into the authorities right now!"

"Debbie!" Principal Grant insisted as he eased off the clutch and accelerated through another intersection. "This isn't the time to lose our cool! I don't fault you for this. But you will keep your emotions in check, do you understand me? We have a little boy to find, and I *will* have your full attention! Am I making myself clear?"

As though being alarmed out of sleep, Debbie immediately resumed her role as kindergarten teacher. Glancing into the passenger side mirror, she discerned something out of place. A crouched small figure could be made out through the now lessening fog, approximately thirty meters behind them.

"That's him!" Miss Tindale boomed as she swiftly craned her neck to see through the rear windshield. "Stop the car! That's him!"

The pair lunged forward in their seats as Principal Grant stomped on the brakes. Unbuckling her safety belt, Miss Tindale left the passenger door ajar behind her and bolted down the street. "Ahmyn! Ahmyn, we've been looking everywhere for you!"

Without acknowledging the frantic woman addressing him, Ahmyn continued to run his pointer finger along the velvet feathers of a young robin that lay motionless in the grass. Beginning at its crest, he traced a line along the bird's neck and down to the tip of its tail.

"Ahmyn," Miss Tindale panted, arriving at the little boy's side, "what are you doing here? You are supposed to be at school. We were all so worried about you."

"He said sometimes we have to let them go," Ahmyn said softly to himself while gently stroking the bird's feathers.

With hands on her knees, Miss Tindale crouched down to be closer to her student. "Ahmyn, you shouldn't bother with that bird. It could make you sick."

Still making no eye contact with his teacher, Ahmyn transitioned from his hunched over position to sitting cross-legged in the cool grass. "But she is my friend."

"The bird?"

"I wanted to save her, but he said sometimes we have to let them go."

Debbie struggled into the sitting position herself and placed a hand on the boy's shoulder. "Who said that, Ahmyn? Who said we have to let them go?"

Principal Grant had now parked beside the pair and had his cellphone to his ear. "Ms. Renshaw? Yes, we found him. He's just a few blocks from the school. He appears to be just fine. You're just getting to the school now? Alright then. We'll meet you in the office in just a few minutes. Alright." With the flick of a switch on the console, the passenger window lowered. "I just notified his mom, Debbie. She's going to meet us back at the school."

"It's time to go, Ahmyn," Miss Tindale stated. Rising to her feet, she extended her hand. "Take my hand, Ahmyn. We need to go now."

"I hope Mom won't be sad," Ahmyn uttered hopefully, looking now into his teacher's green eyes. "I was only doing what he asked me to."

Allowing Miss Tindale to help him to his feet, Ahmyn walked beside her to the waiting sedan. After getting Ahmyn securely buckled into the back seat, Miss Tindale resumed her seat in the front.

"Hey." Principal Grant looked calmly in Debbie's direction. "We found him. Good eye."

Pacing like a hyena in the school's front office, Avery was concluding a phone conversation with her mother when she saw Ahmyn walking barefoot down the hall with his teacher. "He's back at the school now, Mom. I'll see you in a few minutes. Bye."

Rushing out the office entryway, Avery made no effort to hold back the tears as she scooped up her child. "Ahmyn, I'm so glad you're okay! You had me scared to death!" Spinning in a circle as she stroked his thick black hair, she savored the feeling of his warm cheek pressed firmly against her own. "Please don't do this to me again, Sweetheart. Please." Avery then made eye contact with Miss Tindale and the Principal. "Thank you so much for finding him. This has been so terrifying. I feel like I can't ever let him out of my sight."

"It was certainly quite an eventful morning," Principal Grant said, looking back and forth between Avery and Miss Tindale. "Why don't we all have a seat in my office, if that's alright?"

Nodding her head, Debbie followed her boss's gesture and led the way. Taking up the rear, Principal Grant closed the heavy oak door behind him and straightened his tie. "Please have a seat." He then strode over to a coffee maker on a slender table by the far wall. "Caffeine, anyone?"

"I think I'm already wired enough as it is, thank you," Avery commented, easing Ahmyn onto her lap.

"No, thank you, Mr. Grant," Debbie said, leaning forward in her chair.

"Ahmyn, how about a piece of chocolate?" Principal Grant said cordially, extending a foil-wrapped rectangle to the boy.

"Thanks," Ahmyn said quietly, cautiously receiving the gift.

"Here, Honey," Avery said, "I'll open it for you." Avery then noticed something peculiar as her son relaxed his grip on the candy. "What's all over your hand?"

Taking a sip of coffee from a Styrofoam cup, Principal Grant stepped in for a closer look. Miss Tindale leaned over to examine it as well. Avery then lifted Ahmyn's hand to her nose and inhaled. Shaking her head and scowling, Avery sniffed a few more times and rubbed her forefinger through the dark crusted coating. "It kind of smells like blood. Ahmyn, are you bleeding somewhere? Yeah, this is blood."

Lowering her child to the floor, Avery began turning him about, pulling up his pant legs and shirt, looking for a wound. At this, Ahmyn's insecurities with the events of the morning began to surface, and tears commenced spilling down his face as he wept. "Why are you mad at me?"

"Oh, Sweetie, we're not mad at you," Avery said, pulling him close. "We're just worried you got hurt. You left the playground, Honey. We thought someone tried to take you away. We were worried you were in trouble. And you have a lot of blood on your hand." Wiping the tears from his cheeks, she combed his hair back with her fingers. "Where did the blood on your hand come from, Ahmyn?"

"I was just doing what he told me to, Mom!" Ahmyn bawled, burying his head in his mother's chest. "I'm supposed to do what he says."

Her son's words sent fear blazing through Avery's system like wildfire. "What are you talking about, Ahmyn?" She then shot a terrified glance at the principal and Miss Tindale, each looking equally vexed and concerned. "Who is he talking about? Ahmyn, you have to do what *who* says? Who's been talking to you?"

Ahmyn's bloodshot eyes pleaded with his mother for understanding. "Don't you know?" he whimpered in desperation.

"No, Sweetheart. I don't know. Are you saying someone told you to leave the school?"

"Yes," Ahmyn replied.

"Who told you to do that, Ahmyn?"

Ahmyn swallowed and took a step backward, maintaining eye contact with his mother. "My father."

"I'm sorry," Avery choked. "Who?"

"My father."

Cupping both hands over her mouth as she gasped, Avery felt the blood drain from her face. "I don't understand."

Terrified by the grief in his mother's eyes, Ahmyn resumed sobbing and smashed his face into Avery's thigh.

"Forgive me," Avery said, hoisting up her child into her arms, "but I'm afraid I've had enough for one day."

Principal Grant opened the door and watched the distraught mother and weeping child disappear around the corner. Turning back to Miss Tindale, he tilted his oversized head to one side. "So odd."

"I agree." Debbie nodded. "The whole thing. I'm just glad it's over."

"We found him, yes. And thank goodness for that." Returning to the cup of coffee on his glass-topped desk, he sipped reflectively and then called after Miss Tindale as she was nearly to the door. "But Debbie?"

"Yes," she said, halting her step and turning.

"Something tells me this is far from over."

CHAPTER 28

Allison pulled up right as Avery exited the school with Ahmyn in her arms, his head nestled against her neck.

"I'm so glad he's okay," Allison exclaimed as she climbed out of the driver's seat. "What on earth happened anyway? How did he leave the school?"

Avery handed her small-framed child over to Allison and opened the rear passenger door, straightening out the red and yellow booster seat. "We'll talk about it when we get to the apartment. I'm sorry. I'm just really upset and confused right now."

"Alright," Allison consented, lowering Ahmyn into his seat. "Here, let's get you all buckled up, okay, Handsome?"

Before kissing her grandson's cheek, Allison sensed the uncertainty in Ahmyn's eyes. "I'm so glad you're safe, Sweetheart. I hope you won't scare your poor grandmother like that again."

As Allison put the car in park, she couldn't help but query her daughter. "Did he say what prompted him to leave like that?"

"Let's please talk about this at home, okay, Mom?" Avery blurted.

"No need to yell, Aves. I'm just trying to figure out what happened, that's all."

"Yeah? Well so am I!" Avery sobbed, trying to choke back the tears. "How am I supposed to keep my son safe?" she whispered. "Mom, how am I going to prevent this from happening again? Do we take him out of school?"

"Oh, Aves," Allison smiled. "Do you have any idea how many times I've wondered these very same things about you? This is nowhere near the end of it."

"Well, thanks, Mom," Avery said sarcastically, wiping her tears on her forearm. "You know that makes me feel a lot better."

Concluding their short commute back to the apartment, Avery lifted her now sleeping five-year-old from his booster seat and carried him inside. Laying him upon his bed, she removed his shoes and covered him with a light flannel blanket while Allison prepared some tea in the kitchen.

"He's out," Avery said quietly as she took a seat in their makeshift dining area. "I'm sorry about all that in the car. I just didn't want to talk about it in front of him. It was making him upset at the school. He started crying, and asking why he was in trouble."

"So you said he didn't appear to be with anyone else, right?" Allison wondered, placing a small white steaming mug on the table for her daughter.

"They said they checked the security feed and didn't see anything like that. They said he simply took off his shoes and socks and then just walked off on his own. They found him five blocks or so away from the school, all by himself."

Allison took a seat across the table and methodically sipped her tea. "It just doesn't make any sense, does it?"

"Ahmyn said some things in the principal's office that really bothered me though," Avery continued with angst radiating from her eyes.

Allison raised her eyebrows while swallowing some more of her aromatic beverage. "Oh?"

"He said he left the school because he was told to."

"Like on a dare or something?"

"He said – " Avery paused, feeling extremely uncomfortable repeating it.

"What?" Allison pressed. "What did he say, Avery?"

"He said his – father – told him to leave."

Allison furrowed her brow and placed her mug of tea on the table. "His *father*?"

"Yes. That's what he said. He was only doing what his father told him to do." The look of complete shock on her mother's face mirrored Avery's own feelings. "It sounds crazy, doesn't it?"

Sitting back in her chair, Allison took a deep breath and exhaled slowly, clasping her fingers together upon her lap.

"I mean," Avery's voice quivered, "I have to wonder, has one of the whacky neighbors been talking to him without me knowing? Who's been telling him this stuff, and why wouldn't Ahmyn tell me about it sooner?"

"I can't think of anyone that would be talking to him," Allison said, racking her brain for any clues. "He's always with either you or me."

"It's true. He's never really been out of our sight before." Avery sighed, finally lifting her white mug and cautiously sipping. "It makes me never want to bring him back to school ever again, Mom. You know how nervous I was about it. I was freaking out before, and now I'm completely scared to death to ever let him go back."

"Is it possible he saw some other kids' dads drop them off at school and so he just sort of made it up?"

Avery pondered the idea for a moment while forcing herself to take another swallow of the mint tea. "I don't know, Mom. Part of me really feels like I need to believe what he was saying. He acted distraught and surprised that I didn't already know what he was doing and why he was doing it. He freaked out and started crying. He was beside himself that he was getting in trouble for leaving and doing what this person supposedly told him to."

"But his father though? Something tells me he just made it up. He obviously wasn't trying to be naughty or anything. Kids do interesting things sometimes. They're in their own little world."

"Deep down I feel like someone really did talk to him though. It's really scaring me. Who's been talking to him?"

"I don't know, Avery." Allison took another deep breath and pulled her nearly white hair into a ponytail. "Point is, we really don't have a lot to go on right now. This is the first time he's ever acted like this. I really think we need to just take things a day at a time."

Shaking her head, Avery buried her face in her arms upon the table for a moment, then looked up at her mother. "I don't feel like I can ever bring him back to school, Mom. He's obviously not safe. How is it that a kid can just walk off the playground without anyone noticing? I should never have trusted anyone else with my baby. Mom, he's my baby. He's my baby and I need to feel like I'm keeping him safe. We could have lost Ahmyn today, Mom! I could have lost him for good to some psychopath!"

"This is what we'll do," Allison said firmly, looking her daughter directly in the eye. "Talk with Ahmyn's teacher and tell her you'd like to help out in the classroom. You could be one of the room mothers or something. That way, we can feel better knowing that you're right there with him. If he tries to walk off, you'll know."

It made sense. Avery felt a mild sense of relief knowing that she could keep a close eye on Ahmyn even while he was in school. Realistically, as much as she wanted to keep him cooped up in the apartment, it wasn't a long-term solution. "I guess I could do that, couldn't I?"

"Yes." Allison inhaled deeply and sighed, reaching across the table for Avery's hand. "We really got lucky today, didn't we?"

"It was too close, Mom. I felt like my whole world was ending. It was only fifteen minutes that I didn't know whether or not he was okay, but – it felt so much longer. It was like everything just – stopped."

"That look in your eye," Allison said, smiling softly. "Our children become our whole world, don't they?"

"It's so true," Avery said. "I honestly can't imagine life without him."

Gently snoring in his bed, Ahmyn was soon accompanied by his mother, who laid beside him wrapping her arm snugly about his small frame.

CHAPTER 29

The remainder of the week proved to be very encouraging and calming for Avery. Ahmyn's kindergarten teacher, Miss Tindale, was grateful to have Avery's support in the classroom, and Avery felt much better not having to allow her child out of her sight. New and peculiar revelations soon began to manifest, however.

While the students busily worked on a coloring project, Miss Tindale spoke quietly with Avery in the back of the classroom. "He sure is a smart little guy, isn't he?"

Avery smiled and shrugged her shoulders. "That's what every mother hopes, right?"

"He was so shy during our brief introduction appointment a few weeks ago, I wasn't really able to tell how much of a foundation he had."

"Yeah," Avery reflected, "you know, he's kind of funny like that. Sometimes he's quite reserved, and then other times he's a bit more social."

"But wow, I really have to commend you on all the reading you must have done with him during those preschool years."

"Oh?" Avery looked confused.

"Well, the very first morning the kids took a sort of acuity assessment, just to see where they are. We were having a bit of trouble with the software, but the results actually came back in this morning. The entire Republic has to take the assessment, and Ahmyn scored higher than any child his age that's ever taken the assessment."

Avery's eyes widened as she looked over at her son and then back at his teacher. "You're kidding."

"Not at all." Handing Avery a two-page printout, Miss Tindale began to explain. "So this little triangular icon shows benchmarks for all the areas they are tested on. And this circle icon is Ahmyn. As you can see, he's at the very top of the graph in all ten areas."

Avery stared at the charts in disbelief, slowly turning back and forth between the pages. "Are you sure this is right?"

"Well, you taught him," Miss Tindale chuckled. "So this can't be too much of a surprise, can it?"

"This might sound bad to you, but I don't feel like I taught him a whole lot, or anything like that. Sure, we've been over the alphabet, counting to ten, and writing his name, but nothing beyond that. I just figured he'd learn it in school. You know? I guess you're thinking reading will come a lot easier to him then? What do all these graphs even mean exactly?"

Miss Tindale's expression was flooded with bewilderment. "Certainly you must have known he could read?"

"Oh. He can't read yet. I guess maybe a couple of words here and there."

With thin raised eyebrows, Miss Tindale pointed at one of the graphs. "What these results mean, if they're accurate, is that Ahmyn isn't going to learn anything in kindergarten. So we'll double check, just to be sure. But essentially, he might as well be in first grade. According to this, he's already reading at a first grade level. And that's at a minimum. His test proctor was only with him for the first few minutes because it was clearly evident he didn't need help reading or understanding the questions. He didn't get a single answer wrong."

Avery wasn't convinced. "I've never even seen him read anything except for what few sight words he's done in the classroom with all the other kids over the past few days. I'm pretty sure he's right on par with the other kids."

"Have him read you a book this evening. See what happens."

Rendered speechless by what she was hearing, Avery turned and watched her little boy quietly coloring a large letter D with a bright yellow marker. *He can read?*

"Certainly better to be ahead of the curve, right?" Miss Tindale said, leaving Avery with the telling results in hand.

∞

Later that evening Avery was setting out some mismatched dinnerware and pulling spaghetti off the stove. "Ahmyn, no naps! I can't have you waking up at four in the morning, Buddy."

Passed out on the couch, the five year old had fallen asleep watching the Nature Channel, one of his favorite activities of late. Breathing deeply and poised nearly to roll right onto the floor, Ahmyn didn't budge at his mother's mandate.

Avery arrived at her son's side and gently hoisted him into the sitting position with her wet hands. "No naps right now, okay, Mister?"

"Mommmmm, I'm tirrrrrrrrrrrrred," he managed to mumble without opening his eyes. Slumping his small chest atop his tiny thighs, Ahmyn teetered onto his left side.

"It's time for dinner," Avery insisted, tugging him back up and planting a big kiss on his right cheek. "Grandma's almost home too. C'mon. Time to get washed up for dinner. Let's go, Ahmyn. C'mon. Up, up, up."

Leading her boy by the hand to the bathroom, Avery slid a red wooden stepping stool in front of the sink with her foot. "Get washed up and then come out to the table, okay?"

"Okay," Ahmyn sighed, rubbing his eyes.

Minutes later, Allison arrived home looking like a rag-doll. Without a word, she shoved the front door closed and headed straight for the couch, where she laid out full-length and closed her swollen eyes.

"Mom, not you too!" Avery chuckled with hands on her hips.

"What?" Allison moaned. "What's wrong?"

"I just had to pull your sleepy grandson off the couch to get washed up for dinner. And now there you are. Same exact thing." Back in the kitchen, Avery grabbed some tongs and set them out on the table. "There's no way you're cleaning Lowry and Sons tonight. I'm doing it."

"No, Aves," Allison protested. "I've got it. I just need a few hours sleep is all. It's my night. I'll take care of it."

"You need more than a few hours sleep, Mom. Now get over here and eat something before you pass out." Drying her hands with a white paper towel, Avery smiled as she watched Ahmyn shuffle over to his grandmother's side and give her a hug. "You too, Ahmyn. Time for dinner."

The cleaning business that Avery also continued to take an active roll in didn't facilitate the three of them having dinner together but a couple of nights a week. But sitting down together whenever possible was important to Avery. It was something her father Richard had always insisted on, and something Avery had always enjoyed.

"So apparently today was a bit overbooked?" Avery said through a bite of noodles and savory meat sauce.

"Yeah," Allison nodded while twirling a fork full of spaghetti. "The garlic bread always turns out better when *you* make it."

"Whatever, Mom. Yours is better. But thank you for saying that. Ahmyn, are you making a sculpture over there?"

Taking an occasional nibble, Ahmyn had been methodically piling his serving of spaghetti atop his piece of garlic bread. "It's our apartment," he declared. Placing a piece of carrot from the

212

salad he hadn't yet touched on top of the pile, he then took a large swallow of his chocolate milk, which left a glistening residue on his upper lip.

"Well," Allison laughed, "I've never really thought of our apartment quite like a mound of spaghetti, but way to be optimistic, right, Aves?"

"Nicely done, Ahmyn," Avery smiled. "Try to eat as much of our apartment as you can though, okay? I don't want you telling me you're hungry twenty minutes after dinner is over."

"How many bites?" Ahmyn queried with fork in hand. "Two?"

"More than two," Avery said, serving herself some more salad.

"How about ten times nine, minus eighty-five?" Ahmyn suggested.

Both surprised at what he'd just rattled off, the two women glared at him for a moment while their tired minds computed the answer.

"And how many would that be?" Avery questioned incredulously.

"Five, of course," Ahmyn smiled, taking another gulp of chocolate milk.

With wide eyes and mouth agape, Allison cocked her head in silence and stared at her grandson. Avery glanced back and forth between her mother and child, then placed both hands on the table as she swallowed.

"Is that what they've been learning in school, Aves?" Allison questioned in disbelief. "I don't think you were learning multiplication until at least second or third grade."

Shaking her head, Avery removed an elastic from the front pocket of her jeans and pulled her shiny black hair into a ponytail. "No. Definitely not."

"I was going to say," Allison chuckled as she stood up. "The handsome little goober had me going there for a second."

"That's the thing though, Mom," Avery said quietly, looking her mother firmly in the eye. "I don't know how he's done it, but Ahmyn seems to know a lot more than we realize."

Avery's eyes were reflective and uncertain, prompting Allison to resume her seat at the table. "Go on," Allison said.

"I didn't believe it at first when his teacher showed them to me, but his test scores from the first few days at school – were off the charts. No one his age in the entire Republic has scored higher than him. *Ever*."

Allison looked to her left at Ahmyn, who was chomping an oversized bite of spaghetti, then back at her daughter. "Well, that's a good thing, right? Better that than the opposite."

"Well, yes. Obviously it's a good thing. I'm not saying it's bad. I just don't understand where he learned it all. I certainly didn't go out of my way to teach him anything more than the basics, and I don't think you did either."

"Oh, c'mon," Allison smiled, "you have to give his grandma *some* credit, now, don't you?"

"Yes, Mom. You know that's not what I'm saying."

"Can I be done now?" Ahmyn grinned, his little face decorated in sauce.

"Yes," Avery consented. "What are you going to do with your plate?"

Trotting the short distance into their tiny kitchen, he carefully slid his plate into the sink, then zipped to the couch to watch the Nature Channel.

"You know that Emma Shrine novel you've been reading?" Avery went on.

"Yeah," Allison said hesitantly.

"When we got home from school I saw it sitting on the coffee table and decided to see if there was any truth to what Miss Tindale had been telling me."

"You don't mean to tell me Ahmyn sat down and read Emma Shrine to you?"

"He can read it, Mom," Avery said emphatically.

"Noooo," Allison chuckled in disbelief.

"I didn't have to help him at all."

"You're telling me my five-year-old grandson is reading at a college level?"

"That's exactly what I'm saying. He read ten pages before asking me if he could stop."

Padding slowly across the beige carpet, Allison took a seat next to her grandson. "Ahmyn, your mom said you read to her today."

"Yep," Ahmyn said, hardly breaking his attention from the documentary on manatees.

"How did you learn to read so well?" Allison continued, placing her right arm around his little shoulders.

"I don't know, Grandma," Ahmyn shrugged. "I just know."

"Did someone teach you?"

"Nope. Nobody taught me." Ahmyn kept his focus on the television. "I like manatees, Grandma. Don't you?"

"If you like them, then so do I." Kissing Ahmyn on the forehead, Allison wandered over to the table to assist Avery with the dinner cleanup.

Pushing up the faucet lever, Avery began rinsing out the saucepan and washing residual lettuce fragments down the disposal. "So what are your thoughts, Mom?"

"I don't know, Aves," Allison sighed as she set down a stack of four mismatching plates next to the sink. "If he really is that smart, maybe we should just have him do online school or something. I mean, if he's not going to learn anything, what's the point? What do you think?"

Opening the dishwasher, Avery began inserting the silverware and plates she had just rinsed. "He seems to be enjoying himself in the classroom, at least from what I can tell. The other kids really like him. The social interactions are good for him. I don't know. It's just so early. I mean, I'm still kind of in a daze from everything. In so many ways, the whole thing is just so – I don't know – mysterious. I feel like he's from another planet all of a sudden. Don't you? I'm thinking to myself, who is this kid? Seriously."

"That's our little Ahmyn, isn't it?" Allison smiled as she wiped the table down with a paper towel. "Oh, Sweetie. I'm so beat. I haven't been this tired in a long time. Is it okay if I say goodnight?"

"Totally," Avery insisted, kissing her mother on the cheek. "Go to bed."

"Are you sure you're feeling up to doing Lowry's tonight?"

"I've got it, Mom," Avery smiled, ushering Allison down the hallway. "Now get some sleep."

"Wait," Allison said, turning around. "Not before I kiss my little prince goodnight. Oh, Aves. Look. The poor little guy's out like a light." Pressing her lips against Ahmyn's warm cheek, Allison clumsily resumed her course toward the bedroom.

Forty pounds seemed a lot heavier to Avery when it was all dead weight. Carefully lifting her sleeping son from the couch and conveying him to his bed, she then helped him into some alligator-themed sweat pants and a white t-shirt.

Snugly tucking him in, Avery leaned over and whispered into his tiny ear. "Goodnight, my mysterious little boy. I love you."

CHAPTER 30

With a clipboard and pen in hand, Frank Harvey's heavy footsteps were the only sound in the old warehouse. Taking inventory of what goods the New Hope Food Bank had on hand was becoming much easier than he ever wanted to admit. Things were different when he'd starting volunteering ten years prior. That was when local donations from businesses and community drives had managed to keep the operation afloat. Back then people in need – people like Frank – had somewhere to turn. But tonight, looking around the nearly empty warehouse, Frank felt keenly the impact of the current economic recession.

Shaking his head as he entered a small office in the corner of the warehouse, he placed the wooden clipboard onto a metal desk with a clank and checked the computer for any pending deliveries. Rubbing his eyes, Frank let out a long sigh. Nothing. Not for at least a week. "We're going to dry up," he said aloud. "Who am I kidding? We're already there." Closing the office door behind him, he trudged toward the exit. Inhaling deeply, he turned around to take a quick final glance at the scantily stocked room one more time, thinking somehow that simply wanting it to be full was worth something.

Locking the steel door behind him, Frank headed for his rusty green pickup which was parked ten meters from the entrance.

"Hi, Frank."

In an instant, the forty two year-old's heart rate had doubled and he wheeled around, peering through the darkness for the source of the high-pitched voice. "Who said that?" he stammered.

"I did."

The young voice was to his left, inside a small pocket of short evergreens. "Where are you?" Frank gasped, trying to get his breathing under control again. "Can I help you with something?"

"I'm not scary, Frank," the voice insisted. "So you don't have to be scared. Look over here. See? I'm not scary."

Emerging from the shadows was a small child. As he came forward into the dim glow cast by the parking lot lights, Frank observed the boy was barefoot, wearing a white t-shirt and some dark sweatpants. Grinning widely, the dark-complected child carried something between the stub of his right arm and side what looked like a can of some sort.

Frank's mind was spinning like a merry-go-round as he tried to piece together where he supposedly knew the child from, if he even knew him at all. And what was a kid his age doing outside at three o clock in the morning? "Kid, I'm sorry, but do I know you? And what are doing out here in the middle of the night all by yourself?"

"I brought you something," the boy said, extending with his left hand a jar of peanut butter.

Bewildered at the interaction he was having, Frank received the gift, standing speechless for a few moments. "Thank you. The world could use a lot more kids like you. You really shouldn't be alone out here though. It's not safe. Where's your house?"

Moonlight danced across the boy's face as clouds raced by overhead. "I'm never alone. He's with me all the time. Well, aren't you going to bring it in?"

"Oh," Frank mumbled, scratching his head with his free hand. "Of course. Thanks again, kid. You sure you can make it home alright?"

"You're welcome. And thanks for doing what you do. You're a good guy, Frank."

Pulling out his keys as he walked, Frank was racking his brain trying to figure out how this kid knew his name. *He's not Kathy's neighbor, is he? Hmmm.* Facing the floor as he walked in, Frank advanced a few paces forward before he stumbled into a six foot tall barrier. Looking up to regain his bearings, he felt his jaw drop while the jar of peanut butter slipped from his fingers. *What the?*

Directly before him was a double-high pallet full of peanut butter. And behind it was another pallet filled with hundreds of boxes of macaroni. Turning his head back and forth in amazement, Frank firmly closed his eyes, rubbing them intensely for a moment, now fully convinced he was running on too little sleep. Slowly extending his weathered hand, he touched the shrink-wrapped bundle of food before him. It felt real. It looked real. But it certainly couldn't be! Just minutes ago he'd conducted an inventory that took him less than fifteen minutes to complete. Now he was standing in a warehouse so packed with food there would barely be room to accommodate the forklift.

Silently walking every overflowing aisle in disbelief, Frank finally returned to the front of the warehouse. Lying on the ground was the jar of peanut butter the peculiar boy had given to him. He picked it up, wiped the dust from its label, then opened the entrance door to take a peak outside. "Kid? You still out there?"

All he could hear was the soft rumble of the nearby freeway. No trace of the little visitor. But what remained with him was an overwhelming sense of peace. And the image of that face burned in his mind's eye – the mysterious boy who knew him by name.

∞

Avery's drive home had been a blur. Three hours of cleaning Lowry & Sons law offices had been exhausting, to say the least. It seemed muscle memory was the only thing that got her home. Securing the deadbolt behind her, Avery dropped her purse and keys on the floor and groped through the darkness for her room.

Before entering her and Allison's room, she stepped briefly into the room directly across the hall to check on Ahmyn. What she saw left her heart on the floor. Moonlight spilled onto her son's empty bed, while a gentle breeze from the open window rustled the curtains. "Ahmyn?" Flicking on light switches as she went, Avery checked the bathroom, front room, kitchen.

Barging into her bedroom, she firmly placed her hand on Allison's shoulder. "Mom, where's Ahmyn?"

"He's not in his room?" Allison stammered, shielding her eyes from the lamp Avery had just switched on.

"Ahmyn!" Avery screamed as she reentered his room. "Buddy, where are you?"

Placing her hands on the window sill, she could see the screen had been removed. Sticking her head outside, her frazzled nerves were partially relieved. "Ahmyn, what are you doing out there? Get over here, please."

Startled at the sound of his mother's voice, the child looked up from what he had just written in the dirt with his finger. "You're mad at me again, aren't you, Mom?"

"Honey, you scared the crap out of me. What on earth are you doing outside by yourself in the middle of the night? Now get over here. You have to come back inside. Right now. C'mon. Hurry."

Rising slowly, Ahmyn hung his head and padded through the dirt and patches of nearly dead grass. "I don't like it when you're mad."

Avery's long black hair dangled in the moonlight as she motioned for her son to come. "I just don't understand why you decided to climb out your window in the middle of the night. You can't be doing this, Ahmyn. It's not safe. Someone could kidnap you and steal you away from me."

Grabbing his arms just below the shoulders, Avery hefted her child back through the window to the safety of his room. "You even pulled off the screen and everything. Seriously, why would you do that?"

"You'll get mad if I tell you," Ahmyn sighed, looking helplessly into his mother's eyes.

"Sweetie," Allison said, entering the room, "we have to know. Why did you go outside like that?"

Climbing onto his bed, Ahmyn sat down and looked back and forth between the two women, but said nothing.

"Please, Ahmyn," Avery pleaded. "We won't be mad at you. I promise. Please just tell us."

"He told me to," Ahmyn said, closing his eyes.

"Mom, stay here," Avery demanded. Rushing into her bedroom, she retrieved the wooden baseball bat from under her mother's bed and bolted through the front door and around to the back of the building. "Who's out here, huh?! Huh?! Who's out here?!" With the wooden club cocked and ready to swing, Avery spun left and right, looking for anything that moved. Desperate, and terrified, Avery gritted her teeth as she screamed. "You stay away from my son, you hear me?! Leave my son alone!"

She looked frantically for any footprints leading up to the window but found nothing. Panting and sobbing as she went, Avery rounded the four-plex three more times before returning inside. Dropping the bat beside her purse and keys, she joined her mother and son in Ahmyn's room.

"Who's been talking to you, Ahmyn?" Avery demanded. Kneeling down before her child, she cupped his hand in hers.

"Avery, he told me his dad has been talking to him," Allison said with concern in her voice.

"Ahmyn?" Avery pleaded. "Who has been talking to you? Who is telling you they're your dad? Was he here tonight? Did he come to the window or something?" Looking to her right, she peered through the glass, paranoid they were being watched.

"You can't really see him," Ahmyn said calmly.

"I need to know who's been telling you that they're your dad, Ahmyn," Avery insisted. "Who has been telling you that?"

"No one told me." Ahmyn took a deep breath and looked his mother in the eye. "I just know."

"Listen to me, Sweetie." Avery tried to not sound harsh. "I don't know who your dad is, okay. I'm sorry. Is that what this is about? Other kids at school have dads. And you wish your dad was a part of our lives. Is that it?"

"He *is* in our lives," Ahmyn said. "He's here right now."

"Can you show him to us?" Allison questioned.

"No," Ahmyn went on. "You can't see him."

"I don't understand," Avery said intently.

"When you look at me, it's like you're looking at him. When you look at me, you're looking at my dad too."

"Sweetheart, that doesn't make any sense," Allison said.

"I'm sorry I made you sad." Burying his face into his pillow, Ahmyn began to cry.

"Buddy," Avery continued, "you have to promise me you're not going to leave in the middle of the night like that. It's just like school. We can't have you going wherever you want all the time. It doesn't work like that."

With wet eyes, Ahmyn momentarily looked up from his pillow. "I always do what he says, Mom."

Avery placed her thumb and forefinger on her brow and shook her head in frustration. "But what about what *I* want, Ahmyn? What about me? What about your Grandma? We're the ones who have to look after you, Sweetheart. We're the ones who need to keep you safe. Don't you think you need to do the things *we* ask you to?"

Motioning with her eyes and swinging her head toward the door, Allison persuaded her daughter to back off.

"I love you, Ahmyn," Avery said, tucking him in. "I hope you know that. If you feel like you need to go outside, please ask permission first."

Avery left her son's side reluctantly, but was completely depleted. Stumbling after her mother into their room, she crashed into bed and was unconscious the moment her head hit the pillow.

CHAPTER 31

Four relatively uneventful months passed for the 'A Team', as Allison liked to refer to her little clan. There had been some serious discussion about bringing Ahmyn in to see a child psychologist, but taking action was hindered initially by the fact that they absolutely couldn't afford it. Not only that, but Ahmyn was such a pleasant child to be around. He was intelligent well beyond his years, the cause of which remained a mystery, and Avery didn't want to make her son feel as though there was something wrong with him.

Shortly after ringing in the new year, it was time to celebrate Richard's birthday, something Allison and Avery had continued to do since his death ten years prior. It consisted of having dinner at the steakhouse Porter Joe's, which had been Richard's favorite restaurant.

The low din of conversations, clanking silver, and the aroma of all things delicious saturated the air as the trio sipped water at their table.

"What may I start you off with to drink tonight?" asked a young bearded gentleman wearing a neatly pressed white shirt and black slacks.

"Yes," Allison smiled, looking up from the menu, "I'll have a strawberry daiquiri, we'll have a kid's root beer, and a raspberry lemonade."

"Certainly, Miss," replied the server. "May I just quickly see your ID?"

"Oh, I don't look old enough, do I?" Allison teased, reaching into her shiny bright pink hand bag.

"Absolutely not," the server grinned. Taking a brief glance at Allison's York driver's license, he handed it back to her with a smile. "Alright then, I believe you."

Within a few minutes the server returned with drinks and a small warm loaf of honey wheat bread. "And what entrées shall we prepare for you tonight?"

"Ahmyn, are chicken strips okay?" Avery asked.

"Yes," the child replied, keeping his focus on the coloring project he was working on.

"Your Baumini eight ounce, medium well, with rice," Avery added.

"And I'll have the Jasper's Deluxe, well done," Allison said, handing the server her menu.

"Ambitious choice," the server commented. "Are you certain you can eat all of that?"

"Ha! Of course not. It was my husband's favorite dish. Every year on his birthday I order his favorite drink and meal. He loved this restaurant."

"I think that's fantastic," the server smiled, then paused. "I'm so sorry he can't be with you."

"We are too," Allison said, shifting her focus to the table.

"I'll go get this going for you then."

"Ahmyn?" Avery said, playfully nudging her son's shoulder. "What are you drawing over there?"

With the box of three crayons he'd been given when they were first being seated, with green, blue and red, Ahmyn had been drafting a pair of stick figures. "This is Grandma and Grandpa."

"Oh?" Avery said, while her mother leaned across the table to have a closer look.

"What are Grandma and Grandpa doing in the picture?" Avery questioned.

"They're kissing each other, in the kitchen back there." With a green crayon in hand, he pointed toward a pair of swinging doors that led to the back of the restaurant.

Allison sat slowly back in her chair with wide eyes, looking back and forth between her daughter and grandson. She could feel her eyes begin to moisten as she reflected on the location of the first time Richard had kissed her. The first time she'd ever laid eyes on the man who was to be her husband was in the kitchen of Porter Joe's, nearly thirty years ago. She was an eighteen year old hostess, and Richard was a cook.

"Have I told you that story, Ahmyn?" Allison questioned, using a napkin to dab the corner of her eye.

"Must have mentioned it at some point," Avery suggested, removing a piece of lint from the sleeve of Ahmyn's green shirt.

Shifting in her chair, Allison straightened out her silky blue blouse and placed her hands on the table. "I wish you could have met him, Ahmyn. You would have had so much fun with him. He loved kids. He sure had a fun time teasing you, didn't he, Aves?"

"Yes, he did," Avery confirmed, nodding her head.

Looking up from his coloring project, Ahmyn tilted his head in response to his grandmother's comment. "Oh, I know Grandpa."

"Oh, do you?" Avery chuckled.

Reaching across the table, Ahmyn handed his grandma the finished product. Shocked and unable to hold back the tears, Allison stared at what was written across the top of the page in green crayon: *'You really are too wonderful, Allison. Thank you.'*

They were the first words Richard had ever spoken to her, and had been in response to her buying him a chocolate shake at the end of their shift.

Deeply perplexed and feeling as though her lungs had been replaced with a thirty pound dumbbell, Allison looked back and forth between the words written by her grandson and his cheerful face. "I don't understand," she managed, wiping a tear from her face with her wrist.

"I didn't want to make you sad, Grandma," Ahmyn said sympathetically. Stepping down from his chair, he stepped over and nestled his head against Allison's shoulder.

"Isn't that the first thing Dad said to you, Mom?" Avery questioned.

With her mind still spinning, Allison looked at her daughter in disbelief. "Word for word."

"Ahmyn," Avery began, "you have quite the memory, Mister. Very impressive. Mom, I swear, if he hears something once, it just sticks with him forever."

"Have you told him that story about your father and me? Because I'm pretty sure I never did."

"Well, one of us must have."

Now at his mother's side, Ahmyn pulled on her yellow cotton shirt sleeve and leaned in to whisper into her ear.

"Leave?" Avery scowled. "No, Sweetheart. We're not leaving. We just got here. We're celebrating Grandpa's birthday."

"You told me to tell you if I have to leave," Ahmyn rebutted. "Remember?"

Rolling her deep brown eyes in frustration, Avery felt a jolt of panic pour over her like a bucket of ice water. Throwing a frantic look in her mother's direction, Avery smiled nervously at her child and tried to dissuade him. "This really isn't a good time, Honey. Mom, tell him we're not leaving until we're finished with dinner."

"Alright, you three," announced the server, "we have drinks." Carefully placing a round black tray on the table, he distributed the orders accordingly. "A daiquiri, lemonade, and a root beer for the little tyke. Oh, and off he goes."

"Ahmyn!" Avery called, clamoring to her feet and spinning after her fleeing son. "Ahmyn, get back here!"

Sliding with ease through clusters of guests waiting to be seated, Ahmyn pushed open the exit door with his mother and grandmother in hurried pursuit. Scurrying a quarter block down the street, the child inserted himself amidst a group of folks boarding a city bus. Following the others, he stepped onto the vehicle and inserted two dollar-slugs into the change receiver, taking his ticket as it printed.

"'Scuse me, son," said the white-bearded operator, "you're not riding alone, are ya?"

Ahmyn shook his head as he continued on. "No. My dad's here."

"Oh."

"Ahmyn, wait!" Avery panted as she and Allison tromped up the steps. Pulling some coins from her handbag, Avery paid for hers and Allison's fare, then promptly took a seat beside Ahmyn, who had found a comfy spot by the window about midway back.

"Ahmyn, that was completely unacceptable what you did back there," Avery whispered sternly into her son's ear. "People can't just get up after they've ordered food and leave like that. And what were you going to do? Just get on a bus without us? Ahmyn, seriously, what is going on with you?"

Keeping his gaze fixed ahead, Ahmyn spoke calmly. "I did what you asked, Mom. I told you when I needed to leave."

"I said you needed to ask my permission before you leave, Ahmyn. You didn't ask my permission back there. You told me you were leaving, and after I told you not to, you just took off! I feel like you don't think you need to listen to me. Climbing on a bus like this all by yourself? This is so dangerous. Kids can't just go running around whenever they feel like it. How am I supposed to keep you safe, Ahmyn? Geez. What are we doing here, anyway?"

Sitting directly across the aisle, Allison watched intently as her daughter did her best to handle the situation. Contrary to the way she'd imagined it, being a grandmother wasn't any less taxing than being a parent. In some ways, it was harder.

Placing his hand upon his mother's yellow shirt sleeve, Ahmyn smiled at her with conviction. "This is the reason I was born, Mom. This is why I came into the world."

"Reason?" Avery questioned. "What reason?"

"To do whatever my father asks me to."

There it was again. That ludicrous assertion. It was such a troubling claim. And it drove Avery out of her mind. The words 'child psychiatrist' were now swelling in her consciousness. *This has to stop. I can't take it anymore. We don't have any other choice. He needs to be seen.* "It's time to go home, Ahmyn. We're getting off at the next stop."

Nodding in confirmation, Allison reached up and pulled the cable which signaled the operator to make the next stop.

"We need to wait," Ahmyn said, gazing longingly up into his mother's concerned eyes.

"No, Ahmyn," Avery said sternly. "I'm sorry, but it's time to turn around. We need to go."

"He said they would be coming. He said I needed to meet them on this bus. Just wait and see."

Reaching across the narrow aisle, Allison placed her hand on Avery's knee. "Let's just wait and see what he's talking about, don't you think, Aves?"

"Sure," Avery said, shaking her head. "Fine."

As the half-full bus halted at a stop light, Avery pulled out her phone and began running a search for child psychiatrists. Finding some relevant results, she handed the phone to her mother without a word and raised her eyebrows in expectation. Allison glanced at the screen and shrugged her shoulders undecidedly.

The bus was now in motion again, and the passengers all swayed in unison as the driver eased into a left turn. Nine blocks later to the north, the operator pulled over for another routine stop. Ten or so people made their exit, then a few more boarded, the last of which was a shaggy blond-haired boy, about nine or so, leading a balding man by the hand.

The boy's simple clothes were soiled and a few sizes too big. His pants pocket swallowed half of his arm as he hastily dug around for the fair with his free hand. The operator waited for the pair to take their seat before accelerating.

"This way, Dad," the boy said, helping the man along.

Staring blankly forward, each step the man took was very cautious. "Excuse me," he said quietly, unintentionally brushing against another passenger. "Sorry. Pardon me."

Helping his father into his seat, the boy stood in front of him, holding a support pole.

Smiling as he stood up, Ahmyn looked on with satisfaction. "That's them, Mom. That's Burke and Talmage."

"Who?" Avery questioned as her son pushed his way past her and into the aisle. Reaching out to detain him, her arm was pushed down by Allison's firm but gentle hand.

"Just watch," Allison asserted. "Let's see what he does."

Avery's heart felt like a frightened bird flying aimlessly about its cage as she watched her boy with the utmost anticipation.

Ahmyn carefully stepped down the aisle toward the front half of the bus, making certain to support himself with his hand as he went.

"Talmage?"

Startled to be hearing his name, the young shaggy-haired boy turned to his right to be met with the piercing, yet calming, gaze of a boy who appeared to be around half his age. The unfamiliar child's brown hair hung nearly to his chin, and he supported himself by clasping an adjacent pole between the nub of his right arm, which ended above where his elbow should have been, and his chest.

"Talmage," the young child continued, "I've been waiting for you and your dad."

Talmage's eyebrows made an inverted V as he glanced between his father's perplexed expression and the smiling face of the strange boy. As the moments passed, he began to experience an overwhelming sensation of hope. It was a peculiar feeling – something he hadn't been well accustomed to. And like a warming pot of water on a hot stove, the feeling was slowly expanding in intensity.

"I'm here to help you," the boy affirmed.

"Who is it, Talmage?" the man queried, looking blankly ahead. "Who wants to help us?"

"Burke, my name is Ahmyn," the strange boy replied. Slicing through the ambient din of mechanical noise and muffled conversations, his voice penetrated Burke's consciousness and sounded like the most refined of musical instruments.

"I'm sorry, Ahmyn," Burke replied, "but have we met? I think I would have remembered your name. It's not very common, is it?"

"I know how hard things have been for you and your family, Burke."

As the words were spoken, and without knowing why, Talmage and Burke knew they were true. Left speechless, Talmage began to cry.

"Burke, close your eyes," Ahmyn said calmly.

The emotionally overcome man promptly did as the boy asked. Then reaching up for Talmage's face, Ahmyn wet his forefinger and middle finger with glistening tears, then gently wiped the liquid upon each of Burke's quivering eyelids.

Keeping his eyes closed, Burke discerned a cool sensation as the water evaporated from his eyelids. And then it happened. The change. A vivid shift from nothing – into something. Without success, his mind tried to process the information. It was something completely new. With eyes still closed, he raised his hand and pressed it against his eyelids. The familiar nothing had returned. Then removing his hand, the new sensation resumed. He possessed no words to describe it. His mind simply had nothing with which to identify the change. Again and again, Burke placed his hand upon his closed eyes, then removed it. Nothing, then something. Nothing, then something. Nothing – then something.

With his mind at a complete loss, Burke ever so carefully began to open his eyes. The moment he did was initially horrifying, and he immediately recoiled, using his hands to keep out the imposing splendor.

"Dad?" Talmage spoke softly, placing a hand on his father's bristled cheek. "What's going on?"

Grasping his child's fingers with both hands, Burke slowly peered through quivering eyelids. "Talmage?"

For the first time in his life, Talmage made eye contact with his father. Gone was the wandering, blank stare – that aimless gaze he couldn't connect with. No. This was real. There was no doubt, his father was looking at him. His father could see him! And Talmage had never felt so alive!

"My boy!" Burke exclaimed, tightly embracing his child. "How can this be? I don't understand. How could this happen?" Glancing about, he was astounded by the overwhelming beauty of all the human faces surrounding him. Every line, every shape, the dazzling textures, the way people were moving and breathing. It was more than enough to put his system into overload, and he could feel his strength fleeting. Slumping to his hands and his knees, Burke began to weep uncontrollably. "I can see."

"Dad!" Talmage said, trying to help his father back up.

Through heavy tears, Burke gazed up into his son's face once again. "I can see! I can see!"

Pulling on his upper arm, Talmage helped his father grasp one of the support poles, with which Burke used to struggle to his feet. Looking around at the other passengers, Burke cried at the top of his lungs. "I can see!"

The response from passengers in the proximity was a mix of vexed faces and curiosity.

"What's going on back there?" the operator spoke into his intercom. "Please keep the noise level down."

Resuming his seat, Burke watched his son step toward the mysterious child who had touched his eyes and spoken to him in his own language.

Talmage's voice quivered as he placed a hand gently on Ahmyn's shoulder. "Thank you so much. How can it be?"

Ahmyn smiled back. "It is a gift. A gift from my father."

Burke slid toward Ahmyn and reached out with both hands, grasping the child's head gently while kissing his forehead. "I still don't understand. I can't understand this. I don't know how this can be possible."

"Burke?" Ahmyn said, looking the man in the eye. "If you believe – all things are possible."

The bus then veered slightly to the right as the operator applied the brakes. With a minor jolt, they came to a complete stop.

"Dad, this is us," Talmage said to his father, helping him up. As the pair shuffled toward the exit, each looked back longingly at Ahmyn who waved as they departed.

Moving closer to the window, Ahmyn looked on as Burke raised his hands to the sky and shouted at the top of his lungs.

With mouth agape and her mind drowning in an ocean of questions, Avery sat close by, gazing at the back of her son. Having followed closely behind Ahmyn as he had approached the father-son pair, she had focused all her attention on the perplexing interaction. She hadn't been able to understand a word of what had been said, but her consciousness was dancing around the outcome.

Without speaking, Avery turned to Allison, who was sitting to her right. Allison opened her mouth to speak, but said nothing. With wide eyes, Avery turned back to observe Ahmyn watching through the window as the operator again departed. She carefully traversed the aisle to the opposite side of the bus and placed her hands on her child's shoulders as she sat.

"We can go now, Mom," Ahmyn stated as he turned to face his mother.

"Sweetheart?" Avery managed.

Ahmyn peered into his mother's desperate eyes, but said nothing.

"I don't know what to say."

"You're wondering how I know their language."

"Yes. Yes I am."

"You don't know how I made his eyes work."

"That is what you did, right?"

"Yes, but you don't want to believe it."

"I want to believe it, Ahmyn, but I don't know how."

"Let your heart do the hard things, Mom. The part your mind can't."

Glaring earnestly into her son's eyes, Avery paused for a moment, her mind clutching for bits and pieces of the past, trying to make sense of it all. "Is this what you've been doing when – when you leave without asking?"

Ahmyn didn't directly answer her question. "Trevor was shot in the face."

Avery cocked her head to the left. "The taxi driver?"

"Yes. And you used to have metal in your back."

"Well yes, but – "

"The little girl at the doctor's office when I was a baby."

Looking out the window at the passing mirage of gray sidewalks and the heartless cityscape, Avery replayed the perplexing scene in her mind. "She couldn't hear. She couldn't hear and then – "

"Yes," Ahmyn confirmed. "Evan at my first birth day. And there are others."

"Others? Ahmyn, I'm really confused right now. Extremely confused. And I'm kind of scared. Sweetheart, what are you trying to tell me? What are you saying? I mean, yes – I hear what you're saying, but – but I'm in denial. You're saying you can – fix people. That you can – cure them? No one can do that. It isn't humanly possible."

"Before humanity existed – I am."

CHAPTER 32

Like a ragged stuffed animal upon the floor, Avery sat slumped against the side of Ahmyn's bed. Waiting. Watching. Waiting for that moment when he would decide to climb out the window or slip out the front door. Watching for her child to go carry out the ambiguous bidding of a person she'd never seen – an individual who Ahmyn spoke of often.

It had been three weeks since the bus incident, and as far as Avery was aware, there had been no more – occurrences. But possessing this knowledge came at a price. Sleep. Not that she would have even tried to stop him. Avery knew – that is, believed she knew – that Ahmyn's taking off would produce something good, something phenomenal. But she was his mother, his protector. If Ahmyn insisted on going somewhere, she would be right there by his side.

The surroundings of the room then began to dissolve into a completely different scene as her desperate need for sleep overtook her. She was traveling in the back seat of a police car of some kind. Just ahead two other cars could be seen, their lights throwing red, blue and white beams in all directions. And through the rearview mirror a similar image. To her right was a young man in his early twenties donning a bright orange jumpsuit. Chains dangled from his left wrist and descended to his ankles, which were also connected by the shiny chain. With head bowed, his dark brown wavy hair concealed his face. After a moment, he sat up, revealing his identity. It was a face she knew well.

"Ahmyn?!" Avery gasped. "Ahmyn, it's me!"

Keeping his gaze fixed straight ahead, her son made no response.

"Sweetheart, what are you doing here?" Avery persisted. "Where are they taking you?" Slowly extending her right hand, she cautiously attempted to touch his shoulder, but to no avail. Her hand just disappeared into his person.

The police caravan was now approaching an ominous towering facility Avery had only ever seen on television. Peregrine Penitentiary, the Republic's most notorious maximum security prison. Bristled with miles of spiny razor-sharp fences and barbed wire, the blackish gray mountainous façade stood fearless and impenetrable, overlooking the lifeless desert over which it presided with unchallenged authority.

Black armored figures holding semiautomatic rifles stood in tight configuration within the first set of massive unforgiving security gates. As they slid open, the procession immediately descended underground. Very little light penetrated the cab of the vehicle as Avery tried to make sense of her surroundings. After about two minutes, the car halted. She then nearly jumped out of her seat as heavy knocking on the window to her left commenced. With lungs heaving and her heart zooming, Avery peered through the tinted glass. Looking now to the right again, she found she was in complete darkness. And again came the knocking, only louder this time.

"What?!" Avery screamed. "What do you want?!"

Throwing open her eyes, Avery reeled into a one-eighty to confirm Ahmyn was still in bed. He was. Then another round of persistent loud knocks. Glancing at the green numbers on the nightstand clock, which read 1:37, Avery clumsily rose to her feet and threw on her white robe before rushing to look through the peep hole in the front door. The dim yellow porch light was barely bright enough for her to discern who it might be. It appeared to be a pair of police officers. A male-female duo.

Keeping the door chain latched, Avery cracked open the door. "Uh, can I help you?"

"Ma'am," spoke the female, "we received a domestic violence call from a child. Are you safe?"

"I'm not sure what you're talking about," Avery responded with wide eyes. "We didn't place any call here."

"Is this apartment B?" the male cop questioned.

"This is, but could it have been apartment D, maybe? They're on top and to the left."

"Thank you, Ma'am," the female officer said with a nod. "We'll try that."

A cautious curiosity was now tugging at Avery, and she left the door ajar while she listened carefully to the sound of the two officers ascending the metal stairs. Within moments there was another loud knocking, this time on the door upstairs. Training her ear more carefully, Avery listened even more closely. Muffled yelling could be heard above, then the officers knocked forcefully again.

"Open up," the male officer boomed. "This is the police."

Like cold water trickling over her, chills spilled down Avery's back and arms as she continued to listen. The muffled yelling persisted for a few more seconds, and then it fell silent, and stayed that way for a few moments. Avery thought she heard the word "no" screamed with a woman's voice from inside the other apartment, and then Avery winced as it came – a sound that had been bored into Avery's memory nearly six years ago, only this time it was deeper. Like an angry clap of thunder from overhead it came. BOOM! BOOM! Glass shards clashed with the metal railing then crashed onto the ground below.

Avery slammed the door, locked it, then immediately returned to check on Ahmyn, but was mortified by what she found. "Ahmyn!" Rushing across the room, she stuck her head out the open window. "Ahmyn, where are you?! Please come back here!"

During this time, she heard the muffled sound of another shot. With heart racing, Avery climbed through the window and frantically looked in all directions for her son. Certain he couldn't have made it far, she padded along the side of the apartment building toward the front. As she rounded the corner, her stomach launched itself into her mouth. In a crumpled heap upon the ground and drizzled in glistening red was the blonde female officer she'd seen only minutes before. Against her better judgment, Avery proceeded up the stairs toward the upper level. As she did so, above and to her left, she saw him. "Ahmyn, get back down here! Somebody is shooting a *gun* up there! Come back!"

Jumping up the metal steps in threes, Avery gripped the railing as she swung to her left to finish the second half of the ascent. At this moment, two hundred pounds of force sent her into the air as a bald man with a young girl over his shoulder plowed into her. The blow to her skull as it came into brutal contact with the cement beneath her put her into a dizzying frenzy. Rocking back and forth on her side, Avery held her hands up to her throbbing head. Ringing filled her ears and an overpowering ache reverberated through her back and limbs.

"Brian!" Ahmyn shouted from his perch. "Brian, stop right there!"

Slowing his gait, the burly bald man turned to face the person who had just screamed his name. With a rifle in one hand and the crying girl over his shoulder, he tilted his head and looked at the curious child standing beside the male cop who lay lifeless and bleeding.

"You can't run from me, Brian!" the child asserted, pointing his finger. "Put Miata down. Now."

Never before had the man felt so compelled to oblige anyone. It was as if he had no choice but to obey. And a child? Following the boy's orders, the man slowly lowered his barefoot stepdaughter to the ground. Immediately darting away, the yellow nightgown and curly red hair flashed up the stairs and into apartment D.

Continuing to point his finger toward the bald man, Ahmyn seemed to roar like a young lion as he spoke. "Drowning in the ocean is better than what awaits you."

At that injunction, the man cocked the shotgun with a straight face, placed the barrel vertical against his chin, and turned to the street. The night air was then once again shattered as hammer ignited powder, while the man's body was sent sprawling backward into the grass.

While Avery struggled incoherently up the stairs to find Ahmyn, eight-year-old Miata Jones was dialing 9-1-1. Her motionless mother lay face-down upon crimson soaked carpet in the front room. And two officers were down – one just outside the door, and the other on the ground below. Per the request of the dispatcher, Miata remained on the phone as she awaited the arrival of the paramedics. Breathing deeply and sitting against the blood-splattered wall, she ran her fingers through her mother's beautiful dark red hair. "Please be okay, Mommy," she whispered. "Please be okay. Mommy, please be okay."

Closing her eyes, Miata tried to imagine herself in a fairytale palace. It was a tactic she had become accustomed to using at home. A safe place. A happy quiet place. She could go there and be protected from the darkness that surrounded her. But it didn't always work. And this – this was one of those times. Then she heard her name.

"Miata?"

Opening her eyes, she saw the quiet boy who lived downstairs. She hadn't even noticed him as she darted past him moments ago. Without responding, she just stared into his peaceful gray eyes. He smiled at her and walked inside.

"I can help your mom, Miata," he said, kneeling into the wet carpet.

Miata didn't understand. And yet, she fully believed him.

"Is it okay if I help her?"

Nodding her head, Miata lowered the cordless phone from her ear and watched the strange one-armed boy.

Placing his hand upon the top of her mother's head, he ran his fingers backward and down her spine, stopping at the small of her back. As Miata watched him do this, she felt somehow, and contrary to just moments prior, that her mother was now in the room. It made no sense at all. Before, it was only her body. But now – somehow now, she was back.

"Take her hand," the boy said calmly. "Go on. Take it."

Miata did so, and was comforted and surprised at how warm her mother's hand felt in her own.

"Now tell Teja you love her."

With tears streaming down her face, Miata did so. "Mom, it's me, Miata. I love you. I love you so much. Please be okay. Please get up."

It almost scared Miata as she felt her mother grip her hand. She couldn't see her mother's face as it was draped with her hair, but she began to stir, turning her face in Miata's direction. "I love you too, Miata." There was an enduring pause. It was so quiet. So still. Like the morning after a heavy snowfall. "Where is he, Sweetheart?"

"The neighbor boy? He's – " Miata glanced around the room, surprised to see the young boy was gone.

"What boy?" Teja asked. "Where's – Brian?"

"I don't know, Mom," Miata whispered. After he shot you, he kicked my door down and brought me outside. But the boy who lives downstairs – he, he screamed at him to let me go."

Teja continued to lie on her stomach, clutching her daughter's hand. "I might not have much time, Honey. I don't even feel any pain. Oh, Sweetheart. I might not make it. I'm so sorry I haven't been a better mother to you, my love. How am I going to live with myself?"

"Mom, please don't cry. You're going to be fine. You're not going to die. I promise."

Just outside the door, officer Nolan Hicks was pushing himself up from a pool of his own blood. Seeing his fallen comrade below, he reached for his radio. "Shots fired at 320 3rd Ave! Officer down. I repeat, shots fired at 320 3rd Ave. Officer down!" Looking through the open door of apartment D, he could see a woman and young girl sitting against the wall. "Hey, where's the gunman?! Is he still inside?"

The little girl shook her head and pointed outside.

Deeply surprised he possessed any strength at all, Nolan used the rusty railing to pull himself up. With his firearm poised and ready, he carefully made his way toward the steps. Just then, he could see a little boy with wavy brown hair crouched over his partner. "Hey, kid! You really need to go back inside! There's somebody with a gun out here! Go back inside!" As he rushed down the steps he spotted a shotgun and the white-shirted gunman sprawled out in the grass, his mangled head glistening in the pale yellow gleam from a streetlight overhead.

Upon reaching the ground, he holstered his pistol and then halted in his tracks. The boy was gone, and his partner was moving slightly. "Connie? Connie, stay still for a second. Let me help you." Crouching at her side, Officer Hicks couldn't believe his eyes. The shirt of her uniform had been sliced to ribbons by the round of ammunition and shards of glass that had hit her. She was completely soaked in blood. And yet – she was looking him in the eye, and blinking. And breathing.

"Did you get him, Nolan?" Connie asked wide eyed. "Where is he? Did you take him down?"

"He's down. It wasn't me, but he's down. Blew his brains out all over the yard."

"Nolan, you're hit."

"It certainly looks that way, doesn't it? It doesn't even hurt though. Doesn't make any sense. I've taken a bullet before. But this – I just don't get it. You should be dead, Connie. And so should I."

∞

Allison returned home from some late-night cleaning two hours after the shooting, just as a bewildered group of cops and paramedics were preparing to leave the scene. Parking on the street, she briskly traversed the poorly-cared-for lawn and entered the apartment. "Aves?! Ahmyn?! What's going on?"

Exiting Ahmyn's room, Avery rushed down the hall and embraced her mother. "We're okay, Mom. Things are okay."

"It looks like a war zone out there, Aves."

"It was, Mom," Avery insisted, finally releasing her grip on Allison's back. "Let's talk over here for a minute."

Leading the way to the kitchen table, the pair took a seat while Avery began to explain. "So I don't know all the details, but the upstairs neighbors were fighting and somebody called the police. The guy upstairs lost his mind. He shot both of the police that were knocking on his door, then he shot his wife."

Allison sat with her jaw nearly to the table. "What about the little girl up there?"

"She's not hurt."

"And Ahmyn?"

Shaking her head, Avery looked down and sighed. "So during all of this, your grandson decides to pull his escape artist tactics again."

"What?"

"I was out here listening to the commotion for a moment, and he decides to climb out the window again."

"No."

"So at this point I've already heard the shotgun go twice, and I want to stop him before he walks into the middle of all this. So I climbed out the window and see him climbing up the stairs. I tried to stop him but get knocked over by the guy neighbor up there while he's running away. I hit my head so hard on the cement – I couldn't tell which way was up."

"I can't believe – he walked up there like that," Allison said in awe. "He must not have known what was going on."

Avery raised her eyebrows and tilted her head incredulously. "I'm not so sure, Mom. He knows things. He knows things he shouldn't."

Allison nodded and looked down for a moment. "None of them are dead, are they?"

"No. No, they're not. Well, except for Brian. The creep. Blew his head off right there in the front yard apparently. Ahmyn stayed away from him. Didn't touch him."

"But the others though?"

"Yeah. They were all walking around just fine. With blood all over their faces and arms. You should have seen the looks on the emergency crew's faces. If it wasn't for him – with his brains all over the grass out there, I think they would have thought the whole thing was some sick joke. I still don't think they get it though. What really happened. You know? I mean, seriously,

Mom. No wounds? And all that blood? How do you explain that? I don't understand it myself. I could feel the crack in my own skull. I could feel it. I blacked out from the pain. And now it's gone. All that blood is still dried in my hair right now. I woke up to Ahmyn's hand on my face, and his smiling face looking down at me. How is he doing this? I mean – I still don't believe what I'm seeing. What we've experienced, what I've experienced. What I've seen. It has to be him. He's the only one there. He told me that he can do it. That he's been fixing people. But I still can't make myself believe. There must be some scientific explanation for it. Dad used to say there's a scientific explanation for everything, right?"

"Of course there's an explanation. The question is, are we capable of understanding it? Where is Ahmyn now?"

"Asleep in his bed. I super-glued his window shut. Not sure if it will even work, but it seems pretty solid."

"My head is spinning right now, Aves. I'm exhausted. I'm so glad you two are okay. I'm so tired. I just can't process any of this right now. I'm just glad you two are okay. I need to go to bed."

As Allison stood, Avery shot out of her seat and waved her hands. "Mom, wait. There's something else."

Allison turned to face her daughter and sighed. "What is it?"

"Teja and Miata, the mom and daughter from upstairs – they're asleep in our room right now."

"You're kidding, right?"

CHAPTER 33

While contractors were busily making repairs and replacing carpet on the upper level of the apartment fourplex, an awkward breakfast was under way in apartment B.

"So, are the pancakes okay?" Allison said from the stove, trying to break the silence.

"Very good, thank you," Teja said hastily, nodding her head and wiping her mouth with a napkin.

"Good," Miata peeped, keeping her eyes on her plate.

"Sorry we don't have a little more to offer," Allison went on, flipping the next batch on the griddle. "We're much overdo for a trip to the store."

"Don't be silly," Teja said, pulling her thick red hair into a ponytail. "You've already done too much. Hopefully, they'll be done up there by this evening. At least, that's what the landlord said."

"Butch has always been pretty good about those kinds of things. Repairs and all. Gosh, if it weren't for him, I don't think we'd have stayed here as long as we have."

"Your daughter and grandson sure are nice."

"I'll let them know you said so. Sorry they had to slip out so early this morning. There's this field trip to the zoo Ahmyn's really been looking forward to. If it weren't for that, they probably would have stuck around today. Miata and Teja. Such pretty names."

"What do you say?" Teja said, lightly nudging her daughter.

"Thank you," Miata grinned through a bite of buttery pancakes.

"I'm sorry, I'm just talking your ear off over here," Allison said as she began rinsing out the batter residue from a green mixing bowl.

"It's so nice to have a pleasant conversation with someone," Teja said, taking a sip of cold milk. "With all that's been going on lately, it's not really something I've had a lot of exposure to. Let's just say that."

"If there's anything we can do, I hope you won't hesitate to ask. We'd really like to help you any way we can."

"We appreciate that. We certainly don't want to outstay our welcome. Like I said, the repairs should be done by tonight. There's a lot of stuff we need to try and sort through. Need to try and figure out how much longer we're going to stay here. Where to go next. You know. Those types of fun things."

"Of course. Absolutely. I know at least for us, it seems like we've been flying by the seat of our pants for as long as I can remember. It almost feels like second nature. We sure hope you'll stay as long as you need to. We're happy to help."

"Allison, Miata and I were talking last night and – "

Turning off the sink, Allison grasped the orange towel hanging from the oven handle and held eye contact with Teja. "Yes?"

"Is – is it true? About – about your grandson?"

"We would appreciate it – if we could keep that between us," Allison said quietly, laying the towel on the counter. "But yes. As much as I don't understand it – it appears to be true, yes."

"Miata said I was – gone. Dead. I saw the blood on the carpet and the wall. It was there. I saw it with my own eyes. It was everywhere. And my shirt. It was pretty much blown off my chest. And the police. I watched the whole thing. I watched him blow them away. The lady cop went backwards right over the railing. There's no way anyone could survive that – being shot at point blank. There's just no way."

"I'm very glad you're still alive, Teja," Allison said. "And I really hope this can stay between us."

"Okay. We won't say anything. Some good came from all of this though. It sounds kind of horrible, but I'm just glad he's gone."

"I need to use the bathroom," Miata said as she arose and stepped away.

"He can't hurt us anymore. He can't hurt my daughter anymore," Teja said, padding the corners of her eyes with the napkin. "The reason he lost it yesterday was I called him out. I figured out what he was doing."

"You really don't have to tell me, Teja," Allison said, slowly shaking her head. "You really don't need to."

"She's going to be messed up for life. And it's partially my fault. No. It's all my fault. I'm the one who let him into our life. Miata said she didn't want me to. I did it anyway. I went and married him too. Why was I so stupid? How could I do that to my own daughter? Expose her to that?" Looking blankly ahead, Teja folded the napkin in half and laid it down. "I deserve to be dead."

"Hey now," Allison said, taking a seat in front of Teja, "you shouldn't say things like that."

"I'm sorry to dump all this on you. It's just that I'm – still in some shock over all of this. I let him into our *home*. I'm the one who let him in. I'm the one who *married* him. She'll never be the *same* – because of me." Swiping up the napkin, Teja quickly wiped her nose and stood up. "I'm sorry. I'm telling you much more than you ever wanted to know. I think I need some air."

Heading for the door, Teja halted at the sound of her daughter's voice.

"Did you tell her, Mom?"

Turning to face her child, Teja opened her mouth to speak, but couldn't find the words.

"Did you tell her about your cousin?"

Allison looked at Teja expectantly, then at Miata. "Cousin?"

Taking a deep breath, Teja turned to Allison. "My cousin – she, uh – she's married to Darius Viyergo."

"*The* Darius Viyergo?" Allison said with eyebrows raised. "Okaaaay."

"Miata thinks that – he and Ahmyn – that they should meet."

CHAPTER 34

Miata's pale skin warmed as water from the bathroom sink flowed over her hands. It soaked the blonde hair of her Diana Doll which she held under the tap, bringing with it brownish swirls that trickled down the drain. With Diana in her left hand, she pumped the hand soap container with her right and began rubbing the glistening blue substance into the frilled blood-stained dress that adorned her princess doll. Working it into the fabric, she was making progress.

This will work, she thought. Pumping some more soap, she rubbed it into the doll's hair, vigorously sliding her hands back and forth. Focused and driven, she was determined to rinse away her mother's blood, thereby renewing the doll she'd had for as long as she remembered. She was convinced that with enough effort, she could remove the stains. She could make it as though – as though it never happened.

Everyone else in the apartment slept as Miata worked tirelessly for fifteen minutes to purge the unsightly blood from Diana's hair, dress, and limbs. Her eight-year-old fingers began to ache as she persisted. After repeated washes, she was unsuccessful at removing the stains. Her prized doll was tainted. The doll that used to bring her comfort, who used to bring her to her princess's castle, would now only remind her of that night. Of what he had done. To her.

Laying Diana in the sink, Miata watched the water continue to wash over her face, unable to remove the stains. Closing her eyes, her chest began to tighten and quiver while innocent tears were drained, as it were, directly from her aching heart. It was too dark a reality to cope with. She dreaded the prospect that she may never be free. How could she be? The past was the past. It could never be erased.

"Miata?"

Gasping, Miata reeled to her left to see Ahmyn standing in the doorway. He said nothing. But looked her directly in the eye.

"Sorry," she said, hurriedly wiping her tears on her pink pajama sleeve. "You probably need to use the bathroom, huh?" She immediately pulled Diana out of the sink and wrapped her in the yellow hand towel that hung on the opposite wall. As she attempted to leave she was halted by Ahmyn's outstretched arm and his palm toward her.

"I know why you're crying," Ahmyn whispered, lowering his arm.

"I wasn't crying. I was just – "

"Miata. I really do know."

"It's just that – "

"You can't get the blood out of her dress."

"Yes." Looking down at the towel that concealed Diana, Miata couldn't stop the tears from returning. They poured down her cheeks and trickled through her nasal cavity, descending like first rain drops onto the towel.

"And the pain from your heart."

Looking immediately toward him, she felt Ahmyn searching her soul. She was the dark of night, and his eyes – were the sunrise, filling her with wonder. He could see everything. She felt naked before him.

"Am I a bad person?"

Ahmyn shook his head slowly while he smiled.

She believed him. But that didn't alter the emptiness inside.

"Do you want him to suffer?"

Miata paused for a moment before responding, and reached over to turn off the water. "That's what my mom keeps saying.

That he'll suffer for what he did. She must have told me that a thousand times."

"Do you want that? Do you want him to suffer?"

Miata said nothing for what seemed to her like hours as she truly considered this peculiar boy's question. Is that what she wanted? "No. No. That's not what I want."

"Then what do you want?"

"What I want is – " Miata looked down at the towel, and pulled it back from across Diana's blood stained face, then covered it again. "Well, it's not something I can have."

"Miata?" Ahmyn said, smiling as though he'd been her friend since birth.

"Yes?"

"What do you want?"

"For it to have never happened. See? I can't have that. It already happened. That's it."

"You can have that."

"How?"

"That's why I was born. I can take it away."

His remark made no sense.

"That is my entire purpose."

"What do you mean?"

"Do you trust me?"

"Well, yes. Yes, I do."

"Then hand me your doll."

Without hesitation, Miata extended the towel-wrapped doll toward him.

"Close your eyes," Ahmyn said.

Miata obeyed. Immediately she felt a timeless warmth descend upon her from all directions. It was unearthly, and yet, she'd never felt so safe. So – at home. Without a doubt, she was a

252

princess. And it wasn't just an imaginary place. She was precious. Beautiful. And pure.

"Put out your hands," he whispered.

Slowly opening her eyes, she saw Diana looking back at her. Her hair was perfectly curled. Her dress gleamed like new. She even had shoes again. Shoes Miata had long since lost. And the stains were gone. Like – like it never happened.

CHAPTER 35

New Haven International Airport was particularly busy just before the turn of the new year. It was at the height of this traveling frenzy during which they had chosen to embark. The trip would be brief – two days. But it was thought to be plenty of time. Time enough for Ahmyn to interact with Teja's dying cousin, the alleged prophet's wife. And time enough for Darius Viyergo to possibly provide some insight about Ahmyn.

The prospect terrified Avery. What might he say? Would he say anything at all? And yet as soon as the idea to meet him had been presented, Avery was convinced – they absolutely needed to meet him. It had been only one week since Teja and Miata had spent those few nights in their apartment, and Avery truly felt she was at the cusp of discovery, of bridging the synapses of understanding about her son – who he was, and *what* he was.

It had taken nearly three nerve-wracking hours to check in and clear security. Avery had gripped Ahmyn's hand the entire time, anticipating when he would try to disappear into the endless crowd. Now arriving at the gate, Allison crouched down to look her grandson in the eye. "I love you, Ahmyn."

"I love you too, Grandma."

Wrapping her arms about his small frame, Allison lifted him off the ground and held him firmly to her chest. "Will you make your grandma a promise? Will you promise to stay close to your mother the entire time?"

"Yes," Ahmyn said, kissing Allison's cheek.

Avery looked at Allison with bewilderment in her eyes. "Mom, are we crazy for going through with this?"

Lowering Ahmyn to the ground, Allison pulled her daughter in for a brief hug. "Are we crazy, Aves? I don't know about you, but I'm not sure I can remember the last time I felt sane. Just being alive is – well crazy, isn't it? Everything we do, I feel is just one mad grab after another for survival. But I feel good about this. What that means, well – I don't know."

Avery smiled and took Ahmyn's hand. "I wish you were coming, Mom."

"Its fine, Honey. I'll be fine. Besides, somebody has to clean all those toilets at the law firm, right?"

∞

It was Avery's first time on a plane. The seats were a little less comfortable than she had imagined. In fact, they were a lot less comfortable. And a lot smaller too. There wasn't enough overhead carriage space for her carry-on, so it was under Ahmyn's feet. He sat by the window, gazing with fascination at all the other planes zooming about on the runway, pulling into or out of their respective hangars.

"This is fun, isn't it, Mom?" Ahmyn exclaimed with delight. "Whoa, look at that one coming in!"

Avery leaned over to get a better look. Like a massive mechanical bird, a white 747 came roaring overhead. Through the windows on the opposite side, the incoming jet could be seen making ground contact nearly a kilometer away.

"What does flying even feel like, Mom?" Ahmyn queried, looking earnestly up at his mother.

"Well, I don't know, Sweetheart. But we're going to find out pretty soon."

Within minutes, the scene outside the window began to slide away as the plane backed out of the hangar.

"We're moving, Mom!" Ahmyn said gleefully.

Avery's stomach tightened as what felt like ice water trickled down her entire abdomen. Gripping the hard-edged armrests, she kept her eyes fixed straight, right through the back of the curly white head of hair in front of her. "Is your seat belt buckled, Buddy?"

"Yes, Mom," Ahmyn chuckled. "You already asked me that."

"This is your captain speaking," came a gruff voice through the intercom. "Our journey is about to begin. Please continue to remain seated until the red light in the front of the cabin goes out, which will be in about eight minutes. Thanks again for choosing SkyLine Airways, and we hope you enjoy the flight."

"This is going to be fun, right, Mom?" Ahmyn repeated.

Avery gritted her teeth and forced a smile. "Oh yes, Sweety. It'll be tons of fun."

Avery's shoulders were thrust into the back of her stiff chair as the plane lunged forward. Keeping her eyes glued forward, she could see the pavement in her periphery passing faster and faster. Then a rock seemed to drop in her gut as the nose of the plane tilted upward. Avery was trying not to breathe and her eyelids wrinkled like raisins as she kept them clenched closed.

"Mom, we're flying!" Ahmyn exclaimed, pressing his nose into the oval window to his right.

Unwilling to release her iron grip on the arm rests, Avery felt as though it was her heart that was propelling the plane. With sputtered breaths, she panted loudly, drawing the attention of nearby passengers.

"This is the worst part, Miss," said a gray-haired man in business attire to Avery's left. "You'll be okay."

Without turning to face him or opening her eyes, Avery forced a sliver of a smile while exhaling through her gritted teeth. Meanwhile, to her right, Ahmyn acted like a kid at a theme park, practically bouncing up and down, pointing, pulling on his mother's arm, and exclaiming ooos and aaahs.

Five minutes had seemed like far longer to Avery, but finally, the plane had completed its initial ascent, and the rock in her gut slowly dissolved, allowing her to breathe more normally. Opening her eyes, she looked over at Ahmyn, who was now kneeling on the seat with his face against the window.

"Ahmyn, you're supposed to have your seat belt on," Avery whispered loudly.

Smiling back at his mother, Ahmyn pointed toward the front of the cabin. "No. See? The red light is off." Instantly resuming his watchful post, Ahmyn continued to add smear marks to the window. "This is sooooo fun."

Having regained some of her composure, Avery couldn't help but chuckle at her son's enthusiasm.

"At least you have him to help you get through it, right?" said the gray-haired man to her left.

"Yeah," Avery smiled. "He's quite the character sometimes."

"This flight isn't too bad," he continued, pulling some black-rimmed reading glasses from the pocket of his pastel yellow shirt. "I make this trip twice a month. Goes by pretty quick."

Avery's stomach was feeling practically normal now, and feeling obliged to speak with the friendly stranger, she did her best to be cordial. "Do you travel for business, then?"

"Yeah." He shifted in his seat to face Avery more comfortably. "I service MRI machines at a couple of hospitals in Durham. Keeps me busy enough."

"That sounds interesting. Wow. I apologize for making such a scene. I've never been on a plane before and I didn't really know what to expect. Apparently, it sort of freaks me out. I guess I should have known. I've never done very well on rollercoasters either."

"Honestly, there for a second I thought you were going to throw up. I've seen that happen to a few folks over the years." Setting down his novel, he clasped his hands and nestled his elbow on the arm rest. "So how old is your little rascal over there?"

"Ahmyn," Avery said, giving him a nudge, "this gentleman is wondering how old you are."

Spinning a one-eighty, Ahmyn looked into the friendly eyes of the man across the aisle. "Oh hi, Daryl. I don't really have an age."

The man's blue eyes doubled in size under his raised eyebrows. "I don't recall introducing myself, but I guess I must have. But yes, it's Daryl Benson."

"He's a good guesser," Avery quickly responded. "And he's six. Six years old."

"Well, it's very nice to meet you, Ahmyn," Daryl said, extending his hand.

Ahmyn immediately reached across Avery and took the man's hand, holding it for a few seconds before speaking. "When you get home, Daryl – Tyler will be okay."

At these words, wells of moisture began to gather in Daryl's eyes. "I'm sorry. Did you say – Tyler?"

"Yes," Ahmyn stated, keeping his grip on Daryl's rough hand. "Your son."

"How do you – "

"Ahmyn," Avery interjected, "I think maybe we should – "

"He'll be better, Daryl," Ahmyn continued. "You'll be able to hug each other again."

Paralyzed where he sat, Daryl's tear-filled eyes were fixed on the boy's, who was penetrating his very soul. *How does he know Tyler?* In his mind's eye was his nineteen year old son, his best friend, who had been mangled in a terrible motorcycle accident by a drunk driver eight months prior.

"He'll play golf with you again," Ahmyn said, gripping Daryl's hand tighter.

Giant tears rolled off the man's face, soaking into the worn blue carpet below. How vividly he could visualize that first set of clubs he'd given his son on his tenth birthday. They'd played nearly every weekend since.

"And you'll eat raspberry shakes at Clive's."

Daryl's entire frame quivered as he listened to the words uttered by this child. "I truly hope," Daryl managed, "I truly hope you're right."

"If you believe," Ahmyn said, "there is no good thing you can't see. I promise." Releasing the man's trembling hand, Ahmyn turned back to watching through the window.

Speechless, the man nodded graciously at Avery, who was dabbing at the corners of her own wet eyes, and resumed a front-facing position in his seat. Closing his now reddened eyes, Daryl leaned his head back and took a deep breath, trying to convince himself that the conversation he'd just experienced was actually real.

Avery turned toward Ahmyn, watching him in amazement. In this moment, like so many times before, she wondered – is he really *my* son? He was so much more than human. He was – purer, a more perfect being than all other people. She was terrified to ever be without him, horrified at the thought of not being able to protect such a confusingly wonderful individual from harm, and the only known person in the world to share her same blood.

She grinned at the sight of his bare feet. It used to bother her. The fact he'd never wanted to wear shoes. But she'd come to appreciate it. She respected it. In a way, it seemed like Ahmyn's way of conveying he didn't see himself as better than this world.

Avery knew he was. But perhaps he was trying to help her see something. Learn something. Or possibly the simplest explanation was true. Maybe he just didn't like shoes.

Resting the side of her head against the seat, Avery reached out for Ahmyn's left foot. Rubbing her thumb against his heel, she closed her eyes and within moments, was asleep.

∞

A thick eerie silence pervaded the cabin of SkyLine Airways flight 462. As Avery opened her eyes, she felt the warmth of Ahmyn's body draped across her lap. He was out like a light. Trying not to wake him in the process, Avery carefully retrieved her phone from her back pocket to determine how long she'd been asleep. About two hours.

It was particularly dark outside for being only five o'clock. Leaning toward the window to her right, Avery curiously peered outside. Like an enormous blade, the spanning silver wing sliced through the atmosphere, carving a path through the darkening skies. Keeping her eyes fixed outside, bursts of distant light began to penetrate the thick blanket of clouds that enshrouded the plane. The low rumble of thunder could shortly thereafter be discerned, growling and moaning like an awakening dragon.

From the cockpit, Captain Ross Withers was perplexed and astounded at the scene unfolding before his eyes. "Kevin, are you seeing this?"

With eyes the size of tangerines, co-pilot Kevin Starling nodded. "Yes, Captain. Have you ever seen anything – "

"Never," Captain Withers interjected. "No. Never."

Barreling through the thick mist, the plane had emerged into a vast fishbowl-like void in the clouds, the perimeter of which was discernible due to the lightning that sharked out violently and beautifully from its black borders. The noise created by the lightning could be felt as the vibrations swept over the jetliner. Again and again, brilliant jagged knives tore inward from random locations around the massive black cavern in the sky.

Back in the passengers' cabin were gasps of concern and fear-stricken faces. Afraid to look outside any longer, Avery sat frozen in her seat, firmly holding her sleeping son against her abdomen.

"Pretty spectacular, isn't it?" came a familiar voice to Avery's left.

Avery slowly turned to see the friendly face of Daryl. "Is this common?"

"I don't think – "

All conversations were then violently interrupted by a deafening clap, which incited screams from many of the passengers. A half-second later, the only light entering the cabin came from the ongoing bursts of electric wrath from outside.

"No," Daryl continued. "This isn't common. I've never seen the lights go out like this before."

"Should I be worried?" Avery questioned, clutching a still unconscious Ahmyn.

"I'm experiencing a slight degree of uncertainty, yes."

The raspy voice was now back on the intercom. "This is your captain speaking. As you've been able to tell, we've entered a bit of a stormy patch. It appears the cabin lights were affected by some lightning that came in contact with the plane. Not to worry, though. We have a crew member checking on the fuses right now to see if we can't get them back on for you shortly. Please be certain to fasten your – "

An even more imposing explosion of light and sound then blared through the plane, accompanied by more screams from the passengers, and followed by a poignant shove from underneath that launched people out of their seats.

"Please keep your seatbelts fastened until further notice. It may be a bit uncomfortable, but we'll get through this just fine."

The plane then endured another deafening assault from the demonic lightning storm, and another.

"That's right, Honey," Avery said to her slumbering child. "Just sleep through it. We're going to be okay. Just sleep through it."

"This is definitely a rough patch," Daryl went on, "but the planes are built to withstand these kinds of beatings. We're gonna be fine."

Keeping her eyes closed, Avery didn't respond to her fellow passenger's attempts to mitigate her anxiety.

At seven hundred kilometers an hour, the plane was nearing the western edge of the most fascinating five minutes of Captain Ross Withers' life. Plowing through a wall of gray, the plane swam through a sea of near pitch black for ten minutes. Meanwhile, with a small flashlight he held with his teeth, the plane's technician tinkered feverishly to remedy the cabin's blown fuse.

With expressions of relief from the passengers, the lights in the cabin flickered back on.

"That's probably the end of it right there," Daryl said, looking at Avery's presently pasty complexion. "They'll always try to maneuver around or out of those kinds of things. That's what they're trained to do." He looked down warmly at Ahmyn and smiled. "Wow, I wish I could sleep like that."

"He has a gift," Avery said, reflecting on just how far reaching that statement actually was.

"Yes, he does."

"You have to be kidding me," Captain Withers said, dragging all ten fingers through his thick wavy black hair.

"Nature's forces are really out to get us today, aren't they, Captain?" murmured the co-pilot in disbelief.

They found themselves in yet another colossal spheroid, illuminated by the same onslaught of lightning from the perimeter. But what began to materialize before them defied comprehension. At thirty-two thousand feet, they shouldn't have been witnessing a grimacing cyclone thrusting upward from beneath – but the black pillar was clearly not concerned with what it should or shouldn't have been doing. Snaking a terrifying path toward the unseen cosmos, it tapered slightly toward the top, spitting out venomous blinding shards of pink, blue, and yellow in all directions.

Passengers watched in horrific amazement as swirling cylinders of doom began protruding slowly from the perimeter of their prison cell in the sky. As lightning shrieked and roared about the plane, whimpers and gasps were uttered by the terrified humans aboard Flight 462. Barreling through the unforgiving skies in a case of steel, they were as protected as a wooden glider soaring through a forest fire.

As Captain Withers forced the plane to veer to the north side of the deadly twister ahead, a menacing surge of force then pounded the rear right side of the plane, thrusting the interior of the plane into the shoulders and heads of the passengers. The impact greatly reduced the forward momentum of the jetliner, rendering it more vulnerable to the awful vortex raging in the center.

Ahmyn awoke to a forceful blow to the right side of his head. Instinct immediately took over, and with his hand upon the throbbing region of his skull, he rotated in his seat to gaze out the window for a moment. "No, no, no," he said, shaking his head in disgust, "this is not the time!" Unbuckling his seatbelt, he arose and began to scramble past his mother.

"What are you doing, Ahmyn?!" Avery insisted, pushing him back into his seat. "It's not safe to get up right now. They said we need to keep our seatbelts on."

"Mom, everything's going to be fine," Ahmyn said, placing his hand upon her shoulder.

Avery immediately thought of what he had told her on the bus – 'You don't want to believe it.' How could she? And then another shrieking boom as lightning hit the desperate plane once again. Without the tiniest flinch at the explosions thundering about them, Ahmyn rose again, and made his way up the aisle. When he was three or so meters away, the cabin went dark again. Except – Avery could still see her child. A soft vivid glow beamed about him, illuminating his path. Leaning out into the aisle herself, Avery watched earnestly as he approached the door that separated coach from the next section of the plane. She stood upon the tilted floor and followed after Ahmyn as swiftly as possible.

Nancy Allred, the flight's senior flight attendant, was sitting adjacent to the door that separated the cockpit from the cabin. Preoccupied with the unpleasant terms on which she had left home earlier that day, she was coming to grips with the very real possibility that she may never be able to make amends with her sixteen year old daughter. She would never be able to apologize for being so hard on her.

In the darkness, she saw something that caught her off guard. A boy – a glowing boy, for that matter – was approaching up the aisle, with a woman in tow. As though his skin had been infused with moonbeams, he came closer, looking unstoppably determined to enter the cockpit. Without a word, Nancy watched as the child extended his hand and opened the door. And somehow, it didn't surprise her that this mysterious figure had no difficulty turning a handle that she knew was locked.

Ahmyn's presence illuminated the cockpit as he entered. And he fixed his eyes on the terrifying scene that lay before the helpless pilots. "Silence!" Ahmyn screamed with unrivaled authority.

The stunned pilot and co-pilot whirled around and were speechless to behold the vessel of light before them.

"Silence, you spawn of wrath!" Ahmyn continued, holding out his hand toward the storm. "Now is not the time of your vengeance! I *command* you to be still!"

An earsplitting screech tore through the sky like a wounded dragon forced to recoil. Then, like chalk washing from the sidewalk during a downpour, the thrashing storm of darkness bent on vanquishing the plane simply dissolved before their eyes.

"Be at peace," Ahmyn implored the plane's operators as the radiant sun burst through the dissipating clouds.

With mouths agape, the pilots watched in silence as the boy promptly exited the cabin. And while both men puzzled over the experience for the remaining two hours of the flight, neither of the men could find the words to discuss it.

As SkyLine Airways Flight 462 pulled into its destination hangar, the passengers began to file off. Daryl Benson grabbed his carry-on from the overhead compartment and turned, looking in momentary silence at Avery, with Ahmyn asleep across her lap. "What type of individual is your son, that he can command the elements?"

Expressionless, Avery ran her fingers gently through Ahmyn's thick black hair. "I have no idea. But I intend to find out."

CHAPTER 36

Avery quietly watched out the heavily tinted windows of the luxury sedan in which she and Ahmyn were being chauffeured. As the polished black vehicle crawled through some late afternoon downtown traffic, Avery admired the ultra-modern feel to this relatively young and tech-savvy city. Glossy, amorphous skyscrapers towered toward the skies, while sleek bullet-like passenger trains hummed overhead on frictionless electromagnetic rails. She'd seen glimpses of places like this in the media, but it was something else entirely to be in the middle of it all. There didn't appear to be a trace of rust, or a smudge of dirt anywhere.

"Excuse me, Phil?" Avery said, leaning forward in her seat.

"Yes?" the clean cut gentleman in his twenties said, adjusting the rearview mirror onto his passenger.

"Do the Viyergos live in one of these fancy buildings?"

"Not quite," he answered while easing into a right hand turn. "They're in an older part of town, on the outskirts of the city. It's much prettier there."

"It's nicer looking than all this?"

"This city is creepy, if you ask me," the driver explained. "It's all shiny on the outside. But on the inside, it's something else entirely."

"How long have you lived here?" Avery asked.

"Ha," the driver forced a chuckle. "I don't live here. Wouldn't even if I could afford it. I guess I just prefer the old-school stuff. Everything around here is just so – I don't know – fake. Synthetic. It creeps me out."

"New Hope is a lot different than this. You'd probably like it there."

"Maybe I'll check it out at some point. It's not like I'll be driving my grandparents around for the rest of my life. They're both in their eighty's, so, yeah. But you never know. They could live to be a hundred, for all I know."

"You're Darius Viyergo's grandson?" Avery said incredulously.

"I'm one of them. What? Were you expecting something more?"

"I just didn't realize we were riding in the car with a celebrity. That's all. I can't tell you how nervous I am to meet them."

"I can understand that. But they're pretty much just normal people. You don't need to be nervous. In fact, my grandparents are the nervous ones right now."

"Oh?"

"He's never publicly mentioned it, but within the family, there's always been talk of a single mom and a little boy that would contact him from all the way across the Republic."

"Certainly, we wouldn't have been the first mother-son duo to contact him."

"Oh, no. Definitely not. But the idea was that it would happen later in grandpa's life. And let's face it, it can't get much later in his life than this. And just the way Aunt Teja was so somber on the phone when she told us about you two. It just – fits."

"What exactly did she say about us?"

"The way I heard it, not much. The gist of it was, 'I really think you need to meet these two' – something like that."

"That was all?"

"I'm pretty sure, yeah."

"Did your grandpa ever say anything about what the purpose of the meeting would be? Anything about what either party would gain from it?"

"Not really. Grandpa said the boy would likely be some type of leader. And not necessarily a political leader either. I've always had it in my head that they would be pivotal individuals. You know, people like my grandpa. The kind of people that sort of get under other people's skin. But in a good way. Does that make any sense?"

"A little. Yeah."

As Ahmyn slept, Avery processed the conversation she'd just had. She reflected on her own life, particularly the last seven years, and knew – this meeting, with the most controversial man on earth, was going to enhance her perspective. Whether for good, or for ill.

CHAPTER 37

"Darius, Honey?" Jaslyn Viyergo spoke softly as she lay with her face toward the ceiling.

"Yes, Dear?" Placing his dark weathered hand, upon his wife's, he was careful not to disrupt the IV that protruded from her forearm.

"Will you have Bernice push the bed into the sunlight when she comes back in?"

"Absolutely."

"Oh boy," Jaslyn gasped a moment later, clenching her wrinkled eyelids shut.

Darius shimmied forward in his wheelchair, his furrowed brow saturated with concern. "Oh, Jaslyn."

Jaslyn exhaled through gritted teeth. "Yes. Oh, wow, that's cold. It feels like ice cubes are being forced onto my eyes. Ouch. It's been coming in waves. Every couple of hours or so."

The most recent of only twenty documented cases worldwide, Jaslyn Viyergo was in the final stages of a fatal neurological phenomenon, the onset of which was indicated by the misfiring of the olfactory nerve, which produced the distinctive scent of storm clouds overhead. For some, and in Jaslyn's case, this symptom had persisted for over a year before the next phase set in: the immobilization of the eyes. And within two to four weeks, maddening vertigo, which could only be partially mitigated by lying upon one's back. Unable to keep any food or drink down, most victims would die of dehydration.

"Sorry, guys," said Jaslyn's hospice nurse, Bernice, as she exited the bathroom and rounded the corner with haste. "I'm back." Arriving at Jaslyn's bedside, she glanced at the machine displaying her patient's vitals and noticed the decline in her heart rate. "I'm not thrilled about asking this, Jaslyn," Bernice announced, taking a deep breath. "But I just want to confirm the do-not-resuscitate request is still in effect."

"That's right," Darius confirmed, bowing his head and gently squeezing his wife's frail hand.

"Alright." Bernice nodded. Leaning in to whisper into Darius' ear, she placed her hand lightly on his shoulder. "I don't think we have much time, Mr. Viyergo."

In serene silence, Darius stared longingly at his wife's angelic face. After fifty-three years of marriage, she'd never looked more beautiful than she did at this fleeting moment.

"She wants to be in the sun," Darius managed. "By the window over there."

"Certainly," Bernice replied, immediately wheeling the bed to the opposite side of the room, then helped to position her patient's husband at the bedside.

"Honey?" Jaslyn said, turning her head to the left.

"Yes, Sweetheart," Darius smiled while taking his wife's pale clammy hand in both of his.

"Thanks for the adventure. The last fifty years have been – unforgettable."

"Oh, Jaslyn." Darius' voice quivered while he kissed his love's hand.

"Promise – promise you'll look me up on the other side, – okay?"

"Honey? I can't do this without you. I can't do it alone. They could be here any minute now, Jaslyn. What if it really is him? If it is, then – maybe things don't have to end this way."

"He's the one, Darius," Jaslyn declared. Her voice was a hoarse whisper. "I know he is. And you know what he's – capable of. Death is no obstacle for him."

"Then perhaps this doesn't need to be the end, then does it?"

"This is no end, by any means. I truly believe that. I do." Closing her eyes slowly and opening them again, Jaslyn could now see very little, while the scent of rain was stronger than ever. "I have lived my life, Darius. I'm not afraid of venturing into the unknown."

"I'm terrified of my life without you, Jaslyn. I'm not strong like you."

"I hope you won't be scared. I'm grateful for every chapter of our life together. But this final scene, however long it may be – well, I'm afraid I'm going to need to sit this one out. I won't love you any less when I'm gone, my prince."

"But Jaslyn – "

With a slight tremor, Jaslyn's head wobbled momentarily upon her pink satin pillowcase. With her green eyes open, she almost appeared to be looking into Darius' very soul. But no – he could discern it. Indeed, the utter loneliness crept into his frame like frigid coastal air, stilling his insides with every breath. "No," he uttered. "Please no. Jaslyn?"

CHAPTER 38

"Wow," Phil spoke into his phone while making a left hand turn down a private drive that was shaded by a canopy of deep green foliage overhead. Thick groves of aspen and towering massive spruces brooded over the cobblestone road that wound its way half a mile to the Viyergo residence.

"I'm just pulling in now," Phil continued quietly. "I don't know. I just had a feeling. Last night we had a good talk. I didn't realize it in the moment, but we kind of said our goodbyes. I can't believe the timing though. I have them with me right here at the gate and everything."

Entering a code onto a touchscreen within the car's dashboard, Phil concluded his conversation while an ornate iron gate ahead began to swing open. "What should I do? Okay."

Within ten minutes, Phil was conveying the pair's modest luggage to one of the guest rooms while Avery and Ahmyn enjoyed peanut butter and honey sandwiches with glasses of chocolate milk in the Viyergo's large kitchen. Ominous stained-glass style windows occupied nearly the entire wall to the rear of where they had been seated, though the panes weren't colored. Rather, beveled rectangles poised by iron sinew twisted different paths that converged at the center window, blending into a large circle. No direct sunlight was penetrating the glass spectacle this late in the day, but Avery found herself imagining how fascinating it would look.

Under Avery's sandaled feet was a tile floor every bit as intricately crafted as the enigmatic windows behind her. Thousands of turquoise, yellow, black, and clear triangle tiles danced with the ambient recessed lighting emanating from the eleven foot ceiling.

Predicting future events, Avery postulated, must lend itself to accumulating riches in no short supply.

"What do you think of this place, Ahmyn?" Avery said, lowering the glass of chocolate milk from her lips.

"It's good," came the drowsy reply.

"I've never seen anything like it before. Wouldn't it be neat to live in a place like this?"

"A home is measured by how much the people care for each other," Ahmyn stated with peanut butter trailing outward from the corners of his mouth. "So this – this is a very good home."

"That's very true, Sweetheart." Avery used a napkin to wipe some of the peanut butter and bread crumbs from her child's face.

"Mom?"

"Yes?"

"Our home is a very good home too."

Avery smiled. "I hope so."

Moments later, the dark and steeply arched hallway directly ahead of Avery began to produce a silhouette of someone pushing a wheelchair toward the kitchen. Avery's heart rate immediately shifted up two gears and she quickly wiped her mouth with a yellow cloth napkin. She then hurriedly did the same to Ahmyn.

As the two men entered the kitchen, Avery stood, taking her son's hand to raise him up as well. As they came from the dark hallway into the light, the burn scars on Darius' face and neck were much more vivid in person than they appeared in the media.

"Please don't stand on my account," said the aged gentleman in the wheelchair in a crestfallen tone, motioning with both hands for his guests to resume their seats. "I'm honored that you would go through all the trouble to visit an old has-been like myself."

Clad in a crisp off-white buttoned shirt and green pleated slacks, the silver-haired and chocolate-skinned man looked like he'd just returned from a day at the office. His black loafers even glistened with a day-old polish. Wheelchair aside, his warm expression, completely bereft of guile, reminded Avery of Erik.

Having retaken her seat, Avery looked expectantly into her host's stormy gray eyes, noting how closely they resembled her son's.

"It's a pleasure to meet you, Mr. Viyergo. I'm Avery. Avery Renshaw. And this is my son, Ahmyn." Avery smiled while leaning around the corner of the table and extending her hand.

Receiving Avery's thin satin fingers into both of his massive weathered palms, Darius gazed into her eyes for a few seconds before speaking. "Your name, Miss Renshaw, will yet go down in history as the foremost among all women."

"Is that a – good thing, Mr. Viyergo?" Avery chuckled nervously, looking back and forth between her host and his grandson.

"Please, call me Darius." Then shifting his attention to Avery's right, the aged oracle looked upon Ahmyn nearly with hesitation, as though he was acquainted with some dangerous quality the boy possessed. Such a profound silence swallowed the room while Darius and Ahmyn looked at each other, Avery felt as though she could hear the neurons firing in her own head. It was as if the pair was recapping some kind of history they shared.

As Avery watched them, she detected the odd, almost timeless connection between the two. It was something she had longed for. Perhaps she too could enjoy this quiet understanding someday. As she reflected on the concept, she became agitated.

"It's so strange," Darius started, while seemingly unable to take his eyes from the boy. "How can it be?"

"Grandpa?" Phil said softly, placing a muscular hand upon Darius' sagging shoulder.

"All this time," Darius continued, in his deep resonant tone. "All this time. Could it really be? It's not possible though." He then paused, and began directing his comments to Ahmyn. "I know that must sound strange, speaking of the impossible in front of you. I'm sorry. After all, I know that it's you who provides possibilities. All good things. Yes." Without breaking eye contact with his superior, Darius moved his head slightly in Avery's direction. "Ms. Renshaw, do you know how old I was when I started receiving information about – about future events?"

"I, uh, um – weren't you a child? I thought I heard you say that on television once."

"I was no older than your son. And yet, he – your boy – he has always been the wellspring of knowledge all along. I didn't know before now, but it was Ahmyn who was providing the – I call them disclosures. It's been him all along."

Phil watched in astonishment, as though he'd been hearing his grandfather speak for the first time.

Avery felt the need to interject. "I'm sorry, sir, but clearly Ahmyn is just a boy. He couldn't have told you anything before six years ago. Well, and he's only been speaking for three years, so I guess – I'm just not sure what you're trying to say. I apologize. I'm – I'm just not understanding." Just then, flashing before Avery's mind was the incident on the bus, and Ahmyn's perplexing statement. *Before humanity existed, I am.*

"There are more than a few curious things about him, aren't there?" As though given permission to look away, Darius now focused on Avery, who now scooted closer to Ahmyn. "If you would, tell me about his father."

Here we go, Avery thought. *That* topic again. "Well, I never really met him, to be honest with you."

"That's because no one has!" Darius exclaimed.

"What?" Avery questioned, furrowing her brow. "What do you mean?"

"No one's ever met Ahmyn's father, and yet – *everyone* has seen him."

"Okaaaay?"

"Let me try to explain it this way. The universe behaves in such a way as to achieve balance, does it not?"

Avery was pretty sure she'd heard a statement like that in high school chemistry class seven years ago. "Right. Balance. Yes. So?"

"That's why he's here. Ahmyn was born to make that balance possible."

Avery's bewildered expression was in stark contrast to the exuberant smile upon the puzzling man before her. "So, is he doing that now? Is he finished? Is there more he needs to do? How am I supposed to know what he needs to do? And what exactly is he supposed to balance? Are you sure that – "

"In a very real way, humanity is responsible for Ahmyn's existence," Darius continued. "Before humankind walked the earth, there was no such thing as *unnecessary* pain. Indeed, animals have suffered for millions of years. There's no question there. The living world is a cruel and abrasive place. But if you take humans out of the picture, the pain that exists has a sacredness to it – such that we might not even call it pain at all. Think of it. When a lioness takes down a gazelle, she may inflict what could certainly be called pain upon her prey. But there is dignity in it. She brings that food home to her cubs. It is a sacred thing." Darius paused for a moment, breathing deeply. "Humans, on the other hand, at some point – began to inflict unnecessary pain on each other. And why was it unnecessary, do you think?"

Avery was hesitant to answer the question, afraid she might not provide the answer he was looking for. "I don't know. Is war ever necessary?"

"You have the right idea," Darius went on. "Humankind's defining feature is their rationale and critical thinking. Suffering became unnecessary when humans used their rationale to produce sorrow. Rather than thinking of a better way, they began to invest their time in producing suffering. As a species, we have become far too efficient at causing pain for others, and for ourselves. This is what needs to be balanced. All the unnecessary suffering that has ever been inflicted. That is to say, the impact humanity has had on the world."

Darius could see the fear and all the questions begin to swirl about in Avery's eyes.

"But Ahmyn is just a kid," Avery protested. "How is he supposed to stop people from killing each other? He's one person. Yes, he has some unexplained abilities, but he's still just one person. He can't possibly stop all of humanity from destroying itself."

"Now," Darius went on, raising his hand briefly from his thigh. "I never said he could stop them. And he certainly can't stop the ocean of ill behavior that's already transpired since the beginning of our species. If people insist on making the world a dark and hopeless place, and I assure you, there are those who do – then there's nothing that can be done to stand in their way."

"But what of the balance?" Avery asked, with desperation in her eyes. "How is Ahmyn supposed to offset all of the hatred in this world?"

"There is only one who knows the answer – to that question." Darius took another deep breath and clasped his hands upon his lap.

"Who?" Avery then followed Darius' weary gaze to her right until her eyes were locked onto Ahmyn's.

Ahmyn spoke slowly while gazing intently into his confused mother's eyes. "There is nothing I do, which I haven't first seen – my *father* do."

Placing her face in her hands momentarily, Avery looked up and sighed. "Well, I know we were hoping to also meet your wife, Mr. Viyergo. Is she – able to see us?"

CHAPTER 39

Avery had never imagined sleeping in a room shaped like this. In a king-sized bed with Ahmyn slumbering to her right, she lay awake and restless, tracing with her eyes the ornate crown molding that made a seamless circular trip around the ceiling. It called out to her, from twenty feet above her head, though she imagined it to be much further. She was hopelessly lost in it.

Was she supposed to be tracing it clockwise, or counter clockwise? How fast was she supposed to be tracing it? The flawless circle with no beginning and no end hung above her, while her son's words flickered like starry constellations in her mind. *You don't want to believe it. Before humanity existed, I am. If you believe, there is no good thing you can't see.* And his theoretical faceless – and *nameless* father. There was seldom an hour she didn't vex over that. Would she ever have concrete answers to her questions?

Closing her eyes, Avery could still see the vivid circle, and she began falling toward it, and through it. Her new surroundings seemed foreign and familiar at the same time. She and Ahmyn were headed somewhere. Then her mother's bed appeared to her left.

"Are you sure you're not feeling well enough?" Avery asked with purse in hand.

Opening her swollen eyes, Allison pulled the covers more snugly about her shivering frame and glared back.

"Right. Yikes, you do look kind of green. Maybe I should tell him we need to wait until you're feeling better."

"No," Allison moaned, reaching for the yellow glass of tea on her nightstand. "He's been talking about this for a long time. You need to take him."

"I don't know, Mom. You look awful."

"He said he wanted to go on his birthday. It's the only thing he asked for. He never asks for anything. Just take him. I'll be fine."

"True. It is all he asked for. I just worry about you. That's all." Kissing her mother's clammy forehead, Avery took the empty cup. "Do you want me to get you some more?"

"No," Allison groaned. "Love you guys."

"Well, okay then. Love you too."

Striding down the hall, Avery smiled at Ahmyn as he attempted to entertain himself with a set of tinker toys in the front room.

"See, Ahmyn," Avery said, placing the cup in the dishwasher, "toys can be fun sometimes."

"They're okay, I guess," he answered, returning the pieces to their case.

"Well I couldn't give you nothing for your birthday. It feels weird. You know?"

"Mom, you give me things every day."

"Food, shelter and clothes don't count, silly boy."

"Why not?"

"Well, I don't know." Staring into her son's stormy eyes, she mused on this and other such conversations she routinely had with Ahmyn. She never really felt like she was speaking with a child.

"But thank you for the gift, Mom," Ahmyn smiled, embracing her warmly. Flinging his long wavy brown hair back with the quick turn of his head, he headed for the door. "Are we ready then?"

"I'm ready if you are."

Locking the door behind them, Avery led the way to a red car she didn't recognize and climbed inside.

"Well, Mister," Avery began as she fastened her seatbelt, "it's okay if you feel like you want to take a nap during the drive, because it's going to take about – "

"Two hours and seventeen minutes," Ahmyn said casually.

"Oh. You already looked it up."

"No. Just had a feeling."

Avery took note of the time. 9:15. "Alright then, birthday boy. Off we go."

Ten minutes into the ride, Avery turned off the radio. "You know, Ahmyn, grandma and I have been talking lately, and if you really wanted to get back into public school, we could give it another try."

"You had your reasons for taking me out."

"That's true, but, well – I just think you get so bored at home."

"Trust me, Mom. I'm never bored. I do a lot of thinking."

"That much I know for certain!" Avery laughed. "Probably a little more than an eight-year-old should."

"Thoughts are key, Mom."

Running her right hand through his thick dark hair, Avery smiled at her precocious son. "Okay, Mr. Philosopher. So, I can't help but wonder why the sudden interest in the beach? You've never really been a huge fan of the water."

Remaining silent, Ahmyn turned the radio back on, changing the station to classical music.

"I mean, we tried to put you in swimming lessons when you were younger and you refused to get in."

"I have no problem with water. It's my body though. This mind. It isn't certain about the things I'm certain about. It fears things."

"There you go again. Soaring way over my head."

"Mom?"

"Yes?"

"Thank you."

"For what?"

"For allowing me to be your son."

"Oh, Ahmyn," Avery said, wiping moisture from her eyes with one hand while steering with the other. "Are you trying to make me cry?"

"It's not easy being a mom, is it? It can be really scary." Leaning across the middle console, Ahmyn wiped a large tear from his mother's cheek. "So thank you. For everything."

"You're not going to go and die on me, are you, Ahmyn? You're making me nervous."

"No one lives on earth forever. But no, Mom. Not today."

Something was off. It was as if the drive to the beach had never even happened. But there they were. Avery just went with it. It was as if she were watching a movie of herself, but was right there in the middle of it all.

Shifting the car into park, Avery looked over at her sleeping child, his head resting against the window. The clock read 11:32. "Hey, sleepy," Avery said, gently nudging Ahmyn's shoulder. "We're here, birthday boy."

Opening his stormy gray eyes, which matched the color of the current sky, Ahmyn took a deep breath and used his hand to sweep the hair out of his face.

"I'm afraid the weather isn't the greatest," Avery pointed out as they stepped out of the car. Covering her face with her arm, she tried to block sand from hitting her eyes as a sudden burst of wind kicked up dust and debris from the pavement.

Without a word and with his mother in tow, Ahmyn traversed the empty narrow parking lot and passed through one of the weathered wooden entrance gates. Intermittent patches of green beach grass were dancing in the warm breeze, whipping at their legs as the pair plodded through the sand.

Paying constant obeisance to the moon, vigorous waves continuously and rhythmically crashed against the defenseless shore, pulling and pushing on the earth. Plopping himself into the soft sand, Ahmyn proceeded to methodically remove his shoes and socks, revealing his bronze feet. Avery silently followed suit, taking note at how particularly reflective Ahmyn seemed.

Closing his eyes, he leaned back and eased himself onto his back. Stretching out his arm to his mother, she took his hand and did the same.

"Happy birthday, Ahmyn," Avery said, squeezing his hand. "So this is what you wanted, right? Sorry the weather isn't better."

"This is exactly what I wanted. And the weather is perfect. It's always perfect."

Releasing Avery's hand, Ahmyn arose, and stepping cautiously onto the wet sand, began to move purposefully and quickly toward the unrelenting waves.

"You're not actually going into the water, are you?" Avery said, sitting up. "Ahmyn, those waves are coming pretty hard. Let's just walk up to our ankles." Scurrying to her feet, she scampered after her son, who was already up to his knees in the receding tide. "Ahmyn, stop! That's too far!" As she ran, it seemed as if the distance between her and her child was only expanding.

Continuing his course, Ahmyn raised his arm as he walked. As he did so, the wind swiftly slowed until every blade of grass stood still. The boy was now waist deep in the water, and with Avery splashing in hot pursuit behind him, an approaching ten foot wave, now fifty meters away, collapsed upon itself like a deflated balloon. What was left of its previous momentum gushed

283

past, lifting the two off their feet momentarily. Continuing to move deeper into the now motionless water, Ahmyn was now up to his neck.

"Ahmyn, please stop!" Avery screamed, struggling to reach him. "You can't swim!" In horror, she then watched the top of his head slip beneath the surface. "Ahmyn, nooo!" Taking a deep breath she dove forward with arms outstretched to retrieve her child from the water. Trying to get a visual, her eyes recoiled in pain as they met with the unforgiving saline. Now gasping for breath, she fought to keep herself afloat while desperately trying to spot her son. "Ahmyyyyyn!"

In her mind's eye, she began to hear him. He was speaking softly, calming her. Even as she began to sink, dread was replaced by assurance, and fright with composure. As her descent continued, Avery lost track of which direction was up. Still further she descended hearing Ahmyn's voice. "That is right. Let go of your fears. Your regrets. Your pain. You must trust me. It is time. You must release it. Let me take it from you."

And so she did. Relinquishing control, she placed everything on the altar. Every misgiving and vain ambition. All her weakness. In the fetal position she floated, effortlessly suspended in time and space. Protected in this womb of love, acceptance, and hope, she was finally at peace. It was so familiar. So flawless. So quiet. And then the voice again. Was it him? Or someone else? "What you have tasted – it must be earned. And not by you. Only one can accomplish it. Your son. He alone can defeat the unconquerable, and bridge the infinite chasm, a chasm which was forged by the hatred of man."

The first thing Avery saw when she opened her eyes was moist sand. The right side of her face was smashed up against it. *Ahmyn!* Pushing herself onto all fours, she began frantically scanning the shoreline for her son. "Ahmyn, where are you!"

Then something caught her attention out on the water. A slow roaring crescendo could be heard across the sea, which, since Ahmyn had lifted his hand, had been bereft of waves. Like an endless sheet of glass, the ocean shimmered as the sun burst through the clouds. The air was now completely saturated with the rushing sound of a vast throng of approaching birds. Brilliant white feathers reflected the blazing rays of the sun as the flock completely dominated the sky. Numbering in tens of thousands, they now swirled in unison about thirty meters out to sea. Like a descending pillar of flickering light, they nearly touched the water, then dispersed toward the shore, alighting upon the sand like drops of the sun itself. Left standing upon the motionless water where the birds had been circling was Ahmyn. Gazing into the sky as he walked seaward, he then turned and raised his hand toward Avery, beckoning her to join him.

Stepping cautiously from the shore to the warm water, Avery began moving across the surface of the blue-green expanse toward her son. As she pressed on, a burst of air washed across her face as one of the elegant dove-like birds flew past her head, landing moments later upon Ahmyn's outstretched hand. He appeared to be speaking with the bird, then after nestling his cheek on the tucked wing of the creature, set it free into the sky. Caressing the air with its graceful wings, it was followed by the remainder of the flock.

Bolting past Avery as they began to take flight, the swarm of white rushing feathers was all she could see. With her visual of Ahmyn interrupted and her bearings lost, she began to feel the water rise slowly past her ankles, knees, and hips. "No!" she cried. "Ahmyn?!" Still encompassed in the avian whirlwind, she sunk further still. Now to her middle, shoulders, ears, and then through the white rushing storm, she saw it – his face, exuding compassion, and an outstretched arm.

As she grasped his hand, the scene dissolved before her eyes, leaving her enveloped in quietude and blackness. This endured for some time, until she felt it. The sand beneath her as she lay. Through her closed eyelids she began to discern a red glow, its intensity increasing slowly until it became a bright imposing glare. Turning onto her side, she pushed herself to a sitting position. Squinting while her eyes adjusted to the light, she looked straight ahead at Ahmyn, who was building a sand castle some twenty meters away. Next to him was a dove-like bird, with the whitest feathers Avery had ever seen.

"Hi, Mom," Ahmyn said as Avery approached him.

"Ahmyn, how did you – "

"Did you have a nice nap?"

Avery plopped herself next to him, admiring his handywork. "Nap? How long was I over there?"

"Ten minutes."

"I had a really scary dream."

Dragging his fingers through the moist sand, Ahmyn continued to dig out the mote for his castle. "About me."

"Yes. It felt so real. First I thought you were drowning, and then you were – "

"Standing on the water."

"Yes."

"What did you learn?"

Avery took a fist full of sand and added to the base of Ahmyn's castle. "I'm not sure."

"All of us must wash away the old, and take up the new."

"Like being born."

"Yes. As many times as it takes."

∞

The first thing Avery saw when she opened her eyes was Ahmyn silently gazing at her while he lay wrapped in the sleek black bedspread. He had taken the whole thing for himself.

"I see how it is," Avery mumbled. "Apparently you don't think your mom deserves to be warm too."

"Sorry," Ahmyn grinned. "I didn't mean to."

Avery couldn't remove her eyes from her son's face, nor her mind from the words of Darius Viyergo from the night before. "Buddy?"

"Yes?" His tone was warm and empathetic.

"I'm starting to wish we hadn't come here at all."

Ahmyn closed his eyes for a few seconds, but said nothing.

"I just can't believe – I just can't believe we didn't make it in time to help his wife. That's kind of why we came, wasn't it? I just thought it would turn out differently."

"Sometimes we have to let them go, Mom. Sometimes – they want to be let go."

Avery pondered his statement for a moment, then reflected on all Darius had delineated the night before. "I want to be your Mom, Ahmyn. I don't want to be afraid anymore. I don't want to be afraid of losing you."

Ahmyn took a deep breath. "We can't run from what is required of us."

Avery pondered the puzzle pieces of her life. As they swirled about before her, so much of her experience seemed to be imposed upon her. Required of her. And there wasn't a place on earth she could have traveled to escape the reach of these demands. "But Ahmyn, the things he said about you last night. You're six years old. You're just a baby. You can be a kid, right? Can't you be allowed to just be a kid? The things he said last night – made me feel like you're not allowed to have a normal childhood."

Pushing himself up, Ahmyn continued constant eye contact with his mother. "Do you know how many children will die of hunger today?"

Avery lay speechless, while tears began to emerge from her eyes.

"Do you know how many will die tomorrow? How many children's hearts die every day because their parents, who should love them, neglect and abuse them instead?"

"Oh, Ahmyn," Avery mumbled through thick sobs. "Why do you have to think about these things?"

"In my father's house, every child gets to run and play. In my father's house, every child has a warm bed to sleep in. No one is hungry. No one is scared. But here. This world is different. This world is suffering. Every minute. Every hour. Every day."

Ahmyn was now standing as he spoke, communicating as much with his eyes and arm as with his lips. "Don't you know who I am? Don't you know why I'm here? To provide a normal childhood for everyone, in my father's house. To dry all the tears. To heal the broken hearts. To be a friend to the friendless." With moist eyes of his own, Ahmyn now crouched down toward his mother, placing his hand on her cheek. "Don't be afraid, Mom. No one can take my life from me. I will be here until I'm finished. Until I've done what is required of me."

CHAPTER 40

Years came and went with dreamlike fluidity. Allison's little 'A' team relocated three times, her cleaning business grew, and Ahmyn's behavior continued to be a major source of concern for Avery. More specifically, he continued to exhibit blind deference to public school policy, particularly the concept of not leaving without consent.

It was also true that his time in school had introduced no concept of language, mathematics, or science he didn't appear to already be intimately familiar with. So it became an easy decision to pull him from school and introduce an online curriculum, which he completed as fast as the program allowed. At age ten, he became the youngest person in Western Republic history to hold a high school diploma. This provided some solace for his mother. In the moments when Avery's nerves weren't shot from fretting over where Ahmyn was or when he would return, she was at least grateful it had never been necessary to remind him to do his schoolwork.

As her son grew, there wasn't a single day where Avery didn't reflect on Ahmyn's statement at the Viyergo home. There were times when it gave her comfort. There were also moments when she feared his words. What exactly did he mean? '…until I have completed what is required of me.'

Ahmyn never disclosed the specifics. Could he possibly be offsetting the unnecessary suffering in the world, as Darius Viyergo had referred to it, with unnecessary good? Would it perhaps be by curing the illnesses and ailments of mankind? Darius had explained to Avery that the entire world would know of him – that all nations of the earth would forsake all their worldly possessions just to see him with their own eyes. He would give hope to the decaying human race.

Indeed, Avery's child, during Darius Viyergo's final public statement, was pronounced to be humanity's only hope. "The destiny of the human race," he had proclaimed one week before his death, "rests upon the shoulders of one man. Ahmyn Renshaw holds our future in his hands." When probed for details about the individual he spoke of, Darius' response was as blunt as it was evasive: "He will reveal himself to you when he sees fit."

This final declaration of Darius Viyergo, the deeply controversial international icon that he was, disseminated like digital wildfire, saturating the internet in a matter of days. The burning question in hearts the world over was only natural. Who was Ahmyn Renshaw? Where did he live? What did he look like? An accurate spelling of his name hadn't even been supplied. And most importantly, what enabled him to clutch the entire planet's destiny in the palm of his hand?

Gradually, time would produce some answers.

Despite the abundance of claims to the name and responsibility indicated for this Ahmyn Renshaw, a new presence was beginning to emerge from the global binary sea of ones and zeros. Reports of unexplainable events. Quite famously, a children's cancer unit in the Western Republic began reporting unusually high recovery rates. Indeed, virtually all patients admitted were shown to have been cancer free after only a month of treatment. This track record had been going strong for 2 years. The hospital was in York's capital city, New Hope.

The next anomaly making waves on the internet was a long-term psychiatric ward, also in New Hope, in which all one hundred residents were released within just a few months, completely symptom free. Indeed, patients who had been under treatment for over ten years were released to their families. And the oddities only continued.

New Hope also began to see a vast reduction in panhandling. It being one of the worst cities in the Republic for the phenomenon, within a one year period showed an 85% decrease in panhandlers per capita. When queried on what actions were responsible for the dramatic results, city officials made a clumsy attempt to explain it, but in the end it appeared evident they were doing markedly less than other cities struggling with the same problem.

A mystique began to enshroud New Hope. As though surrounded in a threadbare satin sheet, the outside world could peer through and discern the dancing silhouettes. There was a playful youthful energy emanating from this once decaying city. Global chatter and interest were swelling. What was it about this place? What did they suddenly possess that the rest of the world did not?

The head-turning events continued. New Hope's crime rates were plummeting. This city, which for decades had maintained its reputation for being one of the five least happy large cities in the Republic, was trending toward becoming the most sought after place to live. And those who hadn't forgotten Darius Viyergo's declaration began to insist, Ahmyn Renshaw, if he truly existed, would be found in New Hope, York.

Avery's son was certainly not unknown. A select number of individuals had become familiar with him. There was first, and foremost, Avery's fateful taxi driver, Trevor, who she fondly remembered and with whom she'd regretfully lost contact. Then there was Miata and Teja, who had ever remained close friends of the Renshaws. Ahmyn's Kindergarten teacher, Miss Tindale, would never forget the boy who fled the playground on the official first day of her career. And there were, of course, the handful of medical professionals who had crossed paths with him. Khai Oughten, Avery's trauma surgeon, sent her a birthday card every year, quietly anticipating – hoping – that her child would one day fulfill Darius Viyergo's final prediction.

However, the vast majority who had the life-altering pleasure of meeting Ahmyn – and there were thousands of them – never knew him by name. Whether he was relieving someone of a terminal illness, vanquishing a person's destructive addiction, or restoring a maimed body, he departed with empathy radiating from his compassionate gray eyes, never disclosing his identity. He spent his days in exact obedience to the will of his alleged father, anonymously transforming the lives of everyone he encountered.

With nearly a decade of international adoration, New Hope's contagious and optimistic energy was drawing visitors from across the globe. It had the best air, the cleanest streets, a thriving economy, and the finest hospitals. Just stepping foot in the city was rumored to have measurable health benefits. And if you got lucky, you might even run into Ahmyn Renshaw.

Indeed, years of converging accounts had led to the public perception that there was, in fact, an influential resident in New Hope by that name. Since the very day of Viyergo's final disclosure, there had been people in differing locales around the world claiming to be the individual he spoke of. But they were all loons. A couple of charismatic figures had even been able to amass substantial followings over the years. This individual in his late teens from New Hope, however, was quite different from the others. He didn't publicize himself – at all.

The Ahmyn Renshaw from New Hope, as the plethora of obscure stories alluded to, chose to be homeless. Spending the majority of his time among the underprivileged, he was said to employ ancient meditative techniques which allegedly facilitated a better quality of life. Some accounts even indicated that this young sage, despite his own handicapped condition of only having one usable arm, was capable of curing illnesses. With the simple touch of his hand, as more than a few avid bloggers asserted, he could even give sight to the blind. Scores of others claimed to have been relieved of drug addictions simply by having a conversation with him. He was lauded as an incessant advocate for the impoverished, frequently soliciting large businesses to freely share their profits with those in need. This he had allegedly done since his childhood. And so it was, over a decade of countless published accounts had fueled a growing confidence that Darius Viyergo had spoken correctly. There was, indeed, a man named Ahmyn Renshaw.

And desperate people across the globe were clamoring to reach him. New Hope's glory years were about to be challenged. It happened slowly. Imperceptibly, at first. But just like a virus mounting its mindless siege, once the symptoms began to manifest, it was already too late.

New Hope had become the most fascinating and mysterious city on earth. Best known for its unfailing generosity, this gleaming, powerful beacon of the West towered with arms outstretched to hopeless citizens everywhere. And when those seeking refuge arrived, they brought their diseases with them.

CHAPTER 41

With her penetrating brown eyes fixed on the television, Avery was oblivious to the squawking oven timer. Nor did she notice Allison had returned from work and was standing immediately to her left. All that existed in the world in this moment were her worst fears, distilling on her skin like poisonous icy dew.

"In a stunning turn of events this evening, Major General Porter Rauche has issued a scathing statement concerning one of New Hope's most notable philanthropists, twenty two year old, Ahmyn Renshaw. This is what he had to say during the high-profile press conference just last hour."

"This is a matter of utmost concern for Western Republic national security. One of our most regarded cities is hard-hit with the KPC outbreak. Being the commercial hub that it has always been, New Hope is a perfect vector for the distribution of this disease to virtually every country on earth. And this is exactly what we've seen happen over the last few months. While the majority of the some five thousand KPC related deaths in the Republic have been reported in New Hope, we have growing numbers of fatalities throughout the Republic. The global death toll is said to be close to fifteen thousand.

"While it is true our epidemiologists are optimistic about containing this outbreak, it will not be the last major health challenge we have to face. Heightened immigration into the Western Republic over the last few years has brought third-world diseases to a first-world nation. Interviews and other intelligence strongly suggest that many of the sick immigrants are hoping they will encounter the famed Ahmyn Renshaw. Among the most desperate cases, we have found this to be almost exclusively true.

"Internet hype and word of mouth have made Ahmyn Renshaw out to be something he most certainly is not. Contrary to his own adamant personal assertions, and the claims of others, he is not capable of curing any human maladies. Let me be perfectly clear. Ahmyn Renshaw is not a super hero. He cannot cure any illness. That being said, however, his purely deceitful and extremely persuasive campaign to the contrary have created a serious threat to Western Republic national security. We have issued a warrant for his immediate arrest, and a cash reward of one hundred thousand dollars for information leading to his apprehension."

Avery's overloaded nervous system kicked in, forcing her to resume breathing. Gasping for air, she directed her horrified glossy eyes at her mother's bewildered face. Allison had unknowingly dropped everything she'd carried in the door, including an open can of orange soda which had disseminated into an expanding fizzy pool upon the wood floor. With their eyes locked and mouths agape, their conversation, had they possessed the capacity to speak, would have been one of denial. Certainly, they can't arrest him, can they? Murderers got arrested. Rapists were put in jail. Breaking the law got you thrown in prison. What law had Ahmyn violated? What harm had he ever caused?

Reaching for her phone, Avery sent off a text to the person who seemed to have the most consistent contact with Ahmyn. "Miata, have you seen the news? Do you have any idea where he is?"

"I'm watching it right now," came the response. "And no. I haven't seen him in over a month."

Avery hadn't heard from him in even longer. He never carried a phone and his rare visits at home were always very brief. Turning off the TV, Avery stared blankly ahead, thinking nothing, feeling nothing. And knowing even less.

Minutes later she began receiving a string of texts from Miata. "Oh no. Oh no. They can't. They can't. No. Avery, I'm so sorry. I can't believe this. What are we going to do?"

Removing her shoes and leaving her phone behind, Avery stood and walked barefoot for the door.

"Aves?" Allison called from the kitchen. "Aves, what are you doing?"

Without a response, Avery proceeded slowly onto the front porch and down the steps.

Going after her daughter, Allison rushed outside to cut her off. "Sweetheart, where on earth are you going?"

"To the playground," Avery mumbled without halting.

"Aves, come home," Allison insisted, keeping pace.

Avery kept her eyes forward as she continued. "Mom, I just need a minute. Okay? Don't worry about me. I'll be fine."

Allison reluctantly stopped pursuit. As she turned for home, her limbs gave way beneath her and she was shortly upon her knees, with tiny pebbles and debris digging into her skin. With her chest heaving, tears she didn't even know were there began descending from her cheeks onto the concrete beneath.

Ten minutes later, Avery was sitting in a swing at the local elementary school. With her hands clinging to the steel chain, she rocked herself methodically back and forth with her toes. To her left was a swing for a young child, with the bucket seat and chain latch. In her mind's eye, she could see young Ahmyn giggling while she pushed him in the soothing afternoon sun, laughing right along with him.

A fire engine then came screaming past, the jarring noise of which forced her consciousness to reflect on her current crisis. Ahmyn was no longer in the bucket seat swing to her left. Childless, it wobbled slightly in the breeze that was also tossing Avery's black hair into her face. Would she ever embrace her son again? Ever see him again? Ever hear his voice again? To these and a hurricane of other questions, Avery remained bereft of answers.

Close by was a makeshift hopscotch diagram that had been recently traced out by a now abandoned piece of white chalk. Almost without thinking, Avery departed the swings and stepped carefully toward the writing utensil. Having retrieved it, she then padded over to the red brick façade of the school and began to write.

He chose not his birth among the privileged,
Nor his bed among the mighty.
At the tip of the oppressor's blade was he born,
Nourished by an impassible womb.
Gifts immune to appraisal shall he bestow,
While the passerby must judge him feeble.
With dew of justice distilled upon his heart,
Shall he crush eternal chains to pieces.
Judged to be the source of angst,
He will offer solace to his people.

When she finished inscribing the poem, she laid herself on the blacktop, reading the words over and over again. Ahmyn's destiny was out of her control. It had been since the beginning. Like the breeze that caressed her face as she lay, her son's life had never been something she could cling and hold to her bosom. She gazed into the sky, observing how the famed supernova, Grace, had begun to fade. Submitting to all that remained outside her control, she closed her eyes, allowing herself to dissolve into the ground beneath her.

While Avery lay unconscious a few blocks away, Allison watched the latest news update. Her grandson, Ahmyn Renshaw – had surrendered.

CHAPTER 42

"We have him, Sir," rattled a scruffy male voice through the two-way attached to General Porter Rauche's hip.

"Alright," General Rauche said curtly, with the radio to his mouth. "Don't you let him out of your sight, you hear me?"

"He's not going anywhere, Sir."

"I want him uniformed and shackled in ten minutes."

"Absolutely, Sir."

Returning the radio to its leather holster, the commander straightened his Five-Star uniform in the reflection of the plate-glass window that separated his temporary office from the adjacent firing squad chamber. Removing a tattered brown wallet from his dark green pleated trousers, he opened it, gazing at a picture of a young man that looked exactly like him when he was sixteen. Then slowly closing his wrinkled eyelids for a moment, he returned the wallet to his back pocket and took a seat behind a large hardwood desk, upon which lay a newspaper with the front page reading *Riots escalate as KPC pandemic sows death.*

Before long the voice blared again through the two-way. "We're right outside the door."

"Bring him in," General Rauche ordered.

As his prisoner was escorted into the room, the commander gazed at the internationally notorious figure before him. Thick chains connecting Ahmyn's one wrist to his ankles clanked as he shuffled across the white laminate flooring. Not overly solid in stature, he was nearly a full head shorter than the six armored brutes who followed him into the room. Still, despite what should have been extremely intimidating circumstances, Ahmyn looked General Rauche directly in the eye from the moment he walked in. With shoulders erect and his back firm, his posture was majestic. And his eyes. Like spears they pierced General Rauche to the core, unraveling his thoughts, and discerning his soul.

"You came willingly," the commander said sternly, reciprocating Ahmyn's unyielding gaze. "Why?"

"I do that which my father requires of me," Ahmyn said calmly, in a voice that seemed far older than the face from which it resonated.

"Is that so?" The commander's boots thudded as he walked methodically toward his prisoner. "Tell me something. How did you do it?"

Maintaining eye contact with his captor, Ahmyn said nothing.

"How is it that a single man could turn the *entire world* upside down?" General Rauche stepped closer, now only two feet from the only individual he'd ever feared. With no response from Ahmyn, he continued, speaking slowly and firmly, over-enunciating each syllable. "Answer the question."

In a resolute tone, Ahmyn spoke firmly. "The oceans would obey even you, provided you possessed the faith."

With a quick nod from the commander, the six guards slipped out of the room and locked the door behind them.

As the deadbolt clicked, Porter Rauche's arm came swiftly up and across his chest, his hand slicing down sharply across Ahmyn's right cheek. "Faith doesn't command the most potent military superpower in the world! *I* do!"

Ahmyn then stumbled into the wall to his left as the commander rendered another exacting blow upon his face.

"Now," General Rauche continued, his heart pounding like a jackhammer within his chest, "Are we *completely* clear on who you're talking to right now?"

Regaining his balance, Ahmyn wiped a slow stream of red from his nose and now swollen upper lip.

The commander offered a sadistic grin. "I have no idea how you've been able to fool the entire world into thinking you have something of any value to offer. I really have no clue. Actually, you know what? I do. I do. This planet has been populated with swarms of nitwits since day one, so I'm giving you too much credit. I truly am. All these people need is to see something on the internet, the newspaper, or on TV, and they'll swallow it hook, line and sinker. Governments have been exploiting the gullibility of their citizens since the beginning. But you've done something worse, haven't you?"

Tilting his head back to stave off the blood that poured from his nose, drops of crimson fell from Ahmyn's chin, splashing like rain on the ground below.

"You've toyed with people's emotions. You've pretended to be the answer to all their problems. Haven't you? Haven't you?!"

Staring down his throbbing nose, Ahmyn glared patiently into the commander's frantic eyes.

"Do you know what you are? You're the greatest hoax of all time. You're the very definition of evil. Playing on the emotions of the whole planet like that? You and your sick accomplice, Darius Viyergo. You two are the worst thing that ever happened in the history of man. Just think about what you've done to society! We're splitting apart at the seams because of you! Do you have any concept of the suffering you've caused? The sorrow and confusion?! All the disease and death?! How many thousands more will die because of you?!"

Anger seethed through General Rauche's veins at Ahmyn's prolonged silence. Striking fiercely again, the commander sent his captive sprawling backwards into the door. With both of his large hands, the commander grasped Ahmyn's orange uniform and repeatedly thrust him into the door. Again and again, the back of Ahmyn's skull came into harsh contact with the reinforced glass behind him. "This pandemic is your fault!" roared the commander. "People are dropping like flies all over the world! My *son* would still be alive if it weren't for you!"

Leaving his battered victim slumped at the foot of the door, the heaving commander stood with clenched fists and his arms to the side. "You worthless fraud. Don't you see? I have a moral obligation – to kill you. You're nothing but a scourge. All that remains in your path is desolation. Humanity could never begin to undo the damage you've caused. But if nothing else, your life ends today. Right now. It's time for the world to purge itself of the *poison* that is Ahmyn Renshaw."

With his face toward the floor, Ahmyn raised himself to his knees and breathed deeply. "My life – my life cannot be taken from me."

"What did you say?" General Rauche demanded.

Grabbing the door handle, Ahmyn slowly pulled himself to his feet. Now pointing at the commander, he staggered two steps forward. "It is incomprehensible to you, but you haven't the power to end my life. No one can take it from me."

"We'll see about that." Grabbing the radio from its holster, the commander brought it to his lips.

"Tell me something, Porter," Ahmyn said softly.

Lowering the radio, the commander stared defiantly at the bleeding man before him. "You're speaking to a Five-Star General, and you *will* address me as such."

"Did you say goodbye to Brandy before you flew here?"

Looking into the sympathetic gray eyes before him, General Rauche cocked his head slightly to one side. "*Excuse* me?"

"Because it's going to be a very long time before you see her again."

"This all ends here." Raising the radio he clutched with whitened knuckles, the commander spoke his final order. "It's time."

With a solid click, the door unlocked and two men entered the room. Taking Ahmyn firmly by the arm, they forcibly escorted him into the adjacent firing squad chamber. On the far side of the frigid concrete-walled room was a lone steel chair, bolted to the cement floor. Ahmyn made no attempt to resist his captors as they violently shoved him into his throne of death. Pulling thick leather straps across his ankles and wrist, they secured their prisoner.

"Take your places!" General Rauche boomed as he marched into the room, his face burning intensely with the flame of revenge. With boots pounding across the floor, the commander stopped within a meter of his prize. "Any final words, oh great one?"

"Vengeance belongs to my father, and he will repay."

"I thought you'd say something like that."

"General Rauche, are you ready to die?"

Leaning in closely, Porter Rauche placed a rank canvas bag over Ahmyn's head. "Not as ready as you need to be."

Now heading for the opposite side of the room, the commander took up the loaded rifle which awaited him. "Alright, gentlemen! One bullet for every continent that has suffered because of this man! On my mark!"

Per General Rauche's order, seven rifles were lifted and trained on Ahmyn's defenseless chest.

"They drown in ignorance, Father," Ahmyn said calmly. "Forgive them."

"Ready!" screamed the commander. "Fire!"

Seven hammers then ignited powder. Deafening thunder reverberated throughout the room, accompanied by the pings of bullets ricocheting from the steel chair. With his head still upright, Ahmyn sat erect, seemingly untouched.

The General stepped cautiously forward, signaling with his uplifted fist for attention from the guards. As he approached his prisoner, it was clear he was still breathing. There was no blood. No holes in the uniform. Swiftly turning, the General stomped back to his gun. "We go again!"

A collective fear and confusion was humming through the room as the guards apprehensively raised their firearms once again.

"On my mark," boomed the General. "Fire!"

The results were the same.

"What is this?!" roared the General. "Are we all loaded with blanks?" Deploying a round at a light overhead, the General shielded his eyes as glass rained down upon him. "Again! On my mark!"

Seven rifles were once again trained on Ahmyn.

"My father gives," Ahmyn uttered through the canvas bag over his head. "And he will take away."

At that, as if sitting atop a massive jack hammer, the entire concrete room began to tremble, sending Ahmyn's executioners to the floor. Scrambling over each other for the locked exit, the guards began shielding their ducked heads as the ceiling began to crumble and descend upon them.

Laying on the violently quaking floor and with terror in his eyes, Porter Rauche deployed the rest of his semiautomatic magazine at Ahmyn. He then drew a knife and crawled two feet before being crushed by five hundred pounds of falling concrete.

Peregrine Penitentiary, the monster of steel and cement, demonstrated little resilience against the heaving earth. Like an expiring star, the prison moaned and rocked, shrieking as it painfully imploded.

In what had been the firing squad chamber only minutes prior, the chair to which Ahmyn was strapped was leaning back and to the left. Under the open night sky, Ahmyn was surrounded by death, and encompassed by chunks of concrete clinging to webs of mangled rebar.

Looking upward, Ahmyn choked on suffocating breaths of swirling dust. "Anything is possible for you, Father," he groaned. "If you would approve it, allow this task to pass me by." Strapped to the steel, Ahmyn sat patiently in the dark, prepared to fully submit to what lay ahead. "But as always, Father, I won't allow fear to dissuade me. What you require is supreme. Whatever you ask of me, I will carry it out."

Stale musty air filled Ahmyn's lungs as he took one deep breath after another. With chest heaving, he groaned in agony as excruciating pain began surging through his system. The splintering sensation in his bones subsided momentarily – just long enough for him to notice something significant had changed. "Father?" Ahmyn said in a panic. "Father, where are you?!"

Attempting to shed the canvas hood that concealed his face, Ahmyn threw his head back and forth like a mad dog, but it did nothing. "Father, no! Please, no! Don't make me do this alone! Please don't neglect me! Pleeeeease!"

Moisture began accumulating on his face, and in slow hesitant streams, began trickling down his face, leaving the taste of blood and sweat on his tongue. "Why?" he moaned. "How could you – abandon – me?"

CHAPTER 43

Clenching his teeth in exquisite agony, Ahmyn shrieked under the pulverizing burden placed upon him. Unspeakable grief plowed through his system, harrowing his consciousness so relentlessly that time itself cowered into complete insignificance. In his mind, tortured screams swirled in a hurricane of thick putrid blackness, while horrifying images of the most degrading human behavior flashed before him.

Slipping deeper into the endless storm of lies, hatred, abuse, murder and rape, Ahmyn wept. He wept for all the good that might have been. For shattered homes the world over. For the malice that calloused the souls of mankind. He bled and wept for the darkness bred by selfishness, for children hiding in closets from those who should have cared for them.

"Why, my children?" Ahmyn cried. "Why do you exchange happiness for death? Life beckons you. I am here to gather you into the safe house. I have shelter, food, and clothing. Even now, my arms are open! Will you not be rescued?!"

His lengthy descent through the poisonous hurricane concluded abruptly, leaving Ahmyn crawling across a parched barren wasteland. The aroma of smoke and ash filled his lungs, causing him to wheeze and cough. Too exhausted to stand, he slowly made his way toward a windowless wooden door that stood erect ahead of him. As he came nearer, muffled cries for help from behind the door began to fill Ahmyn's ears.

Trying to quicken his pace across the dusty clay ground, he was instantly knocked to his side as a boot was planted firmly into his rib cage. Doubled over in pain, Ahmyn looked up to view his assailant. Before him stood the figure of a man, cloaked and hooded in black decayed raiment. Hanging on a razor-edged chain about his neck was the emblem of the figure eight. Waving a bony pointer finger at Ahmyn, the hooded figure seethed a hideous laugh and dealt another blow, this time to Ahmyn's face.

Now standing directly above Ahmyn, the figure's voice sounded like two massive sheets of rusted iron scraping across each other as he spoke. "These," he screeched, pointing to the door, "are not for the taking. They belong to me, and none else. They have chosen their reward, and carefully selected their master."

Then with the elegant movement of the demon's arm, the door dissolved into dust, and the churning sky grew more sinister. With intermittent flashes of red lightning, the disgusting landscape became more vivid. As far as the eye could see were imposing wooden posts protruding from the desolate earth. From the tops of each post hung a thick chain which held fast the wrists of emaciated gray human forms, the genders of which were undiscernible. Removing a shard-tipped whip from his decaying girdle, the hooded figure began letting it fly upon his prisoners. Cries of agony and horror saturated the air as the demon went methodically through the endless sea of prisoners, leaving sorrow and desperation in his path.

"Father," Ahmyn whispered while struggling to rise to his feet. "With you, all things are possible. All of these people. Their souls are precious in your sight. Give me the strength to free them."

The shriek of the demon's grinding laughter then sliced the air. "Do you really believe you can save them?"

Looking over his shoulder, Ahmyn could see the cloaked demon in close proximity behind him. A debilitating pain then seared across Ahmyn's back, forcing him to his knees. A chained wooden post then slowly emerged from the ground before him, rising perpendicular to the desolate earth. Grasping his wrist as it rose, it stopped, leaving Ahmyn barely on the tips of his toes. The unforgiving whip then sliced across his face, chest, and neck.

"Aren't you going to save the worthless masses?" the demon laughed while slapping the whip across Ahmyn's flesh again and again. "What are you waiting for? Come down from that tree and save them!" Unleashing greater ferocity with each stroke, the hooded figure sneered as the whip ripped across his prisoner. "You're weak. Just like them. Your eyes plead for mercy. I can see it."

Trembling as he hung, Ahmyn managed to utter four words. "You cannot conquer me."

With whip still in hand, the demon slid like a cobra around the wooden post to face him. "You dare speak to me directly?"

"Shortly you will know a new master," Ahmyn groaned.

"I answer to no one!"

"But you shall cower before the Infinite."

Roaring and gnashing his decrepit teeth, the demon clutched Ahmyn by the throat and tore him from the chain. Like fog swirling in the wind, the pair rushed through the endless sea of desperate imprisoned souls, finally arriving at the edge of a sheer rocky cliff. With his throat still in the demon's vice grip and his feet dangling over an endless abyss, Ahmyn reached for the figure-eight emblem that dangled about the hooded figure's neck, and with a violent tug, yanked it free.

"What are you doing?!" cried the demon.

"Keeping a promise," Ahmyn choked. Opening his mouth, Ahmyn placed the emblem upon his tongue. Holding his mouth agape for the hooded figure to see, the emblem sizzled and cracked, producing smoke and fire. Dissipating within a few short moments, Ahmyn closed his mouth and swallowed what remained. Releasing his iron grip on Ahmyn's neck, the hooded figure fell to his knees.

Now free of his captor, Ahmyn didn't drop into the abyss, but stood upon a white glimmering surface which began to materialize beneath his feet. Ornate shimmering pillars commenced lining either side of the walkway that was stretching off into the opposite direction. As the bridge extended further and further, a bright light began to flash and flicker on the horizon. Growing to the size of a full moon, the orb ascended into the sky directly above the white bridge, throwing its healing beams in all directions. As the light fell upon the chains that bound the hopeless sea of prisoners, their shackles shattered like glass hitting rock.

Beckoned by the pure light, the masses began making their way toward the shimmering bridge upon which Ahmyn stood. Addressing the demon which now cowered before him, Ahmyn pointed into the black pit beneath. "Depart."

Obeying his superior's bidding, the hooded figure hissed and coughed, sending himself over the edge. Howling and twisting as he fell, the demon was swallowed by gaping jaws of black oblivion that awaited below.

The endless ocean of freed prisoners began to change. From their nearly lifeless gray ambiguous appearance emerged males and females with bright beaming eyes, clad in robes of silver. All of them started for the brilliant bridge upon which Ahmyn stood, the bridge that traversed an eternal trench and delivered its travelers to a glorious city on the horizon. The people congregated before him, all with tears of gratitude and love in their eyes.

Trembling as he stood before the throng, Ahmyn's overwhelming joy for their release from captivity was more than he could endure in his exhausted state. He collapsed. And all went black.

CHAPTER 44

At first, all Ahmyn could detect was his own shallow breathing. His chest barely moved as he took short and insufficient breaths. Coughing on the dust-filled air, Ahmyn detected he was bound. Unable to move his legs and arm, he raised his head to ascertain his surroundings but saw nothing. A rough texture could be felt against his face as he moved his head. Then more coughing. Approaching sirens began to materialize in the distance, and the whomping of helicopter blades were now being felt from overhead.

From within the thundering helicopter, Talmage Chesnovich was scanning the disastrous scene below, using a high-powered strobe to spot survivors in the deadly debris. "Bring it left, Chuck!" he hollered to the pilot. "There's someone down there! Swing us 45 degrees! Yes, right there." Talmage trained the brilliant beam directly below. "Do you see him, Chuck?"

Peering through the swirling dust, the pilot confirmed it. An orange clad individual, with what appeared to be a burlap sack over his head, was in sitting position. His head was definitely moving back and forth. "I say we use our energy helping non-prisoners!"

Talmage leaned to speak over his pilot's shoulder. "I'm going down."

The pilot nodded reluctantly and trained the chopper over the ragged opening in the roof while Talmage prepared to lower down.

The imposing noise of the chopper remained directly over Ahmyn's head, while clouds of pulverized concrete swirled about him. His sweat-soaked face then felt the refreshing swath of flowing air rush over his face as the rank bag was lifted from his head. Blinded by the headlamp of his rescuer, Ahmyn clenched his eyes closed. Terrible stinging then ensued as sweat was forced into the corners of his lids.

The man before him then began unfastening the beastly straps, freeing Ahmyn's wrist and ankles. "I need to get this harness around you," said the man. "The only way out is up." With the skilled hands of his rescuer, Ahmyn was secured within moments. Feeling the sensation of the ground cease contact with his feet, he was raised slowly into the safety of the helicopter.

Turning in his seat to get a look at the prisoner, the pilot's heart sank. "You've gotta be kidding me!" he screamed at his partner. "Do you realize who that is?!"

Indeed, Talmage knew exactly who the prisoner was. He had just rescued the most recognizable person in the world. And according to the leadership of the Republic, the most dangerous. "Yes, I know."

"They were keeping him here?!" Chuck barked. "We need to get him off this craft ASAP! Holy crap, they were going to execute him! We need to get him over to base right now!"

Manned by National Guard military, the base referred to by the pilot was the highly-guarded temporary confinement locale being established just west of the now collapsed mammoth prison. All surviving prisoners had been designated to be sequestered there.

"We're taking him to New Hope," Talmage defiantly shouted.

"What are you talking about?" Chuck replied, steering the craft toward base. "We're dropping him down and handing him over."

Standing nearly over his comrade, Talmage slammed his fist against the low metal ceiling. "This man doesn't deserve to die! He is innocent!"

"He's a fraud, Talmage! At the very least! He's caused a lot of trouble for everyone! Do you know how many people have died because of him? His fate isn't in our hands. We're handing him over."

"He is innocent, Chuck! I watched him heal my blind father's eyes when I was ten years old. He's no fraud, and he's no threat! Disease came to the Republic because desperate people were looking for hope. He was their hope!"

Glancing back and forth between the base below and Talmage's passionate eyes, Chuck's muscles and limbs seemed to make the decision for him.

To the confusion of the National Guard team below, the rumbling chopper wheeled around, then plowed eastward, disappearing into the night sky.

"You do realize," Chuck began, looking briefly at his comrade, "we'll be court-marshalled for this. And arrested."

"Then why are you flying him home?"

"I always wanted to believe the crazy rumors were true. But up until now, I never knew of anyone who had actually seen it firsthand. If you say he's legit, then – then he doesn't deserve to die."

∞

"That's right, Drake. This is truly an astonishing scene transpiring before us tonight. I'm standing outside the gates to the notorious Peregrine Heights penitentiary, which appears to have suffered severe structural damage within the last thirty minutes. According to reports, this is the locale where the famed Ahmyn Renshaw was taken after turning himself into authorities not two days ago.

"It seems a very powerful localized earthquake has struck, the epicenter being right beneath the most dangerous prison in the Republic. Naturally, this is an extreme concern for officials tonight as Peregrine Heights has long been the maximum security prison for the most hardened criminals. Approximately twenty-five percent of the individuals incarcerated here are on death row. So these events are of highest concern for officials as they seek to not only account for all of these dangerous prisoners, but the staff as well."

"Thank you, Sandy. I suppose it is unknown whether Ahmyn Renshaw is among the survivors?"

"That's correct. At this point, there are some confirmed survivors who are being treated for injuries. We have not been given word whether Mr. Renshaw is one of them."

"The aerial footage we're seeing is very telling. We've displayed a before-image for viewers to demonstrate just how bad this catastrophe really is. Sandy, it appears that the entire structure of the prison has completely imploded on itself. It's almost unrecognizable. There must have been a great loss of life tonight."

"The likelihood of fatalities is extremely high, Drake. So indeed, the emergency responders and military personnel called to the scene are in extremely precarious circumstances as they try to save the lives of the staff, as well as those who were already sentenced to die. Certainly a very remarkable situation to be in, Drake."

"Again, Sandy Austin reporting on the shocking development at York's Peregrine Heights maximum security prison, which is now in shambles after being rocked by a massive earthquake. More details to follow."

CHAPTER 45

Thirty minutes after Ahmyn's rescue from the shambles of Peregrine Heights, he was plodding barefoot along the blacktop of a high school parking lot. Looking back to view the ascending helicopter, he continued the painful walk toward his mother's home. It wasn't far – a mere two blocks. Limping as he went, his swollen eyes and blank stare were fixed on the sidewalk.

A helicopter touching down in the middle of New Hope at this late hour certainly didn't go without being noticed. Peering through slats in the blinds and drapes, multiple nearby residents took note of the commotion, as did the sickly and haggard group of hundreds gathered outside the Renshaw home. Convened for the purpose of expressing their collective hope for his well-being, it had also become a prevailing belief that simply passing by Ahmyn's home could heal one of their ailments and afflictions.

At the sound of the encroaching helicopter, a few individuals from the pining assemblage ventured to satisfy the crowd's collective curiosity. Startled to see an approaching man donning the orange prison uniform, the group paused in their tracks, cautiously watching. The poorly lit street didn't reveal many details about the apparent prison escapee, but he continued on, walking steadily toward them, his dark hair swaying with each careful step.

"I think it's him," one commented.

"That's not possible," another insisted.

"It sure looks like him."

"Ahmyn, is that you?" one called out.

Fighting the desire to allow her hopes to soar, Miata sat upon a small iron bench on the Renshaw's front porch. To her left was Brayden, her fiancé of two years.

Agitated by Miata's worrying, Brayden placed his hand on her left thigh.

She didn't reciprocate.

"I never really thought things would turn out like this," Brayden said, almost cynically. "Did you?"

"Like what?" Miata curtly replied.

"I thought he was going to save the world or something." Brayden paused a moment, glancing around at the hopeful drabble about him. "Look at us all now."

Pushing his hand from her leg, Miata glared at him in disgust.

"Miata, he's not coming back."

"How can you say that?"

Running a hand over the stubble on his head, Brayden shot to his feet. "Look, Miata, I saw the newscast just like everybody else. If he was truly inside that prison when it collapsed, then he's probably not coming back out."

Miata could hardly bring herself to look him in the eye. Looking at the porch's wooden railing, she spoke with calm conviction. "I don't have to believe that." She paused for a moment, reflecting on her personal experiences with Ahmyn. Taking a deep breath, she stood, looking Brayden square in the eyes. "What Darius Viyergo said is true. Absolutely true. Ahmyn Renshaw is the only hope this world has for a peaceful future. Without him, all we can hope for is destruction, death, and despair."

Shaking his head, Brayden stepped swiftly past Avery to the opposite side of the porch. "Do you realize how ridiculous that sounds? Honestly, all of us really are that brainwashed, aren't we?"

Miata remained silent.

Stepping forward, Brayden threw his hands in the air as he hollered. "He gave himself up, Miata! He sold – us – out!"

"Stop it," Miata demanded.

"If he's so great and powerful, why did he turn himself over? If he was what Darius said he was, then would he have just surrendered? Would an innocent man do that?!"

"I wish you could hear what you sound like right now."

"I wanna believe, Miata."

Miata raised her eyebrows. "Do you?"

"Really I do. But if he's supposed to make everything right, if he's the only answer, then why are things getting so bad? If he can stop this epidemic, then why hasn't he done it? What is he waiting for?" Placing his hands on the railing, Brayden took a moment to observe all the people waiting – waiting for something to happen, to be saved from their current reality. "It seems like when things started getting really desperate – that's when he decided to leave. Miata, I wanna believe."

"It doesn't sound like it to me." Stepping toward him, Miata forced a smile through her tears.

"I do," Brayden insisted. "But he abandoned us. Look around. He abandoned all of us."

"You know what? It doesn't matter what you believe. Let me ask you something. What's keeping you here tonight, anyway? Why don't you just go home?"

Brayden softened his tone. "What? Do you want me to leave?"

Miata waited a moment before responding. "I think *you* want to leave."

"I feel like you're pushing me away."

Miata let out a short irritated breath and shook her head. "Honestly, Brayden, I really don't want to do this with you right now. Go home." Turning toward the house, she grasped the brass door handle.

"So what happens when Ahmyn supposedly saves the world?" Brayden interjected.

Miata was already one foot inside the door, but paused. "What are you talking about?"

"Tell me. I want to know. What happens when he fixes this global mess. Are you going to run off and marry him or something?"

"Goodbye, Brayden," Miata said calmly, turning away.

Brayden followed her inside. "I've seen the way you look at him. It's pretty obvious you'd rather be with him than me."

Miata stared into Brayden's jealous eyes and gave him a fiery look of her own. Behind him and through the half-draped window she noticed the loitering crowd shift their attention to the East. Like a flock of sparrows they began sifting down the street in unison.

Pushing past Brayden as though he were a stranger, Miata barged through the flimsy screen door. Running into the poorly lit street, she jogged around the perimeter of the crowd, desperately hoping, though not truly expecting, to see Ahmyn's face amongst the throng.

Downstairs, Avery was using a spray bottle to mist over her unconscious mother's face. A nearby fan was positioned to blow over Allison in an attempt to keep her as cool as possible. Having experienced fatigue for days prior to Ahmyn's surrender, she was now overcome with the pan-resistant strain that afflicted so many others. Allison was particularly hard hit, being without the ability to even sit up for more than a few minutes at a time. Intermittently throughout the day, she had been insisting – albeit a barely intelligible mumble – that Ahmyn would be returning that evening.

Outside, a surge of relief mixed with worry rushed through Miata as she laid eyes on Ahmyn. Supported on either side by a man and woman Miata didn't recognize, he limped slowly along the road's shoulder. He was clad in a filthy orange prison uniform. Miata's imagination was trying to decipher what chain of events had brought him home, though her delight to see him took stage.

"Ahmyn!" Miata yelled, forcing herself through the masses. "Ahmyn, you're alive!"

Smiling warmly, he locked eyes with her, then seemed to wince in discomfort.

"May I?" Miata gestured to the kind woman supporting Ahmyn at his left.

The woman nodded. "Of course. Yes, of course." Relinquishing the job to the eager face before her, the woman then slipped back into the crowd.

"Oh, Ahmyn," Miata exclaimed, taking careful steps as they made their way down the street. "We're so glad you're back." She craned her neck to the right to look at his face. He said nothing, but seemed to emanate gratitude to be among those who cared for him. "I don't know how to tell you this, but your grandmother – she got sick. And she went downhill fast. She's barely holding on."

"I know, Miata," Ahmyn managed. "I know."

"I'm so sorry," Miata said through tears, toggling her gaze between Aymyn's exhausted expression and the street. "It's been really hard on your mom the last couple of days. First you being taken away, and then Allison catching it. She refused to call anyone. She said that you'd be back. That you would – make things right."

"Within three days," Ahmyn groaned, "my work will be finished."

Miata earnestly looked into his glistening gray eyes.

Word of Ahmyn's return blazed through the crowd like wildfire, torching its way through the streets and into the Renshaw home.

Hearing the clamor outside, Avery reluctantly left her mother's side and walked calmly up the stairs. Exiting through her front door, puzzled at why elation wasn't an accurate way to describe her emotions. Her son was back, they'd shouted into the house. *He's back?* Perhaps. But for how long? There was an end to this story. Avery could feel it in the air. It filled her lungs with every breath. And it was terrifying.

She hadn't even bothered to put on her shoes. Plodding down the middle of the street, she didn't even feel the rough terrain against the skin of her feet.

"Ahmyn's back, everyone!" came an intrusive voice over a loud speaker. "Everybody give him some space. Give him some space. Let the man take a breather and then he'll cure everyone."

As the crowd turned to decipher the origin of the announcement, Miata saw Brayden leaning against his police cruiser with its megaphone mouthpiece in hand.

"Just give Ahmyn a couple minutes and he'll get you all taken care of," Brayden continued.

Miata glared ahead with indignation at a man she wished she'd never met. With a disgusting smirk on his face, Brayden glared back.

"Don't pay any attention to him," Miata said, looking at Ahmyn. "Just ignore him. We're going to bring you inside."

Avery continued slowly toward her son. He was in plain view now, looking directly at her. She smiled, feeling the wet trail of a tear down her cheek. What lay in store, she had no idea, but as she embraced him, she couldn't stave off the horrifying idea that this may be the last time she would feel the warmth of her child. She wanted to speak, but by doing so, it felt as though she was surrendering him to whatever fate lay in store.

But Avery knew full well that this moment was the same as any other in Ahmyn's life; she, *his own mother*, had no control over the outcome. His birth, childhood, and early adulthood to this point were all a tapestry of events required by some unseen force. There was a cosmic will at work, calling all the shots. This much was clear to Avery. It had taken a long time for her to learn this truth. To accept it. To surrender to it.

Ahmyn, however, had always been strictly obedient. And not out of fear. He seemed to know very early on there was something grand about his presence on earth. In a seemingly pointless existence, he had purpose. He had a momentous agenda. He was born with it. It seemed his itinerary was plainly laid before he had ever been conceived.

They were now directly in front of the Renshaw home. Miata refused to look at Brayden who resembled a python about to strike.

The yard and curbs were riddled with people taken ill.

"Release me," Ahmyn said. "I can stand. Please let me stand on my own."

"Alright, everyone," Brayden announced, almost sneering, "looks like Ahmyn is ready to fix our dilemma. He will now cure every single one of you. Anyone who has anything wrong with them. Just step forward. Ahmyn is here to save us."

It was completely silent as the throng looked to Ahmyn, awaiting his response.

An aged woman with gray frizzled hair stepped forward, holding an infant in her arms. Her voice quivered as she spoke. "Please. He's all I have left. He has it. Please cure him."

Ahmyn began to extend his hand as he cautiously stepped forward, but then halted.

"Sir?" the woman pleaded.

"There's a lot of people here, Ahmyn," Brayden stated harshly. "They're all relying on you. If you're going to save us, now is the time."

Ahmyn looked longingly at the child, but said nothing. Remaining still, tears began seeping from the corners of his eyes.

Placing her hand on his shoulder, Miata smiled warmly. "You don't have a lot of strength right now, Ahmyn. We need to get you inside. Let's go inside."

"Ahmyn has the ability to simply speak and everyone here can be cured," Brayden insisted over his police cruiser megaphone. "Surely, he won't leave anyone out here to fend for themselves. You're not refusing to help that defenseless child, are you, Ahmyn?"

"Leave him alone, creep!" Miata yelled back. "You don't have the right to tell Ahmyn what to do or when to do it!"

"Aren't you going to heal the baby?" said another woman from the crowd.

"Maybe he can't really do it," said another.

"Oh, no," Brayden rebutted. "He's perfectly capable of doing it. The rumors are all true. But maybe he's had a change of heart."

"Come on," Avery said, placing her hand on Ahmyn's back. "We don't need to listen to this."

Ahmyn turned to his left and began for the steps that led to his mother's house.

"Maybe he doesn't care about us all as much as we thought he did," Brayden said with indignation. "Tell us, Ahmyn, because I'm sure we'd all just love to know. How is it that you are the only survivor? I'm sure we've all heard about it, haven't we? Ahmyn Renshaw was locked away in Peregrine Heights. And while he was there, the entire structure collapsed on itself! How is it that he gets to walk away, while everyone else, including the innocent employees, are left trapped?!"

Ahmyn stopped on the steps and turned.

"Forget about him, Ahmyn," Avery insisted. "Let's go."

But Ahmyn stood still, silently facing his accuser.

"We all know how powerful Ahmyn Renshaw is, don't we? He can heal any disease. We've even heard rumors he can bring people back to life! That's impressive. Let us ask you something, Ahmyn. What else are you capable of? Did you cause the earthquake?" Brayden paused to let the questions sink into the minds of the onlookers.

"Don't listen to that freak," Miata screamed, pointing defiantly at Brayden. "He's insane. He doesn't know what he's talking about!"

"That's very kind of you, Miata, to defend him so fiercely. But it seems pretty clear you probably have some conflicts of interest here. As for the rest of us, we have the right to know, don't we? Ahmyn, did you cause that earthquake, leaving yourself as a survivor?" He paused again before continuing. "Did you kill – those people?"

Ahmyn looked directly at Brayden. "What you plan to do, do it quickly."

"Isn't that interesting?!" Brayden pointed out, almost laughing. "He isn't denying it! Well, makes sense right? A lot of the people in that prison were criminals. Who needs them?"

"Just because someone's in prison doesn't mean they're a criminal!" a man piped in.

"Now, let's just hold on, folks," Brayden said. "Let's ask him one more time. Ahmyn, did you cause that earthquake? Did you kill all those people?"

"Ahmyn has never hurt anyone in his life!" Miata shouted to the crowd. "He didn't kill anyone!"

"He needs to answer the question," Brayden continued. "We deserve to know the truth."

"My life ends when I decide," Ahmyn declared. "Not a moment sooner."

"Did you hear that, everyone?" Brayden said looking around at the throng. "That sounds a lot like an admission of guilt, doesn't it? Is this how Ahmyn plans on saving the human race? By killing all the people that aren't as perfect as he is?! Survival of the fittest, right? He obviously knows what he's doing. He's punishing us by getting our hopes up, then crushing them when we're at our most vulnerable. He doesn't care about us! He's here to punish us!"

"Ahmyn, aren't you going to help us?" came a voice from the crowd.

"Please, Ahmyn!" came another.

"He doesn't have the strength!" Miata shouted. "Can't you see? He can barely stand!"

"He's better off than they are!" Brayden retorted, pointing at the people around him. "What are all these people supposed to do? It's not like anyone can go to the overflowing hospitals!"

"He can't just go around curing every single person in the city! It takes too much out of him!" Miata pleaded.

"Alright, Ahmyn," Brayden went on. "So you don't have it in your heart to take care of these people?"

"He's never turned anyone away," Miata spoke out.

"Shut up, Miata," Brayden barked. "What's he doing right now?" Brayden walked across the street and stepped up to Ahmyn, pointing accusingly. "The miraculous Ahmyn, the chosen, the elite, the one who can cheat death – he's now powerless? Of course he's not powerless. He simply has other plans for the human race. To let us all die off."

With no emotion in his face, Ahmyn glared back and said nothing. From the corner of his eye he could see his mother, her face pleading, aching, yearning. Taking a step back, he began to limp slowly toward the house.

"Is that really what you plan to do, great one?" Brayden chided. "You're just going to walk away from all these people who believed in you? You've spent all these years building up everyone's hopes! You had so many people convinced you were actually going to make things better for humanity. I was starting to believe it myself!"

Running down the stairs, Miata shoved Brayden violently and screamed, "Leave him alone!"

Retaliating instantly, Brayden dealt a sharp blow across her face, sending Miata sprawling towards the stairs. Gasping at the altercation transpiring before her, Avery crouched down to help Miata to her feet.

Ahmyn glared at Brayden, whose face screamed with resolute hatred.

Brayden looked to his left and right. "Are we really going to stand aside and make way for Ahmyn's plans for us? And just what exactly does he have planned for us? He hasn't done anything for humanity! Nothing! We went from bad to worse, and it's because of him! How can we expect to move on and heal if we keep clinging to the lies of Ahmyn Renshaw?!"

"Kill him!" screamed a voice from the swelling mass of people.

"He's abandoned us!" came another.

"Stop it!" Avery screamed from the porch while she and Miata endeavored to help Ahmyn inside, but Brayden and three large men stood in their way, holding them back.

"Go home, everyone!" Miata shouted. "Ahmyn never did anything to harm any of you! Just leave him alone!!"

"No, Miata!" Brayden yelled in return. "We aren't going to let this man lie to us anymore!" Then firmly taking Ahmyn's arm, he and the other three began to drag him into the street.

"Let go of my son!!" Avery shrieked as she fought frantically to free him.

Miata squirmed past more individuals of the convulsing throng and managed to jump on Brayden's back, raking her finger nails across his face. "Let him go!! Ahmyn! Don't let them take you!!"

One of Ahmyn's captors then pulled out a pistol and whipped it across Miata's skull, knocking her to the concrete.

What had begun as a helpless crowd of desperate people was now a pulsing demonic mob, seething hatred as they screamed, "Kill him! Kill him! Kill him!"

Avery struggled to get free but was held back by dozens of imposing hands pulling at her arms, torso, legs, and hair. It was the darkest of dreams, the deepest of nightmares, moving in extremely slow motion. Ahmyn's stormy eyes were fixed on his mother's, his brown wavy hair swaying back and forth like a pendulum as he tried to break free. Being now forced against the side of a nearby van, Ahmyn's arms were pulled up and held out about parallel to the ground.

"Ahmyn!!" Avery screamed. "Don't let them do this to you!"

A frenzied cluster crouched at Ahmyn's feet, holding them fast, while the mob continued to bawl, "Kill him! Kill him! Kill him!"

Raising his head slightly, Ahmyn looked to the sky where thick distressed clouds were rapidly gathering. In an act of surrender, he then faced his aggressors and closed his eyes while he smiled. It was as if Ahmyn had granted permission to pull the trigger.

Suspended in a state of deep reflection, Avery recalled with adoration the first time she ever held her newborn son. That moment of pristine joy melted over her during the present chaos. Her exhausted mind was processing her immediate reality very slowly, and she watched with relative lack of alarm as a round of ammunition entered Ahmyn's abdomen.

Imagery of Ahmyn's first steps were dancing before her eyes now. Clumsily, he wobbled the short distance from Avery's hands toward Allison's, laughing as he accomplished the feat. Another bullet was then discharged, plowing into his chest.

All of his childhood birthdays were now flashing in and out of view. Colorful cakes, gifts he was never very thrilled about, streamers and music. And gunshots. Then Ahmyn's teenage years were at the forefront of Avery's mind. The days when he began to spend more and more time away. The sleepless nights, wondering where he was, and when he'd return.

And more bullets.

Avery's mind had finally caught up with the horror that was unfolding before her. One after another, a flurry of rounds from multiple sources were tearing mercilessly through Ahmyn's defenseless flesh, rendering him nearly unrecognizable in a matter of seconds.

As if under a demonic trance, a portion of the deadly throng was raiding a nearby backyard. Amassing a horde of wood and tires, they piled them high in the street, soaking it with gasoline. Ahmyn's bleeding, broken body was then hoisted atop the heap.

Avery felt as though she were slipping into unconsciousness. The scene was going blurry. The mob no longer held her back, and she staggered forward, falling to her knees. Shock was setting in. Trembling as she crawled, she still believed she could save her son from the inevitable. An overpowering wave of heat then flared into her face, forcing her back. Grimacing black plumes of smoke erupted from the blazing mountain and Avery knew – it was over. All was lost. Ahmyn was gone. Her child – was dead.

Drenched with sweat and panting, Brayden stood before the flames as they snarled and soared into the dark night air. Ten meters to his left lay an unconscious, bleeding Miata. A slight distance further knelt a weeping Avery, the mother of the man he'd just helped annihilate. As if seeing the horror for the first time, Brayden stumbled wide-eyed to the hood of the van where he'd helped restrain Ahmyn moments earlier. The pistol in his left hand gleamed at him as he leaned against the van. He had forgotten he was holding it. The flames mocked him as they reflected off the polished steel of the gun. With his finger on the trigger, Brayden positioned the barrel against his left temple – and fired.

CHAPTER 46

It was unacceptable. The most precious blood ever to roam the earth had been spilt by humanity. The retribution meted by the tortured planet was incomprehensible. Nature, it seemed, *did* have its own mind. And the elements, though not coerced, mourned and refused to be comforted. Writhing under the gravity of her incalculable loss, the earth reeled to and fro as if in death throws for hours on end.

The pathetic structures of men toppled helplessly to the earth into heaps of rock, steel, and ash. Enormous clouds rose from the debris, only to be wafted away and scattered by raging tornadoes. Hurricanes throbbed across all oceans and seas simultaneously while volcanoes heaved molten vomit. No human settlement on earth went unaffected. And death – death drank deeply.

∞

Avery slowly awoke to rhythmic wet impulses on her left cheek. Face down on the cold basement floor, she was pinned by an old oak table that had collapsed on top of her. Window glass was strewn throughout the scene, while massive cracks in the concrete foundation exposed the soil without. Thick in the damp air was the distinctive powerful aroma of the additive in natural gas. Cradled against Avery's chest, wrapped in a white bath towel, was the ornate urn Allison had long ago since asked Avery to make for herself. It was a soft gray, inlaid with brightly colored flowers spiraling around then tapering at the top. The contents were a small portion of Ahmyn's remains – whatever Avery could scoop into it before the violent earthquake and tornadoes began.

"Mom?" she called out. "Mom, where are you?"

Allison's absence was vexing. Avery had pulled her unconscious mother under the table for protection during the quake.

How long have I been lying here? It was difficult to say. Sunlight peered through the small windows, illuminating the relatively barren basement with a faint, pleasant glow. Aside from the leaking pipe above her head, everything was remarkably still, so completely quiet. Stark was the contrast between the present moment and the many terrifying hours that preceded it. But as she lay there, amazed to still be alive, Avery knew – there wasn't much to look forward to. Perhaps the deadly quakes and relentless storms would resume. And even if there was some respite from them, all the destruction that certainly waited outside seemed unbearable to Avery's tortured mind.

It took almost all the strength she could muster to slide herself out of the path of the dripping water. The continuous cold slaps in her face were maddening. Her belly yearned for food, while her back stung from the sharp edge of the heavy table. Completely exhausted, Avery glanced at the white towel under her arm. She knew it wasn't real, but in her mind's eye she could see her little boy nestled beside her. His stormy gray eyes penetrated hers as he reached up to touch her cheek. *I love you, Ahmyn,* she whispered. *Thank you so much for allowing me to be your mother.*

Struggling to raise her own left hand, she intended to touch her infant's perfect face, then gasped as he vanished before her eyes. All that remained was the urn, wrapped in a white bath towel. *No, Ahmyn, please don't be gone!* The events of the prior evening then began to play over and over again in Avery's head. How he was betrayed and murdered in cold blood. How she tried desperately to stop them. And how they threw his innocent body to the flames! The years with him were so few! With what little energy she had left, Avery wept. Why hadn't she been able to protect him? Her crying was barely louder than a pathetic whimper, but was overheard.

"Avery?"

Avery didn't notice the voice at first.

"Avery, is that you?"

Avery began to listen as intently as she could. "Mom?"

There were light footsteps descending the wooden stairs.

"Avery, Allison? Are you two down here?"

It was a familiar lovely female voice.

"Avery, it's me."

The voice was now projecting from the bottom of the stairs, but all Avery could see was a light. An extremely blinding circular light. Squinting her exhausted eyes, Avery tried to make out who or what it could be, but the glaring beam prevented it.

"Oh my gosh, Avery! Are you okay?"

The intense light then took its place two meters away on the floor and no longer pointed directly at her face. It was Avery's old million-candle flashlight.

"Here, hold still while I get this table up."

Avery felt the relief of the weight as it was lifted from her back. As she turned to confirm who had found her, sunlight danced across red wavy locks, framing blood-smeared, lightly freckled cheeks and dazzling brown eyes.

"I have always absolutely loved your hair," Avery commented in a raspy, horse tone.

"You can have it," Miata replied. "It's given me nothing but trouble."

The two looked at each other for a moment in the quietude and smiled.

"Wasn't your mom down here with you?" Miata asked as she crouched down to remove the table from atop Avery's back.

"She was," Avery managed. "I have no idea where she could have gone."

"We'll find her, Avery." Extending both her arms for support, Miata helped Avery slowly to her feet.

"Oh, wow," Avery panted as she stumbled into the cement wall.

"Whoa, watch it there," Miata said as she helped to steady her.

"Talk about feeling light-headed."

"You and me both."

"You wouldn't mind grabbing that urn down there, would you?" Avery asked.

"Who's is – " Miata cupped her hand over her mouth. Having been knocked unconscious during the struggle, Miata hadn't witnessed Ahmyn's fate.

"It's him." Avery spoke barely above a whisper.

"No!" Miata gasped. "Somehow I always thought that he would – " She paused for a moment. "I don't know what I'm trying to say."

"They shot him to pieces," Avery mumbled as she gazed blankly across the room. "Then they burned him."

"Oh my gosh, Avery." Miata gently placed her arms about Avery as tears rolled down both of their cheeks.

"He didn't deserve to die," Avery sobbed. "I can't go on, Miata. I have nothing left. Nothing left to live for anymore."

"I know it must seem that way right now."

"Do you know what he used to always say?"

"What?"

"He would tell me everything was going to be alright. Every time he would leave for months on end, he would say it." Avery placed a feeble hand on Miata's shoulder. "Why did he say that? Nothing is alright. Only misery awaits us out there."

Miata sighed and took a deep breath. "What would Ahmyn expect from us right now?"

"Not to give up hope."

"I think you're right. Hey, what do you say we get you out of this basement? It's not safe down here."

"I'm not sure I want to know what upstairs looks like."

"Not to worry. I won't spoil it for you."

With the spotlight in one hand and the urn in the other, Miata offered her arm to Avery for support. Walking across the shards of glass and through puddles of water, they arrived at the foot of the wooden staircase. As Miata directed the bright beam upwards, it revealed a dangerous ascent. Chunks of drywall were scattered about, while the stairs themselves had become largely detached from their support beams.

Slowly and carefully the two made their way to the main floor. The damage before Avery's face was incredible. Absolutely nothing had remained it its place. Not a dish remained in its cabinet. Not a window remained intact. Major portions of the ceiling had caved in, leaving the floor littered in rubble.

"Not quite the way you left it, is it?" Miata said, forcing a laugh.

"What I wouldn't give for a drink of water right about now," Avery commented as she surveyed the scene.

"Seriously," Miata agreed. "Shall we check the fridge? Maybe there's some bottled water or some juice or *something*."

Walking cautiously across the debris, the two women arrived at the fridge, the door hanging slightly ajar. Helping Avery rest against the green island counter top, Miata turned off the spotlight and placed it, along with the urn, on the counter space adjacent to the fridge.

"Ah, yes!" Miata exclaimed as she revealed two bottles of water and a half-gallon of orange juice. "This should help a little."

As Miata turned from the fridge, she could see Avery's eyes fixed on something in the opposite corner of the kitchen.

"Miata," Avery began, "am I seeing things?"

Following Avery's gaze, Miata gasped and dropped the bottles of water as she rose.

"Maybe we both are," Miata remarked.

Both were dumbfounded at what they saw on the counter to the left of the sink.

"Is that a vase of – daisies?"

"I think so."

"Where did they come from?"

"I have no idea. I'm confident they weren't there before I went down to find you."

The two walked the short distance toward the colorful arrangement, completely puzzled by it. Each instinctively brought their faces up to the pristine vivid flowers and inhaled their sweet aroma. For a brief moment, each forgot the chaos that surrounded them. Their bliss was harshly interrupted, however, when the silence was shattered by the urn as it made earsplitting contact with the tile floor.

Both women gasped in unison and immediately crouched down, picking up the pieces.

"I'm so sorry, Avery!" Miata pleaded. "I know I didn't put it on the edge. I don't know why it fell like that."

"It's fine," Avery insisted. "Nothing we can do about it now."

As they continued to gather the shattered fragments, Avery began to cry. Miata couldn't help feeling responsible. But it was peculiar too. There was broken pottery, but where were the ashes? Then it came – the unmistakable and overwhelming peace. Avery had felt it the night Ahmyn was born, and on the plane when he had miraculously calmed the deadly storm. Miata knew the feeling all too well herself; it had consoled her during the times when she had needed it the most. And now beyond the feeling, was his voice.

"What if I were to tell you everything is going to be alright?"

Turning about, the two astonished women rose slowly to their feet. Neither could believe their eyes. It was impossible. Certainly, this wasn't – *real*. Ahmyn was *dead*, his body shamelessly marred and desecrated. And yet, there in the destroyed front room, he stood, barefoot, with his broad smile, completely unharmed, wearing dark blue jeans and a pastel yellow buttoned shirt with sleeves folded to his elbows.

"Do you believe it *now*?" Ahmyn calmly asked as he walked toward them.

"I don't understand," Avery's voice quivered as she supported herself against the island. "Miata, is he there? Do you see him? Do you see my son?"

"Yes, Avery. It's him."

A moment later Ahmyn placed a hand on each of their foreheads, his left upon his mother's, and his right upon Miata's. Each felt their respective pains quickly recede into nothingness as they were made whole. It felt as if each had just awoken from a perfect night's rest, rejuvenated, and more alive than they had ever been.

It was as Ahmyn now embraced her that Avery fully realized her son had not one, but *two* functional arms and hands. She had dreamt of this moment. She had felt this moment before – the night Ahmyn was born. When she thought all was lost, when she thought she would never get to see her son, it was *this moment* that had been impressed upon her soul. Somehow, twenty-two years ago, she had already experienced this warm embrace, this infallible comfort, this immaculate peace.

"Ahmyn, I never thought I'd see you again," Avery sobbed. "How did you do this? How is this possible?"

"Does reality require an explanation?" Ahmyn replied.

"But I don't understand how any of this is happening. How is it you're alive again? I'm worried my mind is playing tricks on me. I want so desperately for this to be real."

"What does your heart tell you?"

Avery tried to speak, but nothing came out. As long as she had this moment to cling to, it didn't matter what the future held. This moment was real, and nothing else.

"Grandma told me to say hi," Ahmyn smiled.

"Ah," Avery sighed. "So you've seen her?"

"She's no longer burdened by this world."

Avery was surprised to feel no sadness at the news. "Good. I'm – happy for her."

Warmth emanated from Ahmyn's vibrant smile.

"You're not going to stay, are you?" Miata asked as she wiped tears from her eyes.

"Oh, Miata," Ahmyn replied. His voice was kind and reassuring.

As Ahmyn reached now for her, Miata embraced him with all her might, pressing her face into his chest. It felt too good to be true. Such love and acceptance radiated from him, such unbiased understanding. In what often seemed to be a purposeless, harsh, and unforgiving world, hope was also to be found.

"Please don't leave us, Ahmyn," Miata pleaded.

"I've never been absent, Miata," Ahmyn said softly.

Despite his reassurance, Miata knew Ahmyn was too pure, too selfless, too perfect for this world. He wouldn't be able to stay. The world would not tolerate him. It *hadn't* tolerated him.

"Come," Ahmyn beckoned. "Follow me."

Making their way through the rubble, Avery and Miata followed Ahmyn through the front door and into the aftermath of Mother Nature's rage. The neighborhood was completely unrecognizable. It was as if the entire area had been ground in a blender and spat back out again. Massive crevices had formed, half swallowing what little remained of the tornado and quake-ravaged homes. Few trees remained standing, and those that did were leafless and battered. Avery was astonished to observe the horizon, once crowned with its myriad of skyscrapers, now desolate.

The two were having difficulty keeping pace with their leader.

"What about all the other people that may be in the debris?" Avery called.

"The dead need no consolation," Ahmyn spoke over his shoulder.

"And what about the living?" Miata asked.

"They will know where to find us," he replied.

Maneuvering like mountain goats, the three struggled through the endless debris for nearly an hour. Cars, trailers, trucks, and buses had been tossed about like dice, some laying on their side, some on their backs. Many vehicles protruded from buildings and homes. Nothing man-made had withstood nature's wrath.

As the trio traversed what Avery believed to be Aspen Boulevard – what was left of it, in any case – the faint beginnings of a melody began to tickle the air. What a peculiar noise to be heard in such surroundings! Neither Avery nor Miata mentioned it; both simply enjoyed the playful, soothing strain. As to what or who was producing the delightful sound was a complete mystery, but it sounded very much to be a chorus of – children. And an enormous one, at that.

"Isn't that the most beautiful sound in all the world?" Ahmyn exclaimed as they walked.

"What is it? Where is it coming from?" Avery questioned.

"You'll see," Ahmyn responded.

Ahmyn had paused in his tracks and waited for the two to catch up.

"Oh my gosh," Miata gasped as she arrived at Ahmyn's side.

"What is this place?" Avery said in astonishment.

"This," Ahmyn said with outstretched arms, "is a new beginning."

In vibrant color before their eyes was a pristine expansive river valley. The scene was replete with rolling green hills speckled with beautifully colored flowers. Countless clusters of fruit trees and an endless bounty of gardens sprawled as far as the eye could see.

"I know I've never been here before," Avery said with moist eyes, "and yet – it's so familiar."

"I told them I'd be back soon," Ahmyn remarked. "We'd better not keep them waiting."

"Who?" Miata asked.

"Both of you, take my hand!" Ahmyn exclaimed.

Each woman obliged, then Ahmyn led them in a full sprint down the gradual velvet green slope. The delightful singing became louder as they progressed down the hill. Normally, Avery would have expected to be plenty short of breath by now, but strangely, she felt she could go on for hours. Miata couldn't help but laugh out loud as they galloped through the long grass, the sweet-smelling air filling her lungs as they ran.

Now in view was a large bowl-like indent, forming a natural amphitheater of sorts. The marvelous voices of children projected from this central location, producing more than just music; indeed, it seemed to be the essence of wisdom, the purest joy, the pinnacle of understanding.

The throng detected their arrival and immediately formed a straight path leading to the front. The singing persisted, while countless pairs of little eyes were fixed on Ahmyn and his guests.

Releasing his companions' hands at the end of the aisle, Ahmyn turned to face the massive throng, smiling from ear to ear. Thousands of children were gathered, all sitting on the cool grass, beaming right back at him.

"My friends," Ahmyn's voice resonated with ease to all. "Thank you! Thank you for your faith, for your hope, and for the goodness of your hearts!"

Great tears began to roll down Ahmyn's dark cheeks as he continued. "I'm sorry. I'm sorry you've all had to endure so much. I wish there was another way. I truly do. Believe me, if there was any other way – "

Ahmyn was interrupted by the sudden embrace of a small boy in tattered, dirt-stained clothes.

"It's okay, Ahmyn," the boy said meekly. "You did it. You brought us home."

"Bless you, Darian," Ahmyn replied, kissing the child's forehead.

"I personally brought each of you here for an important task," Ahmyn continued. "This is your world now. Long ago it was declared that a little child shall lead them. The war is finished, and that time is now!"

The throng cheered in agreement.

"As the grownups arrive, help them feel welcome. Most of them will look very confused. Teach them what you know. Will you do that for me?!"

The crowd boomed with approval.

"Now there's somewhere I have to go. But before I do, I want to personally thank each of you for being such good friends to me. This world has been cruel to us all, and I'm so grateful that you never gave up hope."

In quite an orderly fashion, as if having auditioned beforehand, each child took their turn in succession to speak with

Ahmyn. He was crouched down on one knee, so as to be more at eye level. Placing a gentle hand on each boy and girl's shoulder, he shared a few words tailored to each individual. A warm embrace was then exchanged, making room for the next child.

It was serenely quiet during this procession. Avery and Miata sat cross-legged in the grass a short distance away, watching in awe as he addressed each child by name. They were, at present, the only adults in sight.

As each finished their turn, the little ones quietly made their way back to sit in the grass, some occasionally whispering to each other. Avery questioned a dark-haired girl with a button nose who happened to sit beside her.

"Do you know where Ahmyn is going?" Avery asked.

"Oh yes," the girl beamed with delight. "To the realm without shadows."

"And where is that?"

"Not far."

Miata listened intently to the conversation between Avery and the little girl.

"Why is he leaving?" Avery continued.

"He has to go. He's preparing a place for us." The little girl then took Avery's hand in hers. "You're his mother, aren't you?"

"Yes," Avery replied, trying to hold back the tears.

"Don't cry, Avery," the dark-haired girl urged. "He's preparing a place for you too. A most beautiful place. You can't even imagine it."

"I appreciate you talking with me."

"You're welcome."

"What is your name?"

"My name is Kendra."

Avery was startled by her response. Gazing into the little girl's eyes, she felt as though she could see herself looking right back.

"You seem worried, Avery," Kendra pointed out, still holding Avery's hand.

"I guess I am. Maybe a little. Yes."

Smiling as big as ever, Kendra continued, "Would you believe me if I told you everything is going to be alright?"

An overwhelming peace flooded through Avery's body at that moment.

"It really is, isn't it?" Avery said.

"It *already* is."

Time seemed so different in this place. In what seemed like only minutes, Ahmyn had spoken with every single child in the audience. Now walking toward his mother and Miata, Ahmyn helped them both to their feet.

"Oh, Ahmyn," Miata cried as she embraced him. "Do you really have to go?"

Ahmyn simply looked at her and smiled. He then embraced Avery and whispered, "Thank you for allowing me to be *your* son."

"The privilege was mine, Ahmyn."

"Was?" Ahmyn replied, placing his hands on Avery's shoulders. "I will *always* be your son. That will *never* change."

Ahmyn turned from the group and walked a few meters in the opposite direction, his long dark hair wafting in the breeze.

"Ahmyn!" Avery pleaded. "Please don't go."

Facing the crowd again, Ahmyn looked directly into Avery's eyes. "I will not leave you comfortless."

"Won't you take us with you?"

"Kendra, will you please look after your daughter while I'm gone?"

"Of course," replied the little dark-haired girl with the button nose.

Avery looked down in surprise as she felt small warm fingers take her by the left hand. A glorious beam of light then broke through the sky. It focused directly on Ahmyn, who then began his ascent up an unseen staircase. The throng of children, with eyes raised to the sky, resumed their chorus in full force as Ahmyn climbed purposefully upward, disappearing into the blinding light.

ABOUT THE AUTHOR

B.K. Peterson grew up in the Salt Lake Valley as the oldest – albeit the least mature – of seven children. He managed to surprise his parents by graduating from Copper Hills High School in 2000, and further astounded his friends and family by earning an Associate Degree in General Studies from Salt Lake Community College, and later a Bachelor of Science in Biology from Utah Valley University in 2011. It was during the seemingly endless bus rides to and from UVU that he conceived the idea for The Beckoning.

He and his wife Brittany reside in West Valley, Utah, where they struggle to maintain order in a home with three growing boys.

ACKNOWLEDGMENTS

I began this project in the summer of 2009, uncertain of just how long it would take to complete. The Beckoning would have remained an unfulfilled hope if not for the unwavering support of my lovely Brittany. She has ever been a wellspring of encouragement and love.

Thanks to Kevin McCafferty and Rex Peterson for your editing expertise, and to all those who kindly offered their time as beta readers. You were a critical source of motivation and support.

Finally, a special thank you to Janelle Dunn and Jeff West. Your continuous words of encouragement and genuine enthusiasm gave me the added strength I now realize I couldn't have done without.

www.ingramcontent.com/pod-product-compliance
Lightning Source LLC
Chambersburg PA
CBHW021444240626
47153CB00001B/293